F

A Runt's Tale

In the Beginning...

By Faeghan B. WhiteWolf

F WhiteWolf

A Runt's Tale, In the Beginning…

Faeghan WhiteWolf

Introduction

The purpose and goals of the book:

Simply put, to entertain...and perhaps teach.

Dedication

For my family and friends.

Acknowledgment

For those who assisted me:

I would like to express my thanks to a number of people; for my daughter, Ashira and her friend, Eliana, who proofread the books along with various other Middle School friends, for Adina and other High School kids, for my adult friends and family members, who also proofread the books (Greg, Cassandra, Crescent, Mike, Brandon, Sezmo, Leann, Rose, Andres, Michael, Jack, Luan, Bobbie, Tara, David, Eric, Dian, Anna, John, Joy, Roxan, Scott, Shary, & Mitch), for my wife, Baihlah, who let me have some peace and quiet to write and minimized the 'honey-do' list, for my sister, Dian Curran, who's knowledge of astrophysics was invaluable, for my friend, Eric Roesinger, who's knowledge of history and many other topics was amazing, for the members of NIP (Novel in Progress), for the members and guest speakers at WLOT (Writers League of Texas) Austin, for the members of SCBWI (Society of Children's Book Writers and Illustrators) Austin, for the members of the CHADD (Children & Adults with Attention-Deficit / Hyperactivity Disorder) Austin Adult Support Group, for the members of Wellness with a Disability Adult Support Group [provided by JFS (Jewish Family Services) at the JCC (Jewish Community Center)], for the members of CBI (Congregation Beth Israel) Austin, and for many others. I would also like to thank Serif for creating so many products that are useful to writers and designers; PhotoPlus X7, DrawPlus X8, PagePlus X8, and WebPlus X8. I have used at least one of these since the X4 version came out. Every map, drawing, and photo manipulation in the books were done with their awesome software.

Forward

A note from some readers:

A realistic view of an alluring realm, drawn completely from the memories of a humble man with a monumental life.

- A.E.

Part of a 'fully realized world', resembling the fantasy works of Ursula K. Le Guin, George R. R. Martin, and J. R. R. Tolkien. In style, the series resembles Remembrance of Things Past, by Marcel Proust, often called "The greatest novel of the twentieth century", and of which Virginia Woolf said, in 1922, "Oh, if I could write like that!" Rememberance is a massive, seven volume story with 2,000 characters, stretching over decades.

- I.R.

Like a cross between Robert Lynn Asprin's MythAdventures series and J. R. R. Tolkien's Lord of the Rings trilogy, with some Pythonesque humor thrown in...hilarious!

- R.P.

The appendices remind me of Tolkien's Silmarillion. Lots of useful back information. I noticed some similarities with Piers Anthony's Xanth series, also.

- R.R.

Like J. R. R. Tolkien, you have created your own alternate and complex fictional world. Good work, good luck, and keep writing.

- D.B.

Preface

How the story came to be:

I'm going to toot my own horn for a bit. In 1984, some kids, that I knew from jumping for the swing at Blue Hole in the small town of Wimberley, Texas, approached me with a proposition. They told me about a Role-Play game called Advanced Dungeons & Dragons. They needed a Dungeon Master and thought that I was smart enough to do a good job at it. It sounded intriguing, so I looked over the 3 books that they loaned me; the Players Handbook, the Dungeon Masters Guide, and the Monster Manual. I was really interested. I read Gary Gygax's Role-Playing Mastery. I agreed to do it and got my own set of books and polyhedral dice. This genre of gaming is called 'tabletop gaming'. I created a multi-page character sheet, because there was nothing available that was anywhere close to being detailed enough for me. I started designing a thoroughly detailed world, called a 'campaign setting', almost immediately.

These were high IQ kids, all in a range of 9 to 11 years old, which were struggling in school for no apparent reason. If the medical profession had known very much about ADHD, dyslexia, and dysgraphia at that time, then the cause for the kid's difficulties would have been easier to diagnose and handle. I was not aware that I also suffered from the results of those same neurological brain pattern differences. Their parents knew that I had also had some difficulties in school, but had overcome them and excelled. I explained to them that I could use the game to assist their kids in skills that they needed to learn to do better in school. They hoped that I could do so and supported an apparently useless and time wasting activity.

I loved the 'acting from the waist up' aspect of the game and learned to do many different accents, voices, and mannerisms, both male and female. I acted out all of the Non-Player Characters completely and made them live for the players in the group. I made it so that we rolled the dice only when absolutely necessary by having the kids research their characters skills to the point that they could realistically act them out.

In fact, they had to completely research every aspect of their characters including period; clothing and armor, weapons and fighting styles, hair styles, food, lodging, transportation, laws, customs, etc. They had to write up a thorough history for their character that showed cause for the character to be the way they were in the game present. They had to do drawings of everything that was important in their character's lives and draft up building plans of their various properties as they became more well-to-do. If their character spoke a language, other than English, they had to learn it also and act it out. Being rural Texas, most of the players were bilingual English/Spanish to varying degrees, some completely fluent. For every level of mage spell, they had to come up with 4 lines of poetry that described what the spell was doing, and had to be able to say it correctly, from memory, while under stress, during a fast paced battle scene. So, a 9th level Mages spell had 9 sets of 4 lines of logical poetry. A 18th level Mage, able to do 9th level spells, had 34 spells that the player had to memorize. For clerics, they had to come up with ceremonies and prayers of the same complexity and purpose. They had to learn how to rapidly calculate many different kinds of problems. They learned physics. They had to learn about architecture and structural engineering. They had to learn how to design businesses from the ground up and every aspect of how they functioned. They had to learn historic battle strategies and how to lead NPC's (Non-Player Characters). Players with Thief characters had to actually know how to do all of the thief skills, same for the Bards...yes, singing, songs that accomplished the goal, and playing instruments. The list of things they had to learn was extensive, to say the least. Of course, they had to completely "act from the waist up' when they played their characters with fixed and stable accents, voices, and mannerisms. We also stood to act out fight scenes in slow motion using prop weapons, one move at a time. We did have to roll the dice for a few things. Their characters were complete persons that learned, grew, and changed over time. When they gained a game level, they had actually earned it. As a result of all of this, their schoolwork became a snap and their grades went from C's, D's, and F's to A's and B's. Their parents were ecstatic. The game group totaled about 15 players. They graduated High School mostly with honours and only a few did not go on to get graduate degrees.

A historical note for the young readers is due. There were no home computers, smartphones, tablets, etc. (that's right, no GOOGLE or Wikipedia to instantaneously look stuff up, shocking, IKR) back then and almost nobody had their own typewriter, so all of this was done by hand, with pencil, ruler, and paper, and the research was done in libraries...in books...I'm sure that you have seen them around, perhaps at your Grandmother's house, those funny looking rectangles with a stack of paper inside...with words on them? What I can crank out in one day on an AutoCAD program now took me at least a month to do with pencils, rulers, and paper back then.

So, when I took the game group, which had the unfortunate and overlong name of Fantasy Adventure Role Playing Game Club of Wimberley or F.A.R.P.G.C.o.W., to GenCon in Milwaukee, Wisconsin, in 1985, our standards were in the exceptional range. We only found 1 organization there that could play at our level. That being, the RPGA Network (International). We joined and became involved in their various campaign style tournament play formats, including; Living City, Living Jungle, Living Death, Living Greyhawk, and Virtual Seattle. I continued to go to GenCon each year until about 2000. I coordinated specific tournaments there, judged tournament play, and played in them. I earned enough points in tournament play to get as high as Paragon Level Player, and in Judge up to Grandmaster level. I was the Regional Director for Texas and coordinated small conventions all over the area, including the adjoining states.

The point of this whole history is that I had a 3" binder with about 15 thoroughly complete Living City characters in it when I retired from RPGA. These characters were so complete that they had essentially taken on a life of their own. When I played them, it was almost like they became real. Almost like a duality, me and the character overlapping. Actors seek this complete immersion in a part.

Over the years since, I have thought occasionally about those characters, the friends that I used to know so well. I finally gave in, in the spring of 2014, and started writing down their stories, as seen through Scram Runt's eyes. This is Scram Runt's story. These are his friends. The difficulty is to take all of the various adventures that they shared and took part in individually and get them down on paper in a logical, organized fashion.

In the process of translating a game world, Ravens Bluff, The Living City, into something that is no longer that, but is similar, into an alternate timeline of our earth (with many differences in its history, and thus, its present), into a non-fantasy location on the map that will work, changing the city's name and layout, changing the governmental structure, changing the metaphysical laws of a game rule system into something more realistic and logical, somewhere in between typical fantasy and reality, explaining scientifically why the 'magical' creatures exist, has been a longish process. During this process, the characters had to morph to fit the new rules. They handled it well, but it broke them and their story free to flow and morph into something different than what they were in that world.

Authors talk with dread about 'plot bunnies' and how they can derail a plotline that has been meticulously planned out. I laugh at that. This whole book series is ruled by 'plot bunnies'. It has grown on the pages like a living creature, like vines growing along a fence, with many abrupt changes in direction, twists, turns, braiding and separating on a whim. I am continually shocked by how it turns out in any scene or chapter. It is almost as if I am the observer or reporter that is frantically trying to record the story as it plays out under its own guidance. I gave up long ago trying to plan out any given chapter prior to writing it. As long as it flows smoothly and makes sense, I really don't care about trying to control it. Something will happen and I will say, in shock, "Where the heck did that come from?" and then I'll think about it and realize that it does make sense. Though, it does annoy me somewhat when secondary characters get written completely out of the story when I had plans for them in the future and thought them integral. It's also kind of unnerving when new secondary and main characters 'pop' in suddenly and when main characters decide to change their future without consulting me and I have to alter what few ideas that I have for the plotline to match their chaotic whims. I call this style "organic writing", with the story being a living, growing entity. 'Real' writers have a variety of bad reactions to this style…

This kind of thing used to happen when I was judging tournaments. I had a written 'scenario', almost like a script for a play, which included a set number of somewhat rigid 'encounters' that usually had 2 or 3 possible outcomes, depending on the actions and reactions of the players characters. I was supposed to subtly steer them in the right direction so that they stayed within the storyline as put forth by the author. Sometimes, they simply would not steer. Some judges would freak when that happened. I never let them know that they had veered off of the plotline. Sometimes, I could nudge them back to it, but that was rare. I just let them wander along and made up the storyline and NPC's fast enough to react to their actions. Sometimes they would ask me at the end of the 4 hour tournament if they had accomplished all of the goals as set forth in the scenario, and I would calmly tell them that they had left the 'Scenario' a couple of hours back. They were usually a little stunned by that, but I got a really good score from them when that happened.

They also loved to get 2 or more NPC's, all played by me, into conversations, or better yet, arguments, with each other and they would just sit back and watch the show...dastardly players...LOL You try to act out a conversation between several characters, each with their own accent, personality, and set of parameters sometime to see what it is like.

I hope you guys enjoy the character's story. They are the authors of their own lives and existence, not me, I am just their window to this world...

Epigraph

Society is founded on
Cooperation & Conformity.
Those who don't Cooperate,
end up ostracized,
in one way or another.
Those who don't Conform,
end up making changes,
hopefully good ones...
Be a good non-conformist.
Learn everything.
See the problems
and work toward a solution...
together.

Map

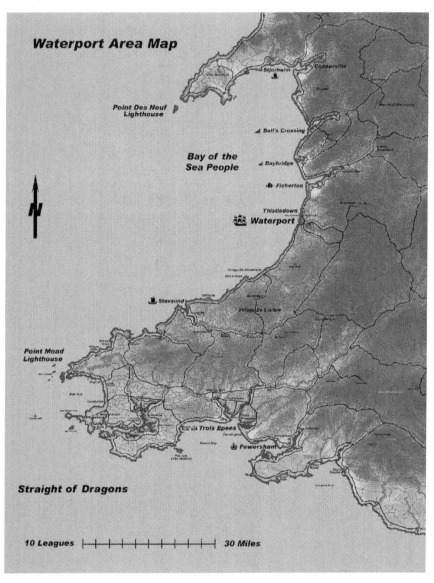

Prologue

28 Frostshine, 5245 (245 Turns of age)

The Memoir of Captain Reginald Rumphrey-Bon Vent, Esq. (AKA; Scram Runt, the Whirling Dervish, the Patch Collector, the Engineer, Dada, and other names.) of the fair City of Waterport. Jack-of-all-Trades, Master-of-Many.

I, being still of relatively sound mind and surprisingly advanced age, have, after much reflection, decided to pen my memoirs. This is the first installment in the series.

I am told that we, as a species, have advanced to the point that a new age is considered to be dawning, an age of Renewal, I feel that I should take advantage of these auspicious tidings to record a bit of our history.

These musings will probably be of little significance to anyone but my various offspring and what few friends I have managed to accrue over the Turns. I really cannot imagine anyone else being interested in the least in a recounting of the miniscule accomplishments of such an insignificant personage as myself, though my life has been described as a cascading series of strange events with even stranger consequences, a chain reaction of cause and effect gone amok and awry, an algorithmic barrage of creatively extrapolative, frenetic activity, but... it certainly has been fun!

Well, here goes...

P.S. My fifth Mate, Kichawi, says she will get around to it someday. My fourth Mate, Kizzy, who is supposed to be all Human, but is somehow still alive and quite young looking after all these Turns, has read it, but kept her comments to herself. My Secondary Mate, Tilly, read this in its entirety. She said that it helped her to "comprehend the zany complexities of my convoluted mind". My darling Primary Mate, Madeleine, refuses to read this manuscript. She says that she lived it, so why should she read about it, and, she reminds me that she will live at least two hundred Turns longer than I and that her memory is working just fine, thank you...I bet she gets bored someday and reads it. What do you think?

Table of Contents

Chaptre 1. In which I Recount My Beginnings

To the best of my knowledge, I was born in the Turn of Our Lady, 5000, shortly after the millennium. We have since, arbitrarily assigned my date of birth as the twenty eighth of Leafall. To say that I am of humble origins would be a vast understatement. I began life as an absolute nothing, at the bottom of the barrel, the very dreg of society...a "Street Urchin", if you will...no, less than that, a bipedal animal.

My first few Turns were evidently spent scrounging for 'food' and avoiding larger predators in the sewer system of the city. I functioned essentially as the other animals with which I cohabited. I was naked and grimy, except for a wild thatch of long tangled hair. I did not know who or what I was. The only sounds that I uttered with any concept of meaning were a mimicry of the various fauna that lived in that environment.

I had many survival skills at my command. I could see extremely well in very low light conditions and could see the glow of anything warm. I could move so silently as to surprise practically any creature. I could climb as skillfully as any spider. I could swim like a fish and hold my breath for several minutes. I could lie in wait, absolutely unmoving, and attack with extreme speed. I used my teeth and 'claws' to kill my prey or just simply bashed it. I could throw objects with deadly force and accuracy.

My 'lair' was an abandoned basement connected to the nearest sewer tunnel by the partial collapse of an adjoining wall high above the water line. There were many old things in the room...what I would come to know as crates, boxes, chests, barrels, and other miscellaneous containers. I had no clue of their former function as most of their contents had turned to dust over the Turns, but they were fun to play with. There was a skeleton dressed in rags in one corner that I vaguely remembered to be the remains of my mother. I must have been about 3 when she died. I had made a sort of altar surrounding her remains, replete with the nicest and prettiest cast off items that I had culled from the sludge flowing by outside my home, a veritable treasure trove of artifacts from the mysterious realm above (the more civil and gentile folks who lived on the surface). I would sit for houres near the sewer grates listening to them make their strange sounds. I would mimic them and try to figure out the meaning of the sounds. Occasionally, there would be a lot of loud rumbling up above. I found out later that these were thunderstorms. I learned to hide in my home when this happened so as to avoid the rush of water that would flush through the sewer system, scrubbing it relatively clean for a while. The water actually tasted good when this occurred.

My home was invaded by giants!

I was used to occasional loud noises transmitting through the solid arched brick roof of the sewer system or through the walls from spaces beyond, but one day, I noticed an almost continuous racket coming from the other side of a wall several tunnels over from the one to which my home was connected. It sounded like several creatures were pounding on it with something hard. This went on for several light periods, when it was noisier up above. While I was watching from a cross tunnel, they finally broke through.

They were HUGE! They towered over me, more than twice my height, and were massive. Other than their ears, eyes, and bulkiness, they appeared to be similar to myself! They wore dark Coloured coverings on their bodies, various containers, and carried things in their hands. I had never seen clothing before, so was somewhat confused by this. The light coming through the hole and the lamps they were carrying was blinding.

I ran in terrour as did all of the other denizens of the sewer system in the immediate vicinity.

After they switched to lanterns that emitted red light, I was able to follow them as they explored the sewer system that I knew so well. It was funny to watch them blunder into the lairs and hunting territories of various predators that I had dealt with for Turns. They used tools, weapons, and Magicks of various sorts to dispatch these creatures with alacrity. I was well impressed and vowed to get one of these deadly implements for myself.

They talked endlessly amongst themselves and drew pictures on a large roll on parchment. I was familiar with drawing, for I had covered practically every flat surface of my humble abode with art depicting the things I saw and knew. I started to make connections between the sounds they made and various objects or actions. It was very enlightening.

After they had mapped the entire system, they started to transport objects to and from their 'lair'. Usually, this was done between the Harbour to which the sewage flowed and their room, but it also occurred between various sewer grates. I had never before known that these could open, being too small of frame to lift their massive iron bulk. They seemed to be more active during the periods of darkness when it was relatively quiet up above.

One light period, I got it in my head to sneak into their lair to see if I could find one of those deadly implements. I realized that this was a very foolish thing to do, but I really wanted one badly. My possession of one of those wonderfully deadly tools would forever shift the balance of power between myself and the other predators in my hunting environs in my favour and, incidentally, make my potential survivability much higher than it was at present.

This escapade had to be well planned and executed extremely carefully, so I began by peeking in the doorway to their lair in an attempt to learn as much about the interior as possible prior to sticking my neck out, as it were. Whenever there was any movement inside, I would scuttle a few feet away, slip quietly into the stinking soup that flowed by, and hide there, under the surface while breathing through a hollow reed.

After several light periods, I finally summoned up enough courage to slink warily into the giant's lair. I prepared for this harrowing endeavor by removing as much muck as was possible from my hair and body during a period when the sewer ran with clear water. Having finished my ablutions, dried thoroughly, and steeled my courage, I felt ready for my grand adventure.

I started by scanning the opening and the area just inside thoroughly, searching for traps of any kind. There were many creatures that utilized strands of webbing and other less palatable bodily excretions or extensions of themselves as alerts and triggers for snares and other forms of traps in the area. I was well familiar with these and quite adept at avoiding their dangers. In doing so, I noticed a thin strand extending across the doorway at approximately a hand span height. I peeked in to the left and spotted where it was attached to the wall inside the room. On the right side of the doorway was one of their strange devices for the purpose of killing. The strand went to the wall behind it and back to the device. The device had a pointy object in it that was clearly intended to impale anyone foolish enough to hit the strand with any force. I gently tested the strand and found it to be made up of an extremely hard substance and coated with something black.

I checked the area beyond the strand, found it to appear safe, solid, and natural except for one of the flagstones. This one had small holes about a finger joint apart covering its surface. It was cleaner than the surrounding stones and had no collection of dust and other debris in the crack between it and its peers.

I gathered myself and leapt over the strand landing adroitly on the flag to the right of the odd section of floor. I froze in silence and searched with all my senses for a reaction to my abrupt arrival. There was none.

The room was laid out in giant proportions with a huge tall platform (that I would later understand to be a table) several smaller platforms (stools) and several long, low, large, flat mounds of fragrant dry yellow sticks (straw). From the impressions in the latter and the body odor scents clinging to them, the giants must occasionally sleep there. There were mounds of personal belongings by each bed. The room was relatively clean and clear of debris. There were crates, boxes, barrels, kegs, bags, flasks, and other, more odd containers stacked against one wall. I had learned from experience that many of these containers usually held liquids of various types, ranging from delicious to bland to nasty to potentially deadly. I had learned through trial and errour to be very careful when tasting these substances and usually used other creatures as taste testers before imbibing of them myself. I would pour a little out on a dry spot and watch the reaction of my fellow sewer denizens to the substance. If they ate it and survived, then it was palatable to me also. Some of the boxes held vegetables and fruit of various types, much fresher than the ones I usually got to eat that had been thrown away down a sewer grate. There were also some smoked meats whose fragrance set my mouth to watering profusely. The best meat that I usually had was when I would sneak out the end of the sewer tunnels into the Harbour and catch fish and other creatures that were much cleaner than what I could catch in the sewer system. I did not want to leave any traces of my visitation to their lair, so I contented myself with eating the small scraps of food off the floor or storing them in my carry bag. There was an angled ladder of sorts, later known as stairs, which exited the lair upwards to a door fastened with something on the other side. I could not open it by any means at my disposal.

Back down in the lair, I climbed up onto one of the stools and perused the surface of the table. There were wooden utensils...mugs and bowls with spoons in front of each stool, some funny cards with pictures on them, a needle with coarse thread like my mother used to use, and a flat smooth piece of stone. Nothing looked particularly interesting except the pictures, so I figured that I would look for some in a less conspicuous location later.

While I had yet to learn even the most simplistic concept of numbres, let alone higher mathematics, I did figure out that the same numbre of Big People as four of my fingers laired here. Back then, if a numbre was bigger than my two hands worth of fingers, I could not conceptually handle it.

I very carefully searched the personal belonging for anything useful that I thought they would not miss. In one of the piles, I found something incredible...one of their amazing weapons that I would later understand to be a fancy lady's double-edged silvered steel dagger, with finger guard and butt of the same material, the length of my arm! It was beautiful! It had a slender blade and hilt of carved bone that I could grip quite easily with either one or both of my hands simultaneously. It was housed in a fine, deep red leather sheath with a matching leather belt. I just had to have it. I realized that this weapon would look positively dainty, almost like a toy, in the hands of any of the large, rough giants. I hoped that they would not miss it. I also found a couple of really nice, small brown leather belt pouches that fit rather well on the belt. I transferred my collection of throwing stones into one of them. I was very accurate and proficient at throwing things and could usually knock out my future dinner with a well-aimed rock prior to throttling it and eating it raw. I had discovered this talent one day when I became cornered by a small vicious humanoid with too many teeth and muck Coloured skin. While scrabbling around for something to hit it with, I had grasped a chunk of broken brick. Instinctively, I had heaved it with all my miniscule might at the leering monstrosity. To my astonishment, I hit it square between the eyes! It dropped instantly, felled by my blow. Whether dead or just knocked out, I did not differentiate. It did not appear very palatable, so I unceremoniously shoved it off into the muck to disappear slowly beneath its turgid surface. I never ran into any more of its kin, so I surmised that it had been a scout and when it did not return, its group decided not to invade the sewage system. Good riddance! Life was tough enough without those creatures to deal with. But I wander from the topic at hand. Please have patience, as Elders tend to do that frequently.

Where was I? Oh yes… I had been watching the giants, so I knew how to use these items. I still did not have a firm concept of clothing. I thought the giants silly for wearing such items and thought that they would be rather uncomfortable and binding. I did take a small blanket for use during the cooler part of the Turn when the cold, white fluffy water would drift down through the sewer grates. It generally stayed within a comfortable temperature range in the sewers with only minor variations due to outside weather, but occasionally, ice would entre the sewer system from the upper end where steams from the mountains flowed in.

I had found and collected a huge assortment of odd things that had been made by the big people over the Turns, stored them in my lair, and actually been able to figure how to use some of them. What I had collected today was better than anything I had collected previously by a long shot. I was elated!

I slipped quietly out the hole in the wall after checking to make sure that everything appeared undisturbed and headed for the lair of my arch nemesis to test out my new weapon.

Chaptre 2. In which I Best a Dire Foe

In one of the dead-end side tunnels, there lived a male sewer rat of gigantic proportions. He was very nearly the same weight as myself. He was the King of his mound and the father of almost all of the pups born to his clan. He was intelligent and very vicious. His followers were smaller by a bit, more timid, and fairly easy to scare off or handle in a fight. They made a fine meal also. Him, I ran from regularly.

I had decided, in my infinite lack of wisdom, to instead of working my way up utilizing lesser creatures as targets for my new blade, training myself as I went, I would de-throne the King Rat with my first attempt. I was so naive back then, it's a wonder I survived to old age.

In the sewers, most of the larger tunnels had a paved walkway of sorts on both sides of a 'river' in the middle. These walkways would flood frequently as the sewers also functioned as storm drains.

I found out later in life while researching the origins of the city that when it was a rural farming village, these were open steams with first, dirt and later paved roads paralleling them. The more substantial houses of that time later became basements for the new buildings when everything was paved over and the streams with their adjacent roadways became vault roofed sewers. One reason they did this, was that the streams had become stinking quagmires of offal, waste, and pollution that were offensive to the delicate senses of the more refined peoples of the town. Mine, and the Big Peoples lairs were both leftovers from that long lost era.

I scouted for the King and found him trundling along one of the walkways. His eyesight was not great, but his nose was excellent, so I masked my smell with a dip in the drink and circled around until I could approach him from downwind, though a slight breeze was all we ever experienced in the sewers. When he paused to refresh himself by devouring a fairly fresh corpse of some indeterminist creature that he sniffed out in the muck, I climbed up the curved stone wall until I was above him.

I leapt with all of the silent agility of the feral cats that hunted the sewers for small game. I pounced upon my prey with vengeance in my heart to eradicate all of the Turns of fear of this fell creature. I landed alright, knocking him flat on the pavement and forcing the breathe from his lungs, locked my legs about his middle and my left arm about his neck and prepared to draw my amazing blade to deal him a death blow, thus ending his reign forever. That is when my beautiful plan went awry.

He regained his air, squealed a shriek of pure, unbridled rage and went berserk! He jumped straight into the air, writhing like a salted worm, hit me with his tail, and then wrapped it around my neck while trying to unlatch my legs with his hind feet. It's a good thing that I never got my blade drawn or I would very likely have dropped it or impaled myself. I grabbed his neck with my right hand and clung to him for dear life!

When he landed upon the stones, he went into a frenzy of rolling and tumbling, squeaking in ear shattering blasts of sound that would have been paralyzing had I not already been immobilized. I was bruised and battered all over by his antics. I nearly lost consciousness. Then...

He rolled off into the water! I barely had time for a quick gulp of the fetid, but life giving air before being submerged by our combined weights. He, on the other hand, was not so lucky as he was at the end of a long screech as he said farewell to the land of the breathing forever. With no solid surface to kick against, his gyrations ceased. I was finally able to draw my blade and pierce his amazingly muscular body repeatedly in the neck and chest area. Minutes later, as my breath was nearly spent, with a final spasm, the King Rat died.

I re-sheathed my dagger, dragged his body up to the surface by one front leg and wearily made my way to the side, barely able to swim the short distance. As I was attempting to drag the Kings lifeless corpse up on the walkway, a huge hand gripped my right shoulder and its twin reached past me to grip the body with ease and hoist it unceremoniously out of its watery grave, all the while saying, "'ere now, le' me give you an 'and wi' dat." Of course, I could not understand the Big Person and only heard a series of low-pitched sounds emanating from the creature. I froze in complete panic and voided both feces and urine simultaneously (the smell was lost in the overall stench of our environs, though). The Big Person patted me on the back and said "Dere dere, now. Wats a wee tyke li' yourse'f doin' down 'ere?" At that point, I passed out from sheer terrour and was blissfully unaware of my surroundings for houres.

Chaptre 3. In which I Experience a Change in Life

Spring, 23rd of Greenapproach, 5010 (10 Turns of age)

When I blearily floated into consciousness later, I found myself a changed person.

My hair had not been cut for many Turns and had been down nearly to my feet. It also had not been washed, except for dunks in the muck, or combed it all that time and had tangled into dreadlocks. The other creatures of the sewers had probably thought that I had tentacles growing out of my head.

My hair had been cut very short and I had been bathed with clean water for the first time in my memory! I had several strips of cloth tied as bandages here and there with strong smelling salve under them on the wounds. I was wearing an over-large natural linen tunic and my weapon had been cleaned and was belted again about my waist!

The four Big People were seated at the table talking amongst themselves. The King Rat was cooking on a spit over the fire and smelled delicious. The biggest of the four looked to be describing my fight with the King with animated gestures as he told the story in his babbled communication. He was grinning as he conveyed the saga to his peers.

From what I learned later, he had been heading for the docks when he spotted the King Rat and paused to decide whether to cross the muck to avoid it or attempt to scare it out of his way. While he was deciding, I struck. He witnessed the entire fight and was very impressed by it. I had been so engrossed by the stalk, that I had been oblivious to his presence!

When he spotted me peering at them in fear and flicking my eyes at the hole in the wall that was my escape to the sewers, he beckoned me over to him with a grin on his face. He had to do this repeatedly, as I was distrustful, to say the least, of their intents, but I had learned to read body language in my interactions with the beasts with which I had co-habited for Turns and his appeared benign. He tried to explain everything to me, but deduced from my completely baffled and uncomprehending expression and my attempts to mimic the sounds he was making that I; 1. Could hear, 2. Could speak, and 3. Could not understand the language he was speaking or any other of the several that they tried. He pointed to my weapon, put his hand flat on his chest, and then held out his hand to me in a giving gesture. "You ca' keep dat. You earned it." My language lessons had begun! Over my long lifetime, I have become fluent in many languages, having found that I have a natural knack for the spoken and written word. From humble beginnings, I have become a scholar, nearly a sage, and known far and wide.

I found out later that one of the men wanted to kill me and dump my body in the sewer because he thought that I would squeal on them to the constabulary. Another wanted to sell me into slavery for the profit. A third wanted to sell me to a house of ill repute. My benefactor stilled their various ideas by explaining to them that he thought I had a lot of skills that their profession values highly, that he thought I was exceptionally brave, and that they were to raise me in a kindly fashion and teach me the arts with which they were skilled. "I li'da li'l bugger. 'e's sneaky as a bedbug an go' da 'eart o' a lion. If you lot e'en look a' 'im crosseyed, I'll twist yur 'ead off yur neck wi' me bare 'ands! We 'ave a' appren'ice."

It would appear I had fallen into a den of thieves...

Chaptre 4. In which I become acquainted with My New Family

This group, it turned out was actually a sub chaptre of the local Thieves Guild propre. They had been assigned to set up a smuggling operation utilizing the sewage system of the city as unobserved thoroughfares, as it were. They had discovered a trap door in the floor of a warehouse in the wharf district by accidently stepping on it while clearing out disused debris after renting the space. They had been planning to do the same smuggling operation above ground at night, but changed their plans after the discovery. This was a much safer, though smellier, method to achieve the same goal.

A note about my new Brothers in The Trade is in order. These four could not have been more different from each other if they had tried. To begin with, three of them were of foreign stock. I discovered these details during a conversation that started with them trying to figure out what I was, how old I was, and where I was from originally. As I said earlier, I picked up languages easily and rapidly. In about two Sevendays, I had generally mastered the Common tongue spoken by all of them, though their individual languages still evaded my comprehension.

They surmised that I was of some sort of Halfling stock, but with some Elven lineage also. They said that my slightly almond shaped, slanted, hazel Coloured, heat sensitive eyes, slightly pointed ears, and general hairlessness gave the Elf heritage away, but that, though slenderer than usual, my bodily build and plain brown curly hair were reminiscent of the average Halfling. My skin was not as pale as it should have been having never been exposed to sunlight previously. I later developed a lighter version of the "permanent tan" of a Forest Elf. They said that there were several kinds of Halflings; the Humkin, Dwarfkin, and Elfkin. They assumed that I was of the latter type. They told me that there was a Forest Elf Tribe living in the area and I was probably from the Halflings that lived close to them. If that were so, then I would age rather slowly compared to the average Human. Everything seemed to be compared to Humans as they were apparently more numerous than all of the other races combined and were therefore used as the measuring stick in all comparisons. They simplified all of this by telling me that I would probably be half to three quarters the height of the average Human when I reached full maturity, nut brown, and always appear slightly exotic, but that I should be able to blend in or camouflage my appearance for heists. I might even be able to grow a beard someday.

To begin with, Waterport was a port city, hence the name. Commerce from the world over flowed through its Harbour Districts on a daily basis and a thriving community of extremely diverse peoples had established quarters in the area amongst the warehouses, shipping, and import/export businesses, along with the less seemly businesses that catered to the more base needs of the people that frequented that bustling area. Street vendors were everywhere and market squares were thronging with shoppers in search of the amazing array of items available. Support crafts specific to the maritime nature of the area were represented by Craft Halls and Guilds of all types. The Thieves Guild was also housed in the area and handled all of the illegal activities that never seem to be absent from Human communities. They did not tolerate outsiders or freelancers plying The Trade within their jurisdiction. The local constabulary had more officers and sub-stations in this area than in all of the other areas of the city combined. They only managed to keep the more honest and law abiding people in check, though. It was sad to watch their efforts.

My new 'friends' were the perfect example of the areas diversity.

My 'Big Buddy', Brud the Strong, was a local. His Father was a Blacksmith, his Mother a Sail Mender, and he had been a Dockworker prior to being hired by the Guild to transport heavy objects. He was immensely strong with massive, corded muscles bunched beneath thick, coarse, and ruddy complected skin showing many scars from his labours. His hands were massive and calloused with thick, coarse nails.

He was tall enough to have to duck his head to walk through doorways. He had a thatch of thick, short, raggedly cut dishwater Coloured hair above beetled brows and piggish, close-set, mud brown eyes. His nose was wide and pugged. His scraggly beard did not help his appearance. His teeth were rather large, gapped, and crooked. He usually wore a coarsely woven tunic and hose with peasant shoes or went barefoot. He always wore a rough leather hat of some sort. He said it protected his head from damage from bumping it so often. He tended to use any handy object as a bludgeoning weapon, when he used weapons other than his body at all. Overall, he appeared mean, brutish, clumsy, and slow witted. This was not accurate. He was actually at least average intelligence, good natured, generally kind hearted, and a lot more quick and agile than he appeared. He was generally tolerant of everyone unless they made him angry, then he could literally dismember them with his bare hands...scary to behold. Fortunately, they had to do something rather drastic to irritate him. He suspected that somewhere up his family tree, an Orc was hidden. His parents appeared fully Human, so the traits must have skipped a generation or two. His ear-to-ear grin, while scary at first, could warm your heart to the core. He liked to hug people, which, if done without warning, could scare them enough to make them pass out or pee themselves. He was listed as a Mugger Specialty and Muscle by the Guild. He was motivated by survival. He had voted to keep me. He actually managed to live to old age. I did the eulogy at his funeral maybe a hundred or two Turns ago and survived the hugs of his children and grandchildren as well, though one of his daughters did accidently pop my back, thus removing a painful knot that had been there for Turns, ever since I had been catapulted into a castle during a siege to open the gate from within for the purpose of rescuing a Baron and restoring him to his rightful place. Let's see, what was the name of that place? It started with an 'R'. Oh, my, I have digressed yet again. I must tell this tale in chronological order. No chaotically bouncing around within my Turns allowed. That would be confusing!

The next fellow in this merry band was Makebe. He was from somewhere to the south. He never divulged precisely where, though extreme heat and dryness tended to be a thread in his tales of home. He had the most amazingly dark skin, nearly black, and almost no body hair, though he shaved his head and face daily. He oiled his skin with scented oils and stayed rather cleaner than the average person in our fair city. He had bright, metallic gold eyes and wore gold earrings and a nose ring to match. He was tall, lean, and lanky. He had evidently been sold into slavery as a child and trained to fight in The Pits. He had either run away, killed his master, won his freedom, or paid for his freedom, depending on who you asked. He used 2 Hook knives and could throw them if needed. The strange thing was that, if they did not stick in something, they returned to him. They were kind of like the more common scythe, but the blades were wider and double edged with odd angles. He tended to wear dark Coloured patterned cloth robes with a wide dark silk rope sash about his middle and sandals. He had many hidden pockets in his clothes for his smaller tools and carried a cloth shoulder bag for the larger ones. He was extremely graceful and lithe. He was absolutely neutral and tended to view other people as tools only. He was motivated by money. He was listed as a Cat Burglar specialty by the Guild. He had voted to sell me.

The third in the set was a nasty piece of work. Sarek the Sly did not trust anyone and was not to be trusted. He was from somewhere to the east, an area of mountains and high desert. He was short, slender, and wiry with black ringlets of shoulder length hair. He had a swarthy complexion, long lashes, a black shadow of a beard, and was generally very hairy all over. His ears were large with gold earrings. He had a hawk nose, high cheekbones, hollow cheeks, and the blackest eyes that I have ever seen on a Human. In my opinion, they mirroured his soul. He usually wore a dark satin shirt with the rest of his clothing being made up of supple, form fit black leather. There was a secret to this leather garb. Between the soft suede leather inner layer and the harder, slicker outer layer was a layer of fine steel netting! He was armoured all over! Add to this the fact that he carried a huge numbre of short, double edged steel daggers and throwing knives all over his body and you get a living weapon. He was practically a surgeon with those knives, but not in a positive sense as he never would have healed anyone for any reason. He was like a cat...he would play with his prey for an excessively long time, slowly torturing them to death with amazingly precise cuts. He was vicious and cruel, and I grew to despise him. He was motivated by the challenge. He was listed as a Cutpurse or Pickpocket and also an Assassin by the Guild. He voted to kill me. Turns later, after I heard that he was the 'artist' behind a particularly despicable act of malice, I tracked him down and ended him with a blowgun dart to his unprotected face (incidentally, but significantly, spitting in his face) that was coated with an extremely fast acting neurotoxic venom. I carried the tiny blowgun with its miniscule dart between my cheek and gum so he had no warning of his impending doom. I then made a large anonymous monetary donation to the grieving family through a relief organization that was a front for some of my various activities. I felt very good that day.

The last of the group was an odd duck, a genius actor with a larcenous streak. Trentish the Face was so beautiful that he could pass for man or woman equally well and did so quite frequently in his dealings with his marks. He was also a makeup artist and seamstress/tailor of advanced skill. It was always a game with him for even us to not be able to recognize him. He had trunks of costumes available at need. In his natural state, he had flowing, wavy, thick, shoulder length golden locks, perfect, creamy complexion, and light hazel eyes. He had dimples, perfect white teeth, and was slender, not very muscular, and extremely graceful. He had no body hair or beard at all. There is a suspicion that he has some Elven heritage. He was a chef, dancer and artist of renown. He could speak, read, and write at least five languages and could do many accents. He was an alchemist and created many, almost magical tools, weapons, tricks, and traps for our use. He could cold-read any person or situation. Nobody knew from whence he originated. He was an extremely complicated person, to say the least. His weapon was his mind, so any weapon he happened to be carrying was probably just for show, though he was a master fencer. When he thought there might be real danger, he carried a Foil for protection. He usually shredded someone's dignity with this weapon, but in dire straits, could kill quite efficiently with it. He was motivated by the score. He was listed as a Confidence Man or Grifter by the Guild. He voted to sell me to a Brothel.

I was to spend several Turns off and on with these folks learning their skills and Trades. They all thought that I had skills in their particular specialty areas, so a friendly competition ensued, each competing to teach me the most. The result is that I became the penultimate Thief, eventually outdoing them all, and thanks to Brud and Trent, maintaining a modicum of 'good' in my nature.

Chaptre 5. In which I Learn My Trade

My teachers had been told to lay low and confine their activities to the smuggling operation that they had set up, so they had plenty of time on their hands and were quite bored. Training me was a fun diversion and kept them out of trouble. We also spent a lot of time playing cards and dice, so I inadvertently learned those gambling skills and could manipulate a game quite handily in short order. Since I was too small to be a Mugger and I had no previous experience with tools or buildings to be a Burglar, and I had no knowledge of life outside of the sewers to be a Con Man, Sarek became my first teacher. Trent acted as the Mark during my training in Pickpocketing, Putpocketing, Cutpursing, and Sleight-of-hand. He absolutely loved dressing up for all of the various parts and made it quite challenging for me to locate the various stashes of loot that were placed in and on the sometimes outlandish outfits and the jewellery that he wore. He acted out the parts completely. It was quite a show!

I also learned from Sarek the Shell Game (done with a dry pea and three half walnut shells) and Three Card Monte, done with three very beautiful, hand painted playing cards). Brud usually acted as the Shill during these training exercises since he could appear very honest and slow-witted. Simultaneously, Trent was teaching me spoken, read, and written Common Language and made me practice Calligraphy (fancy writing) daily. All of them taught me a form of sign language specific to Thieves.

It has occurred to me that my reader may not be familiar with the nefarious world of the Thieving Arts, so I shall elaborate upon the topics above, thus defining them more thoroughly. Sleight-of-hand is the general term for any skill that involves making any small object appear or disappear from the Mark's (the target person's) sight or switching two different small objects. It is used in many Short-Cons (quickly completed, simple Confidence Scams) and many types of Illusion Magic. Have you ever had a Street Magician show you his empty hands, then pull a coin out from behind your ear?

Cutpursing is the act of surreptitiously slicing the bottom of a coin purse and catching the coins that drop out quietly enough so as not to alert the Mark. It takes a very sharp small knife to do this correctly.

Pickpocketing is the act of sneakily removing some item of value from a person's body without them being the wiser. Putpocketing is the reverse of this, and is actually harder to accomplish.

A Shill is a second Con Man who assists by being part of the audience and interacting with the Show Con Man or Scammer to Hook (get someone interested beyond the point of reason) the Mark into losing his money.

The Shell Game and Three Card Monte are similar in that in both cases, the Mark is attempting to keep his eye firmly affixed to one of the three objects that is being manipulated in a way intended to confuse the observer. The Con can use Sleight-of-hand to remove the pea entirely or place it under a different shell. In the case of the cards, he can remove the target card and replace it with one identical to the other two cards. Either of these ruses makes it hard to impossible for the Mark to accurately locate the pea or the target card. If the audience is leery of placing a bet, the Shill will do so, and the Scammer will make sure that he wins, thus showing the crowd that it is possible to do so. The Team can also have a Pickpocket working the crowd of observers and handing off the loot he procures to a Bagman, who is also part of the crowd. In this version, there are four Team Members working the Con. When we did this, Sarek was the Scammer, Brud was the Shill, I was the Pickpocket, and Trent was the Bagman. It worked flawlessly as we were all in costume so as not to be recognized later.

Unlike most kinds of petty crime, a confidence game, or con, takes an enormous amount of skill and forethought to pull off. When done right, in many cases the Grifters, Con Men, who perpetrate them, have not actually done anything overtly illegal—they've simply used lies and manipulation to get the Mark to willingly hand over his own money.

They all agreed that my small, dexterous, fast hands were perfect for this type of work. Over the period of several moonths of intense study, I quickly mastered these skills to the level of Journeyperson.

Chaptre 6. In which I View the World Above at Last

Fall, 10th, Harvestgold, 5010 (10 Turns of age)

The day finally arrives when Sarek and Trent finally thought me ready to experience the 'world above', as I had always called the mysterious region above the city sewage system. They warned me that it would be very bright and dressed me in a ragged, long sleeved, wool tunic with a hood, to protect my head, and ragged leather breeches. Any colour that this attire once possessed, had been stolen by age and abuse. Both were a dusty grey-brown, and would blend in very well into any surroundings. This became my colour of choice for sneaky clothing for the rest of my life. My Blade, Razor Knife, and pouches were stashed under the long tunic, which hung nearly to my knees. I had a coil of thin rope about my waist. Sarek was dressed as a workman in rough leathers, a wig, makeup, and an overlarge cap. Trent reformed himself as a plump, middle-aged peasant woman with a grey-brown wig and makeup.

They took me up the stairs, listened carefully for several minutes while peering through peep holes, and unlocked the door before daybreak. It was cool and grayish dark in the warehouse with the pinks of the rising sun coming in through the windows high up on one side of the room. The place was huge! I had never before seen such a large open space. It smelled dusty and stale, but the usual malodorous reek of the sewers was missing. It was filled with carefully stacked storage containers of various types that were marked with Company Logos, contents lists, and wax seals of the Harbour Masters that had sealed them. Most of these were naturally counterfeit, as this was a Smuggling Operation, after all.

Some of them contained Contraband (illegal items), or stolen property that had been sent here to be Fenced (sold illegally) or was being shipped to another town for the same purpose. Some contained foreign currency that had been collected here as part of the Money Changing Operation and was being shipped back to Thieves Guilds that were part of the network in the countries of origin or incoming Waterport coinage. The Thieves Guilds also had artists and jewelers who spent all of their time crafting fake versions of various art pieces, counterfeit money, and forged official documents to ship to areas that could not spot them as forgeries. The art pieces were sold at auction for large sums of money. Some contained live animals that people collected or that were used in the production of some product, such as highly venomous creatures whose harvested venom would be used on weapons of assassination. Gambling equipment also arrived this way. The variety of items was literally infinite, whatever people wanted. The shipping fees were a drop in the bucket compared to the profit from the transactions. At any given time, that relatively small warehouse could have more wealth housed in it than all of the other warehouses in Waterport put together. Needless to say, our little Smuggling Operation was an important cog in the local Thieves Guild machine. Recently, Repeating Crossbows, called Cho-ko-nu, from the Far East had been a hot commodity, selling like hot cakes.

They showed me around the upstairs part of the Operation, the warehouse and office, which contained the fake set of sales and shipping records, known as 'The Books' (the real set was kept downstairs where the constabulary would not find it). The building had a set of double doors, large enough for a transport wagon to entre, and a regular sized door for foot traffic at the front facing the street. These were barred and locked. There was also a hidden door behind a swinging bookshelf in the office that led through a cramped, lightless hallway to a nondescript door that exited to an alley between the buildings filled with garbage, debris, rats, cats, and the occasional stuporous drunk. We utilized this exit. I had never smelled such a salty breeze of pure, sweet air before! It was amazing! The strip of sky above me was filled with fluffy pink and white clouds and very bright blue! My eyes stung and ached, and I immediately started to get a headache. They told me to keep my head down until my eyes could get adjusted. I took their advice and pulled the hood up over my head.

We made our way to the nearest market square and spent the day simply observing all of the activity. They taught me how to read the scene, the people within, and the interactions between them. We spotted other members of the Thieves Guild plying The Trade. We all communicated together using Thief Sign language, which is minimally noticeable unless you can understand it. It was amazing how much communication was occurring simultaneously in that area. There were several different spoken languages, Merchant Sign, and Thief Sign. People were talking in a spoken language saying one thing while they spoke in a sign language saying something entirely different. It was very confusing!

After I stole our first meal of the day from the fruit vendors, while we were sitting and eating, some little girl, that was nearly as big as me, though they told me that she was probably about two Turns old, sidled up to me, squatted down beside me, and stared at me with huge eyes in an emaciated face. Needless to say, I shared the fruit with her, much to Sarek's dismay and Brud's glee. He had found us at about mid-morning. Even though he could not really help out with that phase of my training, I think he just wanted to see how I was doing and liked to hang out with us anyways.

Brud told me that there were a lot of homeless kids in the city. He said they usually did not survive for very long unless somebody took them in and it was very seldom somebody nice who did so. I vowed to Brud that someday, when I was rich, I would take in all of the homeless kids and care for them.

The big little tyke stayed by me the whole day, usually holding my hand, and ate until her stomach bulged. I stole her, and the rest of the guys, some really good food, meat pies with vegetables and gravy in them, baked tarts, and other delicacies. We developed a pattern. One or more of the big people in our group would keep a vendors attention while I would reach up to the display area of their stand and snag the food which I would pass to the girl who carried the loot in her skirt. One of the Big People would be signalling me under the table with sign as to what to grab and where it was located. They would try to block the view of my hand with a piece of clothing or a part of their body. If I was spotted, the taller members of our party would not be blamed and the vendor would usually yell something like, "SCRAM RUNT!!!!", as I ran away through the crowd with my little shadow scampering behind me, which is how I got my first name. The Gang had just been calling me

"Boy" since they found me, but they loved the new moniker so much that they immediately started calling me "Scram".

As the sun started to set, we made our way back to our underground lair. The girl followed. The guys asked me if I was going to keep her. I told them that I would like to, that I would be responsible for her and see to her needs, but that it was entirely up to them to make the decision if it was OK, because I was still a kid. They said that she was too young to train in The Art, but if nothing else, we could pass her along to one of the women that worked for The Guild in the big Guild Hall.

They let me in on a little secret. Any person that had been accepted into The Guild as a member, had equal status, no matter what their age. As long as they broke no Guild Laws, their decisions would be honoured by other members. If a group of members had to make a decision, they voted, and the majority or the strongest or most dangerous member usually won the vote. If anyone disagreed, they could challenge the winner to a duel. The challengee got to choose weapons, type of duel, and whether it was to first blood...or death. If you recall, when I had been voted in, Brud won the vote. Nobody wanted to challenge him because he would have chosen 'Bare-handed', 'wrestling', and 'until first broken bone'. They knew that they would have lost dramatically, and very painfully, so I became a member.

In the case of the girl, I don't think that they really cared one way or another, except Brud, who backed me with a grin and slapped me on the back so forcefully that I lost all of my wind. The others just shook their heads ruefully and accepted the decision. We had a mascot. We named her Shadow. The other three teased us that we had already started The Orphanage...

We had figured out that I had seen about ten winters at the time that they had found me. They said that age was normal to begin apprenticeship training in any craft. They said that boys were usually stable Journeypersons by the time they reached an age sometime in their twenties, at which point, they sought a Mate. Girls usually Handfasted at age fourteen, unless they were also apprenticed to a craft. They teased me that since I was already listed as a Journeyperson, I should seek a Mate! They said laughingly that she could hold me on her lap and pet me like a lap dog or ferret. I told them that I would think about a Mate when I was a Journeyperson in every specialty of The Art. That shut them up. Trent muttered that I could probably achieve that lofty status.

A Runt's Tale, In the Beginning…

I was pretty exhausted from my big 'first day out'. I had a thousand new images, concepts, and bits of knowledge in my mind to sort out. I slept very well that night, with a good feeling in my heart.

Chaptre 7. In which I Greet the Day

Winter, 21st, Coldstart, 5011 (11 Turns of age)

The next day dawned chill and grey with a thick fog filling the streets of the city. I had been awakened early due to the scuffling and squealing of a couple of large male sewer rats just outside of the cellar in which we lived. I did not feel like enduring the decidedly unharmonious racket of my fellow thieves' snores, so I crept up the stairs and opened the miniature trap door that my friends had installed in the middle of the large trap door at the head of the stairs. I then climbed up to the door in the roof of the warehouse and on to the peak of the roof to look around and was enraptured by the scene that met my eyes. It was as if the clouds had come down to Oerth or maybe the ocean had risen to engulf most of the town. The lower parts of the city were almost entirely covered by a subtly seething mass of dense, grayish-white vapors and I was floating on them! The sky to the East was awash with lovely shades of pinks and lavenders shading into greys and then to intense dark blue to the West. Only the buildings that had more than three floors and the tops or the towers of the city wall between the Merchants Quarter and the Dock Quarter were visible as islands in the sea of rose tinged mist. The hillsides above the Merchants Quarter rose majestically above the new sea of mist clothed in the houses and mansions of the rich and powerful and the stone façade of the Castle that loomed over the town below, protected from the infringing mass of Oerth clouds by the city wall above the Merchants Quarter. It was beautiful.

Remember, I was still new to the effects of light, having only recently emerged from the sewers with their almost perpetual gloom.

A Runt's Tale, In the Beginning...

The masts of the tallest ships in the harbour with their furled sails looked like forlorn dead trees sticking up out of the mists. I spotted a young fellow on one of them, probably doing the same thing that I was, and waved to him. He waved back and gave me a thumbs-up gesture.

At that moment, the sun broke through the intervening vapors, glowing molten red and sending beams of light lancing across the undulating landscape, it was amazing!

Swiftly, it rose into the arc of the sky, shining first orange, then yellow, and finally blazing white! The mists responded appropriately to the various hues in a chorus of colours and shadows until they also shined with such a blazingly bright white glow as to dazzle the eyes into tears beneath the bowl of the clear, azure sky. I truly felt joy; I could not ever remember having such a feeling before in my life. It was definitely a good day!

I clambered back down to the cellar like a scampering monkey that I had seen in the market the day before and ran head-on into three very grumpy sleepyheads and a hungry child who were in no mood for the antics of said 'scampering monkey'. It was like being doused in icy cold water like what ran in the sewers during the springtime when the snow and ice melted in the mountains above the city...brrrrr.

So, I went about preparing a lovely breakfast of lumpy grey porridge gruel (made from a bag of wormy flour meal that I had found. I left the worms in for more meat.) with small bits of salted and smoked bacon in it to give it something approaching a 'flavour', though the bits of sand did give it some texture (the bacon had fallen off a passing wagon and subsequently been run over by others of that ilk. I had washed the horse dung off of it and pulled out the embedded straw, dirt, and pebbles to make it presentable for our meal.) Ummm, ummm, yummy! ("blech", "blah", "phooey", "splutter"). To this wonderful main course, I added some nearly rotten fruit that I had found in a trash pile in the alley outside (I had to scare a hungry pack of wharf rats off of it to acquire this delicious desert. I left the worms in, again for more meat). I just knew that my friends would be forever grateful for this amazingly filling and refreshing repast...not?...oh well, I tried. They attempted to be kind, but still had some difficulty explaining to me that my life in the sewers had evidently given me the constitution of a dragon and that they were mere humans that required more refined tastes in 'food'.

Shadow was the only one that did not complain and actually asked for seconds by holding up her empty bowl and saying, "um um?" which translated loosely as, "That was very delicious. I enjoyed it immensely. May I please have a second serving as I have not quite dined sufficiently?"

I felt that they needed to be re-educated concerning the deliciousness and health value contained in the various insects of the world. I mean, who in their right mind could turn down a lovely platter of crispy cockroaches fried in giant slug grease, and delicately seasoned with a bit of sea salt from the encrustations on the piers in the Harbour? Would that be out of the question?

After breakfast, we continued an ongoing discussion pertaining to appropriate weaponry to add to my growing arsenal of deadly implements. Due to my relatively short and slender stature and general lack of musculature, the possible list was somewhat limited. I had always been excellent at throwing small items and due to the tutelage of my cohorts, I had become quite skilled with a dagger, both thrown and in the hand. We decided that head-on confrontation was simply not my forte and they were right. I was much better at things that required speed and agility. I much preferred to surprise attack from behind or drop down from above and anything that kept me hidden (camouflage, darkness, fog, smoke, and more.) was an asset that much added to my life expectancy. I also much preferred to keep the enemy at a distance and use anything, like poisons, to make me more deadly. And so, after much deliberation, we decided that I would next learn the sling.

Chaptre 8. In which I learn a More Deadly weapon

Winter, 21st, Coldstart, 5011 (11 Turns of age)

A sling is a simple instrument consisting of a piece of leather, forming a pouch, connected at both ends to a braided leather string or slender strap. The length of said strings depended on the size of the slinger (the person wielding it). It was an ancient weapon, dating back tens of millennia and still quite deadly. There was a story, an urban legend of sorts, pertaining to a street urchin that had fired a small sling stone with perfect aim through the visor slit of a knights helm, hitting him in the eye, and thus killing the thoroughly armoured man with one blow. I liked that tale. Any time the little guy wins, I tend to appreciate it more.

In theory, the use of a sling appears rudimentary, but in practice, it is quite another ball of wax. After Brud and Trent had crafted one of appropriate size for me out of materials at hand, we went up to the alley to practice. These were the instructions that I was given by Makebe, "Tie wahn end of de tring aroun' you middle finger, poot a stone in de pouch, hold de udder end of de tring in you hand, swing eet aroun' you haid a few time and let go de tring. De stone weel fly away an hit sumting hahd." At that point, they all ducked behind some handy obstruction, which should have given me a clue that it was not as easy as it sounded.

I placed a rotten melon on top of a stack of crates against the city wall that divided the Merchant Quarter from the area that contained the mansions of the aristocracy. I stepped back about twenty feet, did as instructed, and let fly with my deadly missile.

My first attempt was a complete fiasco. The stone went straight up, causing all of us to scramble around trying to avoid it as gravity returned it to Oerth in a precipitous fashion. My second attempt was not much better as it flew way too high, nearly striking a patrolling City Guard that was walking the top of the wall. He was so armoured and bundled against the chill, that it probably would not have hurt him even if I had hit him. He responded with a loud "Oi!!!!" and scowled at me furiously. I apologized profusely and explained that 'I wanted to learn how to use the weapon so that I may be like him, my heroe, and protect our fair city from the ruffians without.' His face changed to a smile and he said, "Good on ya, lad!" This brought a "Well done!" from Trent and an approving nod. He always appreciated a well-executed con. My third attempt resulted in nearly asphyxiating and clubbing myself senseless as I accidently wrapped the string around my neck in mid spin and the rock collided with my skull! My fourth attempt shot behind us, hitting a passing horse, that happened to be pulling a loaded wagon, in the rump resulting in a startled whinny and the poor creature taking off in an uncontrolled, lumbering gallop down the crowded street to the accompaniment of screams, curses, expletives of various sorts, and a variety of crashing sounds. At least the Guard did not see this happen as he was out of sight. All that I could say was a not so eloquent "Oops", at that point. We hid in the alley until things got sorted in the street. Brud could not stop laughing and nearly gave us away.

The guys laughingly explained to me that I had to be careful as to exactly when I released the string so that the stone would sail true to the intended point of impact. I continued to practice the rest of the day and by the time the sun started to go down, I could at least hit somewhere within a few feet of my intended target consistently. A few of the City Guards had been watching, cheering, and placing bets for some time. One of them had tied a shield to a rope and moved it up and down the wall as a "movin'tahgit" to make things interesting. I actually managed to hit it a few times. One guy said "Wat pooah blighters shield dat is! Ees got a dented ta shite one now! Har Har". He was not so happy when the others explained that it was his shield... They tossed me a few pence before dispersing. Brud, Sarek, and Shadow had gotten bored and left a lot earlier to take care of business. Makebe was slumped snoring on a pile of old potatoe sacks due to no longer having to dodge errant missiles. I kicked him awake, took a few of the sacks, and went to scrounge every scrap of leftover 'food' that I could find in the recently cleared market square nearby.

I practiced every day for at least a moonth in between my other duties and eventually became perfectly accurate with the sling. The bored Guards assisted me by coming up with increasingly harder targets. Toward the end of my training, they were tossing multiple small objects, like potatoes, into the air simultaneously for me to hit. I could manage up to four before they made it to the ground. They tossed down to me a City Militia Tabard with the crest of the city and a stylized sling emblazoned on it, added my name to the roles, and gave me a rolled up scroll. They told me that I now had access to the Guard facilities up at the castle and invited me to visit any time. They wanted to teach me how to use a bow. At the time, it did not really occur to me that I now worked for two diametrically opposed organizations that were endlessly at war with each other...The Thieves Guild and The City Guard and Constabulary...hmmm, something to think about.

The guys were a little shocked when I showed up in the cellar wearing my glorious new tabard, assumed that I had stolen it, and were amazed when they found out that I had actually earned it. They immediately started figuring out ways to utilize it in scams of various types. I informed them that I took it seriously, much to their confusion, and would not allow it to be sullied by less than honourable actions... It would seem that I had somehow grown a conscience.

I scrubbed myself good that night, put on my best clothes, my new tabard, wore my nice dagger belted openly around the tabard with my sling and bag of stones attached to it and proceeded to the castle the next day. It was quite beautiful with the sun reflecting dazzlingly off of the icicles and freshly fallen snow, which happened to cover up most of the grime that marred the surfaces of the city streets and buildings. I walked down the, by then, well known street to the daunting city gate.

Chaptre 9. In which I Travel to the Castle

Winter, 25th, Snowshell, 5011 (11 Turns of age)

The first hurdle was getting past this gate between the Merchants Quarter and the 'Fancy Quarter", as I called it. The guards eyed me up and down and the captain read my scroll (better than I had been able, too squiggly, Trent was the only one of us that could read it). He had me stand to attention for inspection, after showing me how, taught me how to salute properly, explained propre etiquette and behaviour for young gentlepersons of the Guard, taught me how to address 'my betters', fed me a meal when they broke for lunch break, and sent me on my way up the rather steeply inclined roadway between the fabulous mansions of the wealthy and powerful. I was extremely polite and obsequious with everyone that I met during my trek. The ladies in their carriages thought that I was 'darling' and tipped me with better coinage than I had ever seen before. The men thanked me for 'protecting their fair city' from the 'vandals', the Thieves Guild...my other job, that would tear it down and also tipped me. By the time I made it to the castle gate, my purse was so full, it hardly jingled. I stowed it inside of my pants for fear someone would steal it. I was richer than all of the guys put together! I calculated that all I had to do to make a very good living, was to be cute looking and suck up to the 'Fancy People' while walking up and back down this hill once each day. Then, my newly grown conscience kicked in and squelched the scam idea.

I proceeded to the castle gate, which was even bigger and more scary than the earlier one. There was a full contingent of guards posted there. I marched smartly up to the gate commander, saluted, and said

"Private Scram Runt reporting for duty, Sir! The Private is to be given archery training so as to better protect our fair city! The privates papers, sir!" I then bowed and presented the scroll as instructed. The Guard Major smiled in amusement and returned my salute. He then took my papers and read them with one eyebrow raised. I learned later that one of the Guards that had trained and befriended me was a scion of one of the noble houses and had caused all of this to happen. He then ordered one of his men to escort me to Guard Barracks and training area. The Guard asked, "I' dis da kid, Sir?" and the Major nodded.

As we walked, he said, "so, yer da Wirlin' Dervish, huh?" I was completely perplexed by this until he explained that I had attained a reputation amongst the Guards and a nickname, 'The Whirling Dervish' due to the speed at which I spun the sling and fired and reloaded without slowing.

I thought that I had been awed by the beautiful mansions and villas that I had viewed on my hike up the mountain to the castle, but I was not prepared for the castle and its grounds. It was magnificent! Splendid! Huge! I felt like a small insect. The Guard that was leading me noticed that I had stopped and was staring with my eyes very round and my mouth hanging open. He laughed and said, "Don' worry, kiddo, you'll get used ta it. Now come along right propre." The castles towers went up so high that I got a crick in my neck trying to see to the top! Everything was made of stone. He escorted me through yet another gate into a tower in the wall around the castle itself, down some stairs, past a bunch of Guards playing cards at a table, and into a subterranean corridour. We turned right into another corridour and walked past a wooden wall on our right and a large rack of everything deadly that can be thrown or shot… crossbows & quarrels, bows & arrows, hatchets & axes, knives, darts, javelins, slings & a wide assortment of stones, bullets, darts, and other weapons. on the left, to a doorway into a range.

When we arrived at the practice range facility, I was shown one of the shields that I had used for practice, with the entire centre indented deeply, by a grizzled old Dwarven Guard that the other Guards treated with respect bordreing on awe and told "Show meh, laddy" in a rough, heavily accented voice.

I then put on the show of my life with my sling and stones. I hit everything perfectly. I won't bore you with the details, but it was fun! I then started practicing with the other ammunition besides stones and found that I was even better with the small round metal bullets than with the larger oblong stones. I could hold a lot more of them in my loading hand. Instead of completely releasing the string, all I had to do was have it attached to the tip of my middle finger and just simply open up my hand to spill the bullet out of the pouch and on its way to the target. This made it even faster to reload and fire again. I was punching holes through metal shields with those! The older trainers exchanged significant looks with each other on that score. I had taught myself to use the sling with either hand, but was faster with my right and more accurate with my left. They figured out that I could fire one bullet per one to one and a half seconds with my right hand. They appeared amazed for some reason. They told me that I would be in training for a while and that I needed to go back down the hill the next day to let my parents know that I would not be available to help them in their shop for several moonths. They thought that I was the child of a merchant and thus apprenticed to the family business! What an odd thought.

Then, they showed me a most amazing thing...bathtubs...with hot water!...and soap!!...and clean smelling fluffy towels!!! They gave me a fresh City Guard uniform to wear afterwards and we all ate together in the barracks dining area. The food was great! I could not figure out why some of the men complained about it. They assigned me the top bed of a bunk and a trunk to store my things. The bed was so huge that I got one of the bigger guys to put my trunk up on the bed with me. They thought that was funny for some reason.

I fell asleep on clean sheets, on a mattress, in a bed, with a pillow and blankets for the first time in my life! What an amazing day! Wow! I had so much to tell the guys.

Chaptre 10. In which I Become a City Guard

Winter, 26th, Snowshell, 5011 (11 Turns of age)

The next day, I marched down the hill, being cute, saluting and bowing (and collecting tips) all the way. I had a backpack now and had loaded it with 'provisions' for the trip and all of the money I had collected. It would seem that there were other Halflings of my size that worked for the city in various capacities, so things were available to fit me. In the Guard, they were usually slingers or archers, but were also good at scouting, signalling, and a few other things. I was now wearing a full City Guard uniform complete with leather padded steel barbute helmet, chainmail hauberk with mail coif over padded leather, steel cuirass breast & backplate, leather leggings, tall leather boots, steel greaves on the lower legs, steel vambraces on the forearms, and leather gauntlets on the hands. I was wearing a full-fledged City Guard tabard over the armour. I also had a wide leather belt on the outside of it all with a purse, a bag of bullets, my sling, my dagger, and a shortsword in a scabbard hanging from it. I had a leather waterskin on a shoulder strap on my right side. There was an unstrung shortbow stowed on the left side of the backpack and a quiver of arrows on the right. There was a small round steel shield strapped onto the broad part of the backpack. Wow, it was heavy, and hot, even if the temperature was hovering around freezing at the moment. The lead instructor, Garan MacForsh, told me that I would get used to it and be the stronger for it. I felt really deadly and protected...but if I fell down, I probably would not be able to get up by myself. That would be very embarrassing. I swore to be very careful not to do so.

When I arrived at the warehouse, I nearly scared poor Trent to death! He actually screamed in terrour! He thought that the City Guard had discovered our secret tunnel into the office and we were being raided! Hilarious! By the time I got through laughing and Trent got through shaking, the other guys had run up the stairs from the basement to see what the hubbub was all about and were staring at me in amazement.

After I filled them in on my adventures (and they figured out all of the weak points that they could exploit in City Guard armour), they started figuring out how my elevation in status could help the Thieves Guild. We figured out that in the least, I could pass information concerning Guard rosters and assignments, routes and timing, shift changes, weapon advancements, structural weaknesses, secret doors, and other interesting information. After all, I did not want any of my new friends to be injured or killed because they stumbled upon my old friends in the middle of some nefarious deed. If my old friends knew exactly when and where my new friends would be, my old friends could simply avoid my new friends. I split the coins I had collected five ways and gave them their cut. Brud scribbled a parental permission slip with his very limited writing ability, so that it looked correct for knowledge and status level, and actually cried (and tested the stress tolerance of my new armour with a hug) when I said goodbye. They said that they would miss the 'interesting' meals that I usually cooked with grins on their faces. Shadow would not let go until Brud pried her loose. I told her that I would be back before she knew it and she calmed down.

As I left the warehouse, I waved at the Guards on the city wall that had started this whole thing, but they did not recognize me until I removed my helm and coif. Then they yelled for the others in that section and had me climb up to the top of the wall at the nearest gate tower to visit with them a bit. They all clapped me on the back and congratulated me on becoming a Guard. I thanked them profusely and showed them how the steel bullets could go right through steel plate. They were awed when I told them that I could sling a steel dart not just through the steel plate, but bury it in the stone wall behind the plate. They exclaimed that they hoped that the enemy did not have slingers like me in a kind of joking and kind of serious way.

I did not realize that I was the cause of a major upgrade in armour quality practically worldwide. It brought about a combination of eastern light weight layered laminate armour with western steel armour and padding. The bullets and darts would still break bones and cause lots of bruising, but they would not penetrate to cause major wounds or death. Then I added poison to the tips of the darts...

Weapons and armour are in an endless cycle of escalation and I have designed both in my lifetime and profited greatly from the sale of each advancement.

I would later in life design a siege engine that utilized a sling like function to propel a large steel dart completely through castle walls. They would call it The Wall Buster. An entire section of a curtain wall could be breached in two or three shots. When I later added highly flammable chemical jells from the middle regions and Blasting Powdre charges from the far eastern area of Oerth to them, it brought an end to extended sieges. An attacking army had only to show up with one of my siege engines and the besieged stronghold would sue for peace. I then added steel sheathing to the walls and I added an shaped-charge powered explosive round within the dart body to penetrate the sheathing and also tips like giant steel screws filled with charges to penetrate the steel plating and then blow up...ah well, when you design weapons and sell them to the highest bidder, it's like playing chess with yourself. You know all the moves and are thus, the only winner. The two opposing forces all die while you watch, manipulate the outcome, and get rich.

There was a span of time when I misplaced my Halflingity. That's like Humanity, but for Halflings and more caring. I am not particularly proud of my accomplishments during that period. I cannot say Elfity, because Elves live so long that they tend to dismiss Humans as "momentary nuisances", after all, an Elf can watch fifty generations be born in a given Human family during their lifetime. An Elf friend of mine once told me that Humans are like farts...they pass quickly, are rude, smell bad, should be ignored in polite society, and are easily forgotten. Ouch!

I just realized that I have lost time synchronization yet again and diverged from the story arc. My apologies, young reader. My mind tends to meander at times.

Chaptre 11. In which I Cause a Change

Winter, 26th, Snowshell, 5011 (11 Turns of age)

After traipsing back up the hill, and putting on a show for my adoring fans the whole way, I had reported back to the barracks to begin my training in earnest.

After two hearty meals and a good night's sleep, the first thing on the agenda was for me to re-learn how to use a sling while wearing the movement limiting full Guard uniform. I quickly discovered that this was almost impossible. I realized that the flaws were inherent in the current design of the heavy, layered armour and that I would have to completely redesign it into something a lot more functional. I remembered how Sarek's armour had the fine steel weave embedded between the layers of leather. That would work very nicely.

I approached the Master Armourer, who was an extremely muscular Dwarf almost as wide as he was tall with his long gray beard in two braids and tucked into his heavy, scarred leather apron. He also had a dour expression fixed on his face. I did this with noticeable trepidation as he was in the process of pounding something out on a large anvil that he was holding with a large pair of tongs. The object was glowing cherry red and spitting sparks with every beat of his hammer. Between poundings, he would poke the object into the bright red coals in the hearth and pump the handle on the bellows to blow air into them at which time they would blaze white hot. When the metal was brightly glowing again, he would take it out and repeat the process. It was very loud and hot!

I watched this action for a bit while peering around the large workroom at all of the interesting tools, equipment, and projects in mid-manufacture. I was so interested in trying to figure out the function of a very intricate item that I failed to notice that the noise had stopped. I was pulled back into the moment by, "Well, wot arrr ya doin' jus' standin' tharrr sack jawed! Eitherrr spit it oot orrr move along, laddy. This ain't no carrrnival side shoo!" At this explosion, I leapt into the air at least six inches and squeaked. The old Dwarf's face split into a huge grin and he started to laugh. He laughed so hard his belly was shaking, his eyes were tearing, and he had to sit down for fear of falling over. When he finally got control of himself, and all of his Journeypersons, Apprentices, and Labourers had bolted into the room to stare in amazement, he wheezed and chuckled for a bit more and looked me up and down. All I could do was stare at him round eyed in amazement. "So, yerrr that new lad they'rrr talkin' aboot, ain'cha?" I squeaked a nervous "I guess, Sir." In a much quieter voice, he said, "So, wot canni do ferrr ya?" I attempted to rapidly get my brain back on track and explained my idea for making light-weight flexible armour for the Slingers, Archers, and Scouts. He squinted in thought and rubbed the bridge of his nose with an amazingly callused forefinger. After a moment, he grinned and said, "I believe yerrr onta soomthin' therrr, lad." He turned and bellowed "Flarrrs!", then realized that his entire staff was standing behind him and chuckled. A slender, balding man stepped forward and looked questioningly at him. "Well, wot do ya think?" The slender man said, "Oi loike it. It could werk very well, but we'll 'ave ta get wi' tha Leather Craftspersons an do it as a joint effert." He looked at me and said, "I usually do tha fine werk, loike chain and ring mail. We are goin' ta 'ave ta borrow a loom from tha Weavers an' figure out how ta weave steel wire inta fabric. Come wi' me an' we'll put our 'eads tagether."

The Master put another Journeyperson and several Apprentices on the project. The Weaver Master sent a Journeyperson and an Apprentice and the Leathercraft Master the same with two Cordwainers. It was quite an assortment.

The Cordwainers were familiar with making leather armour and quickly figured out how to make the joints more flexible by using a subtle pleating method. The Armourers figured out how to 'draw' the steel wire fine enough for our purposes, thick enough to stop a piercing weapon and thin enough to be as pliable as fabric when woven. Many small patches were woven before the end product was achieved. The

Weavers figured out how to loom steel wire without crimping it. By the first of Thawburst, we had a finished product.

The end result of our efforts was the most beautiful sets of neutral Coloured, camouflage brown-grey leather armour that any of them had ever seen. They were quiet, supple, soft to the touch, breathed to allow perspiration to evaporate, and just the right temperature to wear. Each covered all but the person's face and had a detachable mask that that could cover everything but the eyes. They had been modelled after the outfit worn by Assassins from the Far East. The best thing about it was that they could stop any slashing or piercing blade weapon that we had at our disposal to try on it. You could wear them as is or add heavy leather gauntlets and boots along with a lighter steel, modified version of the helm, vambraces, and greaves if you did not want to be as quiet. We later figured out that if you put the plate under the leather and used moccasins and light leather gloves, you could regain the quietness factor. We also crafted a combination sword scabbard, quiver, and bow sheath that strapped to the back and a wide, supple belt of four large pouches to hold equipment. We made a small set for myself and a large set to fit the Captain of the Scout Company and several other sets in the mid-size range, plus one for the Master Armourer, and one for one of the Lieutenants from the Ranger Company, who happened to be an extremely beautiful Half-Elven lady. The extras were for target practice.

There was a big discussion as whether we should try to keep the armour secret, disclose it to only military personnel, or just spill the beans, due to the fact that everybody would eventually figure it out given enough time. We finally decided on the latter, as it would explain why money was being spent on new armour, and invited all of the dignitaries in the city to a showcasing; the Mayor, Alderpersons, Burghers, the General and Captains of the various Companies, the heads of all of the guilds that had been in on the creation plus the Bards College, the Engineers College, and the Aristocracy. It was going to be quite a show. We set the date for the fifteenth of the Moonth and the castle staff and kitchens started planning the banquet and ball to follow the demonstration.

Chaptre 12. In which I Put on a Show

Spring, 15th, Thawburst, 5011 (11 Turns of age)

The day finally arrived for the big demonstration and I was so nervous, I thought I would die. I had managed to get Trent a job choreographing the event and he was fluttering his hands and tittering all while telling me to remain calm. I was to put on a sling demonstration where I punched holes through plate armour and then failed to do the same with the new material. The Captain of the Scouts was to do the same with a bow with armour piercing arrows. The Captain of the Slingers and the Captain of the Archers, both wearing normal armour, were also on hand to first show the status quo. We had made four lifelike manikins out of wood and put the other two sets of armour on two of them and the normal armour on the other two. We also had four shields mounted on tree trunk butts with bulls-eyes painted in the middle. They would be the targets. Stands had been built in the inner courtyard of the castle for the demonstration and the dummies stood against the one wall without stands. Banners were waving everywhere and everything had a festive aire.

People started arriving early and the Jongleurs Society was on hand in full force to keep them occupied. These included Jugglers, Acrobats, Gymnasts, Jesters, and Fools. There was an entire orchestra on hand, not just the fanfare horns. The castle staff bustled about seeing to everyone's needs. It was very festive.

Garan told me just to imagine I was at the castle range with just my buddies around, focus on the target, and ignore everything else.

After everyone had arrived and was seated, the Master Armourer described how I had approached him with the idea and the problems that the innovations solved. He introduced all of the Crafts people that were part of the project and the various disciplines described the work that had gone into the design. The dignitaries asked questions which were courteously answered.

And so, the time finally arrived for the actual demonstration. The four of us were introduced too much applause by the audience. The Master Armourer narrated the proceedings throughout. First, the Captain of the Archers shot at a shield target, trying to see how fast and accurately he could fire. Then the Captain of the Scouts did the same. The Scout Leader was far faster, more accurate, and had better penetration. Next, I and the Captain of the Slingers did the same on the other two shields with first stones, then bullets, and then darts. Penetration was measured for each and fresh shields were emplaced. I won in all categories; speed, accuracy, and penetration. People were amazed at how much faster I could fire and reload. The other guy only penetrated the steel with the darts. We then switched to the dummies. I went up to my two and painted a small round dot in the middle of the forehead and the middle of the chest, and offered the pot to the Captain with a raised eyebrow. He grinned and said, "You ahre very sure of yourself, arn't you, young man? I just grinned back and said, "Yup...Sir." He painted like dots on his targets, accompanied by cheers from the crowd and many bets placed, and we repaired to the firing line. He went first and easily pierced the common armour much to howls of dismay from the bystanders. When he shot the new armour...the arrows bounced harmlessly off and fell to the ground. The crowd went wild! The Master said, "Mind ya, folks, it'll still heurt a lot, boot it won't poke nasty holes in ya!" which brought gales of laughter. The Captain had been very accurate, but had failed to hit either of the small dots, only hitting close to them. Then came my turn. I chose to use bullets, of course and obliterated the red dots with multiple shots that penetrated clear through to the wood and into it. The crowd clapped wildly and the Captain clapped me on the back and called me 'Lancepesades Runt' with a wink. I almost lost concentration over that. Armourers disrobed the manikins so everyone could see the damage that had been done to the wood underneath. Everyone 'oohed' and 'ahhhed' over that. Then, I readied myself and fired on the new material. I pummeled the dots with rapid fire repeated hits...and they all bounced harmlessly off! The ricochets were a nuisance as they imperiled the crowd that was sitting close by. They had to duck, dodge, and hide behind objects, and each other. Fortunately, the bullets were not going very fast when they impacted the bystanders and left no bruises. Everyone clapped and cheered wildly with a standing ovation! When it had calmed down a bit, the Master said, "And if ya poot some light steel plate behind it, ya won't e'en get a bruise!" This dummy was also undressed and only a dented area was noticeable where the dots had been. Everyone was awed by this. Next, after redressing the manikins, we attacked the new armour with slashing and stabbing movements. I used two daggers and he used a short sword and a rapier. Neither of us could cut through the material. The armour was removed and walked around the periphery so that the fans could inspect it closely for damage. The only noticeable damage was to the outer layer of leather, and that could be easily mended.

We had reached a scarier part of the show. The Master Armourer now stepped up to the stage to be dressed by his Journeypersons. After stripping to his loincloth, which brought appreciative comments from all of the ladies due to his amazingly muscular physique and caused him to blush furiously which then brought howls of laughter from the crowd, they placed a harness of thin, soft leather straps over his head. These straps held in place attached thin steel breast plate, back plate, and shoulder pieces. These were form fit perfectly. Next they strapped on place steel armguards, shin guards, a skullcap, and a belt with attached groin protection. Over all of this went the woven suit. On the chest of his suit I had painted a caricature of a Dwarf with his thumbs stuck in his ears, waggling his fingers, his mouth wide open, and his tongue sticking out. He stood in front of the target wall and proclaimed, "Ahs tha old sayin' goos, 'Poot yerrr mooney wharrr yerrr mooth is', soo I'em bettin' thaht this armourrr will kaep mae saefe from all hahrrrm." I and the Captain stepped up and prepared to prove his armour. "Doo yerrr darrrndest me boyos!" he roared at us. The Captain quipped, "I cahn't possibly miss such a lahge tahget." and fired five well placed arrows into the face of the image on the chest piece. The impact of these set the Master back a few inches, but bounced off without apparent harm. The crowd cheered ecstatically. The crowd was prepared for my turn with opened parasols to ward off stray ricochets. I rapid-fired five bullets between the eyes of the Dwarf in the picture, which thankfully, all bounced every which way and pushed the master back even though he was braced. The crowd cheered again. The master was disrobed then to show that he did not even have a red mark on his broad chest from the demonstrations. Everyone was amazed, including us that had built the armour. The master then redressed in his ceremonial garb while we prepared for the next event. In between events, the Jongleurs had performed around us to keep the audience entertained and put on an exceptional show while we worked.

Next, with much drum roll and fanfare, The Master introduced the aforementioned Ranger Company Lieutenant, the one that was a walking work of art, wearing a full set of the new armour. He informed the audience, "Ahnd noow, Lieutenant LeafFeatherrr will give ya a demonstration o' jus' how flexible this new armourrr is!" She had the combo quiver, bow carrier, and scabbard on her back and a dagger sheath crossways at the back of her belt. All of her weapons were of Elven manufacture and style. She used a slightly curved longsword and dagger with a short recurved bow. She gave an all new definition to the term 'form-fit'. Her figure was simply awe inspiring (and the best part was that as a Half-Elf, she was going to look like that for hundreds of Turns!). The crowd went silent in admiration as she walked to the centre of the area. She then bowed in turn to the three sections of the audience, faced the Mayor, and intoned, "I weel now geeve you a deemoanstration of one of zee more coamleecated Katas wheech we use een traineeng." A simple target dummy wearing the normal armour had been set up for her slightly off-centre in the courtyard. She said with laughter in her voice, "Do not worree, you are not een dangere. I nevere mees" The crowd tittered appreciatively. She walked back to the area close to the Mayors seating and turned to the target. If she was this graceful just walking, this was going to be some show. I was standing with the Master and crew off to the side watching. The Master mumbled to us, "Ach! Thaht girrrl coould maeke a dead mahn perrrk oop!" I agreed. I was only about eleven and a half and she was making me have feelings and reactions that I had never experienced before in my life. Just like every other male that had ever interacted with her, I had an instant crush. I wondered what effect a full Elven woman would have on the average male. They would probably just keel over dead at the sight of one with a big smile on their face. After the show, all that I could say was a stunned "Wow!" She launched into the most graceful and acrobatic series of manoeuvres that involved running, tumbling, leaping, and contortionist moves all done at incredible speed and all the while filling that poor target with arrows, slashes, and stab marks. This went on for at least a quarter houre. It was like a lethal dance. I did not know that any body was capable of such movements. When she finally came to a halt, she was standing in the centre with her back to the target facing the Mayor. The target's common armour was a complete shambles, so totally destroyed that the only thing holding it up was the arrows embedded in it. The silence was so thick, you could have heard a pin drop. Without being out of breath, she said, "I hope you eejoyed zee deemoanstration. Saenk you veree much." The crowd exploded into wild cheering and clapping in a standing ovation that lasted for minutes.

We all came out and stood by her and the group bowed in unison to the audience.

Needless to say, the demonstration had gone exceptionally well. Trent was so happy that he was crying for joy. I was badly in need of refreshments and a chamber pot break, but I had to make the rounds, with escort, and meet all of the dignitaries. I don't really remember what I said. I hope it was polite… I'm sure it was…really.

Chaptre 13. In which I Attend a Ball

Spring, 15th, Thawburst, 5011 (11 Turns of age)

After I was refreshed, and changed into my best finery, a 'Dress Uniform', which strangely, already had Lancepesades stripes on the sleeves, we went to the banquet and later, the ball. That evening was generally a blissful blur, but I do remember eating amazingly delicious food and dancing with an assortment of beautiful young Halfling and Half-Elven girls, the daughters of the other Guards and Rangers. I even got to dance with Lieutenant LeafFeather, who was a vision of loveliness in a green silk gown that perfectly matched her mesmerizing eyes and showed off her lightly tanned, exceptionally smooth shoulders and décolletage. Her auburn hair was held back from her face by a gold filigreed band and cascaded in waves down her back. She smelled amazing, too, like a field of wildflowers. I did not care at all that she had to pick me up to dance with me. She talked while we danced (I could not have uttered a syllable had I tried) and told me that she would like to teach me the Katas after I started Ranger Training. She told me to call her Chasseresse. She teased that perhaps someday I would get over being so shy. Her voice was nearly indescribable; multi-tonal, musical, with a bell-like quality. Needless to say, I was smitten. I have an image stuck in my brain to this day, a close-up of her glorious eyes, which are actually multi-hued and only appear green from a distance, surrounded by a soft-focus blur. I would, as time progressed, get to know her very well, but that first image remains unblemished, frozen in time even after all of these Turns. We had an odd discussion Turns later where she queried me as to why men in general were so shy, awkward, clumsy, mute, and stupid, and I had to explain to her that she was the definition of 'stunningly beautiful' and 'breathtakingly beautiful', meaning she literally stunned men and women by her mere presence. She thought that was very odd, but that it explained a lot. She is so naturally unselfconscious that this had never occurred to her, feeling herself rather plain compared to her Elven kin. While this probably was true, In comparison to Human women, she was the opposite. I reminded her that when I had first been around her, I had to look away from her to be able to think and communicate properly.

I awoke the next morning, very late, and figured out that someone had carried me to my bed and tucked me in. I really hoped that I had not embarrassed myself last night. I found out later that I had simply fallen asleep, and one of the older Guards, a friend of mine had helped me to bed.

I was told that after I completed a few moonths of training, I would be assigned to a City Guard Reserve Unit to be on call as needed for active duty, that I needed to train with the other Guards at least once per Sevenday, and that I had full access to the Guard facilities and could stay there if I wished. I would also be promoted to Corporal after completing some of the training and assigned as Head Trainer to a Slinger and Archer Training Squad made up entirely of Halflings and that I was responsible for eventually training the city's entire Slinger and Archer Corp, most of which were part of the Ranger Companies, in my unique style of Slinging. I would also receive Ranger training as a tradeoff.

After a couple of days off, spent helping the guys out with their various larcenous deeds, I would return to start training.

Chaptre 14. In which I Assist in a Scam

Spring, 16th, Thawburst, 5011 (11 Turns of age)

The most memorable thing that occurred during the interlude was when we switched one key for another in a foreign dignitary's belt pouch. We had received a scale drawing of the key via messenger from the Thieves Guild Chaptre in the dignitaries home city several Sevendays before his arrival and approached one of our chaptres Locksmiths, one Farrlaighn MacDarach, for him to make a slightly altered copy of the large brass key, altered just enough so that it would not work, but not enough to appear different. I liked the Dwarf. He reminded me of Brud in some ways. He was not as old as the other Dwarves that I knew and still had black hair and bright blue eyes. He completed the task early and without problems and I had gone with Brud and Shadow to pick it up about a Sevenday before. His shop was an amazing place with a huge variety of strange tools, equipment, machine parts, clockworks, lock mechanisms, and other paraphenalia hanging on the walls, from the ceiling, and covering the work benches and tables. It was fun to just look at it all, but I really wanted to pick some of it up and get a good look at it. He did not consider people taller than himself, so poor Brud had to crawl on his knees to keep from banging his head on stuff. I was shorter than him, so had no problem navigating the space. He spotted me eying everything with interest and said, "Ye can coom bahk aenytieme ya wahnt an' loook arrrooun', lad. Ye loook lieke ya hahve taeachable hahnds." I vowed to take him up on the offer at some point. We got the key and went to get prepped for the con and switch.

The day the diplomat's ship arrived we were ready and in place. I had hired a group of street urchins to target the dignitary with their pleas for alms and I was loitering about the docks with them and Shadow in wait for our target. I was disguised as a barefoot girl in a

63

ragged tunic. Trent was in costume as an old rag woman who sat sorting her wares. Brud was in disguise also and working with the dockworkers unloading a ship on the same pier. Makebe was playing his drums close to where the pier met the dock just for back-up. Sarek was wearing desert robes complete with face mask and was strolling around shopping at the various street vendors, also for back-up.

The ship sailed in about midday and docked fairly quickly. The gangplank was lowered and everything was tied into place. The dignitary's staff descended and made the arrangements for a carriage and unloaded his trunks while the Captain of the ship dealt with the Harbourmaster. I was starting to get a bit edgy. When was this guy going to show?

When he finally came out on deck, it was with four armed guards surrounding him. Two went ahead down the gangplank and two behind. Once on the pier, they formed a diamond configuration around him. I had already spotted the target beltpouch on his right front, alerted the other kids, and angled to the side so as to be able to slip in between the front and right guard to get at it. I had signalled the other kids to approach from the targets left. Brud picked up a large plank of wood and started slowly up the pier heading past the target group on their right. Trent had collected all of the rags in a large basket and started up the pier in the opposite direction to pass on their right. This all had to look natural.

At the same moment, the urchins mobbed the target from their left, tripping Trent, who's basket of rags went flying all over the targets, I struck from the right, Pickpocketing the target key and Putpocketing our fake version, the guard closest to Brud stumbled into him and Brud dropped his plank in the middle of the melee. The guards exploded into action, drawing their swords and closing in tight about their master facing outwards in a defensive barrier. It was too late. I had already done the deed and faked a fall off of the pier with my loot in hand.

The City Guardspersons in the area cordoned off the pier and helped the private guards sort out the mess. The urchins were shooed away after being checked for contraband. The foreign dignitary checked himself and found everything to be intact and still present. All of the rags were collected back in the basket and Trent was urged to move along as he bobbed his head and thanked them profusely in a querulous voice. Brud got his board back and moved off. The City Guard bawled at everybody to clear a path for the "'mpor'ant ge'leman" and escorted the poor flustered fellow to his carriage with decorum and haste.

It was Makebe's turn next. I clambered up a pier support and surreptitiously passed him the key all the while complaining loudly in a squeaky voice how they had knocked me in the drink. Makebe went to the nearest sewer grate hidden in an alley, where he had stashed his gear, entered, and moved off towards his destination. It was his job to come out near the merchant's house where the large lockbox that the key went to was stored, sneak in, open the box, retrieve the contents, escape without being noticed, and deliver the boxes contents intact to the Thieves Guild Offices for shipment back to the chaptre that had done the request to begin with. He pulled it off without a hitch and we all celebrated that night at a local pub.

When the dignitary arrived at the merchant's house the next morning, he would find that his precious key would not open the lock for some reason. He might take the box back to his home city after he concluded whatever agreement was the front for his visit to our city or he might take it to a locksmith to get it open, only to find it empty. Wouldn't it be funny if he took it to Farrlaighn's shop?

Chaptre 15. In which I Get Trent a 'Real' Job

Spring, 18th, Thawburst, 5011 (11 Turns of age)

Back at the barracks, I scanned the roster and assignment board for my name and had to do the same for a bunch of other guys that evidently could not read very well. This was a problem that I had been unaware of until that moment. I went back down the hill after work that day and asked Trent if he wanted a job tutoring the City Guard in reading and writing. We all discussed it and decided that since he was not absolutely essential to the smuggling operation on a daily basis, only having to keep the books up at irregular times, he could be spared. I went back up the hill for bed and asked around as to whom to talk to the next day. I was told to check in the office for someone.

After breakfast, I went to the office as instructed, saluted, reported, and asked the officer and the old Sergeant sitting there if the Guard could hire a tutor to teach the poor illiterate blokes. They looked at each other questioningly. The officer told the Sergeant to check into the matter and report back to him. I told them that nobody would admit to illiteracy and that if he just asked Guards to read something for him, saying that his eyes had gotten too bad for him to read it himself, he could find out soon enough who could read and who couldn't. The officer teased the Sergeant that that was actually the case. I told them that my old tutor was between clients and was available for hire cheaply. They liked the 'cheaply' part.

Several days later, I was told to report to the office as fast as possible by a young Page that had tracked me down where I was cleaning, sharpening, and repairing weapons in the Armoury. I zipped off to the office and after reporting, was asked how they could contact my friend. I told them that I would be happy to hand-carry the letter to him myself. They said that they had hoped that I would say that and handed me a rolled up parchment with the City Guard Emblem stamped into the red wax seal.

I rushed down the hill and found the guys loitering around the warehouse trying to fill up time. Trent opened the letter, read it and grinned. He read it to us all and immediately started planning a propre disguise for the job. After trying a few out, we came up with one that was easy to wear for a long period, easy to do each day, sturdy, and made him unrecognizable. He came up with an appropriate accent and practiced it until he could stay in character without slipping. He looked and sounded like a middle-aged, scholarly sage in long robes of the type, ink stained hands, a frumpy wool hat over a graying brown wig, and a monocle in one eye. He walked with a cane, which was actually a hidden rapier, and carried a quill case, ink bottle, scroll case, and purse on his belt. This would work!

I went back up the hill that night and informed the duty officer that the new Tutor would be arriving the next day.

While doing my assignment the next morning, I spotted Trent, 'Professor Franz Finklepot', with a neatly dressed Shadow hanging on to one hand, being given a tour of the facilities. I overheard them saying that they would send a carriage for him and his Granddaughter each day and deliver them back each evening, as I approached to say hello to my old 'Professor'.

Another change accomplished that benefitted both the Guard and the Guild. This was a lot of fun!

Chaptre 16. In which I Attend Guard & Ranger Training

Spring, 23rd, Thawburst, 5011 (11 Turns of age)

The city Guard training was fine, but I really enjoyed the Ranger training. This was held at the Guard, Constabulary, Ranger, and Siege Base at Fort Pishnook, called Fart Piss-nooky by the trainees at the various Training Academies that were housed there. The Siege Engineers College was also there along with the Research and Development Department and the War College. The training of everyone in this entire region of the world who did these types of jobs took place here, so the Fort was temporary home to many persons not of the city. I took part in one Sevenday of Guard Training, three Sevendays of Constabulary Training, and two Moonths of Ranger Training.

The Sevenday of Guard Training was kind of boring and basically consisted of walking Guard Duty on the walls or doing Gate Duty on the huge Fort complex. This thing was at least a league long and a half to a third league wide! It enclosed an area almost as big as the city itself. The training area was four leagues long by a league and a half wide, bounded by major roads on all sides with a crossroads village on one end and the city on the other. It ran roughly East-West.

The Constabulary Training was more interesting and included the various Laws of the City of Waterport and the surrounding area, police procedures, traffic control, what was known of the various criminal organizations (this was laughably minimal and wrong in many ways), investigation techniques, evidence handling, crime scene processing, and weapons training, mostly with the truncheon or 'Billy Club' that all Police carried. The trainees worked with the Military Police of the Fort half of each day and were in class or lab the other half.

The Ranger Training was the most fun of all. I had never been outside of the city before and the only green, growing thing that I had ever seen was the occasional flowers in a window box. To be completely surrounded by growing things and animals that did not try to eat me was a real treat. I used my sound mimicking ability to mimic all of the animals that I met with some really funny results.

I learned how to track, hide, stalk, build and set traps, animal and plant lore, and a bunch more. I became expert with the bow and all of the other weapons and tools used by the typical woodland or wilderness Warrior.

One of my graduation tests was to sneak up on a Roe Deer and touch it before it knew I was there. I actually managed it after a couple of Sevendays practice. I also had to pass a test naming and answering questions about every plant, animal, and animal track that we passed as the testers and I sauntered through the woods on a glorious early summer's day. This one took longer to pass. The hardest one was to make it through a furlong of forest being watched by all of the instructors, who were camouflaged and hidden in observation locations. I had two days to make it and took advantage of every bit of it. Even instructors cannot hold completely still forever. I spotted them, found holes in their coverage, and eventually snuck past. I carried a bag of nuts to bribe the Red Squirrels so they would not give my position away by chattering at me.

Night was not very helpful as almost all of us were part Elf and could see heat. I had to keep camouflaging my heat signature with cold mud to keep from being spotted. This mud was a lot cleaner than the stuff I had used for the same purpose in the sewers. It was really fun and I thought that it was hilarious that they did not even know that I had arrived in the safe zone until I jumped up and yelled "BOO!" Most of the students in my class got captured and had to re-do the test, some several times, and some never passed it.

Most of the students had a lot harder time in general passing the various tests in Guard training. I always seemed to quickly learn the required materials and move on to making things more efficient or solving problems that I noticed or something like that. I got bored rather easily, so it was better to be doing something positive than to be getting in trouble for doing stupid stunts.

You would think that not much can change in just a few moonths, but let me tell you, I changed a lot! It was probably due to the excellent and abundant food, the wonderful bed, the almost constant extreme exercise, the heavy load of equipment that I wore every day, and several other factors, but the result was that I grew nearly a span in height (at least five inches and six lines) and added at least seven pounds to my weight…all muscle! When I had started training, they had weighed me at two stone and two pounds and measured me at two feet tall. I now weighed two stone and twelve pounds (since a stone weighed fourteen pounds, that was forty pounds!) and was two feet, five inches, and six lines! I was getting really big! After all, I was eleven and a half Turns old and I had been told that children are supposed to grow very fast at that time in their life. The funny thing was that everybody thought that I was several Turns older. The other folks in training tended to look up to me for leadership and guidance, much to my discomfiture. I figured that I was more mature due to not having had a childhood like they had had, because I was struggling to survive on my own from approximately age three till about age ten. After all, we had only approximately figured out how old I was.

I liked to practice mathematics since Trent had taught me how to count higher than the numbre of fingers on my hands and how to manipulate the numbres. I did math all the time in my head and was getting good at juggling the numbres. The poor Quartermaster had to issue me new uniforms, including the new armour of my design! I had actually outgrown (and worn out) my original set.

All of my friends attended the graduation ceremony, in disguise; accept for Trent, who was already in one. I was promoted to Corporal, as promised, and introduced to my new squad.

More about these guys;

The first one to catch my attention was a bubbly, round, girl Halfling that came bounding up to me, gave me a big hug, a peck on the cheek, and piped in a squeaky voice, "Greetin's to ya, yer Bosship, an' mae tha Laedy o' Luck shine her blessin's down upon ya!" I stammered, "Why, thank you." and blushed furiously, at which point she giggled and patted my cheek, which did not help. "I be Miss Lucky Nell McThyme, at yer service! Squad Healer an' Kaeper o' good spirits." I executed a courtly bow and she giggled some more and blushed herself. "Oh, go on wi' ya, ya charmer." Her accent was kind of odd. It sounded like a blend of Highlander Dwarven, the local Common, and True Common. She was wearing the white robe of a Priestess of the Goddess of Luck, which did not hide her rotund figure. I swear, that girl was as round as she was tall. This did not slow her down much, though, as she seemed to scamper everywhere. She had a curly mop of bright reddish blonde hair, leaf green eyes, rosy cheeks, and a pale complexion. Her eyes sparkled with mischief and she never seemed to stop smiling. You could always locate her by hearing her tinkling giggle. She was even shorter than me. I figured out pretty quickly that she was a Dwarfkin Halfling and later found out that she was from a small village, named Slagdown, close to the mines of a Clan of Highlander Mountain Dwarves. She was the 'mother' of the group and kept us all fed and healthy. On the left upper front on her robe was the double six-sided dice symbol of her Deity and on the right was the symbol of City Guard. On the sleeves of her robe was Lancepesades stripes. Since she did not truly have a 'waist', she had a small mace hooked to a shoulder strap on her left hip from which also hung her sling bag, and purse. Another strap went across the other shoulder and held her waterskin and quarrel case. She had a small crossbow on her back. Underneath of all of this, she wore the new armour. She turned to another Halfling and bubbled, "I tol' ya he'd be nice, did'n' I?"

The fellow to which she was speaking ambled up, came to attention, snapped a smart salute and said. "Private Mendel Padfoot at your service, Sir!" I returned his salute a bit bemusedly, then he turned to Nell and whispered, "How'd I do? Did I do it right?" She giggled and whispered back, "Ya done good, me laddy. I be proud o' ya." I watched this exchange somewhat perplexed as to how Nell could be teaching anyone propre etiquette as I had yet to see her display it herself and felt that I probably never would. She turned to me and said, "I been tryin' ta teach tha lads some manners, lately." And gave me an ear to ear grin. I could not help going into a fit of giggles myself and gasped to her, "Could you teach me some too?" wherein we all giggled till we nearly fell down. Mendel was stout little fellow with a curly mop of brown hair, light brown eyes, and a ruddy complexion. He was from a farming community near the city. He grinned quietly most of the time and appeared to notice everything. He was dressed and armed in the requisite new armour and weapons (bow, arrows, sling, bullets, purse, waterskin, shortsword), but also carried a sheathed dagger on each hip. I learned later that he was quite proficient with them and we spent many an hour sparring.

Another Halfling approached with a mild scowl on his Face and said curtly, "If zee giggle fest is complete, might I introduce myself?" I replied "Certainly" and sobered quickly. I did notice that the other two did not stop grinning and started whispering to each other and quietly giggling. He came to perfect attention, snapped off the crispest salute that I had ever seen, and stated, "Herr Lancepesades Jagger Pfannkuchen reporting for duty, Sir! It vill be a pleasure verking vith you." Needless to say, I was very impressed. This had to be the most muscle bound and chiseled Halfling that I had ever seen. He appeared to have not an ounce of fat on his body. He was also very tall for a Halfling. His straight blonde hair was shorn in a flat-top style. His steel grey eyes appeared to look right through a person. He was very militaristic and warlike in demeanor. Very unusual for a Halfling, to say the least. He reminded me of a hunk of ice. If he ever cracked a smile, it would probably break his face. He wore the most propre new armour that I had ever seen. It actually looked starched and creased. I returned his salute and replied, "Welcome aboard, Herr Pfannkuchen." His eyes appeared to smile slightly at that and I guessed that he must have a sense of humour buried somewhere under that austere façade. He was from a village in the area of the Northern Forest Tribes. They were very tough, warlike, and ferocious in battle, so I guessed that the Halflings in the area were likewise.

The last of the group was still skulking back a ways. Nell leaned in and whispered, "He's kinda shy fer a Halfling." And winked at me. I said, "Come forward, please?" He shuffled forward with his head down, peeking at us through his hair, came to a halt, and mumbled, "Rudd Tinkerton at your service sir." I replied, "Glad to meet you, Rudd." He was as skinny as myself, which was unusual for a Halfling as they tended to enjoy up to six meals a day and were usually quite padded. He had worry lines on his face, which was also unusual. His hair was straighter than the average Halfling, being only wavy. It was nearly black and his complexion had a decided yellowish tinge. I found out later that he was from somewhere to the east and that accounted for the differences. His family were the founders of the town, which was named after them or vice versa and everyone there was Tinkers by trade. He did eventually warm up to me and quit being so shy, but he remained quiet and retiring consistently.

Chaptre 17. In which I Enlarge My Repertoire

Summer, 14th, Perfumedelight, 5011 (11 Turns of age)

As my advanced training, I reported for Kata drills with the lovely Chasseresse, Lieutenant LeafFeather, and found it to be held in the generally unused Ballroom of the castle. Some of the other recently graduated students from my class were also on hand along with my entire Training Squad and some other Guardspersons and Guardswomen.

We started out by introducing ourselves to the group and talking a bit about our learning goals for the course. I stammered that I would like to be able to do the Kata that I had seen our teacher do at the demonstration. She told me that my goals were high indeed and said that it usually took many Turns to master that one. I replied that however long it took, I would be happy to learn from her, the Kata Master.

Why did she have to be so pretty, and how could someone have such a small waist? Where did she put her guts? How did she get her butt and hips to move like that? Her spine must be a lot more flexible than the average person. It was very hard to be around her, but I wanted to do so every day. Ack! I noticed that a lot of the other students, both guys and girls, had the same moon-eyed look on their faces. I resolved to be different from the usual males and females who like girls, act in ways that she was not used to, and perhaps win her interest and maybe, just maybe, her heart. But first, I had to learn to talk to her without my brain clogging up and my mouth freezing...and grow a foot or two. She was a little over four feet tall. I might be able to grow enough to at least match her. This was going to be really hard, but I was bound to do it!

Katas are basically a martial dance. You memorize with your mind a series of manoeuvres that flow from one to another seamlessly, then, practice them repeatedly until your body memorizes them and will do them automatically in battle without you having to think about it. Strikes and blocks can also be individually memorized the same way, but it is better to learn them as part of a Kata. At first, it is incredibly hard, then it becomes boring, and then it becomes effortless and you can move on to the next one. I learned ones for various combinations of sling, bow, shortsword, and one or two daggers. It was exhausting and fun, and exhilarating, considering who my teacher was. I slowly, but surely pulled ahead of the other students, who had plateaued at various stages of the training. When all of the other students, but me, had graduated and it was just me and Chasseresse, she gave me some options to choose from. I could graduate and move on to other training (nooo!), continue training with her whenever she could fit me into her schedule (awkward), or become her assistant trainer and she could continue my advanced training throughout the day in between training the new guys (Yay!). Either way, I would have to keep up training the Slingers in my style and keep running the Training Squad. Of course, I took the third option. The Kata that I was learning at the moment was a few pegs below the one that was my goal to learn, but it was still very complicated, with hundreds of moves incorporated into it.

She told me that there was going to be a ceremony the following day at 1000hrs, so I needed to get my dress uniform ready. I figured that it would be a graduation ceremony just like all of the other students had been through.

After being around her for Moonths, I had become able to talk to her like a regular person, as long as I did not look directly at her, and we had had many long conversations on all kinds of topics during breaks in the training, lunches, suppers, and during the evenings with me getting more and more infatuated with her, even though I was getting used to being around her. She was far more than just her amazing looks and voice. She was a very complex person with a keen mind who studied everything with which she came in contact. She was an avid reader and had read every scroll and book she could get her hands on, even the really esoteric stuff. She was extremely talented in anything she put that marvelous mind to. She was amazingly caring and wise, also. In short, her beauty did not just go skin deep.

She ducked her head in embarrassment and told me, "I am sooo happee zat you choose to stay weez me. You ah zee onlee freen' zat I haf evere had een my whole life. Evereeone has always avoided mee for zum reeazoan and would not carry on a seemple coanverezation at all. I jus' wan' to tell you zat I value you and our time togezere greatlee." At which point, she leaned down, gave me a hug, and kissed me on the check. I very nearly fainted! The room spun and I had to sit down on the floor. She got rapidly down on her knees beside me and said with a worried expression and tone, "Ah you alright ma cherie petit! Oh! You have beeen workeeng too hahd and have not taken good care of youse'f. I must care for you myse'f immeediatly!" Before I could tell her that I had simply been overwhelmed by her close proximity, she called for a large Human Guard and bade him carry me to her quarters. She said that the barracks was out of the question, because it was too crowded and noisy, and had too many nosy people. I did not know whether to protest or go along with it. Going along with it seemed like the better idea, considering that I had dreamed of seeing the inside of her quarters for some time, after all, I was nearly twelve Turns and had been going through some major bodily changes during the last few Moonths.

On the way, she asked a Drudge to have a meal for us both delivered to her quarters. The large Guard deposited me on her bed with a quizzical expression, but did not ask any questions. I said, "I'm fine. I just got overwhelmed a bit there, nothing that some rest won't cure." She said, "Now jus' lie back an' relax, ma cherie, an' I weel see to youere needs. We muust get you cleeaned up zo you may rest." She proceeded to strip off my sweat stained armour in a very fast and efficient manner. I felt like a chicken being plucked be an experienced cook. When I was naked, she pulled the cover up over me and began to prepare for a sponge bath by filling a basin with hot water from one of two taps. The castle had plumbing, hot and cold running water in pipes and toilets over bigger pipes for waste removal. This waste flowed into my old home, the city sewer system. People usually bathed in the large staff Bath House or the Bathrooms in the Barracks, but if they had private quarters, like Chasseresse, they could use the bathtub in their room or do a sponge bath as needed. She evidently thought that I was too tired to use her bath tub. After she got my bath prepped, and looked down at herself in disgust, and said, "Oooo, I am zo sweaty and dirty zat I must also bathe." She started the water flowing into her small bathtub for herself and changed out of her own armour. I was staring at her, of course.

A lack of clothing, in and of itself, means little in our culture, as I'm sure you are aware, but beauty is beauty, and she was the most beautiful young woman in the area. A lot of people should wear clothing, even if they are swimming (swimming with clothes on would be so awkward, though) or it is hot weather, simply because they are so ugly that they should cover it up, but she was the opposite. She noticed that my body was reacting in a definite manner to the visible stimuli. This was a rather new phenomenon for me and I only had a vague idea what to do with it when it acted like that. She started to tear up a little and said, "You do like me! Zat makes mee zo happee. Would you do mee zee honere of being my first lovere?" I blushed profusely, turning bright red all the way up to my hairline and choked out an approximation of 'Yes, please?' too overcome with a huge array of thoughts and emotions all jumbled together to even come close to thinking clearly. She giggled and said, "I always knew zat zee manditoree traineeng een courtisan skeels would come een handee zome day! Eet ees required learneeng for all young Elves. After all, who would want to bee an eegnorahnt, brutish lovere, and while I am not personally experieenced in zees aspect of adult interaction, I'm sure zat wee cahn feegure eet out eef wee try. So, let mee help you weez zat not so leetle problem." I appreciated the fact that she had some inkling of what we were supposed to do, because I didn't and I was very nervous about messing this up, after all, you only get one shot at pleasing the girl of your dreams and I did not want to lose her because I was clumsy, stupid, or inexperienced.

What followed was the most tendre and passionate exploration of each other's bodies and the functions of the hitherto unused parts that I could have ever imagined in my wildest dreams. We were both young and totally inexperienced, so there were some unavoidable awkward moments, but we managed them well and enjoyed ourselves immensely. Turns later, we would look back at that early time period and share fond remembrances. We found the meal outside her door many hours later, very cold and stale, as we made our way to the castle baths to refresh ourselves, and got a giggle out of it. We could not both fit in her little tub, and still being young, we wanted to frolic and play in the water in the large pools of the bath house. We were famished, so ordered another meal and ate like pigs at a trough. By mutual decision, I moved my small amount of belongings into her room that night.

Chaptre 18. In which I Train Constantly

Fall, 21st, Fruitaplenty, 5011 (11 Turns of age)

It turned out that the Ceremony the next day was not for graduation, but for promotion to Sergeant and an award for Excellence in Combat Training for learning more Katas than any other student previously, thus making me a Journeyperson Trainer, and another for Excellence in Design for coming up with the new armour. They were awarded in the Ballroom by the Commanding General of the entire City with Chasseresse assisting and in front of the Mayor and every Captain, Lieutenant, and Sergeant in the entire City Guard along with my Squad. Wow! I was so nervous that my knees were shaking.

I got through the ceremony somehow, and the meet and greet after, and the amazing meal that was served in the Banquet Hall, and the dance that evening in celebration. Chasseresse stayed by my side throughout and there was much whispering and gossip flowing about us. The males were stunned that a runt like me could have won the heart of the most beautiful woman in the castle. They did not realize that all that was required was to look past her stunning beauty to the truly stunning creature beneath. Evidently, no one had ever tried talking with her before. After the festivities, we retired to bed for a well-earned 'rest' from our labours.

The next day, we had another ceremony where I and Chasseresse promoted Herr Jagger to Corporal. He almost showed some emotion at that event. I told him to search for a suitable Private to join the Squad.

We celebrated my twelfth Birthingday at a pub called The Pig in a Poke in the Harbour District on Leafall 28th. We rented a dining room there and invited all of my friends. I made out the invitations and delivered them personally. My Squad went into high gear making food for the party, and they were all talented cooks. Herr Jagger made a beautiful cake. Farrlaighn showed up. Everyone brought their instruments and there was much dancing and singing throughout. I remember a singing contest where several groups competed. I think that the Dwarves won. It was Farrlaighn the Locksmith, Garan the Master Trainer, the Master Armourer, and another Dwarf that I did not know in the group. They made up in volume what they lacked in skill, but they did this one song in four part harmony, in their native tongue that was so sad, even though most of us could not understand the words, lots of people got tearful. You know, I don't remember ever hearing the Master Armourer's given name. Everyone just called him 'The Master' out of respect. The guys from The Guild came in disguise. Trent came in the one that he used practically every day at the castle. He had worn it so often lately that my mental image of him was starting to be that disguise. Tons of folks from the Guard and the castle were there, so the townsfolk were on their best behaviour. Some of the castle kitchen staff showed up with a wagonload of food.

One group of ornery sailors fresh off a ship did try to bust in, but when Brud picked up their leader by one ankle, held him aloft with ease, and gently slapped him senseless, they decided to frequent a different tavern. The party ended up taking over the entire pub and spilling out into the street, where we had a street dance and everyone in the neighbourhood joined in, even the sailors, after getting the 'OK' from Brud along with the signal that he was watching them. After watching him keep the crowd safe all night, some of the City Guard approached him with an offer of training. He initially turned them down, citing that he had a warehouse to run, but about a Turn or less later, he did join and was a reservist for the rest of his life. A swell time was had by all, though some got a bit too much into their pints, and felt it the next day. I danced so much that night with Chasseresse, that my feet were sore the next morning! I could barely walk. Really. It was not just an excuse to stay in bed. Really...I swear!

For the next six Moonths or so, I divided my time between training in the advanced Katas, training others in the easier ones, training all of the Slingers in my method, and learning some new things from Trent, in his capacity as Tutor for the Guard. He had already taught me how to read and write True Common fluently and some calligraphy, but now he expanded it to include book writing and illustration, called illumination, and the forging of official documents. There was a lot of art involved in this and each illuminated book written in calligraphy was nearly priceless. It did not really matter what the words were talking about or the story. Each page of parchment was very expensive, even without having something added to it. It was very interesting and absorbing work and my relatively small, slender, and dexterous hands were very good at it. This was a very fun activity! Under the guise of training, I learned how to do all of the common legal documents and managed to make passable forgeries of several important papers needed by the Thieves Guild. I learned to forge almost anyone's signature and got very good at the various cursive styles of writing. I wrote some poems, illuminated them, and tried my hand at bookbinding. My first attempt frankly looked like a first attempt, but Chasseresse enjoyed it immensely, said she would cherish it always, and rewarded me for my efforts, though, being young, we never really needed an excuse for such endeavors. We were so randy in our youth.

I also practiced my gambling skills with the other Guards. My goal was not to win, but to see if I could manipulate the game so that everyone came out exactly even at the end, so there was no clear winner. This was harder than it appears to be. The other guys were always amazed when this happened. Sometimes, when one of the players needed money badly for some good purpose, like if one of their children was sick and needed costly care, I would manipulate the game so that he or she won big. It was a lot of fun. I never needed any money, so I made sure that I never won, just broke even, not losing or gaining any money during the game. To me, money is just a tool, not a goal in and of itself. It is to be acquired only to be used for basic needs and the fulfilment of worthy goals. Amassing a fortune, just to collect it, is a waste of time and skills. If it does not benefit something or somebody, it is greed, pure and simple.

Chaptre 19. In which I Plan an Outing

Winter, 15th, Snowshell, 5012 (12 Turns of age)

We had one interesting occurrence during that period of very ordinary activities, which introduced me to another of my life-long friends. While training a bunch of recruits in the Katas with Chasseresse, we were approached by the Captain of the Ranger Company and a very Elven looking Half-Elf that I had never before seen. The only thing that gave him away as part Human was the perfectly and very elaborately trimmed beard that he sported. He was very slender and dressed very fussily, even though he was wearing all green outdoors leather clothing. He acted like he should be wearing a tuxedo at a fancy ball. He was amazingly poised and graceful. He had an Elven Longbow and Quiver on his back and a Sabre on his left side. His hair and beard were very dark and his eyes were the most mesmerizing yellow-gold. He had a flawless Ivory complexion that showed off the hair and beard nicely. I found out later that his hair was really bright red, but he dyed it to stop people calling him "Cranberry". If Trent saw this guy, he would probably swoon.

That was a good idea. They would make a cute couple. The Captain introduced him as Cranndair the Warden, meaning that he was the highest level of Constabulary in the woodlands surrounding the City, the equivalent power of a Colonel, and reported directly to the Mayor. We introduced ourselves, he bowed to us both, kissed Chasseresse's hand, shook mine rather daintily, and replied, "How wonderful to finally meet you both, I have sooo looked fahwahd to this day. It will be my distinct pleasure to work with you." He had a very high class accent, a bit unctuous and effete for my tastes, but definitely gentlepersonly, a real classy guy.

We repaired to an office and he began to fill us in on his needs and request. He said that he normally did not require much assistance to police his jurisdiction and could usually handle the ruffians and vandals with ease, but he had discovered a group that was a little bit too big and formidable for him to handle by himself. He described a band of well-armed, organized Highwaypersons that had been a thorn in his side, and their victims also, for much too long. They moved their base frequently, were alert, focused, and hard to track, even in the snow. They reminded him of some sort of military outfit, possibly Rangers, rather than the usual riff-raff that were members of Bands of Highwaypersons. He was concerned about this menace to society. He said that while they had not committed murder, as of yet, they were not above physical assault during their robberies and needed to be stopped.

A slight aside is in order, not all highwaypersons are bad people. There is a legend amongst the Guards of a very nice one, called the "Polite Bandit". About a hundred Turns earlier, people started getting held up by a very large, rough fellow, who wore a sack with two eye holes cut in it over his head, in an area of the South Road, just outside of town. The weird thing was that he only took a small portion of their money, exactly ten percent, or just took a small amount of foodstuffs, whatever they happened to be carrying. He was far too kind hearted and had been known to give things to poor travellers instead of taking. He also was not very bright and trusted the word of his 'victims', accepting whatever they said without argument and thus getting fooled quite often. Curiously, at the same time that the thefts started occurring, people started to notice an improvement in the condition of the road and the sides of the road up to and including the fences of the local landowners. The people thought that the city had suddenly taken an interest in road improvement, but the Guards knew that was not the case. Therefore, they decided to leave him free to do his version of community service. Over the Turns, the frequent travellers on that road figured out the connection between the nicely maintained several miles of roadway and the big fellow that 'robbed' them. They came to think of it as a tax of sorts and this led to the generally accepted concept of taxation for public service. They started to cook him food and bring him replacement tools instead of paying money. He eventually gave up wearing the hood, worked openly, and got to know the folks that frequented his stretch of highway. By the current era, every square foot of public thoroughfare had been staked out by someone. There were signs to inform you when you were leaving the responsibility of one Caretaker, as they had come to be known, and entering the responsibility of another. The Caretakers also kept an eye out for troublemakers in their area and 'squealed' to the Guard if they spotted any. This meant that as a person travelled through the city or the surrounding lands, they paid a 'toll tax' for each section through which they travelled. Most of the Caretakers just nailed cans to a post or wall at the boundaries of their jurisdiction, but some only expected you to pay them if you saw them working. Nobody ever robbed these cans. If someone attempted to, people would mob or shun them, which was actually worse. Some of the Caretakers also gave information to the Thieves Guild, so they were protected by everybody. The caretakers took pride in their area of responsibility and as a result, a competition of sorts emerged between Caretakers concerning how clean, neat, pretty, and well-tended their areas were kept. The condition of the sections had a positive or negative effect on the size of the tips that people paid, so a diligent Caretaker could make a really good living. One of the city holidays that took place in the springtime, in the moonth of Flowercascade, was called 'Caretakers Day'. A parade of one hundred handpicked citizen judges would start at one end of the city and wind its way through to the other side, passing through every street. Some of the citizenry would follow the judges, 'taking the tour' as it was called. As the parade exited each area, each judge would drop one whitewashed pebble into a bucket, watched over by a City Guardsperson, if they liked the condition of the area enough to give it a vote. The 'votes' were counted and tallied by junior members of the Pursers Office after each section was viewed. If more than one section got all hundred votes, there would be a tie-breaker competition where the contestants would do a particular task chosen by the Mayor to beautify the city. The winning section was given an engraved brass plaque to display in their area. Collecting these plaques was a big deal to the Caretakers. A big feast and street dance in celebration of the event would happen that evening. This usually pretty much trashed up the sections that were so beautiful the day before, so I wondered why the Caretakers would allow it, but since the entire population helped clean up the mess, I guess it was not too bad. The businesses would clean, repaint, and dress up their storefronts in preparation for the event, so the whole town got a make-over annually. Just think, all of this got started because one simpleminded farm boy with a small larcenous streak decided to clean up a stretch of highway and needed to make a living while he did so.

So, back to the 'mean' Highwaypersons. We resolved to assemble a merry band of hearty folk to take on the challenge. Chasseresse would bring her Platoon of Rangers and I would bring the Training squad. Let's see, that would make five Squads plus leaders, so, fourteen Privates, five Lancepesades, five Corporals, two Sergeants, one Lieutenant, and the Warden. That makes twenty eight, total. That sounded just right, not too many and not too few. We decided to capture them alive if possible so that we might question them. I had a bright idea. I would try to get Trent to come along so that he and Cranndair could meet one another, and then decided against it, because in his 'Professor Finklepot' persona, it simply would not work. I would have to figure some other way for them to meet.

We sent the word out for everyone to be ready to depart by first light the next day at the East Gate of the city. That sounds early in the day, but you must understand a bit more about the geography of the area to see why it is not actually very early at all. The City of Waterport is sandwiched between a large bay called the Bay of the Sea People to the West, with a narrow sea called the Straight of Dragons further West, that splits the islands in half, and a chain of low mountains to the East. Since it takes extra time for the sun to shine on us over those mountains, first light is later in the morning than you might think. Since the day is divided into four sets of seven houres or bells, midnight being twenty eight houres and noon being fourteen houres, then depending on the season, dawn would happen generally between six houres and nine houres and the mountain to our rear added at least one houre to the equation. Since the season was mid-winter, that would make our start time about ten houres, but there was one more factor to consider in this equation, heavy cloud cover had blanketed the area during the night, so the start time would probably not happen until at least twelve houres or nearly noon.

At least we always knew what time it was. The Temple to the God of Time saw to that. The Clergy there kept meticulous track of time using various sized houre glasses, sextants, celestial alignment spotting devices, and other esoteric machinae. They had a huge bell tower and rang them each houre with the appropriate numbre of bells. When I lived in the sewers, I could clearly hear those bells, that's how loud they were. Twenty eight bells at midnight took a while to ring out.

Faeghan WhiteWolf

Chaptre 20. In which I Get Ready for an Outing

Winter, 16th, Snowshell, 5012 (12 Turns of age)

So, at somewhere between ten and twelve bells, we all collected outside the castle gate replete with all of the necessary supplies and equipment for a winter foray, since the temperature was hovering around freezing and it looked like we were in for a big snowfall. We were all wearing the new armour, but versions that had been dyed in winter colours, a blotched pattern of white, grey-brown, dry hay yellow, and faded green. We were really hard to spot against the snow, rocks, heather, evergreens, and mostly leafless deciduous trees. We had on wool liners for all of the pieces, so we looked a bit bulkier than usual, but we were warm and dry.

Wool is such a wonderful material for clothing in cool, wet climes. One of the biggest industries in the area, both cottage and large scale, was the manufacture of woolen sweaters, mittens, caps, and other garments. The supply side of that industry was also huge, the raising of many varieties and colours of Sheep for their wool and mutton. If you travelled about the countryside, you would see herds of Stout and Striped Sheep practically everywhere that crops were not being grown. This gave the landscape a neat 'mown' appearance.

Herds of Goats, raised for their mohair, milk, and hides, took care of the forested regions (where they ate the brush) and rough & rocky terrain, so even those areas appeared tended.

Some Black Cattle was also raised in the lowlands for beef, milk, and leather, as were Dwarf Hippo. I was told that other areas of the country were much more 'wild' in appearance and less 'park like'.

Herds of Dwarf Mammoths were raised for their shed hair, rich milk, hides, and meat. Dwarf Elephants were raised for all of the same reasons, except the hair, as they had almost none. The hides and meat were only harvested if one of these died naturally, due to people being loath to kill such intelligent beasts.

Quilted down-filled clothing could not be beat for sheer warmth. Down-filled pillows and mattresses were also excellent. Farmers kept herds of Knobbies in the lowland pastures for their molted down, meat, and eggs. In the forests, Herders kept watch over Knobby Longnecks, Crested Longnecks, Cowbirds, and Deerbirds, which were raised for the same purposes.

Fae Glen Forest in Summer

In our packs, we carried an assortment of useful tools and equipment; a breathing tube (for use underwater), a camouflage paint kit, a fishing kit (lures, flies, hooks, lead weights, cork bobbers, 25 feet of line, and a hand spooler), a First Aid kit (bandages, needles, thread, a razor, and ointments), a trowel to dig cat holes, a tin of insect repellant, snow goggles, a tin of sunburn ointment, a skinning knife, a waterproof tinderbox (flint and steel, aromatic evergreen shavings), and a tin of weaponblack. Strapped to the top was a bedroll made of a wool blanket and waterproof tarp rolled together. We also wore two large beltpouches on each side of the belt buckle in the front. They carried equipment that we needed instant access to; a sling with bullets and darts in one, and flash and smoke bombs (made of two chambered glass spheres with reactive chemicals inside all in a crushproof metal case), a metal signalling mirrour, a small spyglass, and some hard candy in the other. Each person seemed to also carry some sort of small musical instrument. I had a metal Penney Whistle, in the key of C, stowed on me. Lucky Nell was teaching me how to play it. I also carried a modified Thieves Tool Kit in a separate bag, slung under my pack, which includes; a lockpick set, a skeleton key, a keymaking set, limewood strips, sharkskin, tarpaper, a wax pad, a wax lined glass vial of acid, small chisels, a small hammer, files, a hacksaw, a small crowbar, a magnifying glass, a flask of oil, a small mouthed funnel, a small telescoping mirrour pole, a folding grappling hook & thin knotted line, spikes, a glass cutter, caltrops, a bag of marbles, and a bag of sneezing powdre.

We had enough dried meat and fish, and travel bread in our packs to last two Sevendays. Water, we would collect along the way and stow in our waterskins. The Halflings also carried an array of spices, sugar, butter, flour, rice, dried beans, dried fruit, and an array of cooking utensils. Halflings never went hungry and tended to eat at least six small meals per day. I figured that it was because we have small stomachs that empty out rather quickly. Human kids are like that. They always seem to be hungry, too. Both groups tended to be partial to sweets, also.

We also had the requisite weapons; a quiver on one side (suitable for twenty arrows), and a combination sword scabbard, bow sheath, and Tracking Stick holder attached to the other side of the backpack. My sword was a shortsword (a straight, double edged, sharp pointed sword with a fingerguard) and my bow was a recurved shortbow of about forty five pound draw weight. I carried a fighting dagger on each hip and two bandoleers of small throwing daggers in an 'X' pattern across my chest. These daggers were of the straight, double edged, sharp pointed, leaf bladed shaped style with blood groove and fingerguard. They were perfectly balanced, made almost entirely of fine steel, except for the slightly knobby leather grip inserts (so as to maintain sure grip, even when covered in slippery blood). I always kept my blade weapons honed to a razor-sharp edge. Due to Sarek's excellent training in dagger fighting and throwing, I was quite deadly, almost surgically so, with these implements. Everything was padded and 'silenced' so as to not make any noise as I moved. All of this was obviously sized to the person that carried it and each person carried the style of weapons to which they were most accustomed and most proficient, so there was a wide variety within our small group. Some carried axes instead of swords and daggers or a combination. The biggest Human in our group, a guy about seven feet tall nicknamed 'Bear', carried bandoleers of small throwing axes...scary...those 'little' axes were nearly as tall as me. He also carried the largest double edged battle axe that I had ever seen. The handle on that thing was about four or five feet long! Three or four of us Halflings could ride around in his backpack, which was about the size of a small cart. I know, because just for fun, we had tried it. He was of Norseman stock from Stavsund and wore his long, light blond hair and beard in braids. He had the brightest, most piercing blue eyes. Nice guy, though, but I would not have wanted to take him on in battle. He had a temper and his normally fair skinned face got bright red when he got angry...very scary. Can you imagine having a whole bunch of Warriors like him running straight at you with bright red faces, screaming battle cries, and waving oversized weapons around? In that case, I would probably just wet myself and faint in sheer terrour. I would find out later in life that he was actually a cousin of mine, on my paternal grandmother's side of the family, so, but more about that later, when I actually track down my blood kin.

Cranndair briefed all of us on the details of the situation using a large map, pointed out where they had struck in the past, where their abandoned camps had been found, the areas on the map that we needed to scout for them, and several possible methods that we might use to capture them. He then did something rather odd. That huge map had appeared almost three dimensional when we viewed it and it stored oddly also. He rolled it up tightly, then spread his arms, placed his palms on the ends of the roll, and pushed both ends in simultaneously. You would expect nothing to happen except maybe crumpling the ends of the tube, but that was not what occurred. The map shrunk between his hands until it was the size of a small rolled scroll! I was so curious, that I actually ached to find out how that worked. I resolved to broach the topic later with him. He stored the tiny roll in a carved bone case at his belt and stoppered it neatly. The stopper made an audible soft 'click' when he did it. I suspected that this was an actual Elvishly enchanted item.

Next, he presented another wonder to us. Out of a pouch on his belt, he pulled nine large, clear, crystal marbles about two inches diametre. He kept one and handed out eight of them to the Corporals, Sergeants, and Lieutenant. People started looking through and in other ways investigating them. He brought his up to his face and clearly spoke the word "all" into it. Each of the others lit up with a soft glow and made a tiny chiming sound. The various reactions were hilarious and varied from staring in shock to yelping to dropping the item to jumping back to falling on their butt. I was so busy watching all of the others that I really did not react, except maybe for a slight twitch of surprise. He smiled slightly and spoke into his sphere. "Warden to all group leaders. Please acknowledge." The image of his face and a slightly tinny version of what he said came through the marble in my hand. Stares of wonder were the predominant response to his query. I had the presence of mind to tentatively respond by saying, "Sergeant Runt of Training Squad here Sir." Chasseresse also responded appropriately. He smiled again and told us that he needed to organize us for communication efficiency. He had us line up by groups, Chasseresse, her Sergeant, me and the Training Squad, and the other four Squads. He then pointed at himself and said, "One", then proceeded to numbre us accordingly, thus making my Squad, numbre four. "When I ahsk fah you to acknowledge, please simply sound off in numericahl ordah by simply holding the communication device in front of youah face and speaking youah numbah. Let us try it again, shall we?" This time, it went much smoother and when it came to my turn, I responded with "Four here." He responded with "Much bettah! You chaps will become proficient in no time at all." I said, "Excuse me Sir? How do these things work?" He smiled and told us that they were a product of Elven technology and were simply shaped and polished crystalline balls that had been attuned to each other in a closed circuit, in other words, they could only 'see' each other, so if we were to try to 'see' the future or do anything else with them, it simply would not work. He told us to cup them in our hands at night so the glow could not be seen and that a whisper was sufficient to transmit. Amazing Elven technology! That they considered this to be normal was a peek into the huge differences between Elves and everyone else. He had us practice communicating between specific groups and to all of the groups. It was fun!

Chaptre 21. In which I Go on an Outing

Winter, 16th, Snowshell, 5012 (12 Turns of age)

We headed out of the East City Gate, accompanied by cheers and yells of support by the Guards manning the gate and the walls, crossed the drawbridge over the moat, and turned left, generally North, onto the road that went around the outside of the City wall. We shared the road with all sorts of conveyances from small two wheeled carts pulled by a goat up to large wagons with three axles and wheels taller than a Human pulled by teams of eight oxen. These were carrying a huge variety of materials and products to and from the city. On the left side of the road was the wide moat of fresh water and on the right, it was lined with fine estates, large well-tended farms, orchards, vineyards, and combinations of all of the above. It crossed three of the streams that fed into and around the City wall on well-designed stone bridges, then curved left, or West, still following the City wall. It connected with the North Coastal Road as it exited the City at the North Gate. There was a huge traffic jam there due to a spillage that had occurred because a large wagon had overturned while trying to make the sharp corner. It had been overloaded with a far too top-heavy stack of twined rolls of hay. The ropes holding the stack on had broken when the wagon tumped. Tempers were starting to flare, with people cursing and yelling at each other, shaking fists, and other imprecations and gestures. and the too few Guards that had been able to respond to the situation were in danger of being overwhelmed. The Warden stepped into the centre of the potential melee, followed by the rest of us, made an arcane gesture with his fingers while saying something in Elven (Chasseresse covered her ears and I followed her example), and spoke without apparent strain in a voice that was so booming and loud that it made my ears ring even though they were covered. "SILENCE!!!!" He then spoke in a normal voice, "If we might have a modicum of order and manners here, please." and proceeded to organize the stunned crowd into a group of large men righting the wagon, several groups calming and sorting the animals, and a large group reloading the wagon. It ended up taking the combined efforts of many people and draft animals to right this tumped wagon. I was put to getting some of the other conveyances through the area and on to their destinations. When they had gotten down to the bottom of the pile of hay, they found a small cart buried there. Everyone expected the worst, but was pleasantly surprised to find a still living, but very angry, straw covered Halfling farmer and his stunned goat under the mass. His load of hens eggs were a goner. The small farmer, while voicing expletives in several languages, marched over to the righted wagon and demanded to know who the owner was. His face was a strange shade of purplish dark red from the level of his anger. It was scary to behold. Several of the people present pointed at the offending wagon driver and backed hastily away. The Apoplectic farmer marched up to the Human wagon driver and kicked him squarely in the shin with enough force to make everyone present say a mental 'ouch' just from watching it. The offending Wagoneer howled in pain and started hopping around on his other foot until he lost his balance and fell over into an exceptionally large steaming cow pie that had been left in the roadway by one of the many oxen. The offended small farmer walked up to him, pointed a stubby finger at his nose and said, "Watch w'ere yer goin, ya clumsy great galoot! Next time, I won't be so fergivin'" and then tweaked his nose. The bad driver yelped in dismay and the crowd roared with mirth. Lucky Nell came over and started bandaging the man's freely bleeding shin while giggling continuously. A small herd of Dwarf Mammoth were busily cleaning up the leftover straw in the road and when they were done, we assisted the Herdsperson in moving them along. The traffic jam was finally cleared and we were on our way North again.

A Wagoneer driving an empty dray, one of the super large wagons, offered to give all twenty eight of us a ride in return for the amount that he would have made if he had had a load during his return trip. The Warden and Chasseresse rode on each side of the driver up top. We started teasingly referring to ourselves as 'The Cargo Crew'. We took up a collection and paid the man for a trip to the next village, a

Halfling town called "Thistledown". This was Mendel's home town and he assured us that they would make us feel right at home. We found lots of leftover edibles, mostly root vegetables of various sorts, which had evidently fallen out of their crates while being transported to Waterport. Most of them did not require cooking, so we snacked quite well during the journey and had lots of room to stretch out in the back of that enormous wagon. These wagons were basically a really big flat bed with slots along the sides for the removable six feet tall side sections to be added. The beds were sixteen feet long by four feet wide. The front wheels were five feet diametre and the rear were seven. The tires were made of one inch thick iron and they had steel axels. They were constructed of solid oak. They weighed seven thousand eight hundred pounds empty and were rated to carry loads up to nine metric tons of cargo. It took a lot of abuse to break one of these behemoths.

We arrived in late afternoon. It was only about a league distance to the village, just past Merchantville and the New Harbour, but oxen, while able to haul incredible weights, move at a very slow pace.

We had been travelling beside a beautiful forested area, to the East, of mostly leafless deciduous trees interspersed with a few evergreens. After hearing the honking, we had spotted a herd of Cowbirds feeding on the conifers. They were pretty impressive. Gigantic wingless birds up to fifteen feet long, from nose to tip of tail, and very tall at the back. They used their hands to manipulate the tree branches on which they dined. The conifer forest had ended about a quarter mile from the stream to be replaced by fallow fields separated by hedgerows, fruit trees, and pole fences. One Cowbird casually stepped over the fence into a pasture and had to be hurriedly urged back into the forest by the Herdspersons. Stout Sheep and Knobbies were grazing in many of the enclosed areas. The Knobbies were cute. They looked like a cross between a turtle, a crocodile, a bird, and a Sheep.

A dirt road intersected the cobbled highway just before the expanse of a stone bridge over a wide shallow stream that gurgled along heading to the sea on our left. This cart path headed East, generally following the creek, but high enough to avoid being flooded during the Spring melt.

The village was hard to spot, due to the fact that most of it was underground. So that was why living in the confined underground space of the sewers had never really bothered me, but seemed to be oppressive to the Big Folk. I could see wisps of smoke rising into the sky, apparently from chimneys, but no structures for them to emit from. I had climbed up to the top of the boards that enclosed the bed of the wagon to get a better look. Mendel spotted my perplexed look and asked what was wrong. I said, "Where are the houses? I just see one big building. Does everyone live in it?" He giggled and replied, "Did you not know, Sir, that we live in Burrows? That is why all of the Halfling town names end in 'down', because they are underground. The Big Folk ought to end their towns in 'surface' and the Elves in 'up'. Dwarves live 'down', too, but a lot deeper than us. Maybe they should call theirs 'deep'. I should suggest this to all the bigger people that I meet. That one big building is the Inn and it's a 'surface', so Big People can stay there. I wonder what it would be like to have all four types living in the same spot, each in their own layer…sort of a vertically aligned town with four horizontal sections. Wouldn't that be fun?" He grinned at this. I was beginning to suspect that the majority of Halflings could be described as "irrepressible" and "chatty", with a few notable exceptions, like Jagger and Rudd, though the Elfkin, like myself, tended to be slightly less talkative.

The dray came to a halt and the Wagoneer called out, "Well, 'ere ye are, such as it is. Could ye do me a favour and ask if they 'ave a load fer me ta Fisherton?" Mendel scampered up the road, disappearing rapidly from view and came back a bit slower accompanied by a grizzled old Halfling that stumped along leaning on a walking stick, several boys to take care of the draft animals, and his parents and siblings. We had been dismounting from the wagon and getting our belongings in order while we waited. What followed was the most amazing bartering session that I had yet witnessed. The Wagoneer and the old Farmer sat down cross-legged in the grass; lit carved wooden pipes loaded with a very aromatic pipe blend, and commenced to haggle. Evidently, there was a load of dried fish in Fisherton that needed to be delivered to Thistledown, a load of sheep in Thistledown that needed to go to Fisherton, and the Wagoneer needed to be paid to haul both loads. Apparently food and lodging on each end of the trip were part of the bargain, also. You would think that this would be easy to negotiate, but these two gentlepersons sparred with each other for houres that evening over the details. After the first half houre or so, they moved the discussion, along with the rest of us to the local inn, The Full Belly, and kept at it until late at night, lubricated by many pints of the local brew.

While this discussion had been occupying most people's attention, Mendel introduced us to his family. They were so typical of Humkin Halflings that it was almost funny. The kids were really cute and asked a million questions. Chasseresse was completely charmed by them and told me in an aside that she hoped that our children took after my Halfling ancestry. Wow! Kids...I had not considered kids.

Mendel had notified the town authorities to our presence, so we were met by a greeting committee that included representatives of the various aspects of the town, local politicians, and a lot of curious bystanders. After we had gleaned every bit of information that was available concerning the Highwaypersons, a party seemed to spontaneously start up. I am told that this is a common occurrence whenever two or more Halflings are in the same area with nothing pressing to do, yup, food and parties go hand-in-hand with Halflings. Musical instruments appeared as if by Magick, the dancing started, and away it went.

I was actually footsore the next morning! I had danced with Chasseresse as long as I could, then just sat back and watched the festivities. Most Halfling music is somewhat raucous and bawdy in nature, but that is not the extent of their abilities. Chasseresse asked the musicians if they knew any Elven music. They did and after a few of the Half Elves joined them, began to play some of the most hauntingly beautiful music that I had ever heard, almost the complete opposite of the usual ballads, laments, reels, and jigs. Many of the Half Elves, including Chasseresse, danced and sang to it. The expression of and the ability to invoke emotion by the movements, lyrics, and melody were phenomenal and evocative. The crowd reacted on queue and unanimously as if they were puppets and a puppeteer was directing them. It was amazing, almost dreamlike. When the musicians finally ran out of songs that they knew, there was not a dry eye to be seen. I will never forget this one little Halfling girl who earlier had been bouncing around playing her miniature fiddle like a fiddle, doing the final violin solo, while quietly standing, which was so sweet, it would have melted the heart of the most vile and evil villain into a puddle of pure joy mixed with sorrow. As I write this, just from the memory, I have accumulated three sopping wet handkerchiefs from crying. As she played, you could have heard a pin drop, it was so silent in the inn. The music was so powerful that it was tangible...it felt like it literally reached into your chest and grabbed you by the heart. There are no words in any language to adequately describe it. When she finished playing, that last note seemed to linger for minutes. Not a sound could be heard, except quiet sobbing for at least a quarter houre. Everyone seemed to be lost in their own private thoughts and ruminations. Chasseresse later told me that all Elven music is Magickal in nature and very powerful. I believe her. That was the end of the party. The young lady just stood there with her head bowed hugging her violin and crying quietly. Everyone lined up and each bowed in turn to her reverently on their way out, hugged each other, and wandered away to bed. A gruff old Dwarf actually got down on one knee and kissed her hand before departing, his long grey beard soaked in tears. We made our way to our rooms and prepared for sleep. As I stood looking out of the window at the moonlit village below with the tiny round windows glowing yellow through the luxuriant plant growth that covered the Halfling Burrows, I spotted the young violinist making her way home along the main path through the village. Three tall, pale, exceptionally graceful and beautiful creatures glided from the shadows into the path in front of her. She recoiled in shock, and then went quiet as she realized that she was in no danger. I could actually 'feel' these beings. I noticed that the other Half Elves in our party were also peering out the windows of our large room at the scene below. Some of them murmured in wonderment at the presence of High Elves in a lowly Halfling village and that possibly the Elven music had actually summoned them. Evidently, out of the many varieties of Elves in the world, this type was the rarest and the closest to the Fae half of their lineage, thus making them the most naturally Magickal. Trying to figure out their gender was also hard. I am calling the leader a 'he', only because 'he' was taller than the other two and slightly more broadly built. All three were exotically beautiful. The three ephemeral beings below actually glowed slightly...amazing. They approached the transfixed young Halfling, bowed to her, and the leader placed 'his' hand upon her head and said something that was too quiet for us to physically hear, but still resonated all around the area, like a silent explosion. A sparkling glow descended from his hand down her tiny body and stayed there. There was a collective gasp from the more knowledgeable of my Half Elf cohorts and shocked whispers concerning a 'Blessing' that had been bestowed upon her. Other townsfolk had quietly appeared in front of their homes and were witnesses to the event. 'He' leaned far down, placed his hands on her shoulders, kissed her on the forehead, pulled her instrument and bow from her unresisting hands, and huddled over it with the other two High Elves.

There was a flash of light and another silent 'sound'. 'He' turned and handed her much altered instrument back to her. From a simple wood Halfling fiddle (called a Kit), probably hand-made in the village, a thing of beauty had been wrought. The tiny violin was now made of a shimmering wood whose grain appeared so rich and deep as to look like you were seeing it through clear water. The instrument was also covered in arcane Elven script and images in a glowing silverish metal inlay with chinrest, tailpiece, fine tuners, bridge, strings, and tuning pegs of the same material. The bow had been altered equally. In Pure Common, with a twinkle in his eye and a subtle smile, 'he' said, "Well, go ahead and give it a try, little one." She stared at it in utter amazement for a moment, then slowly brought it up to playing position. She played a single note. If her music had been enchantingly beautiful earlier, it was now completely magical in nature. Every living creature within earshot froze in place, listening with such intensity that it was a full body, mind, and soul experience. When the note finally ended, an eternity later, a collective sigh went up unanimously from the entire audience. It felt so wonderful, that I wanted the effect of that single note to last forever. I had never felt such peace, wellbeing, and harmony with all creation before. 'He' gracefully waved his hand to include the entire area and proclaimed "An instrument worthy of the Artisan who wields it. May it bring joy to all who 'hear'. We name you Elf Friend and grant you all privileges pertaining to said status, including, but not limited to, training with our younglings in your Art. In return, you bear the burden of sharing freely of your lovely music with all who would 'hear'. Do you agree, young maiden?" She stammered an acquiescence and impetuously hugged his lower leg, for that is the highest that she could reach. He smiled, leaned down, and patted her back. He rose again, ever so gracefully, looked around and said, "We bid you adieu, and may this night remain in your hearts forever." All three then faded into the shadows and were gone. This disappearing act happened in the middle of a large numbre of people and I was never quite sure how they pulled it off. How do three seven to eight foot tall, slender and elegant glowing humanoids in shimmering silken garments simply disappear into a shadow? It was almost like the shadow became a tunnel. I also got the strangest feeling that 'he' had spoken simultaneously in multiple languages and that each person 'heard' 'him' in whatever language they were most proficient. After they disappeared, the 'spell' was broken, and everyone began to chatter animatedly amongst themselves concerning the event. Many of the village children crowded around young Penney to 'oooo' and 'ahhh' over the instrument, though none attempted to touch it. None of my Half Elven fellow Rangers had previously been blessed with seeing a High Elf, and considered them to be almost mythical creatures. Needless to say, they were in total awe over that evenings happenings.

Everyone noticed the next day that Spring had come early to the village. New leaves were popping out everywhere and flowers were blooming in a gorgeous array of colour. What they would only later realize was that this was a permanent state. It was forever Spring from that night onward in that small village area and the temperature was always "just right". Needless to say, the enterprising Halflings took advantage of this opportunity and became the sole source of Spring crops (fruits, vegetables, and flowers) for Winters thereafter. The Wagoneers actually set up a depot and loading area at the juncture of the dirt village road and the coastal highway.

The young lady went on to become a famous Bard, known and honoured worldwide, who, true to her vow, never charged a pence for her performances, but who was wealthy beyond measure simply from gifts that had been lavishly bestowed. She was also known for her philanthropy, due to giving a large portion of it away to worthy beneficiaries and causes. I do not know what this 'Blessing' did to her aging, but after she reached 'young adulthood', she became 'stuck' at that point and has not appeared to age a day since, and she glows slightly to this day. She is the only non-Elf that I have ever heard of to be trained in music by the High Elves. Her music actually has a healing effect on all who hear it. She is a good friend to Chasseresse and me and whenever she is in the Waterport area, I arrange for the venue, advertising, catering, and other necessities for her to put on a grand performance. Handkerchiefs are handed out liberally onsite (people never seem to remember to bring enough of them). Her stage name, as it were, is 'The Enchantress of Thistledown', but we know her as Miss Penelope 'Penney' Honeysuckle. She is also known as 'Elf Friend Penney', 'The Immortal Bard', and Professor Penelope of the Waterport Bards College, as she went on to teach there and be a renowned guest lecturer around the world at various places of learning. They had to soundproof the walls of her lecture hall, due to the mesmerizing effect of her music leaking out and bringing all activity in the area to a grinding halt. It is an amazing feat of architecture, with no windows and six feet thick walls. It is built like an auditorium, with a stage, stadium seating, and perfect acoustics. Unfortunately, it only holds about one hundred persons, so it is way too small for a regular performance.

The next morning, after working the kinks out of our sore bodies and cleaning up with a "spit bath" (Named after the way mothers will spit on a cloth rag and wipe their small children's grubby faces and hands to clean them. In this case, it was actually a "sponge bath" with clean water in a basin and a cloth.); we retired to the Inn Common Area for a rousing breakfast fit for a king. The townspeople evidently gave us some credit for inspiring the life changing events of the evening before and wished to show their gratitude. We went over all of the information on the Highwaypersons that we currently possessed. Evidently, these guys operated East of Fisherton in a heavily forested area and according to Cranndair, moved their camp frequently. The Halflings had only heard rumours and were not able to add to our knowledge significantly, but sent along one of their Woodsmen who knew the area well to assist us in our endeavor. Now, we were twenty nine in numbre.

A bunch of the townspeople were outside to see us off with gifts of carefully wrapped journey food, hugs, and cheers.

I had checked with the Thieves Guild prior to our departure and they had denied any knowledge of these trespassers and given me their blessing, their sanction, if you will, to assassinate them and bring proof of their demise back to the Guild Bosses. I explained to them that the Rangers were intent on capturing them and finding out more about them, probably via our lovely Torture Department at the castle. The Guild Bosses let me know that they would also send a group of Assassin skilled Thieves Guild members led by my 'friend' Sarek the Sly, but that they would be instructed to let us have first crack at the Highwaypersons and would only clean up any of them that escaped our custody. At least those would have a quick death. I pity the ones that get questioned by our Torturers. [*see Appendix I. Torture Techniques of the Era] I agreed and thanked them for their benevolence and spirit of cooperation. I did not tell any of the Rangers that we were not alone in this hunt.

That brought up an odd topic that I had debated with myself and others. Generally, folks tended to be nice, kind, passive, calm, rational, quiet, friendly, and cooperative. They did go armed everywhere, but were very loath to injure and especially to kill. Even when somebody proved that they were evil and mean to the core, people tended to still look for hope and good in them. Even the professional Torturers were nice folks. So, what exactly caused a perpetrator to slip from the 'possibly can be rehabilitated' category to the 'too far gone' category, where torture became a viable option? How can such nice people have such a repertoire of despicable, painful, and debilitating skills and devices? The only thing that I could figure was that they were leftovers from a darker era.

The Guild Assassins were evidently shadowing us, because on our way out of town, I spotted Sarek leaning indolently against a large bare Oak tree surrounded by some kind of dark evergreens at the edge of the forest. He was black against dark greens and blacks, but he glowed with heat in the cool air. When he spotted me surreptitiously glance his way, he signed to me in Thieves Sign, "Nice Party, Munchkin. You look so scary and official. I'm shaking in my boots." I signed back, "Ha Ha, so funny. You guys need to be a lot more hidden. These Rangers are not a bunch of ignorant slackers, like a lot of the City Guard and disguise your heat signature; these guys can see heat like I can. That is how I spotted you, Sir Pink Glow." He replied, "Oops, I see your point." and moved behind the tree. He stuck his hand out and said, "Have fun, oh Sawed Off One, save some for us." and disappeared. Chasseresse had spotted me signing and asked what I was doing. I told her that it was finger exercises, that it kept my fingers limber. She wanted to learn how to do it, so I taught her to sign, "Pay no attention to me. I do not know what I'm doing. I think that I am doing finger exercises. That will teach me to not be so nosy." in Thieves and Merchants Sign and told her that that particular movement pattern is extremely beneficial for the joints, like a Kata. She taught the other Rangers as we travelled in the days that followed. When one of them would do it around people, they could not figure out why certain people would crack up laughing for no apparent reason. I figured that someday, someone would tell them what they were saying.

Chaptre 22. In which I Continue the Mission

Winter, 17th, Snowshell, 5012 (12 Turns of age)

We crossed the bridge and travelled North at a fairly leisurely pace with the woods continuing on our right and the seashore on our left. It was about three leagues to Fisherton and we would get there long before sundown. We foraged as we went and searched for signs of our quarry having been in this area. Some of the other Half Elves knew some useful Magick, simple small 'spells' that were useful in everyday affairs. They had started to teach me and it became a group class where everybody taught each other. Evidently, one had to know Elven to do 'spells', so I had started to learn that also. On that trip, I learned how to raise the temperature of an object. They figured that it would be safer for me to practice on water as my first attempt on a tuft of grass had been a bit explosive and I had a blister to remind me. We had collected some seabird's eggs and nobody really wanted to eat them raw or try to keep them from getting broken, so we put them in a small pot filled with sea water. This was my target... I had to say the Elven word 'Chauffer' (Heat), while focusing my will and intent on the target, while 'seeing' the changes in the material that I wanted to occur and to what degree. That seemed to be very important. Too much or too little and to the wrong sized area and, well you can guess how things can go wrong. On one attempt, instead of gently heating the whole bottom of the pot, I burned a small hole, quite explosively, in the pot. One of the other guys, while laughing as hard as the others, leaned in, uttered a word, and pointed at the damage. It fixed itself immediately to my great surprise. Through her giggles, Chasseresse told me that that one was called 'Mend" and she would teach it to me later. After a few failed attempts, some rather spectacularly, like when I made the water explode all over us, I finally produced boiling water and we all had a lovely snack of boiled eggs as a result. They used another one called 'Essuyer' (Dry) on our clothing and hair after that disastre, but warned me to be very careful with that one, because if you accidently aimed it at the person and not their clothes, you could end up killing them, or at least making them very ill. Even the 'Reparer' (Mend) one could be dangerous. If you aimed it at somebody's mouth, it might seal it shut. I could think of lots of uses for these 'spells', a lot of them not what was intended, like what if you did not like someone and did a 'Reparer' (Mend) on their butthole. That would be hilarious. Halflings really should never learn these 'spells', way too dangerous for the Big People, so I vowed to learn them all...look out world, a Spellcaster with a Halfling sense of humour, run away in terrour, Big People! Hmmm, I wondered if there was such a thing as 'Chill', 'Wet', and 'Break', also? These could come in really handy. What an arsenal; 'Reparer' (Mend)/'Briser' (Break), 'Chauffer' (Heat)/'Refroidir' (Chill), and 'Essuyer' (Dry)/'Tremper' (Wet).

I learned later that these did exist along with; 'Durcir' (Harden)/'Ramollir' (Soften), 'Melanger' (Mix)/'Diviser' (Separate), 'Liquefier' (Liquefy)/'Solidifier' (Solidify), 'Cabosser' (Dent)/'Lisser' (Smooth), 'Nettoyer' (Clean)/'Souiller' (Dirty), 'Parfumer' (Freshen)/'Puer' (Stinky), 'S'Ouvrir' (Open)/'Fermer' (Close), 'Bloquer' (Lock)/'Degager' (Unlock), 'Supporter' (Stand)/'Tomber' (Fall), 'Charmant' (Glamour)/'Brut' (Decrepit), 'S'Etendre' (Expand)/'Comprimer' (Compress), 'Ranger' (Sort)/'Troubler' (Chaos), 'Absorber' (Absorb)/'Repousser' (Repel), 'Reduire' (Thin)/'Epaisser' (Thicken), 'Assimiler' (Sop)/'Deverser' (Spill), 'Pulveriser' (Powdre)/'Regrouper' (Cube), 'Saler' (Salt)/'Poivrer' (Pepper), 'Geler' (Freeze)/'Bouillir' (Boil), 'Organiser' (Order)/'Deranger' (Disorder), 'Envoyer' (Send)/'Recuperer' (Retrieve), 'Feuilleter' (Flip)/'S'Effondrer' (Flop), 'Sceller' (Seal)/'Desceller' (Unseal), and 'Vibrer' (Vibrate)/'Calmer' (Still).

I did eventually learn all of these.

We crossed another stream via the usual stone bridge and noticed some Dwarf Hippos feeding below. The young ones were so cute! We continued on and soon left the woodlands behind, to be replaced with scattered farms growing a variety of crops, from the look of the fallow fields, but the majority appeared to have been hay. Winter rye grass was growing amongst the crop stubble. Stout Sheep and Knobbies were grazing in most of the enclosed spaces. Some fields sported Black Cattle, Dwarf Elephants, or Dwarf Mammoths. A few even had the much larger Deerbirds. This extended for miles to our right. I wondered what they did with all of the grazers when the crops were growing in those areas.

We noticed a distressed variety of sounds coming from up ahead, some low and some high pitched. We discovered that they were emanating from a mother and baby Knobby. The young one had squeezed through a gap in the fence and could not figure out how to get back in. The Mother and several other youngsters were on the inside. We walked up to the baby slowly, so as to avoid alarming it, but we should not have bothered. The moment that it saw us, it rushed over to us with funny honks and whistling squeals, and started nuzzling us and licking our hands. It's back was kind of hard to pet, considering that it was mostly made up of bony plates and spikes, with tufts of feathers sprouting in the gaps between them, bit it liked having its soft, warm tummy rubbed or scratched and rolled over for us to do so. It was so cute! We petted it and lured it back over to the fence where a couple of the bigger guys carefully lifted it up and over to its Mummy. They had a beak on the tip of their snout, but they also had a mouth full of teeth...odd. There was no slobber when it licked us, as its tongue was dry and kind of rough. It reminded me of a Parrots tongue. They smelled kind of like a Parrot, too. Interesting. We repaired the hole and moved on.

We could see, and smell, Fisherton long before we got to it. The town evidently lived up to its name for its major product. Maybe if a person were around the smell long enough, they would get used to it and no longer notice it. Apparently, they salted, smoked, and dried the fish for transport to other regions. I was hoping to eat some that was a lot fresher for supper.

After we arrived at the town propre, we headed for the Inn of the Cross-eyed Flounder for a delicious repast and perhaps some information on our quarry. Like Waterport, this town was built with the Harbour as the focal area, but while Waterport's harbour was a big oval, Fisherton's was a nearly right angle corner with a large relatively narrow bay on one side and a navigable river channel on the other, between the town and a barrier island. This bay was about two leagues, or six miles, long before it, too, turned into a river. I assumed that the bay was brackish water. This gave them a wide variety of types of fish from which to choose. With the cropland and pasture land behind them, they had the best of both worlds.

The harbour was packed solid with fishing boats of all sizes and varieties, from tiny dinghies to two or three person vessels, most unloading their hauls, cleaning up, and packing everything away after a long days fishing. The tide was in so the bay was full. When the tide was out, the bay was empty, except for the river channel flowing through it. As we walked through the wharf area along a wide graveled loading area, watching the bustle of activity, and checking out the various businesses on our right, I could not help but notice a fair amount of communication concerning our arrival in both Thieves and Merchants sign. I guess a fairly large Ranger military unit was cause for notice by the locals. A lot of the Thieves signed a 'welcome greetings' to me and I replied surreptitiously. Evidently, The Guild had alerted them to my description and our mission. Some of them asked if we needed anything and I replied to meet me later at the Inn. The 'chatterboxes' were dispatching runners to take messages to unknown locations for unknown reasons. I was not worried about the Thieves, but could not figure out why the Merchants would be so interested. I mentioned that our arrival was causing a stir and the others agreed that we were being stared at, to varying degrees, by many townspeople. They completely missed most of the activity and it made me wonder if Thieves Guild Training should be mandatory for all Constabulary, and then nixed the idea, because the Guild would go crazy if that ever happened.

We turned East with the wharf and continued for a bit. This area had much larger, multi-person crewed ships docked, whereas the first section we had passed seemed to be for smaller craft only. There were more warehouses and fish processing factories along here also. Fish were being transported every which way.

A large crowd had formed around a huge fish that had been hoisted up by its tail. We went over to gawk. I and the other Halflings, being small of stature, squirmed our way up to the front to get a good look. Sometimes it's good to be small. This thing had lots of sharp teeth and was at least a rod long! [*See Appendix D General Note, Calendar, Weights & Measures] I don't know how much it weighed, but the crane holding it was creaking with the strain. It could have gulped me in one bite. I was told that it was called a Shark. An Artist had been called in to preserve the moment and he was working rapidly due to the fast approaching twilight. The Fishermen that had caught it were arrayed around its head for the painting. One of them must have gotten bored, because he suddenly squatted down and stuck his head in its mouth. The crowd gasped in dismay, then laughed as he wiggled around and yelled help. I remembered a few creatures that I had killed that had bite reflexes even after death, so you had to keep your fingers clear of their mouth or get bitten. If this thing had a bite reflex, the guy would be minus a head...ouch. Those teeth could be used as dagger blades.

The Warden called for us to continue. He had done this often on the trip, because keeping us together, at the same speed, and moving in the same direction was like herding Alley Cats...a lost cause. He never lost his temper with us, though. We made it to the very large Inn in short order. The sign over the door was really funny. All Inns, and other businesses as well, besides having the name of the business spelled out on the front, also had a picture type sign, sticking out perpendicular to the front wall, so that the people who could not read could tell what the business was about. This one had a very comical cross-eyed flounder on the sign that looked very confused. Along the length of the bottom, hung three small signs; a bed, a bowl, and a mug. A steady stream of customers were entering the establishment after their long work day. The common room was very large, at least seventy feet by fifty feet and sported a band stand, lots of tables, and the bar. There were two floors of balconies on three sides above us. Besides the kitchen with the bar in front, the office, and the Inns front desk, there appeared to be some private dining rooms available on the ground floor. We made our way to the bar and the Warden haggled with the Barkeep a bit to rent us one. They came to an agreement and the Barkeep signalled a Waitress to escort us to the room. He used Merchants Sign, so I understood that he told her which room and to be our personal attendant. She was a cute thing, for a Human, and I liked the way the peasant blouse and full skirt she was wearing accentuated her feminine curves. Chasseresse spotted me, and all the other guys and girls who liked girls, avidly watching her swaying derriere as she led us through the crowd. She poked me in the ribs, and laughed when I yelped and looked sheepish. She giggled some more when I explained that I was only admiring the girl's wardrobe and thinking how nice it would be if Chasseresse got some clothing like it. She kissed me on the cheek and said she would buy a like outfit just for me. I blushed at the thought of how stunning Chasseresse would look in that outfit.

After we were seated at the long wide table, and our Waitress had taken our order, the Warden explained to us that this close to their operating area, our quarry almost assuredly had townspeople spying for them, so we would have to be somewhat circumspect in our questioning of the populace. I asked the others if they had ever heard the saying, "the enemy of my enemy is my friend". Most of them had, so I went on to say that due to my early life on the streets, I knew a bit about the Thieves Guild, and since I seriously doubted that our quarry was a part of the local Guild, they would be glad to help us nab their competitors and give us straight information. They were a bit unsure of this, but allowed me to go check it out.

Our meal arrived as we were discussing this. We had ordered a single large baked fish along with a serving of potatoes, carrots, and bread for each of us. It was served on a charred plank and it took two strong fellows to haul it in to our long table. I do not know what kind of fish it was, but it was a whole carcass was about six or seven feet long, basted in a savoury sauce, cooked to perfection, and smelled delicious. I definitely ate before I left on my scouting mission. We had berry Bubble Pies for desert...yummy.

Our waitress brought me some street clothes and I slipped them on over my uniform. I told them that if I found any that were willing to snitch to us, I would be back with them in short order. My search was rather short, for as I exited our dining room, I was hailed, and signed at, by some guys seated at a large round table over in one of the darker corners. Nobody else noticed as the room was filled with loud talk and the clatter of eating, and a poor fellow was up on the bandstand singing and playing a lute, attempting futilely to be heard over the racket.

I made my way over to the table and said, "Hey, old buddies." while introducing myself in detail using Thieves Sign. They introduced themselves in like manner, I sat and we commenced a briefing in hushed tones. I got them up to speed on what information we had accrued and they imparted what they knew to me. One of the fellows at the table was one of the local Guild Bosses, so I mostly aimed my conversation at him. I asked if any of them wanted to volunteer to impart whatever amount of information they chose to the Rangers. The boss said that they had figured that I might have a request like that, so had come prepared. It would seem that one of them was also a representative of the local Merchant's Guild and one of them was part of the local Constabulary, a double-agent, like myself. There was also a fellow from the supply section of the local Guild present at the table to see to our material needs. The first two would brief the Rangers, the second would go with us, and the third would fill equipment requests. I bowed to the Boss and thanked the others heartily.

We made our way through the boisterous throng back to the private dining room, entered, and I informed the crew that I had located some solid informants. Said informants made the appropriate introductions without mentioning their more clandestine connections and began the briefing. The Supply Man took requests and said that all would be delivered in the morning. According to the locals, the Highwaypersons operated in an area starting about four miles NorthEast of town to a point about eight miles away where the coastal road crossed a bridge over the river and turned back SouthWest down the other side of the bay. This was an area where dense, old-growth forest was on both sides of the road, making it into a shaded tunnel through the trees. They were driving the local merchants batty with their depredations, but the local Constabulary had been unsuccessful in capturing or killing them to date. A bounty had been placed on them, both individually and as a group. The Warden declined this bounty saying that we, as members of the military, were compensated well enough by the City of Waterport and that they should give the money to a local charity, like maybe a fund to support the widows and orphans of deceased sailors of the town. They looked at one another somewhat perplexed, but agreed to do so. Part of me agreed with the Warden and part of me was aghast at giving away so much money. This seemed to be a theme in my life, always of two minds on things, 'good' and 'evil' locked in an endless battle in my brain. Maybe this was why I could easily be a part of opposing sides, like the Thieves Guild and the City of Waterport Guard. I must be weird or something, a neutral being in a world of opposites. Anyway, enough ruminating, our party now numbered thirty persons, a nice round numbre.

After our guests had finished dining and our Waitress had packed up the leftovers of the fish for us to take with (we tipped her extravagantly), we bid them a good evening and arranged with the Innkeeper for a large room for the night.

The next morning, when we went down to breakfast, we found our new accomplice chowing down, surrounded by our requisitions. He was dressed in the local version of Winter Ranger attire, camouflaged leather armour, cloak, bow, quiver, sword, dagger, backpack, beltpouch, and waterskin. He had a letter from the local Chief Constables office thanking us for the assistance, introducing him as Sergeant Rodney Griffinbane, and assigning him temporarily to our command. He also had a checked off listing of our gear requests to go along with the supplies at hand. The Warden later stowed these papers in his map case. He cheerfully called out, "Mornin' Sir, Ma'am, and comrades in arms! Your breakfast will be out shortly." We almost had the large room to ourselves, as the crews of the fishing vessels, that had not eaten at home, had already been here and left at the crack of dawn. Just a few business people, Constabulary, and ourselves present. All of these locals seemed to know about our mission and gave us well wishes exuberantly. After a breakfast of amazingly large eggs, some really delicious steaks that oddly tasted like Chicken, and fresh baked bread with butter, we divided up the new gear and supplies and headed out of town at around nine in the morning. I found out later that the huge eggs and the steaks had been from one of the varieties of large flightless birds.

Chaptre 23. In which I Smell like a Fish

Winter, 18th, Snowshell, 5012 (12 Turns of age)

The air was crisp and fresh, somewhere in the forties or fifties in temperature. All of the remaining snow had melted, which had been left over from the snowfall that had occurred the first day of our trek. I noticed that I no longer smelled the fish. Either my nose no longer noticed it or it was not as stinky this morning. Rodney warned us that we would have to get rid of the smell in our hair and on our clothing or our quarry would smell us coming. I guessed that my nose had become accustomed to the fish smell in town. He said rubbing dirt or old manure on our clothes would work, but that he much preferred rolling around in dry leaves, much cleaner and it did the trick quite well. I agreed personally with the latter idea. You understand, after growing up in the sewers, I was not the least bit squeamish, but my nose was no longer used to rampantly stinky smells, so I would rather not smell them if I had a choice in the matter.

Sergeant Rodney, the poor Thief/Cop that tagged along with us from Fisherton had such a hard time keeping a straight face when viewing the "finger exercises" going on around him and even allowed himself to be 'taught' them, also. During one lesson, he signed, "You guys are so stupid." with a straight face and was promptly told that he had done the wrong sequence of finger wiggles and that he would have to try again, that it was very important to get it just right. I cracked up laughing at that one and had to fake a coughing spell to cover it up.

There were small farms on both sides of the road as we travelled East. In one area, where some slightly sparse woodland came down nearly to the road, we spotted a Slasher walking among the trees.

It looked vaguely like a huge Ostrich. It took us a moment to realize that a person was riding the huge colourful Bird. It took a moment longer to realize that they were herding a bunch of much more camouflaged Deerbirds. I bet that a Slasher could take on a Toothy and any smaller carnivore would just simply be shredded.

I had continued to practice 'Chauffer' (Heat) until I could do it without errour and had started to learn 'Reparer' (Mend) and 'Essuyer' (Dry) also. It was a lot of fun and a source of comedy for my friends, who were also learning ones that they had not previously known.

When we reached the point where the woods started, after about three houres trek up the highway, Cranndair took out his amazing map and asked three of us to each take a corner and pull gently while backing up until the map was of sufficient size to see details. Amazing! It was three dimensional! We stopped at about twenty feet by thirty feet, and you could practically see individual trees. We all came around to the side that showed the area of interest and peered at it while Cranndair and our two local experts, one from Thistledown and one from Fisherton, briefed us on details and our patrol routes. We split up into fifteen groups of two people each, one squad member plus one leader or local expert in each group. Lucky Nell went with me, Jagger with Rudd, and Chasseresse with Mendel. Cranndair made sure that one person in each group had in their possession a 'communication sphere'. Cranndair handed out one two inch diametre green ball to each person that was good with a sling. He explained that these were enchanted plants that worked as 'capture vines'. Aim it at their hands and when it hits, it will wrap around their wrists binding them, same for ankles if you wanted to trip them or necks if you wanted to choke them. He asked for a volunteer, asked him to catch, and tossed a ball at him. When the guy caught it, the ball unraveled into a green vine and rapidly wrapped his wrists, much to his dismay. Cranndair explained that part of the enchantment included being too strong to be cut or broken. He said that the plants were essentially sentient and responded to commands in Elven easily. He walked over to the man and said clearly and distinctly the Elven, "Relacher" (Release) and "Revenir" (Return). The vine unwrapped and climbed up Cranndair's arm like a snake. Wow! How many Magick items did this guy have and how did he fit so much stuff in his beltpouch? He then taught us a few basic commands that we might need during our venture. We pushed the map back into a small page and he stowed it back in his case. We placed bets with each other as to who would find the first sign, first camp, first sight of a Highwayperson, and first capture. This was going to be quite a competition. We wished each other Luck and split up. The Small People had taken advantage of the approximately two hour break and ate one of the many meals of the day, sandwiches made of the leftover fish from last night with fresh bread from that morning.

The roadway in front of us looked more like a tunnel than an open road. Evergreen ivy grew up a lot of the trunks and not all of the Fall leaves had dropped off yet. Winter grass grew where ever sunlight made it through the dense growth overhead. The woods in this area were denser in general than what we had seen so far. Perhaps that was why the Highwaypersons preferred them.

Two groups took the NorthWest side of the highway and another two the SouthEast. They would move out slowly paralleling the road heading NorthEast. Eleven groups headed down a trail that connected with the road perpendicularly {see map} on the SouthEast side and dropped off a group every three hundred yards or so. As each team was dropped off, they would begin their stealthy sweep NorthEast through the woods in search of any sign of the Highwaypersons. We would all end up in a roughly North-South line that extended approximately two miles inland from the river. If any team encountered the Bandits, we could execute a rapid pincer movement and close up around them. Of course things could, and probably would, go wrong.

Lucky Nell could be amazingly quiet, when the need arose, for such an abnormally loud and boisterous person. We were the first group into the woods South of the two team group that was paralleling the highway on the SouthEast side. While the deciduous trees were still leafless, except for some Fall leaves that still clung to the branches, they were packed fairly close together and interspersed with evergreens, so visibility was not very good. I guessed that during the Summer Moonths, this forest would be in perpetual gloom from the dense foliage overhead. Since the thaw had occurred very recently and it had not rained since, any tracks that we found in muddy areas would be recent. After all of the teams were spaced out in line, Cranndair gave the order to move out. We slunk along silently, about a dozen feet apart, constantly checking for a variety of things; tracks, broken plant life, traps, movement, any shape that did not fit, sounds, people smells, carnivores, and other alarming stimulation. Evidently, the Bandits did most of their moving around back in this area, just out of sight of the road, so there was a lot of sign to sort out. After we reported this, Cranndair made his way over to us to help out. None of the tracks appeared to be very recent, all showing signs of weathering, and some overlaid by animal tracks, but there were a lot of them. We spotted several old lines of tracks crisscrossing the area in any given hundred yards. Cranndair said that they habitually walked in a line and stepped in each other's footprints to make it confusing as to how many of them there were, size, weight, load carried, side of the body the heaviest weapon was carried on, and other details. Mostly, we used Ranger Sign Language to communicate with each other. It is a much simpler language than that used by Thieves or Merchants, as those are complete and complex languages, and while those are very subtle and hard to spot, Ranger Sign uses large, easily seen gestures and motions. A little too easily seen for my taste, if the enemy knew Ranger Sign, and was watching from hiding, they would know exactly what you were saying to one another.

We continued slowly NorthEast, crossed a major trail, after making sure nobody was watching before braving the open space, and were just inside the trees on the other side when we received an exited call on our communication spheres. Team Three, on this side of the highway, had spotted a fresh trail leading into the woods in our direction. Cranndair told them to follow it, leaving Team One, Two, and Four to continue paralleling the highway. We, Team Five, spotted Team Three slowly making their way with one of the team looking ahead, up, and to the sides, and the other tracking the sign. We continued on an intercept course scanning more to our right than ahead and almost none to the left.

When we arrived at the trail, Cranndair checked, and figured out that the group was made up of all male Humanoids of varying sizes and weights, and predominately right handed. There was at least two that were very large, most of them were average sized, and there was at least two that were more slightly built. The guy was really good at tracking! I was impressed. He had Team Three switch with us, told all of the Teams to hold position until he was sure that the quarry had not doubled back behind our line, and had me and Nell move parallel to the track on each side about twenty feet away while he continued to follow the fresh trail. He told us to keep our eyes open for side trails branching off or ambushes, if they had doubled back on this trail. He said that some of them could have climbed into the branches, climbed out a numbre of feet, dropped down to the ground, and either left or be waiting in ambush also. They could also still be up in the trees with bows for the same purpose. I was beginning to feel somewhat exposed. He told the other groups to check left and right for the tracks going back SouthWest between their current positions. We did want to box them in and capture them after all.

Since the river was behind us, to the NorthWest, and some pretty steep and rugged mountains were ahead, we were generally going uphill through increasingly hilly terrain. It was still wooded, but there were ever increasing outcroppings of lichen covered weathered grey rock interspersed with the forest. The trail wound upwards through one such outcropping, actually a hill of sorts, where the trees became thinner with small patches of open space filled with heather and grass.

At one point, we surprised a Wolverine, who growled at us and barred its teeth. I automatically went into my 'big Sewer Cat' imitation complete with realistic hissing, growling, and yowling. The Wolverine turned tail and trundled away. Cranndair quietly complimented me while Nell tried to stifle giggles.

I am not sure how Cranndair was able to follow the trail through this area, as it was not muddy at all and the tracks became barely discernible. He did not have to use his Tracking Stick, except for a few times, where it was entirely rock.

We each carried a telescoping, hardwood Tracking Stick, four feet long when fully extended, with one inch markings up its length. This implement is utilized when tracks become hard to spot. If you know the measurement of the tread of the quarry when the tracks are easily visible, then you can use that measurement to look for the next track after one you have found. Uphill and downhill movement makes this span generally shorter, so you must adjust accordingly.

The hill was much steeper on the back side, so the trail became much more noticeable with snapped small limbs, scuff marks where people's feet had slide out from under them, and other sign. Cranndair took out a coil of rope and one of the Magickal Vines. He held the knotted end of the rope close to a sturdy Oak sapling, placed a Vine on the ground between them, and gave the command to grasp. The Vine uncoiled, grabbed the tree and the end of the rope, and coiled about them. These Vines were really useful!

We used the rope to quietly make our way to the bottom without disturbing anything. At the bottom, Cranndair quietly called the release command up to the vine, which did so and coiled back into its default 'ball' configuration, whereupon it promptly rolled down the steep hillside to us. Cranndair grinned, picked it up, and tucked it away. I asked him quietly what would have happened if it had gotten stuck along the way. He replied that you can also use the 'Return' command to cause it to slither back to you. Very nice!

We followed the tracks SouthEast for a bit more until they encountered a trail heading almost due East. The fresh tracks turned and followed the trail while maintaining their strict methods meant to confuse trackers. Since no back-track had been located by the Teams, Cranndair told them to move out again in their original line of march, so that we maintained our line. We continued until the sun started to set and then we stopped and made a cold camp for the night. We had tracked for approximately six houres and had covered about a mile and a half linear distance in a NorthEasterly direction from our point of origin. That did not seem like very far, but then again, our quarry had not been moving in anything approaching a straight line. Cranndair told all of the other teams to spread out somewhat and camp also. They were to split up the watch anyway they saw fit, as long as one of them was awake on watch at all times throughout the night. We were lucky in that there were three of us to split up the time, instead of two, as the other teams were comprised.

During our cold supper, Lucky Nell asked about my parents. I had never really thought about how to answer this question if it came up. I suppose that technically, I would be considered an orphan, but I did not really feel like one. True, I did not know who my father was and could not really remember my mother, even though I had lived for at least seven Turns in the same room as her skeletal remains. But as I considered the question, I came to an odd conclusion. I actually had parents. Adopted parents, but none the less, parents and what a different sort they were. Brud the Strong was my 'father' and Trentish the Face was my 'mother'. This was not as strange as it appeared at first glance. Brud was the perfect father; strong, capable, protective, loving, jovial, patient, kind, and a little bit simple. As was Trent the perfect mother, he could be such a girly guy when he was not putting on an act; loving, caring, complex, emotional, cuddly, an excellent teacher, worried about me, skilled in many things, made sure I was always fed and clean, fussed over me a lot, a little overly protective, and very proud of my accomplishments. Both of them acted the same toward my little 'sister', Shadow. I realized also, that I really loved and cared for them. I resolved to go visit them when we were done with the mission and tell them of my epiphany. The answer that I gave Nell was a lot simpler. I told her that my parents were Warehousepersons in the Merchant Quarter and were really nice. She said that she would really like to meet them some day. Well, that was another can of worms. Trent could look and act like any age and social status of female, but there was not much that we could do with Brud's looks, and they were so much taller than I would ever be, and I did not look anything like them. I suppose that I could be some kind of throw-back to a distant Halfling ancestor and Trent looked Elven enough to have passed on my 'pretty' looks, but why didn't Brud's slightly Orcish looks get passed down to me? Then I remembered that most boys get their maternal Grandfather's looks and most girls get their paternal Grandmother's looks, so that would explain why my completely Human appearing four Turn old 'sister' was taller than me at nearly twelve Turns old. That would make Trent's fake Dad an Elfkin Halfling, his fake Mum a Human, Brud's fake Dad a Half Orc, and his fake Mum a Human. That could actually be plausible! Problem solved. I would just have to brief Brud and Trent on the details of the scam part of this deal. I would have to figure out a backup story as to why my name was Scram Runt. Maybe it was a nick-name and I actually had a real one that we would have to make up prior to the engagement. I told Nell that I would be glad to have her and any other of my friends meet my parents sometime. She giggled quietly and told me that since I was so nice, they would have to be nice, too, "cause tha apple doon't fall too far from tha trae."

Cranndair chose to bed down between two trees, Nell chose to sleep in a large evergreen Holly bush, and I climbed a craggy old Oak Tree and settled down in a large crook. I tied myself in place with some rope, so as to not fall out during the night. We slept without removing any of our gear, so as to be ready in a seconds notice. We divided up the night into two houre watches and rotated these between us, two hours on, 4 hours off.

Chaptre 24. In which I Continue the Hunt

Winter, 19th, Snowshell, 5012 (12 Turns of age)

The night went smoothly and Cranndair, who was the last on watch, woke us up for a cold breakfast of biscuits with butter and cheese. As I was eating, I noticed a slight movement in my clothing, which somewhat startled me, to say the least. I motioned to the other two and pointed at the very slight bulge at my chest, above where the straps crossed. The material was looser there. They stared at the movement and Nell giggled quietly and told me that I had become an Inn during the night. Cranndair smiled at this and asked me if the area was noticeably warmer than the rest of my chest. It actually was! The lump was between the outer Armour and the wool liner. It started moving up my chest until it reached the point where the 'V' in the neck, below my chin, was located. It paused, then slowly poked its head out and sniffed in the direction of the biscuit that I was holding in my hand. It turned out to be a rather cute, rusty brown, fluffy mouse with a white underside! Nell giggled and Cranndair smiled. He told me that it was a Harvest Mouse.

He told us that it happens occasionally that when people, like Rangers and other woodsy folk, are doing whatever in the woods, certain animals will start to follow them around, sort of adopting them. These animals are not fearful, as they should reasonably be, and while not being technically 'pets', they can be trained and utilized as helpers of sorts. Some woodsy sorts collect so many of these followers, that people term them "Beastmasters". Another odd thing is that the 'companions' never harmed each other, even though they may be of predator and prey species. He surmised that I had inadvertently been adopted by a creature of this type. He also said that it was very fortunate that it was a rather small, concealable, and easy animal to have around. Some people get very awkward followers.

I tentatively pinched off a piece of the biscuit and handed it to the mouse, who grabbed it with its teeth, then stuck its front paws out, took hold of the morsel, and started nibbling on it with relish while holding it with both front paws. Nell gave out an "Awwww, so cute it is!" Cranndair said that usually followers fended for themselves, but this one appeared to be a bit more dependent. As it slowly climbed out into my hands, after finishing it's meal, we discovered that it was female, about three inches long in the body with a three inch prehensile tail, which it wrapped firmly around my fingers, that had almost unnoticeable short fur on it. It licked my fingers clean, which brought more giggling and cooing from Nell. According to Cranndair, they were amazing climbers and they could also leap, swim, and burrow, so I really should not worry too much about dropping the little girl. I gave her another chunk of biscuit and after she had completed it and yawned widely, I put her up close to the hood of my armour where she promptly crawled in and made herself comfortable against the back of my neck. It was like having a personal heater! I could hear her now that she was close to my ears. She chattered quietly to herself quite a bit.

Cranndair checked in with all of the teams, who reported nothing out of the ordinary and said that they were ready to continue. He ordered us to check our bearings and move out in a NorthEasterly direction.

We continued following the fresher tracks along the path, which had angled nearly due North, So that we were now crossing the line of march of our comrades. The path petered out after about a mile, but the trail continued in the same direction.

We had been spotting wildlife throughout our stalk, who did not appear unduly afraid of us, as if they knew that we were not hunting them. These included; Fallow Deer, Roe Deer, Wild Boar, Red Squirrels, Rabbits, Mountain Hare, Hedgehogs, Red Foxes, Badgers, Pine Martens, Polecats, Stoats, Lesser Weasels, Sparrow Hawks, Barn Owls, many kinds of smaller birds, Wildcats, Lynx, Grey Wolves, and even a Brown Bear. We noticed that all of the wildlife had rather suddenly gone quiet or gotten scarce. Cranndair checked with all the teams and found that the anomaly was only present in our area. The mountainous region to the SouthEast had veered Northwards, causing the teams to have to bunch up somewhat. We had actually spotted some of the other teams to our left, right, and behind us. He warned them that we might be close and to be ready to complete the pincer movement if we located them.

We moved forward more slowly and carefully. We stopped when we started smelling scents caused by Humans. Whereas we dug 'cat holes' to do our business and covered it up afterwards, the Highwaypersons evidently had not, and we could smell their waste products, along with wet ashes (from a camp fire), rotting food scraps, and even some body odour. It is amazing how keen your nose gets when you are out in nature away from bad smells.

We inched forward, staying very low to the ground, and moving absolutely silently. We came to an impromptu clearing of sorts, where the bandits had cleared an area somewhat to make a camp, but it was abandoned, much to our chagrin.

Cranndair ordered the teams to halt and Chasseresse and Mendel to come to our location. We slunk completely round the area to see where the fresher trail exited and found it continuing NorthEast. We then did a complete search of the camp, found their uncovered slit trench and their uncovered dug out fire pit, counted the places where people had lain down for sleep and the sizes of the imprints, checked individual footprints for details, and gathered every other shred of evidence that we could. In total, we discovered that there were indeed two exceptionally large ones (one of them quite stinky), two exceptionally small ones (possibly Halflings), at least four Dwarves, and at least twelve Humans of various sizes and weights. They should have made it harder for us by wearing all the same style of footwear, as did we. Cranndair noted that they were usually a bit neater than this; covering every hole and brushing the area down with a branch to remove the details of their stay, covering the area with fresh leaves, and other techniques of obfuscation. Either they were getting sloppy or they had been in a hurry. If they were in a hurry, their Scouts had either spotted a fresh target, ripe for the picking, or they might have spotted us approaching. Either way, we needed to hurry to catch up. Cranndair ordered the teams closest to the road to pick up the pace.

We all moved out with the four of us dogging their trail, which shortly connected with a pathway. They were no longer walking in each other's footsteps, so they were leaving a mélange of tracks right in the middle of the path. The path hit a 'T' intersection, where they went left, then another 'T' where they went right, then left, then right again. Then, they veered off to the left into the woods, heading for the road. We warned the four roadside teams about this just before those teams spotted them accosting some travellers on the road ahead of their location.

Cranndair ordered the road teams to move into a good firing position, but to stay hidden, while we came up behind them, and the other teams started to swing inwards to cut them off. Our group moved up until we could see what was going on. We spotted a couple of bandits away from the road watching their back trail, the direction we were hiding, and Cranndair asked me to shoot two Vines at their necks with my sling. I prepped my sling, got two of the balled up Vines ready, and on his signal, fired them off, hitting the two in the necks perfectly while Cranndair did something Magickal with finger movements and spoken Elven. When the balls hit them, they coiled around their throats and started to squeeze. The two dropped their weapons and started clawing at their necks, but strangely, no sound of their struggles could be heard. They fell to the ground as we rushed up and per Cranndair's signal, bonked them on the head to knock them out. Cranndair then removed the Magickal silence and we ordered the Vines to 'Release' and gagged and tied the two up and stowed them in the brush.

We then crept closer to see what was going on. Evidently, somebody had sent a payroll, a payoff, or a payment in gold coins in a small chest hidden under a load of corn in what appeared to be a farmer's wagon, ostensibly on the way to market. Unfortunately, they had not used real farmers to drive the wagon and the two soldiers did not look very much like farmers even though they were dressed as such. The Highwaypersons had not been fooled by this charade. They had not hurt the two "Farmers" or the other one that was really dressed like a soldier that had been hidden under the corn very much, only bruised them a bit and disarmed them. They were in the process of searching the wagon thoroughly while teasing their bound and gagged victims unmercifully. Come to think of it, the Highwaypersons looked like soldiers, also, even though they wore no uniforms. Their fitness, bearing, and mannerisms gave them away. Cranndair nodded grimly upon noticing this also. He motioned us to move into position and communicated via globe for everyone to aim to wound by shooting for the legs with arrows, the knees with sling missiles, and the ankles with Vines. There were eighteen of them, as we had already taken out two of them, against ten of us, but we had the surprise factor.

Cranndair gave the order to attack, and we all fired. Eight of the enemy were hit in the legs with arrows, four had their kneecaps taken out by sling bullets, and four had their ankles tied by Vines by me. A cacophony of screams, curses, yelps, yells, roars, and other expletives erupted upon receiving our missiles. Two of the enemy, the largest and the smallest, were hidden from view when we did the initial volley. The largest one picked up the smallest one, burst into view from behind the wagon, and sprinted into the trees on the other side of the road. Everyone fired at them, but only succeeded in hitting the roadway and trees.

Chaptre 25. In which I Give Chase

Winter, 19th, Snowshell, 5012 (12 Turns of age)

Cranndair quickly ordered the three teams by the road, seven people, to take them into custody, the nine teams, eighteen people, which were closing on us to watch for them, and us four to follow him in chase. As we ran, he notified the others of the two that were hogtied in the brush.

We fanned out and ran into the trees after our quarry and soon discovered that they had changed direction to parallel the road. Chasseresse veered out back onto the roadway in time to see them sprint across ahead of her. She fired six arrows in the space of a few seconds and managed to bury one in the big fellows right butt cheek! He howled in fury, but scarcely slowed down.

She yelled for us to follow and sprinted after them. We crashed out of the trees and pelted headlong into the ones on the other side of the road. The nine teams could hear the bandits crashing through the trees and us doing the same behind them. They headed to cut the bad guys escape off. Unfortunately, the two Highwaypersons/Soldiers ran into a path and followed it to the SouthEast at a sprint.

They were spotted and shot at several times by the teams, but only one arrow managed to find a home in the Giants right shoulder. As each team hit the trail, they in turn sprinted in pursuit. Bear, with his long legs, was outdistancing everybody else easily. The trail veered toward the East and we could hear the sound of rushing water ahead. The mass of us broke into a clearing in time to see the Giant, fully twelve feet tall, with the tiny Halfling clinging to his clothing, step into the shallows, turn to face us, and roar at us in some language that I did not understand, while Bear sprinted at him, roaring back in the Norseman language and brandishing his huge battleaxe. The Giant unlimbered a huge club, studded with steel knobs, from his back and set himself to receive the charge. The Halfling squeaked in terrour and jumped off the Giants back into the rapids and was swept away. Several of our people changed   direction to intercept the little guy.

At that moment, Bear leapt into the air from the embankment of the river with his axe poised for a huge downswing, apparently with the intent of cleaving the Giant in half. Simultaneously, the Giant swung in a horizontal arc, attempting to swat Bear aside and crush him like a bug in the process. In mid leap, Bear twisted to the side and rolled into a forward flip, thus avoiding the club as it missed his back by fractions of an inch. He continued the tumble past the Giants head, uncoiled, and slammed his axe downwards with all of his might into the Giants lower spine, splitting it completely, as he sailed by and headfirst into the roiling river.

The Giant collapsed with his legs completely useless. He started to crawl up the bank while several of our folks threw ropes into the water for Bear to catch hold of. He was saved, but it took six people to haul him out, as was the Halfling that had gone in the drink earlier.

The Giant had crawled out onto the bank and reached back to pull the axe from his back with a grunt of pain by the time that Bear made it back to the battleground. The Giant propped himself up on his arms, looked squarely at Bear and said in True Common in an amazingly deep voice, "You are a worthy foe. I underestimated you. I thought you were charging mindlessly to your death. I honour you as a fellow Warrior. I request a Warriors death, as I am now unfit to continue as one, myself." Bear replied in his accented, but flawless True Common, "I honour you as a Warrior. You would have made a good Norseman. You hold the place of Honour as being the most worthy foe that I have ever faced. I agree to your request for a death worthy of a Warrior.' Bear and several others helped the Giant into a sitting cross-legged position and the two clasped right forearms in farewell. Bear was only a little taller standing than the Giant was sitting. The Giant looked around at us and said, "I am Akicita Wase, a Warrior of the Paha Wicoti Tribe. Remember me to your descendants and tell my story that I may live in their hearts forever. Please tell my Tribe that I died a Warriors Death? I would know my brother Warrior. How are you known?" Bear responded, "I am Bersvend Dagvaldsson, a Warrior of the Stavsund Norse. We will carry your tale of valor to your people. Carry my greetings to Odin, All Father, who rules in Asgard. You will like Thor and Tyr and all three will love you and welcome you as a brother." We all nodded in agreement and a bunch of us were crying. The Giant then raised his face toward the sky and started singing his Death Chant with his arms outstretched and slightly raised. Bear picked up his axe and waited patiently until the other had finished. When the last of the song had faded away and the Giant had lowered his arms, Bear swung his axe with all of his considerable strength and cleaved the Giant Warriors head from his shoulders with one fell blow.

Bear insisted on giving the Giant a sendoff fitting for a Norseman. We built a raft with a sharp prow and a fixed rudder and stacked firewood on it in a huge pyre. We poured a container of Flammable Jell on the wood where he would lie, so that it would burn well. We placed the Giants body on it in a position of repose with all of his belongings. It took all of us to lift him into place. We pushed the raft into the river and set fire to it by shooting a flaming arrow into it. It exploded into flames and sailed away to the sea, borne on the rapid current in the centre of the fast flowing river. Bear stood there for a while with his head bowed.

We still had to deal with the captured Highwaypersons, question them, find out where they hid their ill-gotten gains, recover said gains, and transport them and the loot to Waterport for trial. I had to call off Sarek's Hit Team. We had to escort the latest victims to their destination so that they delivered their gold safely. I had to report success to the local branch of the Thieves Guild and to the main branch in Waterport. We had to report a successful mission to our superiours at the castle. We needed to cook that load of fresh corn and eat it all. I had to learn a lot more small Spells, the Elven language, and how to play my Penny Whistle well. I had to set up Cranndair and Trent so that they fell in love with each other. So much to do and so little time. Oh well, back to work...

Chaptre 26. In which I Clean Up the Mess

Winter, 19th, Snowshell, 5012 (12 Turns of age)

As we headed back to the Highway, collecting the arrows that had missed their targets, and repairing any damage that had been done to the forest, I kept an eye out for Sarek and his people. It was about four miles back to the robbery point from the battle site at the river. Quite a sprint we had done. Lucky Nell was checking everyone's injuries, all minor, thankfully. Cranndair was getting reports from all of the sub-bosses. Bear was carrying the Halfling prisoner as one would a small child. The poor little guy was completely broken up over the death of his big friend and was crying quietly into Bears shoulder. Bear kept patting him on the back to comfort him while looking so sad, that he might cry again, himself.

I had an odd thought while walking back. Most people consider distance to be a 'constant', something measured equally by all yardsticks, while actually, it is a 'variable'. The concept of 'long' and 'short', 'high' and 'low' varies wildly depending on a given person's viewpoint. If a group of people are of a small range of sizes and heights, say an average of six feet tall, this difference is not as readily apparent as is in a group that varies between one foot and twelve feet tall. One average step, approximately six feet, to the twelve feet tall person is about twenty four average steps to the one foot tall person. While keeping in mind that the relative height to; weight, fuel storage, muscle mass, heat generated, and other factors are generally a constant ratio between the various heights, distance becomes the variable, instead of being a constant. There is a huge difference in the expenditure of energy over time and distance! Therefore, given an average height of six feet equalling the map measured four miles, while the Giant had sprinted approximately two miles, I had actually sprinted approximately eight miles. So, it's no wonder that us smaller people eat more frequently and get tired more easily.

About a hundred yards into the woods, I saw, more by heat signature than regular vision, a hand wave at me from behind a tree. I said to the people that I was walking with, Chasseresse, Mendel, and a few others that I needed to "fertilize and water the trees" and that I would catch up to them in a bit. I actually did need to go rather badly, so it was not a lie. It takes a few minutes to get out of the gear that we carry and wear to the point where you can squat easily to defecate, and urinate in the case of the girls. I also had to find a particular broadleaved weed that worked well to clean with afterwards. This procedure was made easier due to a buttoned up slit in the appropriate area of the armour and liner. In a pinch, it could be done without removing any gear. I found the appropriate plant, removed my backpack and some of the bulkier equipment, got the trowel out, and proceeded to dig a cat hole. I heard Sarek's voice from behind me, "You are not going to make a 'Stinky' while we talk, are you? That is just downright rude, you Sawed-Off little Western Barbarian. I'm getting upwind of this." Sarek was laughing as he said this, so it was only his usual jibing. He privately called everyone in this area of the world by that descriptive name. He had an odd, sibilant accent, but spoke flawless Pure Common. I laughed and said, "That is why I am facing upwind, you Greasy Sand Flea on a camels ass. I don't want to smell it any more than you do!" He replied, "Ouch, that one stung more than usual. You are getting better at banter, my little friend." We then discussed our concurrent missions and the reports that needed to be filed with the two chains of command. I filled him in on the details that he and his crew had not witnessed and about how Sergeant Rodney Griffinbane was a double agent, like myself, from the Fisherton branch of our Thieves Guild and that he was aware of Sarek's crew and would make the report to both sets of his superiors when we got back to town. I told Sarek that as we questioned the prisoners and found out their details, I would await his signal each evening, meet with him, and give him the update. He agreed to this and promised to pace us as we moved. I had finished my job by the time we had finished talking, cleaned up, and prepared to cover the hole. Sarek glanced in and faked astonishment, saying, "How could so much shit come out of such a little person, you must be full of it!" He laughed and I replied with a straight face, "I eat very well, thank you, it's those six meals a day with lots of fruits and vegetables that does it. You should try it sometime, maybe some of that shit that you store up would actually come out the right orifice. I'm afraid sometimes that it's going to back up and start running out of your mouth, ears, and nose. Oh, I'm sorry, that already happens, cause you spout shit out of your mouth all the time!" At that, he started laughing so loudly that I had to shush him. He sputtered quietly, "You are getting better at banter. You definitely won that match. I bow to you, oh Wordsmith." At which point, he did a very mocking bow towards me and disappeared into the trees with a wave. I grinned, settled my gear in place, and headed back to the Road. For such an evil bastard, he could be fun at times. It was a really pretty day, and the wildlife had quit hiding and were busy going about their business. I checked on my little companion, rubbed her ears, which made her shut her eyes and shove against my fingers with her head. She seemed none the worse for wear after the battle. She was a cute little thing. I mimicked some male bird that was establishing territory with his rather loud song. He responded and we sang to each other as he moved ever closer. He landed on a tree limb in front of me, cocked his head, and stared at me in disbelief. I was definitely not the bird that he had expected to find. He uttered a small squawk of disgruntlement and flew away. By that time, I had found the road a couple of hundred yards up from the wagon and started towards them. I found one of Chasseresse's arrows on the roadway, searched out the rest of them, and carried them back for her. They had evidently hit the road on a very shallow angle and were thus unharmed by skittering through the dead leaves for some distance.

     People who are not Archers think that all arrows are the same. They are not! To start with, each person has a different 'draw length' (the distance from their cheek to the bow with the string drawn back as far as it will go), so each person's arrows are a specific length, and further, the diametre of the 'shaft' varies accordingly from a minimum of about a quarter of an inch to a half inch in some cases for the really big guys. The size of the 'head' and 'vanes' or 'fletching' vary accordingly and are relative to the size of the arrow. The 'nock', made from bone, also varies dependent on the size of the string used. Each arrow is marked with a 'crest'. This 'cresting' consists of a patterned series of painted lines or stripes around the 'shaft'. The colours, widths, and pattern are distinctive and identifies the owner of the arrow. That is why I knew that these were Chasseresse's arrows, mystery solved. Even if they had been broken, the parts would have been useful. We never wasted arrows. When you run out in the middle of nowhere, you are in trouble. By the way, bows also vary in size (length and diametre), grip size, and 'draw weight' in pounds for each person. When everybody is about the same size, this is not as bad a problem as it was in groups that contains wildly varying people.

Everything looked orderly when I got back to the group. The fake Farmers had been freed and were seeing to their charge, the chest of gold. The prisoners were tied with a method that we had been taught in Ranger training. You place a stout stick across their back and through the crooks of the both elbows, tie their hands together in front, but separated, bring both ends of the rope through their legs, and tie each end around the point where the elbow and pole are in contact, and then together in the middle to keep their elbows from sliding over the ends of the poles. This secures them well, does not give them any extra movement, leaves no rope ends for them to play with, and gives you a handle to hold onto from behind them.

They were lying lined up on the ground for our Medics to see to their wounds. Their ankles had been hobbled with short pieces of rope between them. The ones with the shattered knee caps had their legs splinted with split tree limbs. The ones with arrows in their legs were not as serious as they could have been, because we were great shots and we had been ordered to wound them so they could not run away. Each arrow, but one, had hit the outer part of the thigh in the large muscle that straightens your leg out, thus avoiding the bone and all major arteries. If you can't straighten your leg, you can't stay standing up. One guy had been shot through the large muscle on the back of one calf, though, as he had been standing in a way that his thigh could not be hit. All but one had gone clear through, so the head could be unscrewed and the shaft pulled back through the wound after sulfur powdre had been rubbed on the shaft to cleanse the wound of infection. After each shaft had been removed, a red-hot metal rod had been pushed a short way into the holes on each side to cauterize the wound.

One arrow head had not made it all the way through, but since it was just under the skin, Nell was performing field surgery to free it from the flesh. The patient was lying on his side with his head in a lap with a stick clamped in his teeth against the pain. Nell said, "Reaady? On thrae! Won...tooo..." and she sliced cleanly with her razor. The prisoner gave a muffled yell and glared at her in an accusatory manner. With a cocked eyebrow, she calmly replied, "Waell naow, I didna' wan' ya ta stiffen oop nor flinch eein ahnticipation, naow did I?" She pushed the head through, unscrewed it, powdered the wound, sutured it closed, and cauterized the other end of the hole.

One of the prisoners complained about being shot and Cranndair replied, "Well...If we hahd politely ahsked you to hold still, drop youah weapons, ahnd raise youah hahnds, would you hahve done so? Or would you hahve immediately countahahttacked?" The prisoners looked sheepish and Cranndair continued, "I thought so. While I hahve youah ahtention, allow me to impaht a pertinent piece of infoahmation. We need foah you to tell us everything about youah operation, what you took, wheah it is located, ahnd descriptions of youah victims. Ahs criminals, common Highwaypersons, as it were, you ah subject to the vilest of torture and incahceration in the foulest of Dungeons foah ahs long as you may survive in such confines." The prisoners were looking at each other somewhat frantically upon hearing this. Cranndair continued, "But...ahs prisonahs of woah, you would be treated with the courtesy due a fellow soldiah. You all appeah to be soldiahs, ahftah ahl. If you choose the lattah, you would be returned to youah country of origin, set free, oah folded into ouah ranks, as you choose. Youah fate will be determined by how foahthcoming you ah with us. Choose now!" Immediately, the prisoners started talking animatedly amongst themselves and every emotion possible flew back and forth amongst them. It quickly boiled down to seventeen in favour of spilling the beans versus two that through pride or shear stubbornness refused to tell us anything. One of the seventeen asked, "'scuse me, youah lordship, but could some o'us go one way an' some da udder?" Cranndair grinned and replied, "Of coahse we cahn treat you as two distinct groups. Ahftah ahl, you fine, upstanding soldiahs could hahve hahd youah rahnks infiltrated by a few low-down, dirty, scum-of-the-earth, demented criminahls. Totahl rapscallions' thaht deserve whahtevah punishments ah delivahed unto them!" The two "rapscallions" glared at him, but clamped their mouths shut in grim determination. From the laughter and ribald comments, like "Ya deserve it, ya bloody pricks!", "jus' deserts, I says!", and "Wot goes aroun', comes aroun'!", this illicitated from the POW's, these two were not well liked by their comrades at arms and had not been for a long time. Cranndair intoned in a very solemn manner, "Soldiahs, ah you prepeahed to sweah an Oath of Peace on youah honah ahs Warriahs and Soldiahs of youah Country oah Oahgahnization to which you owe allegiance, nevah to beah ahms against any lawful citizen of Waterport area except in self defence ahnd nevah to kill unless absolutely necessary?" With a resounding, "WE SO SWEAR!", the deal was done.

And so, with that simple mind game, Cranndair avoided any unpleasantness, such as torture, and gained seventeen willing POW's who were very talkative. We removed the uncomfortable sticks from their bindings and changed their ropes so that they had more freedom of movement for their arms. The two recalcitrants got the opposite treatment, with a noose being added to their neck that was attached to their ankle hobble with their legs drawn up. This is a very uncomfortable position to stay in for very long. Your legs start to cramp and you feel like you must stretch them out, but if you do, you choke yourself. They were also gagged with somebody's pair of worn-out, old, dirty, stinky, sweaty socks shoved in their mouths and tied in with a cloth. They had to lie there all night like that...ouch.

We roasted most of that fresh corn and shared it amongst the POW's, the wagon Soldiers, and ourselves while the little Halfling fellow and Bear told the story of the Giant, Akicita Wase's, heroic last battle. There was not a dry eye in the circle around that great fire that night. I noticed that the little guy was not tied and never left Bear's side, hmmm, I bet Bear had adopted him. They did make a funny team with the Halfling being about one foot tall and Bear being about seven feet in height. The musical instruments were pulled out and everybody sang to the various tunes around the campfire. Cranndair spent the evening talking privately with each of the POW's in turn and recording it all.

Miss Mouse enjoyed the corn immensely. I introduced her to Chasseresse, who dubbed her, "Darling!" and fed her some kernels of corn, too.

Chaptre 27. In which I Head Back to Town

Winter, 20th, Snowshell, 5012 (12 Turns of age)

The next morning, we untied the rope connecting the two prisoner's ankles and their necks, so that they could get some circulation going in their legs. We had the leftover corn from the night before for breakfast, and Cranndair called a meeting. He ran over the details of the situation with us all; that Baron Rastmusus Ekridge of Castle RamsHorn had conscripted these fellows and a lot more into his private army by threatening their families, that he had taken over the Barony recently upon the very suspicious death of his much beloved father, that the true heir (his older brother, Lyonel) was incarcerated in a tower, that he was an evil brat and a total degenerate, that our two prisoners were representative of a small percentage of actual followers of the Baron…that he collected bullies, brutes, and other mean folk to his side, that his Soldiers were never paid and had to provide all of their own equipment, that he had set up a Toll Booth along the Highway and was charging exorbitant Taxes of anyone that went through it, that he took almost all of the produce from the serfs in his area leaving them to starve, that he had sent these men to harass trade along the highway in an attempt to shift more trade through his Toll Booth, and that they were just Farmers turned Soldiers and they were very sorry to have caused anyone harm. Cranndair concluded with, "It would appeah thaht this ruffian, this Baron in name only, is a vile pustule upon the face of ouah world and should theahfoah be 'popped' with all haste! Do you men sweah temporary fealty the City of Waterport foah the purpose of removing this threat to life and happiness until the point at which this foul stain has been blotted out?" The POW's responded with a rousing cheer to this. Cranndair ordered them untied and their weapons returned.

After breakfast, we loaded the former POW's into the wagon, with the two prisoners tied to the back by ropes and staggering along behind, and headed for the cave in which the former 'Highwaypersons' had stashed the money and valuables they had taken from the various travellers. We went back towards Fisherton along the highway for a ways and then turned NorthWest onto a dirt road that appeared to bisect a peninsula that protruded into the river.

At the end of the road, near the tip, one of the ex-POW's showed us a trail that went down a steep cliff to a cave where he said they had stowed the loot. Cranndair dispatched several of the bigger guys to retrieve it while he contacted Guard Headquarters in Waterport using a different, somewhat larger, sphere. And here I thought that we would have to get all the way back to the City to report, silly me. He waited until all of the powers that be had gathered in the Guard Office, then gave them a complete report of our mission to date and our current situation. He requested that at least three more Ranger Platoons be dispatched to Fisherton with all haste in enough War Wagons to carry our group and themselves for the purpose of setting things aright in the Barony. He also asked that seventeen sets of the old Guard armour, in appropriate sizes, be sent along with a complete set of weapons. It was about nine or ten miles from Waterport to Fisherton, so even with the time it would take to get the people and gear together and the transport time, we should be able to meet them in Fisherton that evening.

Our medics had been checking the wounds of the men in the wagon and I could hear Nell bantering with them as she worked. The Little People were enjoying a snack...second breakfast.

The War Wagons were really amazing contraptions. They were made entirely out of steel and other metals, so were fireproof, had firing ports with doors on all sides, had a ram on the back (which became the front during battle), had a larger platform on top with a protection wall around it and a catapult or arbalest inside. The tongue doubled as a method for Soldiers to push it toward the enemy, after the horses were removed to be ridden, and it had protective screen that rolled out to protect their heads while doing so. They were normally pulled by eight massive armoured Destrier, War Horses, that were comfortable in harness pulling the wagons and as personal war mounts.

Apparently, a whole fleet of them were heading this way in response to Cranndair's request. Each had a two man team of drivers that doubled as siege weapon Artillererists, very efficient.

After the stolen goods had been loaded in the wagon, we departed for Fisherton.

The trip back was uneventful, so we all continued with our various practice of whatever we were learning…languages, musical instruments, the 'finger exercises', small spells, and other exercises. In my case it was Elven, my Penny Whistle, and more small spells. By this time, I had perfected 'Chauffer' (Heat), 'Reparer' (Mend), and 'Essuyer' (Dry), and was working on 'Chill', 'Break', and 'Tremper' (Wet). All of these were good for pranks, and were used so, frequently. I 'watered' the two prisoners by making the dirty socks in their mouths wet, after a bunch of misfires where their heads kept getting soaked, much to the amusement of their former unwilling conscripts. I 'Essuyer' (Dry)d them off each time, really, I did, and only once made one of them thirstier.

When we rolled back into town that afternoon, Nell and I were in the middle of a duet on our Penny Whistles, and the local kids flocked to us and began dancing around in the street. The other guys joined in with their various instruments and it quickly turned into something like a parade. We marched this way the whole way to the local Constabulary Office, where we ushered our two prisoners in and presented them to the Desk Sergeant. Cranndair produced a bag of individually wrapped hard candy from somewhere on his person and handed it out to our young escorts, much to their glee. This got the attention of all of the small people in our party, so they had to have some, too.

After the Head Constable and his staff had gathered, Sergeant Rodney Griffinbane presented his report, followed by Colonel Cranndair the Warden, and Lieutenant Chasseresse. The Head Constable asked a few questions and then told us that his people had been hearing rumours of the fell goings on to the NorthEast and that this information confirmed them. His people received the stolen goods along with a listing of descriptions of the victims from which they had been stolen. Cranndair made a request, and received a positive response, for medical assistance for our wounded and temporary housing for our prisoners until we could retrieve them on our way home after the rescue mission. Sergeant Rodney requested to accompany us on our rescue mission and was told to take his entire Platoon along as representatives of Fisherton.

Next, we escorted the 'Wagoneers' to their destination, a Merchant's small Mansion, and delivered them safely along with their cargo. The merchant was so ecstatically pleased with us for saving his men-at-arms and his money that he insisted on hosting a banquet for us that evening at his manse! Our housing at the inn would be paid for by the city of Fisherton and the Hospital stay for our wounded, the same, so this was not turning out to be an expensive trip, after all. We would be back at about eight bells for the feast!

We headed from there to the Hospital, where, having been warned of our imminent arrival, they had prepared enough beds to house our wounded. Stretcher bearer teams met us at the door and ferried the fallen into a ward with beds set up in ranks down both sides of the long room, each with a bedside table, metal water pitcher, metal cup, waste receptacle, and a lamp. Hanging on the end of each bed, facing the long aisle between the two ranks, was an empty clipboard. The Hospital was part of the local branch of the Temple of the Goddess of Health and was staffed by Her adherents.

Our wounded received a quick examination and a propre bath, while their clothing was taken to be cleaned at the laundry. Each was settled into their own bed and fed a 'healthy' meal. As the rest of us were about to depart, I had an odd idea...

What if the 'Reparer' (Mend) spell could be used to heal someone's wound? I ran this idea by Cranndair and Chasseresse. Neither had ever heard of anyone attempting to do this before, but thought that the idea had merit.

We explained to the 'patients', and the gathered staff, that if they healed the traditional way, they would not be able to take part in the upcoming battle for their homeland, but if we tried a radical new approach to healing. They would be instantly fit to travel and fight. They heartily agreed to the new approach, in as much as they really could not stand to be sitting idly on the sidelines while the fight for their homes blazed.

The hospital staff, who were quite knowledgeable in herbal remedies, bandaging and splinting, suturing, surgery, and other more normal treatments, were a little more reluctant to attempt Magick, other than the usual Deific sort, to heal, but the part-Fae amongst them convinced the others that it would be worth a try.

As our most skilled Magick using sort, Cranndair was chosen to make the try. A volunteer was prepped with his wound exposed and a chair placed beside the bed. Cranndair sat, meditated for a moment, and Magickally probed the area. The man squirmed a bit and said that it tickled. Two staff held his leg still and Cranndair focused all of his mind on the task at hand and said clearly, "Mend". The force of this caused a 'silent sound' that echoed through the room and brought a gasp from the onlookers.

Evidently, Cranndair had overdone it a bit, because every single thing that had been wrong with the patient, from cavities in his teeth to every scratch and scrape and sore muscle was instantly completely well and healthy! The patient exclaimed, "Oi! I feel bloody good! Best I've felt in Turns! Blessin's on ya, Sir!" and gave Cranndair a hug, much to his discomfiture. The man actually looked more youthful and so healthy that he practically glowed.

The staff was much impressed and wholeheartedly agreed to the new procedure. Next, Cranndair told us the details of the differences between using this simple spell on a broken cup and a living Human.

Chasseresse tried it next, followed by some of the Hospital staff, and finally me. The results varied depending on the Magickal potential of the person doing the spell, but all of the patients were healed of their wounds.

The former patients got dressed in their freshly cleaned clothing and we departed. The staff were completely oblivious to this, as they were entirely focused on a huge discussion of how to implement all of the 'Small Spells' into their daily routines and healing practices and how to disseminate this startling new information to their Order worldwide in as fast a manner as was possible. They tended to name techniques after the inventor or discoverer, so they were calling this one the RCAPM (Runt-Cranndair All Purpose Mend). Funny sounding name, if you asked me.

We made our way to the Inn of the Cross-eyed Flounder, entered, and were welcomed by wild cheering and applause, which bemused us somewhat until the Innkeeper apprised us of the fact that he had gotten the story of our heroism, along with payment for our room and board, from the Chief Constable himself, and had informed the patrons, who told all of their friends, who all showed up to give us a welcoming party upon our arrival. The place was packed…many people were shaking our hands and clapping us on the back with words of praise for our accomplishments. It was very embarrassing.

The Merchant had heard of this and decided to move the banquet to the largest private dining room at the Inn. His staff had been preparing said room all the while that we were taking care of the healing issue.

The Innkeeper hustled us up the stairs to the large dormitory style room that we had used previously, but with forty six of us this time, Rodney was staying with his family at his own cot, and we nearly filled the room to its capacity. The person in command of the War Wagon fleet, along with his second in command, were awaiting us there and monopolized Cranndair's attention for a while.

Staff were waiting to take our clothing to be washed and escort us to the bath house for cleansing, shaves, haircuts, nail trims, teeth cleaning, and massages. Somebody had spared no expense! We found out later that the local Merchant's Guild had donated the money in thanks for us removing the threat that the Highwaypersons posed to commerce. Miss Mouse rode in my hair and settled herself at the edge of the bath to lick herself clean while I was bathed. The bath house attendants were skilled in their craft and I really enjoyed the part where I got to lay back in the pleasantly warm water and get bathed by two somewhat pretty young Human ladies. I really understood at that point how much Chasseresse's amazing beauty had changed my concept of relative physical attractiveness. These girls would normally be considered pretty, maybe even beautiful, by the usual concept of that physical trait. I found them plain at worst and mildly pleasing to the eye at best. They probably thought that I liked other boys, which was fine by me, considering that Chasseresse was in the next bath area and could see me. Her attendants had somewhat stunned looks on their faces. It was really hilarious to watch this. Several times, one of them had to be replaced due to being overwhelmed.

After our spa treatment, we headed back to our room to find our gear and clothing all laid out on our beds, sparkling clean and shiny. We dressed and repaired to the private dining area for the banquet. As we passed through the common area, we noticed that snack trays had also been provided for the local guests, who were busy drinking the Inn dry, much to the pleasure of the Innkeeper. He had been very smart to spread the word. He got free food for his guests and sold massive amounts of drinks for a large profit.

The dining area had been transformed. It was now decked out in an array of finery in the colours and crest of the Merchants family. The long table was set in actual silverware with crystal goblets for the wine. The Merchants staff had probably taken over the Inn kitchens. Our favourite waitress was on hand, at our request and looked her best in a lovely new gown. She curtsied to Cranndair and thanked him from her heart for the honour of being included. He kissed her hand and told her that we would not dream of dining here without the pleasure of her company. The poor girl blushed to her hairline, then turned pale as she nearly fainted. Bear who was standing nearby easily caught her, brought her gently upright with one hand, and fanned her face with his other massive paw. Her green eyes fluttered open to be locked with his brilliant blue ones in an intense gaze that lasted entirely too long. We were all quietly smirking and grinning while we watched this interaction. So, that is what love-at-first-sight looked like. It would seem that Bear had been caught in a bear trap! Oh well, poor fellow, at least she had nice wide hips and would be able to bear him many fine little Norse semi-giants. Just imagine how big Norse babies were! He picked her up, carried her to the table with a silly grin on his face and told her that tonight, she would be wined and dined instead of working. She giggled and snuggled into his broad chest. He placed her gently in a chair and held her relatively dainty hand in his mighty one while talking quietly with her. His adopted 'son' took the chair on the other side of her and gave that arm a hug. What a cute family!

After we were all seated, the Merchant's staff served us a truly amazing seven course meal. We dined far into the night. The group finally staggered, totally sated, up to our room for some very heavy sleep.

Bear and his new lady friend got a private room for the night…

Rodney and I paused on the way and met with the Boss of the Thieves Guild local Branch and his sub-bosses in the Inn common area, which was a lot less full, and gave them a full report. They were satisfied with the results of our quest.

I finally crawled into bed at about midnight and was asleep the moment that my head hit the pillow.

Chaptre 28. In which I Go on a Whole New Mission

Winter, 21st, Snowshell, 5012 (12 Turns of age)

The next morning, after a truly wonderful breakfast in the Inn common area, we headed out of town to meet with the War Wagon party. Bear had a tearful goodbye, replete with lots of hugs and kisses, with his future Mate, promising to collect her on the way back to Waterport. After we were out of sight, he became the brunt of some truly ribald humour, to which he solemnly replied, "She's the one. My true love…" which completely put a stop to the ribbing. Rodney, with his Platoon marching in formation, met us along the way with his usual hearty welcome. The guy was always so cheerful. How did he do it?

I was kind of amazed at the sight of the camp along the road. Each wagon held two squads of five Rangers, plus the two crew members. That would be two wagons per Platoon, plus an armoured Chariot for the Platoon Leader and Sergeant, times three Platoons of Rangers equals six War Wagons and three War Chariots. Also present were four War Wagons and two War Chariots for our party. This makes a grand total of ten War Wagons and five War Chariots for our siege of the castle and one hundred and fifty four trained Soldiers. That poor usurper would not know what hit him!

They were stretched out for at least a half mile along the edge of the road with the Destriers and ordinary horses picketed alongside and munching on grass. The Soldiers were in the process of harnessing the huge beasts preparatory to moving out. This was a somewhat complex process due to the size of the Destriers compared to the

Humans and the numbres involved in each string. While we were watching this show, I noticed an amazing sight approaching our location. It was a very large Knight in full plate armour, shined to a mirrour brightness, mounted on the most beautiful snow white Destrier that I had ever seen, armoured in equally shiny plate barding, and carrying a couched lance with his standard mounted on the deadly steel tip. He was followed by two mounted squires and six pack horses. The morning sunlight, glancing off of his armour, was making it very hard to look at him. I poked Cranndair on the arm and pointed. The Knight cantered up to us and doffed his helm. He had pitch black hair, slightly curly with a ringlet in the centre of his high forehead, blue eyes, bright white teeth, flawless skin, a very manly chiseled jawline, and a little dimple in his proud chin. He said in a loud voice, "I say, would you chaps be so good as to point me in the direction of your supreme commander? I wish to converse with him or her. I am here to volunteer for your little foray, as I am in need of a good battle to test my skills. Perchance, is there any fair maiden's in need of rescue? Any foul villains in need of smiting? I do so love a good smite. Perhaps a dragon or two to slay?" He looked at us hopefully, almost wistfully, and we all looked at each other incredulously while some of us pointed at Cranndair in a dumbfounded manner. The knight responded with aplomb, "Ah, well pointed, lads and fair ladies! Sir, may I present myself, I am Sir Willem De Vie of Fewersham, at your service. May I offer myself to use as you see fit in your noble cause, may justice prevail!" He bowed from the waist as he made this pronouncement. I had never before seen Cranndair at a loss for words. He was actually a bit nonplussed by this fellow's arrival and manner. His mouth was even hanging open a slight bit. It didn't hurt that the fellow was devastatingly handsome and as far as I was aware, Cranndair liked guys way more than he liked girls, if he did like girls at all. After a moment to gather himself, Cranndair responded with, "Colonel Cranndaiah thah Wahden of the Rangahs of the City of Watahport and originally of Ville Des Neuf, at youah suhvice, Sah! We would be vereeh pleased to include youah most noble personage in ouah humble cause," and bowed in return. Wow, these guys were amazing to observe! It was like watching a ball game where manners were the ball and decorum was the court. Lucky Nell broke the austerity of the moment with, "Welcome, yer Shininess! I bet tha enemy sees ya commin' a mile away an' flees in terrour pissin' their pants tha whole way!" while Mendel chimed in with, "Your horse is really pretty, Mister Sir, I don't think that I have ever seen such a pretty horse before!" and handed an apple up to the War Horse, who nuzzled it from his hand and munched it down with enthusiasm, then soft lipped Mendel's head, who giggled and stroked the Destrier on the cheek. Cranndair and Willem both smiled at the interchange and Willem said, "Call me Willem. Would you like to ride up here with me, young Sir?" and in response to Mendel's ear-to-ear grin, reached down, grabbed Mendel's outstretched hand, and hoisted him with ease, pack, gear, weapons, and all up to the rear of the saddle. Mendel was used to the tiny, jug headed, barrel chested, knobby legged, shaggy Halfling ponies, but this was a whole new experience. While he stood on the War Horse's loin and stared around goggle eyed, Cranndair and Willem chatted in a less formal manner and the rest of us went back to watching the preparation for our departure.

After a couple of houres, everything was ready. We all formed up on the roadway by units for the official start of the campaign. After each squad leader reported to the Platoon Sergeant, who reported to the Platoon Leader, who reported to the Campaign Leader, Cranndair, up the chain of command that all were 'present or accounted for', we were ready for the briefing. Cranndair introduced Sir Willem and told us that they would share authority in the Campaign. Cranndair would be in charge of strategy and logistics, and Willem would be the Battle and Heroics Commander. Cranndair briefed us all on the details that we had been able to acquire on our own plus some that had been tortured out of our two prisoners during the night. The members of our party that had once worked for the villain had given us the entire layout of the castle and its surrounds, so we were prepared for just about anything. We were to recruit the unwilling conscripts along the way and take the 'true believers' prisoner so that they could stand trial. We had chains and shackles for that purpose. Justice was our goal, not carnage.

We broke ranks and loaded onto our assigned wagons and chariots. I and Chasseresse had a chariot to ourselves while her gruff old Platoon Sergeant and Lucky Nell shared another. Maybe she could lighten his mood. Mendel stayed on Sir Willem's War Horse and they chatted affably the whole trip.

The ride from Fisherton to Longbridge of about ten miles, or a little over three leagues, was uneventful, so we practiced our various Small Spells, musical instruments, and languages. Chasseresse and I played with Miss Mouse. We discovered that she had a very ticklish belly. The troops rode on top of the wagons or inside with all of the windows open, considering that it was a sunny day and solid metal vehicles get a bit warm, even in the end of Winter.

We arrived at Longbridge without incident and caused quite a stir as we rumbled through town in our large, heavy wagons, pulled by the massive steeds. Willem, on his War Horse, and Cranndair, on a Grey War Horse led the way magnificently. We continued on through toward our goal and made camp in the late afternoon just before where a stone bridge crossed a rushing stream about three miles, or one league, from the castle. We had gone about six and a half leagues, or twenty miles, that day. We had allowed no traffic to pass us and sent three of the faster moving War Chariots ahead to secure the bridge, so as not to warn the villain of our imminent arrival and we blockaded the road now, so no through traffic could occur at all. The spies would have to swim across that icy, fast-flowing stream if they wanted to report to the villain.

We made camp for the night alongside the highway to the right in the edge of the woods and along a trail that followed the stream to our right. We picketed the horses in a grassy area between the highway and the river on the left. We set up a command tent by the bridgehead and rigged a roadblock out of three tree trunks blocking the road at that point. Chasseresse and I finally had a little privacy, in our own small tent, and we made the most of it, as neither of us had to pull watch that night.

Chaptre 29. In which I Go to War

Winter, 22nd, Snowshell, 5012 (12 Turns of age)

The next morning, every leader type person met in the roadway outside the command tent for a planning session. The rest of the guys were either on guard duty, tending the animals, cooking breakfast, policing up the trash, digging slit latrines, doing wagon maintenance, sharpening weapons, doing maintenance on the siege machines, or some other useful chore.

Cranndair brought out his map and four of the guys expanded it to a size large enough to see details. We crowded around the side of the map closest to Castle Ramshorn and studied the area. The ones of our party that knew the area well started to explain details. As they did, those details showed up on the map, almost as if the area was coming into focus. If the new guys had been shocked by the Magickal properties of the map before, their shock increased at this new twist.

We decided to send two Squads plus two local guys, equipped with mountaineering gear, across the bridge, then to the right up the East bound fork, then North up a trail that wound through a valley, and then West over a small mountain that backed the castle to range themselves in positions ready to rappel down upon the battlements. We also decided to send two of our Squads with a Squad of the local guys along the river to secure the North road on the other side of the castle and to make contact with trusted dissidents in the village of Ekridge who would then take into custody any 'true believers' that were outside the castle. When these were in place, the rest of us would approach the castle from the front with the War Wagons, array them for siege, and ask the usurper if he was prepared to parley with us. If we could get a note to the dissidents inside the castle, so much the better. These twenty seven folks gathered their gear and supplies and headed out over the bridge.

Throughout the day, whenever traffic came up the road from the Southwest, they were told that they had a choice of either turning around to seek an alternate route to their destination, camping further down the road until the campaign was concluded, or going back to town. Since there was no other road going this direction, most chose to camp or go back to Longbridge. When traffic came from the other direction, they were boxed in by guards that stepped out from cover behind them and allowed through the gate, but not allowed to return toward the castle.

The next morning, we broke camp really early and moved out towards the castle.

We rolled slowly up the road toward the Toll Booth. When we were approximately a quarter mile from it, hidden around a bend, the lead War Wagon continued while the rest of us stopped, dismounted, and rapidly moved off through the woods to flank them. We left a skeleton crew to man the wagons left behind. This wagon had an old tarp covering it from front to back and side to side. It was a very poor job of camouflage though and would fool only the most simple-minded.

We were in position on both sides of the road when the wagon hove into view. Some of us were up trees and some were behind cover on the ground. We could tell the difference between the usurper's followers and the conscripted farmers. The former were lazing about, drinking wine, and playing cards, while the latter were guarding the gate across the road. They were armed with crossbows, longswords, and daggers. One of them walked out into the roadway with his hand raised up in a signal for the driver to stop, which he did, bringing the horses to a halt with about ten feet to spare. Since the driver was not wearing his uniform, he did not look very militaristic at all. He waved at the guards and grinned jovially saying, "Good day ta ya Gov'nor, I 'aven't seen a roadblock 'ere before." The guard replied in a bored tone, "Tis new. Tis a toll gate and ya owes us a fare ta get t'rough. Le's see, eight pence fer tha 'orses, a tupence for ya, and a shillin' fer tha wagon. Wots yer cargo, so's I can value it?" He said all of this while walking down the line of horses toward the wagon. When he reached the side of the wagon, he lifted the tarp and found a three inch long, three bladed, razor sharp arrowhead protruding from each of the four firing ports and aimed directly at various portions of his anatomy. He heard, "Shhhhh" from inside the wagon. He gulped, wide eyed, but said nothing. Eight of our guys quietly exited the back of the wagon and stayed out of sight. When they had the surprised guard covered, the other four exited. One of the locals in the group recognized the poor fellow and waved him over behind the wagon saying, "Jake, are ya wi' us or agin' us?" Jake nodded, grinned, and gripped the other's hand in greeting. He was told quietly to go lure the usurper's men out into the open from the rude hut in which they were indolently ensconced. He walked back towards the gate saying, "Hey bosses, I need ya ta help me value dis cargo, I dunno wot i'tis." The grumpiest looking boss person growled, "Aw'right, ya useless bag o' shite! Ya canno' do nothin' right wi'out whinin' ta us ta he'p ya, ya lazy bugger! C'mon, me boyos, le's go save tha idiot farmer," while heaving his bulk up out of the old chair that it had been very comfortably occupying until he was so rudely interrupted. He and his two cronies sauntered out of the hut, around the barrier, and toward the wagon. They did not even bother to bring their weapons. He growled again, "Wot are ya grinnin' at, ya fool?" just when the twelve Soldiers fanned out from behind the wagon with bows drawn, the tarp was pulled off and onto the ground baring the arbalest and crew on top, and all of the Soldiers on both sides of the road stood up with bows drawn. One of his two cronies actually wet his pants. The guard grinned and said, "Tol' ya I was 'avin' trouble valuin' it, but now I can see dat it looks like freedom, ta me!" The other conscripts had raised their hands in the air, but after that statement, they lowered them and gave a quiet cheer. The locals from our group chatted excitedly with the recently rescued ones and caught them up on the recent developments, while they roughly bound and gagged the usurper's men and parked each one on a cross bar directly under one of the Destrier's butts, so that every time it relieved itself, the stuff landed on their former bosses' heads. They called it 'Road Apple Delight'. The horses did not much like them there and kept swatting them with their tails. They informed us that unfortunately, all of the conscript's children had been collected and taken to the castle to keep the conscripts in line. This was a rather nasty wrinkle!

We called Cranndair and apprised him of the new situation. He had the rest of the army move up to our location. After they had arrived, he questioned the new guys extensively. While he was doing that, he got a call from the local Squad that had gone to Ekridge. They had located all of the usurper's men that were in town, captured them, and recruited all of the former conscripts and even most of their wives, who refused to stay away when there was a chance to save their children. They were nearly to our location with prisoners, new Soldiers, and a lot of food. Their skirmish was being touted as The Battle for Ekridge! They marched up to us, carrying the strangest assortment of weaponry that I had ever seen, and a really big woman with stern features, blazing blue eyes, and iron grey hair roared, "Whar are tha rest of 'um? I'll not tolerate those ruffians a second longer in our land!" while waving a log splitting axe that must have weighed twenty pounds easily in one hand. We all kind of involuntarily took a step backwards, so fierce was her demeanor. Bear just grinned and said, "She's Norse."

After they arrived, we got to hear details of the great battle that included heroic tales of Grannies armed with rolling pins bashing the bad guys over the noggin, young women with pitchforks poking them in the butts, and one matron who took three of them out with an iron skillet! The women and a few men had marched their much battered prisoners in proudly, all tied together with a motley array of materials, including one guy who looked practically mummified in bailing twine! I laughed so hard at that one that I nearly fell over.

We sorted out the prisoners, got the scoundrels properly chained and shackled, tore down the Toll Booth, fed everyone, and when all was ready, started up the gravel road to the castle. We were told that there was a large field in front of the curtain wall and that the other two sides of the enclosure backed up to a nearly vertical cliff with parts of the castle built into it and up it a ways.

When we arrived at the field, it was still several houres before noon. The guards on the walls started calling out excitedly and gesturing towards us. We ignored them and proceeded to set up our skirmish line by backing the War Wagons up in a line about four hundred yards from the wall, unhitching the Destriers and readying them as War Mounts, spreading most of the archers out in line with the wagons, setting up a siege camp behind the line of wagons, and other chores.

I noticed that the curtain wall was not very imposing, being only about a rod tall (see Appendix D, Weights and Measures). It had common square crenellations on top and appeared to be more of a nuisance than a serious impediment to purposeful movement. The stones were not even smooth, with lots of noticeable handholds. I could have scaled it in absolute silence in way less than a minute.

Towards the end of the set-up process, we heard, "I say, you theah, wot is the meaning of this hubbub! It's too damned early in the morning and I did not ordah a cahnival. How da'ah you set foot upon my sovereign lands without permission! I shall be forced to expel you personally if you do not remove yourselves immediately!" broadcast through a megaphone tube. We could see the tube easily at the bottom of a crenellation in the top of the battlements, but only the top of a sleeping cap behind it. The speaker was in his pajamas!

Cranndair, mounted on a dapple grey Destrier, and Sir Willem, on his gleaming white War Horse, cantered past the wagons and approached to within a few dozen yards of the gate to the fortress. The Archers followed in a line stretching across the field behind them. Cranndair loudly intoned, "Rastmusus Ekridge, you ah heahby chahged with…" and proceeded to read off a litany of bad things that the guy had done. When he finished, the usurper insolently and totally without remorse replied, "Yes, yes, all that is well and good, but I am still stuck on one salient point. Who the Helheim ah you and wot right do you have to accost me on my own sovereign lands concerning internal governmental functions, decisions, and policies? Have I stepped outside my bordahs and hahmed anyone in any way? Have I attacked any other sovereign nation, state, or city? I think not, and you should depart forthwith and remove yourself from my beautiful field that will soon be filled with the loveliest of wildflowers. Spring is coming soon, you know. Did you not see the signs along the well delineated roadway telling you to 'Keep Off the Grass'? I have a standing rule on pain of death that there is absolutely no walking on my grass allowed!"

Cranndair called up to him, "Actuahlly, you hahve, sah! You hahve sent a military foray into youah neighboahs lahnds, and caused them to attack innocents!" The usurper replied in shock and dismay, "I have certainly not! Prove it!!!!" Whereupon Cranndair motioned for the former Highwaypersons to step forward. Upon seeing them and being prompted by one of his underlings as to their identities, the pompous villain said, "Oh Drat!!!! That was supposed to be a secret! Who squealed? They need to die! I just knew that was a bad plan. Father always said, 'Play in youah own yahd, don't pee in youah neighbours.' I will kill the idiot personally that made me decide to authorize it. It is all his fault! After all, I would never make such a foolish mistake." At that point, Sir Willem bellowed in a gentlepersonly manner, "You may now choose to give up your stolen lands and title, remove yourself peacefully from the castle, and submit yourself to fair justice or I, Sir Willem De

Vie, Knight Errant of Fewersham, shall smite you forthwith! Oh…and, by the way, we shall also lay siege unto you and your villainous crew. Now, be a good chap and open the gate so that we may entre? I do so hate bashing through walls. It dulls the edge on my sword. Unforgiving stuff, rock…" He turned towards Cranndair and said in a somewhat quieter voice, "I do really believe that the vile fellow deserves a good smiting, or at least a spanking, don't you?" Cranndair grinned and suppressed a chuckle. The 'good chap' replied with a sneer in his voice, "You must think me insane! Why on earth would I let you in? Wot can you possibly do to make me open the gate?" A voice called out, "Yer Baronship, they 'ave go' a lot o' arbalests and catapults aimed at us!" The usurper replied in a querulous voice, "They 'ave siege engines?!?! W'y didn't you tell me that?!?! You idiot!!!! Somebody kill him!" This was followed by the 'thwack' of a crossbow firing and a short scream of agony, then the thud of a body hitting the paving stones of the courtyard. The usurper then said in a petulant manner, "I sweah, I am completely surrounded by incompetent idiots! Why can I not find efficient underlings to do my bidding?" One of the Halfling Slingers or Archers, from the pitch of his voice yelled, "Cause yer a complete loon? And nobody sane would work fer ya? You'd probably kill yer Mama fer overcookin' yer buscuits." The response was, "Now the peasants are talking rudely! Somebody kill that fool!" One of his men raised up in a crenellation to fire his crossbow at the Halfling and received three arrows, one in his right eye, one in his neck, and one in his chest. He dropped like a stone. The usurper screamed, "I SAID SOMEBODY KILL THAT LITTLE FOOL!!!!!!" but no more of his men made themselves visible. "Very well, you are all fired! I do not want any of you around me ever again. You may leave now. I SAID LEAVE!!!!" but none of his men opened the gate or left. We next saw the megaphone disappear from the crenellation and heard muttered imprecations that got softer with distance, "Move aside, lummox! Out of my way! W'y are you still here? I told you all to leave. Oafs, probably too stupid to understand me." Cranndair and Sir Willem looked at each other with perplexed expressions on their faces. A small white cloth tied to a spear appeared above the battlements for a moment, but precipitously dropped as another crossbow quarrel pinioned the bearer. If they kept this up, they would kill each other without us firing a shot, but unfortunately, the ones being killed were probably the unwilling conscripts. Sir Willem spat, "Dastardly, that!" He was starting to actually get somewhat angry!

As they cantered back to our lines, Cranndair told Sir Willem, "You know, you could use othah implements bettah suited foah bashing through stone walls than that lovely, immense blade of youahs." Sir Willem responded with sudden interest, "Really? Do tell…" and they continued chatting all the way back to the command tent.

We retired to our camp, set up a watch schedule, started cooking supper at the mess tent, established latrines, set up the tents, and all of the leaders met for a planning session.

Our guys on the heights above the castle reported on the internal layout of the castle, supplemented by the memories of the former conscripts, and we drew a diagram on the top of a Battle Table. They could not sneak down to the castle due to the numbre of enemy that were stationed below, some specifically looking up at the cliffs. We had to get someone inside, fast, before the usurper could react well to our presence.

As all the Big People mulled over the situation, I piped up with, "We could play a game of Halfling Toss on a grand scale…" The bosses turned to look at me perplexed. I explained that when we were bored and could not find a ball to use, we would use Halflings as balls in a game of toss. It built up the big guys muscles and we Little Folk enjoyed it as well. The big bosses stared at me wide-eyed for a second, then broke into laughter along with, "Jolly good!", "Bravo!", "I would 'ave never thought…", and other exclamations.

I pointed at the drawing of a large pile of hay at the back of the courtyard up against the wall of the castle. "Do you think you could hit this?" The Dwarven Siege Engine Master stared at the drawing critically, and slowly said, "It'll be a bit o' a challenge, boot I t'ink it's do-able."

I said, "I volunteer to be the first. If it works, you can chuck the rest of my Squad in after I take out any guards that are in the immediate vicinity. The guys on the cliffs can tell you when to fire or any adjustments to aim that are necessary. We can quietly take out a few guards and get the gate open. All of our troops can be waiting in the dark up against the outside of the curtain wall ready to storm in or over with grappling hooks and take the rest hostage. Our guys on the cliffs can drop down at the same time that we come in the gate to take out the guards on the upper areas. They can search for the usurper's chambers and take him hostage."

I was watching them to gauge their reaction, "I am sure that we will succeed, considering that most of his men are conscripts that will turn on their captors the moment they realize that we mean them no harm and that their families are secure. Our local guys can yell for them to do exactly that, the moment they are inside the wall."

They continued to listen, "If, for some reason, the attack utterly fails, and there is absolutely no other way to take this sadistic nut out, the catapults can be ready to fire on the castle itself behind us. They can be loaded with that Liquid Fire stuff that even burns stone. The arbalests can be aimed at the bases of the towers to crumble them. Either we succeed in capturing the bad guys and saving the true Baron or we leave behind a pile of charred rubble. We will not have died in vain."

I noticed a few positive responses, "So, in summary; One, Our troops sneak into position along the base of the wall. Have the local guys in front ready to shout. Two, Load and aim five catapults with my Squad. Load the others with Liquid Fire and aim them at the castle. Have Archers ready to fire flaming arrows to light the stuff. Three, Aim the arbalests at the bases of the towers. Four, Launch me. Five, I take out the close guards. Six, Launch my Squad, one at a time. Seven, We take out the gate guards and open the gate. Eight, Storm the castle. Turn the conscripts against the bad guys. Nine, The guys on the cliff drop down, take out the top guards, and search for the villain. Ten, Secure the prisoners. Eleven, Search the castle and find the true heir to the Barony. Twelve, Save the true Baron and restore him to his rightful place."

I looked around hopefully, "So, what do you think of the plan? Will it work?"

I noticed that almost everyone was staring at me in awe and wonderment and there was dead silence. Very strange...they probably thought that it was a stupid plan and were about to laugh at the silly little Halfling, the ignorant little kid, the upstart. I swore to myself that I was not going to cry. I hung my head in shame and started to slink toward the back of the crowd.

Then Cranndair said, "Young Sah, wheah hahve you been hiding that astute mind of youahs? The enemy should quake in sheah terrah upon word of youah coming. I humbly bow to youah military strategy, cunning, mental fortitude, and courage! I heahby promote you to the rank of Lieutenant. This field promotion to take effect immediately." And he actually did bow!

Needless to say, I was stunned! You could have knocked me over with a feather. They actually liked the plan! Chasseresse gave me a hug and a kiss that promised more, when we could get some alone time. The guys clapped me on the back and congratulated me. I made sure that Miss Mouse was safe from their clapping. Sir Willem said bemusedly, "A much better plan than mine! I was simply going to charge the gate, smash it to splinters, and smite any who attempted to thwart me in my quest to save the...who are we saving again?" This bought a giggle from several of the guys and a chorus of "The Baron." Sir Willem continued with sadness, "Not a Baroness? This is a gentleperson, I take it? Not a damsel in distress? Tsk, tsk, a shame. I do so love rescuing fair maidens. Gentlepersons are somewhat problematic. A handshake is just not the same as a hug and kiss from a beautiful girl..." This brought mixed reactions from the onlookers. Lucky Nell impetuously jumped up on the table, grabbed the shocked Nobleman, hugged him around the neck with her stubby arms, and planted a big kiss on his cheek, saying, "There naow, ya have yer hug an' kiss, Sir Knight! That ought ta maeke ya feel a bit better!" to the uproarious laughter of all present. The Knight, having collected himself, gave her a flashing smile, bowed to her, took her chubby little hand in his, kissed it, and solemnly intoned, "My Lady, may I be your champion in the coming tournament? May I fight in your name and for your honour? It would please me greatly to do so." Lucky Nell blushed furiously, turning bright red clear to her hairline, ducked her head in extremely unusual shyness, shuffled her feet, and peeked up at his face through her eyelashes, then burst out in a rush with, "Sur'an' ya can, ya charmer!" to a chorus of more laughter and some applause. Sir Willem picked her up gently and easily and placed her back on the ground saying, "My Lady If I may be of assistance." Nell looked up at Chasseresse and said, "I loike him! He's a kaeper!", which made Chasseresse giggle. I said, "I'm sorry for leaving you out of the plan, Sir Willem. If everyone would be so kind as to insert 'Sir Willem leads the charge heroically through the open gate on his mighty steed and smites any and all who stand in his way!' in between numbre seven, opening the gate, and numbre eight, storming the castle." This brought applause and cheers from all present and a courtly bow from Sir Willem.

We discussed how noisy it would be, should we just chuck me or test it with less easily damaged objects first, should we disguise the Halfling missiles, should we shoot a bunch of stuff at them so they did not notice the Halfling missiles, when should we do it, and other considerations.

We finally decided to chuck a melon first, with the guys on the cliff as spotters. The orders were disseminated amongst the troops, then we gathered our gear. Each one of my Squad went to a catapult to be weighed precisely so that the Siege Engineers could add this data to their calculations. They had a large scale with a centre post, a balancing arm, and a basket hanging from each end of the arm. We sat in one basket while they placed measuring 'stones' made of lead in the other until the ends were balanced. Thus, they knew exactly how much each of us, and the poor melon, weighed.

After supper, when the shadows were long, we sent out a couple of scouts to huddle at the base of the wall and listen to the enemy. They had each taken the end of a roll of twine with them. When they got into each position, as directed by the Engineers, the twine was pulled taut and marked by a tied ribbon with the catapult's numbre on it. This was repeated for six catapults. The Scouts released their ends and the Engineers rolled the two balls of twine back up while marking on a slate the measurements for each catapult. The twine had foot and yard markings on it, so the Engineers knew exactly how far it was to the wall from each catapult. The Engineers then brought out more slates and an abacus and began to make the calculations for each of the six squishy missiles.

We had lots of time before the attack, which was planned for the wee houres of the morning, so we brought out the musical instruments and had something of a pre-battle party, which we hoped would put our enemy at ease. Music is so soothing. Our two base-of-the-wall scouts reported lots of grumbling from the enemy guys, who were all watching from the top of the wall. Apparently, they wished that they could take part in the festivities and talked very badly about their captors, who were lazily not on guard, but were somewhere in the castle. Some were even bantering about an idea that they should abandon their posts, go over the wall, and join us, but then they remembered that their families were being held hostage. Our Scouts reported all of this and it was decided to let the conscripts on the wall know that their families were safe. One of the scouts positioned himself directly below one of these conversations and called out to them, "Yer families from tha village are safe an' most of um are in our camp he'ping us to rescue yous guys! Pass da word amongst yerse'ves. It's safe fer ya ta join us." After the initial shock of hearing this coming from outside the wall directly below them wore off, they talked among themselves and decided to escape to our side. They asked a few questions, which were answered. They wanted to see their families. The word was passed to the women, who stood in the firelight of our bonfire and waved at their men. We asked about them opening the gate, but unfortunately, it was locked with two large padlocks, reportedly way too big for my Thieves Tools. We would have to steal the key. The top of the wall and the field in front of it were bathed in moonlight, but the courtyard was in shadow, so they kept a few of their guys in sight on the wall, in case a boss woke up and peeked out of a window. They looked for rope, but could find none. We asked them to find a large tarp and for a bunch of them to hold the edges of it with it positioned over the hay pile. They pulled one off of a large wagon that was parked in the courtyard and complied. We figured that it would be too noisy to throw grappling hooks over the wall, so the rest of our troops moved out stealthily, staying in the shadows, to position themselves at the base of the wall.

Chaptre 30. In which I Rescue a Baron

Winter, 23nd, Snowshell, 5012 (12 Turns of age)

Next came the harrowing part. The Siege Engineers fired the melon over the wall, but it splatted with a squishy sound on the cobblestones of the courtyard. Everybody held their breath and listened intently for a response from the bosses. Thankfully, none of them awakened. Apparently, they were wine besotted. The distance variable was relayed to The Engineers, who adjusted their aim and fired another melon. This one hit in the middle of the tarp with a soft thud. The Engineers adjusted the aim of all of the catapults that were to fire my Squad members accordingly. I coaxed Miss Mouse into transferring to Chasseresse temporarily with a bribe of sweet berries, gave my sweetie a really good kiss, and climbed into the catapult's bucket without apparent trepidation, but with my insides quaking like a bowl of pudding on the back of a jouncing wagon rolling over cobblestones. I really hoped that I would not piss my pants during this. I jauntily saluted Cranndair from the bucket and gave a thumbs up gesture. I did not try to speak, as my quavering voice would have given me away.

The catapult arm was released and I immediately felt like I weighed a ton. I was smushed into the bottom of the bucket by the increased gravitational force. It was painful! I should have been lying flat of my back in the bottom of the bucket. Then suddenly, the arm reached the padded stop and I was free of the bucket. I was flying! I righted myself and watched as the field sped by below. So this was what it felt like to be a bird. I sailed over the wall, missing it by a few feet, though it looked a lot closer, heart stoppingly closer, and into the darkness of the courtyard. I rolled into a ball and hit the tarp with stunning force! The pile of hay under it cushioned me as much as the tarp. They helped me out and held me up until I got my bearings. We all listened for wakeful noises from the bosses, but heard none, after several minutes had passed. I relayed the details of the experience to my Squad members, exactly how to do it correctly to avoid injury. I was using the Communication Spheres. They sure were handy.

Due to her Faith in the Goddess of Luck, Nell had to go next, since her Deity required the taking of chances. She did a quick prayer over the guys and jumped in the bucket, positioning herself as I had directed. The catapult fired and she sailed in for a landing. She did not hit the exact centre, but did manage to land quite nicely and appeared to be completely unfazed by the experience. She whispered that it was really fun and she wanted to do it again after the battle. This brought quiet chuckles from the tarp holders, who were shaking their heads at the antics of the crazy Halflings. Mendel came next and thought it to be quite an enjoyable experience, but one that he would not want to repeat. Sensible fellow. Jagger did it without comment, as was his way, but Rudd declined at the last minute, which was fine, as it was a very dangerous thing to do.

We talked with the conscripts to find out what they knew of the locations of the bosses, the usurper, and the true heir. The only one that they knew for sure was the tower that held the prisoner, as they were not allowed in the castle propre and had been housed in the stables and courtyard. They also informed us that the prettiest young men and women from their village were kept in the castle for whatever vile purposes the evil sorts desired. This fact had been driving them a bit nuts as these were, for the most part, their sons and daughters.

We decided to rescue the true Baron first, because of his familiarity with the inside of the castle, then the girls, who could tell us exactly where the bad guys were and especially the location of the key. They all went back to their places on the wall or at the doors. I inspected the padlocks on the gate. They were truly works of art and I realized why when I saw the Dwarven Makers Mark on them.

We crept up to the door that they had indicated went to the correct tower. It was locked. I took off my pack and retrieved my Lockpick Set. The other guys watched with interest as I deftly picked the lock, slipped the kit into an easier to reach front beltpouch, and put my pack back on. Nell asked where I had learned to do that and I explained that having grown up on the streets, I had been around a lot of Thief sorts and that I had picked up some knowledge from them along the way. That seemed to satisfy her and Mendel, but I don't think that Jagger was convinced. Oh well, I would have to talk with him later about it.

We slipped into the entryway and quietly shut the door securely behind us. We were all wearing our hoods and masks, with the skin around our eyes blackened with weaponblack, and the lighter coloured patches of the camouflage on our uniforms had been darkened with charcoal, so we were invisible for the most part in the gloom. Jagger carried a bag of rope and gags for our soon to be prisoners. I could see heat, but the others could not, so I was on point. We let our eyes adjust to the deeper gloom, then moved out towards the stairway that went up the prisoner's tower. I hoped that there were no artificial light or extreme heat sources along our route. These would probably be in the form of fire. Once my eyes were adjusted to lightless conditions, seeing a fire would flash blind me and it would last for a while.

We turned right and went through a Great Room, another hallway, turned right again, through another hallway, and through a door into a round room with a spiral staircase leading up in a clockwise fashion. We had listened at every door that we encountered, but heard no sounds of occupancy, nor had we met anyone so far. This was odd, where were they?

The stairwell was curved like this to hinder attackers fighting upwards and aid defenders as they backed up the stairs. This was based on the premise that most people are right handed and wielded their main weapon in that hand. If left handed or ambidextrous people were attacking, the defenders were in trouble.

We crept up the stairs, quieter than rats, and came to a room without a door at the top. The stairs just went through a hole in the floor and stopped. We could hear snoring coming from the room. I stuck my head up and peeked into the room. There was a large, ugly Human, with the worst case of stinky feet that I had ever smelled, asleep on an overlarge cot against the wall. I did not feel like getting in a fisticuffs fight with this lummox, so I pulled out my small blowgun, inserted a sleep dart, and shot him in his big, fat neck. His eyes popped open and he slapped at the dart, probably thinking that it was a biting insect. Then, he swooned and started to snore again.

We climbed into the room and looked around. Nell asked me about the blowgun and I told her that I had learned about them on the streets, also. Jagger was looking more skeptical by the minute. We saw a ladder leading up to a trapdoor in the ceiling. It was closed and padlocked. I climbed the ladder, held on with just my legs, and picked that lock, also.

With Jagger's help, we were able to quietly lift the large door and peek inside. We saw a rather handsome fellow wearing a filthy nightrobe staring at us from a rough pallet of hay. The room was nasty and it stunk badly. He said, "Children? Children wearing masks? What, pray tell, are you two doing in my cell? Did the ruffians send you with my breakfast?" I told him that we were Halflings, not children, and that we were there to save him. He looked a bit confused over that, but smiled in gratitude. We climbed on up and started to help him up, but the smell was horrific. This fellow had not had a bath in a very long time. I did several 'Nettoyer' (Clean) spells on him until he was completely fresh from head to toe with not a smudge on his nightrobe. He was amazed by this, for some reason, and thanked me repeatedly. Sometimes I forget that Mundanes do not understand Natural Magick and have no abilities in the use of it. I use Natural and Deific Magick many times each day and think nothing of it.

We helped him down the ladder and he helped us roll the fat guy off onto the floor, after I 'Nettoyer' (Clean)'d him up a bit, just because he stunk so badly and was too filthy to touch. I realized that I had grown finicky since I left the sewers. That was funny. He landed face-first with a thud, but did not awaken, then we tied his wrists and ankles and gagged his mouth.

Jagger was still staring at me thoughtfully, so I gave up and told them a partial truth. I told them that being a street urchin with no living parents was a tough life. That I had had to do things to survive that I was not, in retrospect, proud of. In fact, it shamed me to remember them. That it would take a lot of 'good' deeds to balance the slate or better yet, wipe it clean. That I had survived to the age of ten by using my wits and living in the shadows. That you either became a victim or you joined some group that would keep you alive as you got older. That the Thieves Guild recruited urchins to train and fill their ranks. That I had been recruited, whether I liked it or not. That I had been trained completely, but had never actually committed a crime, other than occasional petty theft of food. That I got a chance to disappear, when a situation occurred where it would have been unlikely that there were any survivors. That I could do this, because the Guild works in separate 'cells', where only the people in your 'cell' know what you look like or much about you. With the rest of the 'cell' members' dead, I was just another street kid again. The City Guard spotted me training myself to use a sling and helped me. They then sent me to the castle to join the Guard. So, I was not a 'real' Thief, even though I was Journeyperson level in; Pickpocket, Cutpurse, Grifter, Smuggler, and Forger, and Apprentice in; Counterfeiter, Burglar, Trapfinder, Safecracker, and Assassin. Also, from the Street Bards, I was an Apprentice; Fencer and Jongleur. I told them that I would be glad to teach them the skills that I had accrued if they were interested, as they could see how useful they were to Rangers. They nodded appreciatively and Jagger stepped forward to do a forearm grip handshake with me and clap me on the shoulder with his other hand. It was the first time that I had ever seen true respect shining in his eyes. He had always fastidiously respected my rank and station, but had never before respected me, the person. I was somewhat taken aback by this, but clapped him on the shoulder in return. He never said a word, but I could tell that he was apologizing for underestimating my 'toughness', 'goodness', and 'honour' and that he would never question my skills again, that he considered me to be a true Warrior. Wow, that felt good!

We retraced our steps without incident and presented the Baron to his people in the courtyard. They welcomed him back and remarked over his cleanliness. He explained excitedly about the spell I had done and one of his men asked me to give his head a cleaning. I did, and it must have fixed whatever had been wrong, because the fellow was really happy about the results. The Baron told us where the best bedrooms were, which were probably where the bad guys were. He also told us where the servant's quarters were.

We silently headed that way, through the kitchen and the scullery, and found a narrow, dark hallway with small, locked doors leading off of it. I unlocked the first, opened it, and found four women and a few children crammed into a room not much bigger than a broom closet, all staring towards the door in a frightened manner. I left Nell to explain things to them and moved on to the next door until they were all unlocked. It turned out that some of them were the castle staff and some of them were village girls and smaller kids. They had all been abused in various ways and some wanted to help us catch the brutes that had done it to them. We gave them the bag of rope and gags and asked them to point the way to the first bad guys room. They followed us at a distance and were fairly quiet, due to being fairly lightweight, for

Human girls, and barefoot. I oiled the door mechanism of the first room, opened it silently, and we all crept in to surround the bully that was sleeping in the rather nice bed. He was flat of his back with his mouth wide open and snoring loudly. We each jumped on an extremity and Jagger stuffed a gag in the guy's mouth before he could yell. I had a dagger tip touching the tip of his rather pointy nose and he stared at it cross-eyed for a second before relaxing. He didn't put up too much of a struggle while we tied him up and frisked him for weapons, especially after he tried to pull an arm free and got clouted in the back of the head with the pommel of a shortsword by Jagger. We placed him in the middle of the floor, where he could not get to anything useful. The girls had helped us tie him up and asked if they could do it themselves on the next one. We agreed and the whole group went to the next room to repeat the process. This one was not as easy, considering that the guy was all tangled up in his covers. The largest girl solved the problem by picking up the iron poker from the fireplace and swiftly clubbing the lout over the head. Needless to say, he put up no fuss as the girls unceremoniously dragged him from the bed and tied him thoroughly. Jagger nodded in agreement with their brutality, but the rest of us looked somewhat unconvinced that it was necessary, especially when one of the girls kicked him squarely in the family jewels with a savagery that was impressive. Mendel and I winced sympathetically.

We moved on to the next room and generally repeated the scenario, except the this one had a dagger under the pillow and when he tried to pull it, got his arm pinned to the bed by Jagger's shortsword. He stopped fighting at that point. He must have been especially brutal to the girls, because several of them took turns punching him in the face. I reminded myself to never underestimate the upper body strength of Human farm girls. They were a tough lot!

The rest of the captures were generally uneventful and then we were at the door to the usurper's apartments. This one was probably going to be a bit more problematic. The girls had decided to go back and drag all of the captured ruffians out into the hallway where they could be watched more closely.

We crept up to the door, listened carefully for a bit, and then I oiled the hinges and carefully attempted to open it. It didn't open and it wasn't locked, I checked. Through the keyhole, I spied a wooden bar across the door! Hmmm...I had wondered what those iron bolt heads were doing on the outside of the door. Oh well, this one was going to take a bit longer. I took out my fine steel hacksaw and as silently as

159

possible started to cut off the eight heads. Then an odd thought crossed my mind. I asked Nell to ask the girls if there was a servant's entrance to the apartments. She scurried off and came back with a 'yes'.

We left her guarding the door with her crossbow cocked and ready to impale anyone that dared to attempt to escape that way and headed back to where the girls were casually torturing their former abusers. Me and Mendel looked askance at that behaviour, but brushed it off as revenge. One of them led us to a cramped back hallway and showed us the door into the apartments. She smiled, curtsied, and told us that she would like to help collect the bad guys. She had the fireplace poker in her apron string. I was not going to try to stop her, so we agreed.

I oiled the hinges and quietly opened the door. I had my blowgun out and ready, but only spotted the heat signature of one scrawny Human in the really large canopied bed. No one else was in the room. We snuck up to the bed, surrounded him and very easily, gagged and bound him. He just stared at us wall-eyed, pissed himself, and swooned. What a wimp!

The girl watched over him with really scary glee while we worked on the next door. I got it open quietly enough, but found that there were four of the ruffians asleep in the room! Too many! I crept into the room and prayed to the Goddess of Luck that I could shoot them all before they woke up. We waved the girl over and pointed at one of them and signed for her to wait. She stood over him with her poker raised high in the air and waited expectantly. We each took one. Jagger and Mendel each had their shortsword and dagger out and ready. I had mine in their sheaths, but instantly ready if I failed to knock them all out. When everybody gave me the thumbs up sign, I poked the one I was standing by with a dart while firing a dart at another ones exposed face. They both made noise before subsiding, but it was too late. The other two started to rouse and the girl clubbed hers over the head with her iron poker. Mendel was the only one that was not able to subdue his, though he tried to knock the guy out with a hard blow to the head with the flat of his sword. The guy reared up yelling and pulling a dagger from his belt, thus knocking poor little Mendel aside as if he were nothing. Jagger threw his dagger while charging, hitting the guy in his shoulder and making him drop his dagger while I dropped my blowgun, pulled both daggers, jumped atop the sleeping form of the bad guy in front of me and executed a tumbling leap across the room and between the guy's legs. As I tumbled through, I spun, uncoiled, and slashed him across the backs of both ankles and rolled clear, thus hamstringing him. He collapsed backwards with a yell of pain and landed on the floor with a loud thump, injuring his tailbone. Jagger landed on his chest, knocking his breath out, slamming his torso to the ground, cracking his breastbone and pinning him while the girl finished him off with a hard kick to the groin. He vomited, then lay there in a fetal position gasping for breath and moaning. I bet he would never underestimate Little People or women again!

We tied up these guys and unbarred the door. The girls crowded in and hauled them all out into the hallway. They had been joined by the rest of the women and children of the castle. We found the gate key, told the prettiest of the girls and all of the children to come with us, and ran down to the courtyard. The children rushed to their Fathers for hugs and kisses. I did a quick 'Nettoyer' (Clean) and 'Charmant' (Glamour) on each of the girls. We told them to make Sir Willem feel like the hero of the day, with lots of hugs and kisses, and unlocked the gates.

As we pulled them open, Sir Willem charged into the courtyard on his fine steed bellowing, "I'LL SAVE YOU!!!!" The girls all yelled "My Hero", and mobbed him. They pulled him off his horse, took his helmet off, got one good look at his amazingly handsome features, squealed with glee, and proceeded to hug and kiss him for what seemed like minutes. When they finally let him up for air, he looked completely groggy. We all yelled, "Hip, hip, hooray for Sir Willem!!!!" He grinned and said, "Now where is that Baron that is in dire need of rescue? Not as much fun as you fine ladies, of course, but an honourable task in need of doing." He proceeded to try to kiss each and every one of their hands while they had a giggle-fest. The Baron said, "Here, Sir Knight, and well indebted to you for your leadership in the noble cause of saving this Barony from a vile usurper and his villains! Now where is that pusillanimous brother of mine hiding? I would have a word with him concerning his recent bad manners."

Our Soldiers had practically filled the courtyard by this time, led by Chasseresse, who handed me Miss Mouse, who gave my cheek a licky bath and chattered to me her distress at being separated. We dispatched the troops with propre shackles to the locations where the prisoners were bound. The castle girls led them while Mendel took some to the tower to retrieve the big stinky one. They were to bring them all down to the courtyard.

The village ladies meanwhile rushed in and had tearful reunions with their menfolk and children.

When everyone was gathered in the crowded courtyard, Cranndair read the charges aloud. He had added some really heinous ones to the list that the girls had told him about. He asked the Baron if he wished to handle their trials himself and see to their punishments or allow us to remove them to Waterport for trial and punishment. The Baron replied that he had neither the personpower, the holding cells, nor the inclination to deal with them further and was happy to be rid of them completely. He hoped that his poor Barony could just pick up the pieces, forget the incident entirely, and get on with their peaceful lives. "We have suffered enough, Sir. I hereby remand them unto your custody. May they never again experience a joyful moment or see the light of day!" to which everyone responded with, "HEAR, HEAR, SO MOTE IT BE! FOREVER AND EVER!" Cranndair responded, "Heard ahnd unduhstood, Sah! Youah will shall be done! Life imprisonment in ouah deepest, dahkest Dungeon with daily torture is what Ah shall recommend to the Court. Ah shall need statements from all of you concerning the depredations of these malefactors ahnd it would help immensely if one from among the young ladies ahnd one from among the conscripts would accompany us to beah witness at the trial." Several people stepped forward to volunteer, but several of us Rangers pointed out the most promising young man and the 'Poker Girl' as the best candidates and I suggested that they be allowed to join the Rangers due to their Warrior tendencies. The 'Poker Girl' had been standing by her parents, the large Norse woman and her much shorter husband. She looked at them both pleadingly. Her father smiled and said, "Li' mother, li' daughter. You 'ave me blessin's, me girl." She hugged her small Dad and squealed with delight. Her Mum next held both of her hands, leaned down, and kissed her on the forehead with tears in her eyes and said, "Make me proud, girl!" I looked at the rest of the Training Squad and asked what they thought about taking the girl in. I got a very positive response from them all except Rudd, who had not seen her in action, and considering his generally pessimistic and gloomy reactions, I would have expected a negative response anyway. Jagger was especially pleased. I asked Cranndair if we could have the girl in our Squad and he looked at us quizzically. He remarked that she obviously was not a Halfling and was curious why we would want to have a 'Big Person' in our group. We responded, almost in unison, things like, "We have fought together!", "We respect her courage!", "She has a Warrior Heart!", and other positive accolades. He looked taken aback, looked squarely at the girl, and said, "You, my deah, must be vereh special to gahnah so much respect in so little time from Warriors such as these! Would you like to join the Training Squad?" She responded with, "Oh, YES! These are my Heroes!" whereupon she rushed over to us, got down on her knees, and gathered us all into one big hug. Wow, she really was a big girl! Her name was Emerentse Brynhildesdotter, but she said to call her Entse, the short form of her name.

I approached her parents with Jagger following me, for some reason. Bear and his small satellite Halfling were also approaching from the side. We arrived simultaneously. He saluted me and said, "Lieutenant, you first" with a grin. That shocked me, I had forgotten about the promotion!

I gathered myself, shook her father's hand, and thanked him. He had tears in his eyes and just nodded to me. He was only about a foot and a half taller than me, though Jagger and he were of about the same height. Jagger followed suit. Next, I looked up at her more than six feet tall mother, and said, "Ma'am, I give you my solemn oath that we will do everything in our power to keep your daughter safe and to train her to be an exemplary Warrior of which you may be very proud!" She got down on her knees, very carefully took my hand between her thumb and forefinger, shook it gently, and solemnly intoned, "I'll be countin' on ya, young Sir, ta do exactly that." Jagger said with conviction, "Ve vill teach her vell!" and shook her hand with enthusiasm.

Next, Bear said something in Norse to both parents, who nodded, smiled and shook his hand. I asked him what he had said as we walked away. He told me that he had adopted her as his little sister. We rejoined the Squad and Bear told the girl the same thing in Norse. She grinned, jumped up, hugged him around the neck, planted a big kiss on his cheek, and told him in Common that she had always wanted a 'Big Brother'. He pried her loose while grinning, patted her on the head, and walked back to his Squad. I noticed that she still had that poker at her waist...hmmm. I noticed our supply Sergeant in the crowd. I ambled over and asked him if he could trade the girl a propre longsword and belt for that poker. He grinned and nodded.

The young man was also eager to join, as both of his parents had been brutally slain by the usurper's men and he not only wanted payback, he also wanted to keep that kind of thing from ever happening again to anyone else.

Our medics checked over all of the former prisoners and treated their injuries and ailments. One of the young ladies was pregnant. Nell asked her if the baby was from a chosen partner or from the thugs. She replied that she had been a virgin before the thugs had taken them as slaves. Nell brewed her some tea and told her that it would make the baby be reabsorbed or aborted, as it was still tiny. The girl drank it with relief, then walked over to the prisoners, singled one out and crowed, "Did ya hear that, ya bugger? Yer get is no more." And spat in his face. The other women yelled for her to make it so that he could never make babies again, but instead of castrating him, she only kicked him extremely hard squarely in the testicles while two of her cohorts held his legs apart. I swear, I thought the man's eyes were going to pop out of his head. He passed out after screaming. Nell checked him out and proclaimed that they were completely squashed and probably dysfunctional. The women cheered.

We had our other prisoners brought from our camp, then chained the scoundrels together, stuffed them against the wall, and had a festive breakfast together as the sun came up, shining clean, bright light upon the scene, washing away pain and fear.

We decided to let the sun 'cook' them that day, with only minimal water provided. We set up a guard roster, to keep the prisoners in check, and retired for some well-earned sleep. I noticed that Sir Willem did not leave the assemblage unescorted. At least two of the young ladies were willing cohorts, the prettiest, of course.

Chaptre 31. In which I Have a Feast

Winter, 24th, Snowshell, 5012 (12 Turns of age)

After about six hours sleep, we awakened and all of us helped to clean up and sort out the castle. After it was 'tip-top' and spotless, the local folks and Sir Willem all went to change clothes. One of the girls loaned Chasseresse some clothing that was more ladylike than her uniform. The staff and the ladies from the village had prepared a grand feast and everyone repaired to the Great Room, where long tables had been set up for the gala event.

Before entering, all of us that had the capacity to do Magick, did 'Nettoyer' (Clean), 'Lisser' (Smooth), and 'Charmant' (Glamour) spells on everyone, because most of us had been in the same clothes for days, were really stinky and dirty, and had not time to clean up or change clothes, if we had some to change into.

The local folks were really impressed with the results that were achieved with a simple 'Charmant' (Glamour) spell. It was like a total make-over and made these rough country folk look like Lords and Ladies of the Aristocracy. Chasseresse never really looked less than 'stunning' due to her natural beauty, but a 'Charmant' (Glamour) spell could make her jaw-droppingly gorgeous.

I noticed that Jagger was especially caring regarding our new Squad member, almost doting...hmmm...that was odd. I had never before observed him to be particularly kind to anyone. I would have to keep an eye on them. He was rather muscular, large, and dashing in a chiseled way, almost giant sized for a Halfling. He was about four feet tall and she was at least five and three quarters' feet. It might work out. Vertical differences in height are less of a problem when placed horizontally, as witnessed by the differing heights of her parents, Bear and his soon to be Mate, and me and Chasseresse as examples. Also, the Humans that Jagger's people hung out with were kin to the Nordic types and also known for their large size and musculature, probably why he was so big, considering that "Halfling" was not just a name, but also a description of our relative size to the Big People that we lived close to. I kind of categorized the two types as Forest Dwelling and Ocean Going Barbarians. Their languages were also similar. Interesting...

The ladies were particularly pleased by the makeover and wasted no time becoming reacquainted with their menfolk. This was probably going to be a short meal and dance.

Sir Willem glided into the gathering wearing the most amazing outfit. It was very manly and at the same time gorgeous to behold. It showed off his physique, while covering him completely. There were several types of fabrics involved. I spotted silk, satin, lace, and velvet easily, all in complimentary shades of blue and white. The boots were shining black leather and knee high. You could have knocked the females and Cranndair over with puff of air. They were completely stunned. Sir Willem's escorts from his earlier 'nap' were the first to react and practically sprinted to his sides, where they each possessively grabbed an arm and held on, alternating between adoring looks at him and glares around the room warning the other girls to stay clear. Sir Willem guided his two 'guards' to a table and doted on them throughout the rest of the evening, alternating dances with each of them, wining and dining them in a show of gentlepersonly manners fit for a Kings court.

When Chasseresse whirled into the room, the usual response happened, one very similar to Sir Willems. I met her in the middle of the dance floor and laughingly proclaimed, "Forget it guys. She's claimed already...and I'll be more than willing to amputate any stray appendages that should happen to come near her, so don't get so deep in your cups that you lose your ability to reason and control yourself. You DO want to wake up in the morning with all of your body parts intact, don't you?" This brought gales of laughter from the guys and made them pay attention to their own sweeties, who had been giving them mean looks when they were gawking at Chasseresse. I turned to her and said, "May I have this dance, my Lady?" She giggled and said, "There ees no museec playeeng." And I replied while kissing her hand, "Your mere presence is music so divine as to fill the heart with joy!" She actually blushed at these words and said with tears in her eyes, "Ma Cherie, I love you zooo much! May wee please be marrieed when wee get back to zee ceety?" I was a bit bowled over by this, but managed to stammer, "Of course, mon Cheri, anything that your heart desires, I will attempt!" I stood and we locked in a very steamy embrace and a kiss that lasted for minutes. A chorus of "ooohs" and "ahhhs" from the girls accompanied this interplay. When we finally came up for air, cheers broke out all through the room. The girls were crying and gathering around Chasseresse while the guys grabbed me and hoisted me up into the air to be carried about the room while they sang, a bit off-key, "For he's a jolly good fellow..." Lucky Nell yelled out, "I'm doin' tha weddin' ceremony! It'll be a doozy!"

The meal was absolutely wonderful. The usurper had evidently had a taste for fine food and beverages and had filled the castle larders to the brim. We ate until we were as stuffed as the large roast goose that had been served, drank wine until we were tipsy, and danced until we were exhausted. Everybody that could play an instrument did so and took turns on the makeshift bandstand. At the end of the evening, The Baron got everyone's attention for a toast, "To our rescuers, may their names and deeds be remembered through the ages!" The townsfolk erupted in cheers. "To my Father, may we honour his memory forever and may he rest in peace knowing that justice has prevailed!" A quieter response with lots of tear filled eyes. "To the citizens of this Barony, may we live in peace and harmony for the rest of our days!" With a mixture of positive responses around the room.

Every room in the castle had been turned into temporary bedrooms for the occasion. We all staggered off to our assigned quarters and 'slept' very well. Chasseresse and I had a large broom closet to ourselves and took advantage of the privacy.

Chaptre 32. In which I Go Back to Fisherton

Winter, 26th, Snowshell, 5012 (12 Turns of age)

The next day, as we all recuperated from our night of debauchery, we staggered to the Great Room for a late breakfast. Afterwards, about half of us pitched in to tidy up the castle while the other half went out to the field to break camp and ready for our departure. When the wagons were all lined up on the road and the castle was neat and clean, we paused for lunch, then exited the castle.

The field in front of the castle was a shambles. It looked like a herd of swine had uprooted and eaten more than half of it. Those big metal War Wagons were really heavy and War Horses were not light either. Cranndair approached the Baron, who was looking with dismay at the carnage, and bowed to him while telling him not to worry, that it would be repaired posthaste.

Cranndair asked everyone to stay off the grass while he did "a little Magick". He then walked to the middle of the field, raised his arms in a sweeping gesture, and intoned something complex in Elven. The ones of us that could understand him gasped in response. One of those 'silent sounds' occurred and rippled out in all directions from Cranndair. As it passed over the ground, an eruption of growth happened behind the wave. When it had petered out, some distance into the woods, everything in the area of effect had been transformed into luxuriant springtime growth! The field was again smooth and a sea of wildflowers of all types had sprouted and grown into a brilliant display. The trees were full of bright green foliage. It was really beautiful. Cranndair sort of wilted and started to slump. Several of us rushed forward and caught him before he hit the ground. He said in a soft voice, "Don't worry. Ah'll be Ahlright in a few minutes. Ah just need to rest a bit." We carried him to his chariot to lie down and brought him water. The Baron rushed up and proclaimed in a very excited manner, "That was amazing, my dear Sir! You are a wondrous Mage! This field shall be called 'Cranndair's Bounty' now and forevermore!" and bowed low to Cranndair who sat up with aid and bowed in return as best he could from a sitting position. "Tis nothing, my deah Baron, just ah little something thaht my Mothah taught me. Ah was ah pooah student, but did mahnage to learn bits and pieces of her wisdom."

After the hugs and kisses, and lots of waving were complete, we packed into and onto our wagons and chariots and moved out. The prisoners were piled in the large wagon that had been in the courtyard so that we could make good time back to Fisherton, where we planned to stay for the night.

On the way back, everyone practiced various skills that we had been working on. I practiced Elven with Chasseresse in our chariot. She explained to me that what Cranndair had done was a slightly lesser version of the spell that the three High Elves had done in Thistledown, and it was actually very high level Magick. She explained that Fae Magick is inherent to the natural state of being Fae, or half Fae in the case of the Elves and quarter Fae in the case of Half Elves, and is very connected to non-Deific 'Nature', so it is somewhat like the Deific Magick that the Humans can do and somewhat not, being much more direct and from the person, not a Deity. Each Elf or Half Elf has a particular Magick Potential built in from birth and can only do Magick up to that magnitude. She suspected that Cranndair was doing both types of Magick or a combination of both. That his Deity was the Goddess of Nature, so the two types of Magick did not conflict. She said that this was a particularly powerful combination. That when he referred to 'Mother', he was probably referring to two different Mothers, his actual Elven Mother and the Goddess of Nature. She said that she only did non-Deific natural Magick, but that if I were to combine the two types, my Magickal abilities would rise significantly. What an interesting thought.

On one of our short rest stops, I climbed up to where Lucky Nell was seated on top of a War Wagon and asked her about Deities. As she fed Miss Mouse some delicious crumbs that she had saved, she said that I had a way too calculating mind to truly worship the Goddess of Luck. That she had heard me pray to several different ones at different times and for different reasons, but that I had never mentioned the one that the Spirits said was my true Deity...Trickster. I told her that I was not aware of Trickster. She said that He was well aware of me and kept an eye on me at all times. That I was a natural Priest of Trickster, whether I liked it or not. She thought this was funny because I was a really nice person and not annoying at all, which Trickster could be, though I WAS very mischievous in her opinion, like a nice junior Trickster and I could be a really mean junior Trickster to my enemies. She said that I was very neutral, like Trickster. That my mind was unfettered, quick, and powerful, not bogged down at all by dogma and mundanity. That concepts and ideas flowed easily and constantly. That I, apparently, could learn anything that I set my mind to and was therefore, very eclectic and far less limited than the average person. That I was always looking for a need for positive change, learning, and growth, just like Trickster. I agreed and asked why He was not called the God of Tricks. She said that He was a lot more powerful than the other Deities and could actually be called the God of Change, Growth, & Learning, but that people just called him Trickster, due to the methods that he usually employed. She said that there are not very many Priests of Trickster, no Temples or Shrines to him, no Priestly Order or rules of His Religion, actually no Religion at all, because he was beyond all rules and made his own spontaneously and they changed constantly to fit the situation and his need to teach. She asked if I had ever spotted anything odd in my environment. I said, like what? She said, like weird sights and sounds. I replied that yes, I had seen a set of mismatched coloured eyes out of the corner of my eye many times, but could not spot them when I looked directly at the spot. I had gotten used to it over the Turns and just ignored it, as it had never posed a threat. She said that was a standard 'look' for him. That He was watching me directly when that happened. She said that I should try acknowledging him and try asking for his assistance when I saw a need for change, growth, or learning...positive, neutral, or negative. I thanked her and switched back to my own chariot at the next stop. Nell really was a very smart and wise person, for someone that constantly took chances as a way of worshipping her Deity.

I gave Chasseresse the news that Nell had been able to figure out who my Deity was and that I had always been a 'Priest' of that Deity. She asked which one it was and I replied that she probably would not like it, because He had a somewhat bad or weird reputation. She seemed unconcerned and asked me if the Deity had mismatched, glowing, cat eyes, one green and the other blue. I replied that yes, this was true, somewhat shocked. She said that she had spotted the smoky, charcoal grey feline watching me often. She had confronted it once and it had spoken in her mind, "Take care of my boy. Teach him well. He is one of my chosen. He will cause great changes in his lifespan. He will find me when it is the right time." I was stunned. She said that it gave off no malevolent energy, so she felt fine about it. I told her that it was Trickster and she replied nonchalantly that she had guessed as much. Amazing, I was surrounded by wise, calm, smart women! She giggled and pointed to the shadows in the chariot behind us. I turned to look and found myself staring directly into the glowing mismatched eyes for the first time. It startled me so much that I jumped a little. I heard in my mind, "Welcome, my son, I look forward to many joyful lessons with you. May you spread change wherever you may go. Do you have any questions?" I started to ask out loud and He told me to just think my questions. So, feeling a bit silly, I asked in my head if I was supposed to wear some kind of priestly garments, like Nell did, and what was His Symbol and colour? He replied that no special garments were required or needed, as He worked undercover and quietly most of the time, like a spy. That if He had a colour, it was neutral grey. That an image of his eyes were the only Symbol that anybody in our area of the world had ever used and only then, left as a warning to someone that if they did not change voluntarily, change would be forced upon them. I realized that I functioned as a neutral spy, favoured grey as a clothing colour, worked in the shadows well, loved to cause positive change, to learn and to teach, and had slanted, cat-like, light hazel eyes! He laughed at my thoughts and sent me a warm feeling, like a non-physical hug. Wow, this was going to be fun!

We made the trip of about twenty miles, or six and a half leagues, back to Fisherton by early evening, parked along the roadway as before, left guards posted at the campsite, and strolled into town to retrieve our two prisoners and report our results to the various powers that be in town.

We made it without incident back to the local Constabulary Office, with bursts of cheers and other forms of positive recognition along the way from the populace. After the Head Constable and his staff had gathered, Sergeant Rodney Griffinbane presented his report, followed by Colonel Cranndair the Warden, Lieutenant Chasseresse, and me, Lieutenant Scram Runt. The Head Constable asked a few questions and then thanked us for sorting out the problem so efficiently. His Gaolers delivered our two prisoners, who were then shackled, chained, and escorted back to the campsite along the road where the others were located.

Sergeant Rodney and his Platoon dispersed to their homes after a brief formation in front of the station where Cranndair, Sir Willem, and others, expressed their thanks to these local Rangers for their part in the siege. A campaign patch would be awarded as soon as the Seamstresses could craft them.

Next, we headed to, what was starting to feel like a second home for us, the Inn of the Cross-eyed Flounder, for a bath, supper, and a nights rest in a comfortable bed. 'Nettoyer' (Clean) spells are alright, but they are not nearly as good as a nice warm bath and freshly laundered clothes.

After our ablutions, without the attendants, this time, we retired to the large dining area for a wonderful meal, not nearly as nice as the feast that we had last eaten here, but filling, wholesome, and good. We were paying for our room and board this time, so we kept the charges to a minimum. Bear's fiancée ran and leaped into his arms as he reached the bottom of the stairs! This was a noticeably athletic move, but unfortunately she did bowl over a couple of chairs and two of our guys in her charge toward the goal. Everyone got a big laugh out of these antics and left them locked in a lengthy embrace as we continued towards the dining area. They sheepishly followed us in a few minutes later to much good-natured ribbing and ribald humour, like, "Geta room! Oi, dats roight, yer ina inn, lucky yew!" After supper, we moved the party to the common area and brought out our various musical instruments. We took turns playing and dancing, along with the locals till late that night. During the evenings' activities, I spotted the head of the Local Branch of the Thieves Guild, plopped down at his table, and gave him a quick report. He was well satisfied and thanked me.

I met with Sarek at a table in the darkest corner of the Inn Common Area after our group had staggered upstairs leaving just the locals in attendance and gave him the update on the military action. He told me that his crew had watched my 'little flying circus act' and found it most enjoyable. He congratulated me on becoming engaged to be Handfasted, which made me wonder just how close his men had been, because he knew way too much. He said all of this with his usual sly smile, his trademark smirk. I wanted to just once, wipe it off his face.

Hmmm. I had been practicing the 'Charmant' (Glamour) spell, so I surreptitiously did it on Sarek by slipping the Common version of the word into the conversation in a logical place. This was easy to do. He had no reaction when I did it, so I assumed that he had not noticed the Magickal surge that went along with the word. He was so used to blending into his environment that he was shocked as he left the table to find himself VERY noticeable to everyone, especially the girls and guys who liked guys. I had such a hard time keeping a straight face and looking worried and perplexed as he glanced back at me with a venomous scowl and tried to shoo his worshippers away. I signed at him, "I felt that spell hit you. Some Mage or Wizard is after you and has spotted you, run for it!" His look changed to one of abject horrour and he ran for the door, knocking people out of his way and looking frantically about. I had never seen him so discombobulated before. Why such a huge reaction? Then I remembered him mentioning that he had a fear of Magick, Wizards, and Fae, because all of his tricks and sneakiness could be easily countered by them and he could not spot their Magickal traps or sense Magick at all. After he made it out of sight, I bailed out laughing, so hard that I fell off the chair and onto the floor. People were looking at me like I was a nut as they picked themselves up off the floor and righted the toppled furniture. That made me laugh all the harder. I managed to splutter, "Sorry, not laughing at you...laughing at the crazy guy." Which mollified them a bit. He had really deserved that! He was always so smugly cock-sure of himself. I heard laughter in my mind and spotted Trickster in the shadows under the table grinning at me. I made like I was going to do the same spell on Him and He disappeared with a poof of mist, laughing the whole time and telling me "Cheeky little bastard. Good job, kid. You got him really worried. He's hiding out. You should see him. The shadows are no longer his friend. He looks like he's having a waking nightmare. Do you mind if I carry on the charade for a bit? Take him down a peg or two?" I thought back, "Go for it, he needs a little demoralization." Next, I wanted to learn the opposite one, 'Brut' (Decrepit). That would be so much fun! Imagine what you could do with that one!

I went on up to bed and crept into the small room for which Chasseresse and I had paid. I thought that I was being sneaky so as not to awaken her. I undressed quickly without lighting the lamp and started to slide into bed. I heard, "I have beeen waiteeng for you." and a soft giggle. So much for sleep...

Chaptre 33. In which I Finally Go Home

Winter, 27th, Snowshell, 5012 (12 Turns of age)

We were all awake, cleaned up, dressed, fed, and out to the roadside camp by ten bells. The caravan was ready to roll out by eleven bells.

Mendel had requested some time off in Thistledown and had asked Nell if she wanted to tag along, so we were going to drop them off on the way back to the city. Chasseresse and I had volunteered our chariot so that they would have a quick way back to the city afterwards.

On the third of the next Moonth, Frostshine, a celebratory ball was planned for all of us and our families. I would have to talk with Trent and Brud to prep them for it. I could get Brud to come as my adopted father, but I wanted to get Trent, as himself, and Cranndair together so they hopefully so would like each other. This was going to be fun! The trick would be getting Trent to just be himself and not play a part.

Chasseresse and I climbed up to the top of a War Wagon for the trip back. We had chosen the one that held Bear and his fiancée, Entse and Jagger, Chasseresse's old Platoon Sergeant, the young man that had volunteered for the Rangers, and a few more from Chasseresse's Platoon. Chasseresse and I discussed wedding plans with Bear and his girl, Beth (Bethilda) Beckett, and it was decided that we would have a double ceremony. Now that would be a real party. We all figured out that Entse and Jagger had gotten a private room the night before and wondered if it would be a triple wedding. Those three girls, plus most of the others in the wagon, clumped together to chatter and the guys split into two groups, one a card game and the other a dice game. Between those activities and playing instruments, practicing spells, and practicing languages, we passed the time easily.

About a league before Thistledown, the caravan came to an abrupt halt. We were in an area where the cliff face was relatively close to the road. We climbed up to see what was holding us up. We spotted Cranndair and Sir Willem leaning over the sides of their War Horses to talk to someone standing on the ground. The Platoon Sergeants dispersed the troops around the caravan in guard positions while Chasseresse and I walked up to the front to see what was going on. When we arrived. We found that the two leaders had dismounted and Sir Willem was hugging a Human girl and patting her on the back while she cried into his steel plate covered chest. We got close enough to hear him say, "Do not fret, young Lady, we will save him!"

We guessed that we had another mission and stepped up to volunteer. Cranndair explained that the girl's brother had been collecting molted sea bird feathers from the nesting cliffs for his mother to make a pillow. He had been placing them in a basket with twine tied to it for his sister to pull up to the top of the cliff and stow in a bag. She had heard him yell and rocks falling. She was afraid that he had fallen and hurt himself. She had called for him without response and that made her even more worried. We had an attachment on the front of our belts for a rappelling ring and were quite adept at it. She and I volunteered to rappel down the cliff in search of the boy. A chariot was backed up to the point where the boy had climbed down. Two ropes were brought up and tied off on the rear of the chariot. Cranndair and Sir Willem were supervising. Several large Human Rangers, including Bear, were brought over to hoist us back up.

We started down the cliff, side by side, slowly and cautiously, so as not to disturb any more loose rock that might fall down and hit the kid below. Evidently, the cliff was made of alternating layers of hard and soft rock. The softer layers had worn away faster from wind and sea spray, making small ledges and undercuts, almost shallow caves. These ledges held the remains of old nesting sites and the whole cliff face was covered with really rank and acrid smelling white and black splatters of bird poop. This place must be very lively during nesting season. Miss Mouse stuck her head out of my hood, looked down, squeaked loudly, and disappeared back inside. We got to the end of the twine and found the basket waiting there, swinging slightly in the breeze. The cliff was slightly undercut a few feet down and there was a place where the edge of a ledge had broken free. We looked at each other and down to the water below without a lot of hope. That water was really cold this time of Turn! [*See Appendix D, Weather] A person would not survive for long in it. They would freeze to death or drown quickly. That could be one very expensive pillow for his family.

We free rappelled further down while looking around for the boy or his remains. At first we did not spot anything, then we noticed a lighter smudge in the gloom and some very odd heat signatures. One was horizontal and of normal brightness. Two different vertical ones were a lot fainter than normal! These two were speaking with each other in a strange whistling and clicking speech. They were swimming in the frigid water with their heads, shoulders, and arms out of the water and holding the horizontal one above it. We hailed them, and they turned to look at us. One swam over to us and I was able to see that it was humanoid, but had rubbery, hairless skin in shades of grey! It spoke to us in very stilted Common, saying,
"Weee...arah...glade...tooo...seee...you! Weee...taughted...thate...weee...woulded...hasss...tooo...keep...heem...drieee...tilla...teee...tide...wented...ahooot!" Chasseresse pulled out her communication globe and asked that a stretcher be lowered down to us. I was a little shocked by these water creatures and asked, "I do not mean to be rude, but what exactly are you?" The one talking to us replied,
"Yoooarah...peeepull...called...usss...Seeee...Peeepull...Youah...coulded...notted...sayee...ourah...reeeal...named."

The stretcher arrived and the Sea Person guided it over to the boy while managing to keep it dry. A third and fourth Sea Person popped out of the water and helped load the boy onto the stretcher and not a moment too soon, for the tide had continued to rise and swamped the ledge he had been on seconds after he was clear. All four held it in place, for if they had let it go, due to the angle it was on, when it swung back out, it would have gone underwater.

Chasseresse coordinated with the lifters, who rapidly hoisted it up as the Sea People maintained its altitude above water level. All in all, an amazing effort. We thanked them and they laughingly told us to pass on to the pair of kids to be careful, because they had been worriedly keeping an eye on the brave pair for several Turns as they collected birds, eggs, droppings, and feathers from the cliff face. They knew that someday, one of them would fall. They told us that the boy's 'not tail' had been broken when he landed on the beach and that he had hit his head.

We called for them to haul us up and bade our new friends' goodbye. When we got to the top, we found Nell and a couple more Medics working on the boy while his sister hovered anxiously about, wringing her hands and trying not to get in the way.

When the boy was awake, we passed on what the Sea People had said to the wide eyed kids and how they had saved the boy from certain death. The kids were full of questions about the water dwelling people and we answered their questions to the best of our abilities. They told us how they had thought that they had spotted people in the water over the Turns, but had never been sure. The kid's parents had been tracked down by some of our guys and they arrived about that time with a wagon and we placed the stretcher in the back. The kids were babbling to them about the Sea People all the while as the Mother fussed nervously with the boy's splint and bandages and talked with the Medics. The Dad shushed the children and apologized profusely for any trouble that they had caused us, apologized for not having anything to pay us with, apologized for the fanciful tales that his children were telling, and thanked us for saving their son. When Chasseresse and I told him that it was not a tale, but was actually true about the Sea People, he became tearful for no apparent reason. He then informed us that when he was a boy, he thought that he had seen them as well, but his parents had convinced him that he was just seeing things and that creatures like that could not possibly be real. I resolved that someday, I would learn more about the Sea People.

When we arrived at Thistledown, Mendel and Nell hugged everybody goodbye and told us that they would be back in town in time for the party.

We continued on our trip to the city and were rolling along fine until we stopped yet again. Chasseresse and I went to investigate and found the roadway clogged with sheep and one Small Deerbird, all munching pleasantly on the verdant strip of grass and bushes along the verge of the road. We fanned out on both sides of the mob and were able to push the sheep quite easily back through the hole in the fence through which they had escaped.

The Small Deerbird, at about ten feet in length and quite tall refused to move. We discussed the matter until one of the guys that had come from Farming stock suggested that we cut the bush off at the base and use it to lead the Deerbird back inside the enclosure. He said that Deerbirds really loved those bushes and not to worry, it would sprout from the stump and be good as new soon. This was a relief. Nobody liked to hurt vegetation. We had been petting the large creature, scratching its pebbly skin through its thick coat of downy green feathers and playing with its crest of longer brown quills that started out small at the back of its head and got increasingly longer down its back until its tail was completely covered in them. It had a red wattle on the front of its neck below its beak and I was told that it was a male. It seemed to like the attention.

We sawed off the major limb that it was munching on and was able to lead it back through the wall. Cranndair laughingly told us that this was actually part of our job under the category of 'Keeping the Peace and Maintaining Order in the Community". We rebuilt the rock wall for the Farmer.

We continued without further incident and arrived in the late afternoon. It felt like a long time since we had left. As our troops were delivering the prisoners to the Gaol and cleaning everything up and putting it away, the leaders went to meet with the Mayor, the General, and other high ranking officials.

We went down to basement level three below the castle that housed the Courts, Gaol, Dungeon, and Torture Chambers. We were shown to a Waiting Area after seeing a Court Scribe for an appointment. Some Drudges brought us a tray of refreshments and we dug in with relish!

When we finally got called in to see the Mayor, General, and the others, it was late in the day. Sir Willem had tagged along with us and he and Colonel Cranndair presented our report while the rest of us waited uncomfortably on the benches behind them. Mostly Cranndair talked and Sir Willem just sat and looked noble. This took a really long time, as we had done quite a few things since leaving the city on our original mission. I dozed off a few times and was awakened by subtle digs in the ribs from Chasseresse's elbow. Cranndair called on each of us at various times to present sections of our report. I told about the castle invasion and a few other spots in the story. The scribes were scribbling furiously all the while and the scratching of their quills on the parchment was very distracting to me.

When the report was finally done, we all stood at attention and the Mayor beamed at us and said expansively, "You ALL have done an excellent job and represented Our Fair City very well to our neighbours!

You are to be commended!" He then told Cranndair to see to any details that were necessary with the Castle Seamstresses so that all would be ready for the celebratory Ball on the eve of the third of next Moonth.

We all saluted and marched out of the Court Room. We were to have the intervening day's off-duty and had to make the most of it. I had so much to do in the interim; I had to get with Brud and Trent, take Chasseresse on a 'real date', go shopping, find a Jeweler and design our wedding jewellery, get an armoured carrier built for Miss Mouse, report to the Thieves Guild (get Trent to disguise me first), and a bunch more.

Chasseresse and I checked on how it was going with the clean-up and sorting of all of the gear and supplies and how our troops were doing. The War Wagons and War Chariots had departed for the Siege Base at Fort Pishnook along with most of the troops. We borrowed horses from the castle stables and rode out of town and East up the road to the Fort. The Destriers were in their stalls in the barns being seen to by the grooms. The War Machines were in their parking area being seen to by a bunch of Siege Engineers and their Apprentices. They were getting a thorough scrubbing and a maintenance checkup. The Rangers were in the Barracks area cleaning and stowing gear and getting themselves squared away. We helped out, which brought shocked murmurs of appreciation. Evidently, it was not common for officers to do the dirty work with the troops. We ate supper with the guys in their Mess Hall and had a grand time. They remained deferential, but seemed to view us with more respect and comradeship than before. Some of the ones that knew me better, teased me by calling me Serg-enant or Lieut-eant, since I was still wearing Sergeant Stripes, but had been field promoted to Lieutenant.

We officially commended everyone on the fine job that they had done during the Campaign and singled out a few for special recognition, to the accompaniment of much cheering and ribbing. We told them that they were all off-duty till two days after the formation, awards ceremony, and ball on the third of next Moonth. We teased that that would give them time to get over their post-party hang-overs. We reminded them to get their dress uniforms ready and bring their families along for the event.

Things seemed to be pretty much in order, so we headed back to the castle, dropped off the horses at the stable, and went down to our room to see to our own gear, get cleaned up, and get some sleep. I idly wondered how Sarek the Sly was handling being targeted by the non-existent Mage...

A Runt's Tale, In the Beginning…

Well our little war was over. It had ended well. Now, we had to get back to the more normal daily activities…but…I hate boredom…What can I do now to stir things up a bit?

Let's see…I have to get Cranndair and Trent together, deal with the Thieves Guild, meet a really big hairy guy, design lots of stuff, get Handfasted, go to college, have lots of parties, start a band, be a Dada, and become a hero. So much to do and so little time…

This ends the first installment in the life and times of Reggie. Look for the sequel to this book, A Runt's Tale, the Next Generation….

Epilogue

A note from Reggie:

Anyway, I set out to write my memoir at the beginning of this and only achieved recording the first twelve Turns of my life, and only two of them in any detail. That is very sad. Either I have too complicated a history, or I'm too wordy, or I may have described it in the propre amount of detail and it is simply going to take a lot of books to accomplish the task. I know not which.

I do know one thing for certain, there are lots more things that happened in my long and adventuresome life that might be of interest to you, my descendants and other possible readers. I do not know for sure, but I shall endeavor to record them. No matter how long it takes...I still have a few Turns left in me. Some of it might be boring. My apologies for that.

Why, I still have to write about; playing matchmaker, getting Handfasted (several times...), having children, designing a City School, going to various Schools, starting a band, starting a business, designing & building lots of stuff, finding my kinfolks, starting a Charitable Foundation, starting an Orphanage, starting Waterport Investigation Services - the Private Investigation Firm, the League of Adventuring Fellows and all of the escapades that my friends and I got into, being the Captain of a Ranger Company, my Assassin and Ninja training, the Relief Organization that I founded, and a bunch more!

With warmest regards,

Your Servant Always,

Mr. Reginald Rumphrey-Bon Vent, Esq.

Conclusion

A note from the Author:

I sincerely hope that you, the reader, have enjoyed this book and the world that it describes within its pages. It was really fun to write. If you enjoyed it, please spread the word to your friends and family. I initially wrote it as a 300,000 word, 600 page monstrosity, but my writer friends convinced me that modern readers prefer more 'bite-sized' books, so I cut it up into 50,000 – 80,000 word chunks.

The common steps in the publishing process include; writing a rough draft, checking and editing to make two to three more drafts of increasing quality, then you hand it over to the pros for professional content editing, professional copyediting, professional cover design, professional production, professional proofreading, professional marketing & PR, professional sales, and professional publishing. I did not follow these steps. I am very dyslexic, so I am very careful the first time I write anything. I wrote the first draft, edited it once, sent copies to a bunch of friends & family members to see how they liked it, designed the covers with my daughter, altered the manuscripts to fit Kindles digital format and later, CreateSpace's print format, and self-published the books to Amazon.

While, it is aimed primarily at our modern, way too worldly readers, aged 11 through 14, Middle School years, I hope that it is not too G or PG rated for High School and older "Young Adults' and Adults which are 'young at heart'. Hey, I'm an Old Fart, and I like this genre and level of risqué-ness, which my Middle School aged proof readers say is too subtle and Elementary School level. It could only be described as 'risqué' at all due to its complete social equality and openness, something that we should aspire to in our version of Earth. It is long past time that we should shed the social strictures and stigmas applied by various dogmatic, rude, unequal, and intrusive religions and laws based upon them. They are antiquated at best and based on ignorance at worst.

That brings up a good question. What exactly is this genre? I think that it is a mixed blend of 'Fiction', somewhere between; Historical, Science, Humor, Legend, Fantasy, Mythology, and the Tall Tale. What do you think?

Faeghan WhiteWolf

I would like to add a new genre of fiction to the pile...Gaming. Any Gamer... Table Top, console, or computer, will immediately recognize that these are Gaming Characters and that I am not so much 'writing' the books as 'reporting' what occurred in Tournament Gaming Sessions over a period of years while adding in the backstory and details that went on behind the scenes.

One thing is for sure. At the end of this book, the main character is 12 years old...and he lives to over 245 years...hmmm...how many books is it going to take to record his life and adventures?

Thanks again for reading,

Faeghan

Appendix A	Scram's Skills, Titles, Awards, & Organizations						
Skills							
Interactive / Reactive							
Group	Section	Specific Name	Sources	Taught By	Turn Learned	Tools Used	Description
Sneaking	Movement	Move Silently	Thief	Sewers	5003 - 5010	Body and appropriate clothing	Walking, running, swimming, and climbing in as near absolute silence as possible.
			Ranger	Ranger School	5010 - 5011		
			Ninja	Sensei			
		Stalking	Ranger	Ranger School	5010 - 5011	Senses	Creeping up on your quarry unnoticed.
	Camouflage	Hide in Shadows	Thief	Sewers	5003 - 5010	Charcoal Grey Clothing	Being inconspicuous around habitations.

Awareness				Environment		
Hear Noise	Find & Remove Traps			Hide in Terrain		
Thief	Ranger		Thief	Ninja	Ranger	Ninja
Sewers	Ranger	Makebe	Sewers	Sensei	Ranger	Sensei
5003 - 5010	5010 - 5011		5003 - 5010		5010 - 5011	
Body			Senses and Thieves tools		Camouflaged Clothing	
Hearing every sound around you and identifying it.			Finding, building, and disarming or avoiding traps.		Being inconspicuous in natural settings.	

Body Language

Thief	Ninja	Ranger
Sewers & Guild	Sensei	Ranger
5010 - 5011		5010 - 5011

Senses

Reading others Body Language, which often varies from their verbal & facial communication.

Alertness

Thief	Ninja	Ranger
Sewers	Sensei	Ranger
5003 - 5010		5010 - 5011

Mind

Being aware of everything around you; every movement, sound, vibration, emotion, interaction, energy fluctuation, and anything that is 'out of place'.

Faeghan WhiteWolf

	Detect Fakery	Persuasion	Distance Sense	Direction Sense	Tracking	Cold Read	
	Thief	Thief	Ranger	Ranger	Ranger	Thief	Ninja
	Trent	Trent	Ranger	Ranger	Ranger	Trent	Sensei
	5011 - present	5011 - present	5010 - 5011	5010 - 5011	5010 - 5011	5011 - present	
	Senses	Senses	Senses	Senses	Senses	Senses	
	Figuring out if something is real or not	Getting other people to do what you want them to do, changing their minds	Innately understanding distances that you have traveled	Innately understanding directions as relates to your present location	Following the tracks and other sign of a quarry	Figuring out a lot about a person or situation without them being aware.	

187

Constitution	Environment	Poison Resistance	Thief	Sewers	5003 - 5010	Toughness	Grew up living in the sewers eating and drinking poisonous stuff.

Intrusive							
Group	Section	Specific Name	Sources	Taught By	Turn Learned	Tools Used	Description
Sleight of Hand	Thieving	Pick Pockets	Thief	Sarek	5010 - 5011	Nimble fingers	Taking things surreptitiously.
	Scamming (Swindling)	Shell Game	Thief - Grifter	Sarek	5010 - 5011	A pea & 3 walnut shells	A game of 'chance'
		3 Card Monty	Thief - Grifter	Sarek	5010 - 5011	3 Playing Cards	A game of 'chance'
			Thief - Grifter	Trent	5010 - 5011	Costumes, props, forgeries, etc.	Tricks to get people to give you their money willingly.

Theft	Sleight of Mouth	Gaming (Swindling)		Cutpursing	Framing
Mechanics	Scamming	Dice (Gambling)	Cards (Gambling)	Coin Theft	Put Pockets
Open Locks	Fast Talking				
Thief -	Thief - Grifter	Thief - Grifter	Thief - Grifter	Thief	Thief
Makebe	Trent	Trent	Trent	Sarek	Sarek
5010 - 5012	5010 - 5011	5010 - 5011	5010 - 5011	5010 - 5011	5010 - 5011
Nimble fingers	Quick thinking	Nimble fingers	Nimble fingers	Nimble fingers & a razor	Nimble fingers
Opening locked things without the proper keys.	Talking your way out of anything.	A game of 'chance'	A game of 'chance'	Slicing open a purse surreptitiously.	Giving things surreptitiously.

				Farrlaighn	5013 - 5014		Nimble fingers

Informative							
Group	**Section**	**Specific Name**	**Sources**	**Taught By**	**Turn Learned**	**Tools Used**	**Description**
Communication	Speak	True Common	Trent	Trent	5010 - 5012	mouth	The purest Common Tongue
		Thieves Cant	Guild	Trent, Sarek, Makebe	5010 - 5012	mouth	Not a true language, simply a specialized vocabulary or slang specific to the interests of Thieves.
		Woodland Elven	Maddy	Maddy	5011 - present	mouth	The Elvish language
		Highlander Dwarven	Farrlaighn	Farrlaighn		mouth	The Highlander language
		Daremo	Sensei	Sensei		mouth	The Far Eastern Common Tongue

Faeghan WhiteWolf

	Calligraphy	Reading Lips	Daremo	Norse	H. Dwarven	Elven	Common
Write	Trent	Trent	Sensei	Bear	Farrlaighn	Maddy	Trent
Read	Trent	Trent	Sensei	Bear	Farrlaighn	Maddy	Trent
	5010 - 5011	5010 - 5012		5012 - present	5012 - present	5010 - present	5010 - 5011
	senses	senses		senses	senses	senses	senses
	Fancy writing	Must know the language being spoken		Written language	Written language	Written language	Written language

Sign			
Signaling	Rangers	Merchants	Thieves
Ranger	Ranger	Guild	Guild
Ranger School	Ranger School	Trent	Trent
5010 - 5011	5010 - 5011	5010 - 5011	5010 - 5011
	senses	senses	senses
gestures	gestures	Subtle gestures	Subtle gestures

The Arts	
Group	Show
Section	Bard
Specific Name	Juggling
Sources	Guild
Taught By	Trent
Turn Learned	5012 - present
Tools Used	Body and objects
Description	The obvious plus catch items thrown or shot at him.

Drums	Penny Whistle	Fire Dancing	Tightrope Walking	Acrobatics	Tumbling
Makebe	Nell	Guild	Guild	Guild	Guild
Makebe	Nell	Trent	Trent	Trent	Trent
5010 - present	5011 - present	5012 - present	5012 - present	5012 - present	5012 - present
Musical instrument	Musical instrument	Body and tools	Body, pole, and rope	body	body
Small hand drums	Small metal 6 hole flute, Key of C	Juggling, dancing, & Katas with flaming objects	Ropes, narrow beams, narrow ledges, etc. (balance work)	Tumbling plus Trapeze, etc. (air work)	Dives, rolls, somersaults, handstands, flips, etc. (ground work)

Crowd Working	Poetry	Singing		Acting	Disguise
Trent	Maddy	Maddy	Trent	Trent	Trent
Trent	Maddy	Maddy	Trent	Trent	Trent
5010 - present	5011 - present	5011 - present	5010 - present	5010 - present	5010 - present
mind	mind	voice	voice	everything	everything
Altering the mood of a crowd				Theatre	

Art		Etiquette			
Assistive		Gentleman			
Illumination	Illustration	Manners	Dancing	Entertain Crowd	Persuade Crowd
Trent	Trent	Trent	Trent	Trent	Trent
Trent	Trent	Trent	Trent	Trent	Trent
5011 - present	5011 - present	5010 - present	5010 - present	5010 - present	5010 - present
Quills, brushes, ink, paints, gold leaf	Quills, brushes, ink, paints, charcoal	grace	grace	mind	mind
Pictures in books	Pictures in general	Gentlepersonly behaviors	Skill in dancing	Lighten their mood, make them happy	Charm them into believing something and maybe acting on it

Group	Section	Specific Name	Sources	Taught By	Turn Learned	Tools Used	Description
Culinary	Merchants	Chef	Trent	Trent	5010 - present	Cooking utensils	How to cook well
Attire	Tailor	Costuming	Trent	Trent	5010 - 5011	Sewing tools	Crafting clothing
Roguishness	Forgery		Trent	Trent	5011 - present	Quills, ink	Making copies of documents
Cartography						Quills, ink, protractors, rulers, etc.	Making maps

Creative							
Group	Section	Specific Name	Sources	Taught By	Turn Learned	Tools Used	Description
Protection	Armourer	Chain/Ring Mail	Armoury	Flars	5011	Smithing	Crafting armour

Knowledge							
Group	Section	Specific Name	Sources	Taught By	Turn Learned	Tools Used	Description
General Knowledge	Nature	Animal Lore	Ranger	Ranger School	5010 - 5011	Mind	Knowledge of animals
		Plant Lore	Ranger	Ranger School	5010 - 5011	Mind	Knowledge of plants
		Hunting	Ranger	Ranger School	5010 - 5011	Mind, body, Senses	Stalking and capturing or killing a target
		Set Snares	Ranger	Ranger School	5010 - 5011	Mind, hands	Using snares to capture or kill a target
		Mountain-eering	Ranger	Ranger School	5010 - 5011	Mind, body, hands	Negotiating mountainous terrain
		Land Navigation	Ranger	Ranger School	5010 - 5011	Mind, Senses	Getting from point A to point B

Trail Signs	Ranger	Ranger School	5010 - 5011	Mind, Senses	Knowledge of trail marking and tracking
Trail Marking	Ranger	Ranger School	5010 - 5011	Mind, hands	Marking the trail for others to read
Rope Use	Ranger	Ranger School	5010 - 5011	Mind, hands	Everything to do with ropes and knots
Foraging	Ranger	Ranger School	5010 - 5011	Mind, Senses	Finding food and supplies quickly and efficiently
Survival - Mountains	Ranger	Ranger School	5010 - 5011	Mind	Knowledge of survival in mountains
Survival - Woodlands	Ranger	Ranger School	5010 - 5011	Mind	Knowledge of survival in woodlands
Running	Ranger	Ranger School	5010 - 5011	Mind, body	Sprinting and long distance running

	Value	Mathematics	
Section	Art Objects	Accounting	Basic Math
Specific Name	Appraising	Accounting	Basic Math
Sources	Thief	Thief	Thief
Taught By	Makebe	Trent	Trent
Turn Learned	5010 - 5011	5011 - 5012	5010 - 5011
Tools Used	Mind, Senses	Mind	Mind
Description	Figuring out the value of an object and how, when, and where to get the best value for an object	Business math	Numbers and how to manipulate them

Combat		
Group	Rogue	
Section	Thief	
Specific Name	1 or 2 Daggers	Thrown Stones
Sources	Guild	Sewers
Taught By	Sarek	Sewers
Turn Learned	5010 - 5012	5003 - 5010
Tools Used	Hand to Hand / Thrown	Smooth rounded
Description	Fighting with Daggers / Throwing Daggers	Throwing small objects with accuracy and deadly force

Bard

Missile Weapon Deflecting	Missile Weapon Catching	Rapier	Foil	Blind Fighting
Sarek	Sarek	Trent	Trent	Sewers
Trent	Trent	Trent	Trent	Sewers
5010 - 5012	5010 - 5012	5010 - present	5010 - present	5003 - 5010
5010 - 5014	5010 - 5014			
Hands	Hands	Hand to Hand	Hand to Hand	Senses
Deflecting thrown or shot missiles	Catching thrown or shot missiles	Fighting with a Rapier	Fighting with a Foil	Fighting in the dark or blindfolded

Warrior				
Ranger			Ninja	
Dagger	Shortbow	Sling	Blowgun	Dodge
Ranger	Ranger	Ranger	?	Trent
Ranger School	Ranger School	Ranger School	Sensei	Trent
5010 - 5011	5010 - 5011	5010 - 5011		5010 - 5014
Hand to Hand / Thrown	Arrows	Darts / Bullets / Stones	Darts	
Fighting with Daggers	Shooting arrows with accuracy and deadly force	Slinging various missiles with accuracy and deadly force		Dodging thrown or shot missiles

Engineering	Warfare	Siege Engineer	Self	Self	5012 - present	Mind plus drafting	Using siege engines in warfare
	Movement	Katas	Ranger	Maddy	5011 - present	Mind & body	Specific Katas for hand-to-hand, sling, bow, shortsword, and 1 or 2 daggers, plus combo versions.
		Shortsword	Ranger	Ranger	5010 - 5011	Hand to Hand	Fighting with a shortsword

Magick							
Group	Section	Specific Name	Sources	Taught By	Turn Learned	Tools Used	Description
Alchemy	Tricks		Guild	Trent	5010 - present	Chemicals & tools	
Roguishness	Traps		Guild	Trent	5010 - present	Chemicals & tools	

Simple Spells	Useful	25 +/- combos	Ranger	Maddy	5011 - present	Mind
	Explosives	Guild	Trent		5010 - present	Chemicals & tools

Titles			
Organization	Title	Turn Awarded	Description
Thieves Guild	Pickpocket		
	Apprentice	5010	The act of sneakily removing some item of value from a person's body without them being the wiser. Putpocketing is the reverse of this, and is actually harder to accomplish.
	Journeyperson	5010	
	Master	Not Yet	
	Cutpurse		

Master	Journeyperson	Apprentice
Not Yet	5010	5010

The act of surreptitiously slicing the bottom of a coin purse and catching the coins that drop out quietly enough not to alert the Mark. It takes a very sharp small knife to do this correctly.

Grifter "Swindler"

Master	Journeyperson	Apprentice
Not Yet	5010	5010

Unlike most kinds of petty crime, a confidence game, or con, takes an enormous amount of skill and forethought to pull off. When done right, in many cases the Grifters, Con Men, who perpetrate them, have not actually done anything overtly illegal–they've simply used lies and manipulation to get the Mark to willingly hand over his own money.

Smuggler

Forger

Master	Journeyperson	Apprentice	
Not Yet	5011	5010	Surreptitiously transporting goods, persons, and creatures so as to avoid scrutiny by the authorities.

Counterfeiter

Master	Journeyperson	Apprentice	
Not Yet	5012	5011	Making as close to identical copies of works of art, official documents, or anything else of value that is usually one-of-a-kind.

	Master	Journeyperson	Apprentice
Burglar	Not Yet	Not Yet	Not Yet

Making fake Bank Notes, Letters of Mark, Deeds, and anything else of monetary value.

	Master	Journeyperson	Apprentice
Trapfinder "Box-person"	5014	5014	5013

Sneaking or breaking into a residence or business and stealing something of value.

Master	Journeyperson	Apprentice	
5014	5014	5013	Having the skills to find, disarm, remove, or create tricks and traps of all kinds, usually, but not limited to a structure.

Lockpicker

Master	Journeyperson	Apprentice	
5013	5011	5010	Having the skills to open or close locks of various sorts without the actual key.

Safecracker

Master	Journeyperson	Apprentice
Not Yet	Not Yet	5013

Having the skills to open safes without the combination or key.

Assassin

Master	Journeyperson	Apprentice
Not Yet	Not Yet	5013

Having the skills to kill persons or creatures efficiently and usually in a specific manner, like making it look like an accident or making it very public and showy, as designated by the person who hires the Assassin.

Bards College

Fencer

Apprentice	Journeyperson	Master	
5011	Not Yet	Not Yet	A specialist Fighter with swords in general and the Foil specifically

Jongleur

Apprentice	Journeyperson	Master	
5011	Not Yet	Not Yet	Juggling, Acrobatics, Gymnastics, Comedy, Clowning

Thespian

Trickster	Chandlers Guild						
Specialty Priest	Master	Journeyperson	Apprentice	Master	Journeyperson	Apprentice
5012	Not Yet	5013	5013	Not Yet	Not Yet	Not Yet
There are very few of these in the world.	Making candles.			Acting specifically, but also includes; Singing, Dancing, Stand-up Comedy, and practically anything else done on a stage in front of an audience. Secondarily includes Make-up, props, wardrobe, lighting, and many other facets of performance art.			

City Guard, Constabulary, & Rangers

Ranks

Rank	Number	Description
Private	5010	The lowest rank
Lancepesades	5011	Second in command of a Squad
Corporal	5011	Command of a Squad
Sergeant	5011	Second in command of a Platoon
Lieutenant	5012	Command of a Platoon
First Sergeant	N/A	Third in command of a Company
Ensign	5012	Second in command of a Company
Warrant Officer	5013	Special skills Officer

Rank	Status	Command
Captain	Not Yet	Command of a Company
Sergeant Major	N/A	Second in command of a Battalion
Major	Not Yet	Command of a Battalion
Command Sergeant Major	N/A	Second in command of a Brigade
Colonel	Not Yet	Command of a Brigade
Senior Command Sergeant Major	N/A	Second in command of an Army
General	Not Yet	Command of an Army
Trainer		

	Journeyperson	Apprentice	Master	Journeyperson	Apprentice	Master	Journeyperson	Apprentice
Katas	5011	5011						
Bow			Not Yet	Not Yet	5011			
Sling						Not Yet	5011	5011

Katas: Training people in the hand-to-hand and weapon Katas.

Bow: Training people in the use, design, and maintenance of the weapon and ammunition.

Sling: Training people in the use, design, and maintenance of the weapon and ammunition.

Bard Skills				Rogue Skills			
Master	Journeyperson	Apprentice	Master	Journeyperson	Apprentice	Master	
Not Yet	5012	5012	5014	5012	5012	Not Yet	
Training the City Guard, Constabulary, & Rangers in suitable and useful crossover skills.			Training the City Guard, Constabulary, & Rangers in suitable and useful crossover skills.				

Pilot		Bear Claws			Cat Claws		
Journeyperson	Apprentice	Master	Journeyperson	Apprentice	Master	Journeyperson	Apprentice
Not Yet	5013	Not Yet	5012	5012	Not Yet	5012	5012
Training people in in the art of flying an Aircraft		Training people in the use, design, and maintenance of the weapon.			Training people in the use, design, and maintenance of the weapon.		

Skills

Siege Engineer			Siege Tactician			
Master	Journeyperson	Apprentice	Master	Journeyperson	Apprentice	Master
Not Yet	5013	5012	Not Yet	Not Yet	5012	Not Yet
Designing, building, maintaining, repairing, and utilizing siege weapons in a variety of situations and for a variety of purposes.			Planning Sieges, use of battle strategies as regards siege weapons and troop tactics.			

Ship Engineer		Aircraft Engineer			Air Force Pilot		
Journeyperson	Apprentice	Master	Journeyperson	Apprentice	Master	Journeyperson	Apprentice
5014	5014	Not Yet	5014	5014	Not Yet	5013	5013
Designing, building, maintaining, repairing, and utilizing ships in a variety of situations and for a variety of purposes.		Designing, building, maintaining, repairing, and utilizing aircraft in a variety of situations and for a variety of purposes.			Flying an aircraft.		

City of Waterport	Not Yet	Master	Not Yet
		Not Yet	Not Yet

Awards			
Organization	Title	Turn Awarded	Description
City Guard, Constabulary, & Rangers	Excellence in Combat Training, Katas	5011	Learning more Katas than any other student previously.
	Excellence in Design, Armour	5011	Designing the new armour.
	Ekridge Campaign	5012	Saving the Barony
	Living Missile Award	5012	For being fired out of a catapult and into a castle

Award	Year	Description
Excellence in Design, Warship	5014	Designing the Behemoth Battle Platform Class
First in Flight Award		First to fly a wing
Excellence in Design, Siege Breaker	5013	Designing the Wing aircraft
Excellence in Design, Siege Weapon	5013	Designing the Wall Buster
Siege Engineers College training	5013	For attending College
Excellence in Design, Weapon	5012	Designing the Claws, Cat and Bear
War College training patch	5012	For attending College
Siege Tacticians Award	5012	For designing the siege of Castle Ramshorn, Ekridge
Cross of Courage	5012	For the above

Excellence in Design, Siege Weapon	Excellence in Design, Siege Weapon	Excellence in Design, Warship	Excellence in Design, Siege Weapon	Excellence in Design, Siege Defense	Excellence in Design, Siege Weapon	Excellence in Design, Siege Breaker	Excellence in Design, Warship Defense
5014	5014	5014	5014	5014	5014	5014	5014
Designing the Repeating Mini-Arbalest	Designing the Turtle	Designing the Interceptor Class	Designing the Repeating Arbalest	Designing steel cladding, castles	Designing the Booms	Designing the Stoop aircraft	Designing Steel Cladding, ships

City of Waterport

Award	Year	Project
Excellence in Design, Building	5014	Designing the Airfield
Hero of the City	5013	Same as above
Excellence in Design, Building	5013	Design and implementation of the concept of the City School Complex
Excellence in Design, Engineered Material	5014	Designing Flame Retardant
Excellence in Design, Siege Weapon	5014	Designing the VTOAL Attack
Excellence in Design, Weapon	5014	Designing the Swordbreaker Dagger
Excellence in Design, Weapon	5014	Designing the Parrying Dagger
Excellence in Design, Engineered Material	5014	Designing Moldable Plastic

Norse	Excellence in Design, Safety	Excellence in Design, Transportation	Excellence in Design, Merchant Ship	Excellence in Design, Transportation	Man of the Year	Hero of the City	Excellence in Design, Merchant Ship
Norse Longship necklace	5014	5014	5014	5014	5014	5014	5014
Designing the screw powered Longship, infers Captain Status	Designing the Floaties	Designing the VTOAL Cargo	Designing the Interceptor Merchant Ship	Designing the Caravan	For all of the stuff in 5013	Same as above	Designing the Behemoth Merchant Ship

Stavsund Engineer of the Gods	5014		Designing the nine Axes with Bear

Organizations

Name	Sub-group	Sub-Sub-group	Turn Joined	Description
Thieves Guild	Smugglers	None	5010	Waterport Smuggling Operation
City Guard & Constabulary	Guard	None	5010	City Watch
	Rangers	None	5011	Country Watch
	Air Force	None	5013	Air Watch
Bards Guild	Jongleurs Society	Jesters & Fools Society	5012	Jugglers, Acrobats, Gymnasts / Comedians, Clowns
	Thespians Society	None	5014	Actors

	Organization	Sub-organization	Code	Description
Scribes Society	Scriveners Society	None	5012	Scribing in general
Scribes Society	Calligraphy Masters	None	5014	Fancy writing
Scribes Society	Illumination Masters	None	5013	Pictures in books
Scribes Society	Bookbinders Society	None	5014	Making books
Scribes Society	Limners association	Cartographers Society	5014	Mapmakers
Smiths Guild	Locksmiths association	None	5014	
Mercers Guild	Street Merchants	None	5013	Business Owner

Traveling Players	Street Musicians	None		
Mechanical Engineers	Siege Engineers	None	5012	Siege Engineer
Alchemical Engineers	None	None	5014	
Magicians Guild	None	None	5015	

Appendix B	Character Sheet		

Name	Deity	Alignment		Build
Captain (Teacher) Reginald 'Reggie' Rumphrey-Bon Vent (FairWind)-Lokisson, Esq.(AKA Scram Runt, The Whirling Dervish, The Patch Collector, The Engineer) of Waterport, DOB 28 Leafall, 5000 (actually 4 Frostshine, 5000)	**Trickster**, Goddess of Nature, Goddess of Luck, God of Thieves, God of Crafts, God of Strategy, God of Trade, Goddesses of Music, Celebration, and Dance (the three Sisters of Entertainment)	Good	Neutral	Meso-Ectomorph

	Gender	Race	Height	Weight
	Male	½ Elfkin Halfling, ¼ Human, ¼ Forest Elf	4'4"	46# / 3 stone, 4 lb

Class
Grifter/Burgler/Pickpocket/ Smuggler/Forger/Trapfinder Rogue, Archer/Scout Ranger, Jongleur / Charlatan Bard, Trickster Mage, Assassin, Priest of Trickster

Specialty
Constabulary, Rangers, Military Designer, Engineer, Scribe, Calligrapher, Illuminator, Sage, Candlemaker, Merchant, Cook, Armourer, Weaponsmith, Musician- Penny Whistle

Hair	Beard	Skin
Medium Brown, curly, medium length	Mustache & goatee (no need to shave the rest)	Nut brown, no body hair

Eyes	Ears	Teeth

Light hazel, slanted, almond, thin slanted eyebrows	Slightly pointed	Even, off-white

Personality

Rationality	Mannerism	Self-esteem	Philosophy	Demeanor
+ Stable	0 Cautious + Relaxed + Studious + Perceptive + Inquisitive	+ Humble	0 Optimist + Extroverted + Altruist	

Intellect	Bravery	Morals	Piety	Motivation
+ Active	+ Calculating + Courageous	0 Normal + Lusty + Aesthetic	- Irreverent 0 Average	+Motivated

Relationships

Manner	Mood / Disposition	Honesty	Length
+ Helpful + Kindly + Compassionate + Courteous	+ Peaceful + Pleasant + Soft-Hearted + Forgiving + Cheerful	+ Truthful	+ Stable + Long

0 Mischievous + Well-Spoken + Sensitive + Trusting

+ Reserved + Even-Tempered + Easygoing

Interests

Hobbies	Loves	Fears	Hates
Altruism	Armour	Sharks	Braggarts
Athletics	Artwork	Torture	Bullies
Community Service	Books & Scrolls	Undead	Greed
Dancing	Coins & Tokens		
Exotic animals	Knives & Daggers		
Fishing	Minerals & Gems		
Foods & Preparation	Ornaments & Jewelry		
Gambling	Porcelain, China, & Crystal		
Handicrafts	Shields & Weapons		
History	Swords		
Horticulture			
Husbandry			
Legends			
Nature			
Politics			
Religion			
Smoking & Pipes			
Wine & Spirits			

Appearance

General	Personal Habits	State of Clothing
0 Typical + Dignified	0 Nonchalant + Organized	+ Clean

Possessions		
Thrift	Quantity	Quality
+ Charitable + Generous	+ Above Average	0 Functional + Practical + Durable + High

Scram's birth name was Reginald Rumphrey-FairWind (Bon Vent), Regi or Reggie for short.

- His Mother, named Abigail Rumphrey, was an Elfkin Halfling from Rootdown. She was a Seamstress in Waterport after the family moved there. She passed over when he was approximately 3 years old from a fever. A catapult ball had demolished the house that they had been hiding in during a Pirate raid, hitting her and fracturing her back and right leg on its way through the house and cellar, and out into the sewer. Her leg fracture was open and became infected. Her family has been Humkin Halfling mixed with Forest Elf, making Elfkin, for many generations back.
  - Her father, named Arnaud Rumphrey, is a Woodcarver of great renown.
  - Her mother, named Genevieve Underbough, is a Housemate and part-time Seamstress.
- Scram's Father, named Lars FairWind (Bon Vent), is a Half Elf from Stavsund. He works as a Sailor and Fisherman in Trois Epees - Deux. They met when Lars came to the Village De L'arbre / Rootdown area to visit with his father. They got handfasted and moved to Waterport to make a life. Scram is their only child. After his Mate and

son disappeared, he moved to Trois Epee - Deux to start over due to having kinfolks in that area. He got rehandfasteded to Lorraine Pascal, another Half Elf, and produced a batch of half siblings.

- o Lars Mother was a Human, named Else Ingridsdotter, from Stavsund. She was an herbalist. She only lived to her 50's and passed over peacefully, surrounded by Lars and his half siblings (all full Humans) and their children. She was exceptionally pretty, for a Human, and very petite for her Norseman lineage.
- o Lars Father is a Forest Elf, named Etienne Bon Vent (FairWind), from Village De L'arbre. He is a Poet. They met while she was searching the forest for medicinal herbs and he was creating poetry about a glen filled with Spring flowers. They never officially handfasted or lived together, but they enjoyed each other's company whenever she came to his woodlands.

At the time of the writing of his memoirs, Scram keeps in contact with his father and 3 surviving grandparents, their respective extended families, and his deceased grandmother's kin.

Scram speaks, reads, and writes, True Common, Western Elvish, Norse, Highlander Dwarven, and Daremo. He also knows 3 sign languages; Thieves, Merchants, and Rangers.

Name	Deity	Alignment		Build
(Princess) Lieutenant Madeleine 'Chasseresse'('Huntress') Feuille Plume (LeafFeather) of Waterport and Village De L'arbre DOB 4983	God of Nature, God of Strategy, Goddesses of Music, Celebration, and Dance (the three Sisters of Entertainment)	Good	Neutral	Ecto-Mesomorph

Gender	Race	Height	Weight
Female	¼ Human, ¾ Forest Elf	4'6"	70# / 5 st, 0 lb

Class
Archer Ranger, Highwayman Rogue, Nature Mage, (Elven Minstrel, stringed instruments)

Specialty
Constabulary

Hair	Beard	Skin
Auburn (reddish brown), long cascading waves	none	lightly tanned, flawless, no body hair

Eyes	Ears	Teeth
Mesmerizing, multi-hued, primarily green, slanted, almond, slanted sleek eyebrows	Small, delicate, pointed	Perfect, white

Personality				
Rationality	Mannerism	Self-esteem	Philosophy	Demeanor

231

Intellect	Bravery	Morals	Piety	Motivation
+ Stable	+ Studious + Perceptive + Curious	+ Modest	0 Optimist + Extroverted + Benevolent	Calm Extrovert Positive Happy
	- Exacting - Precise + Relaxed			
+ Active	+ Courageous	+ Lusty + Aesthetic + Virtuous	+ Reverent	+Motivated

| | | | | Relationships | | | | | |

Manner	Mood / Disposition	Honesty	Length
+ Helpful + Kindly + Compassionate + Courteous + Diplomatic	+ Easygoing + Pleasant + Soft-Hearted		+ Exceptionally Long

Interests			
Hobbies	**Loves**	**Fears**	**Hates**
Altruism Athletics Community Service Dancing Foods & Preparation Gambling Handicrafts History Horticulture Legends Nature Politics Religion Wine & Spirits	Armour Artwork Books & Scrolls Coins & Tokens Knives & Daggers Minerals & Gems Ornaments & Jewelry Porcelain, China, & Crystal Shields & Weapons Swords	Beggars Loneliness Torture Undead Being Bound	Braggarts Bullies Greed Selfishness Stupidity

Personality:

- War-Like
0 Mischievous
+ Well-Spoken
+ Forceful
+ Sensitive
+ Trusting

+ Reserved
+ Forgiving
+ Cheerful
+ Even-Tempered

+ Truthful

+ Very Stable

Appearance

	General	Personal Habits	State of Clothing
	+ Stately	+ Organized + Prim & Proper + Immaculate	+ Clean + Pristine + Immaculate

Possessions		
Thrift	Quantity	Quality
+ Charitable + Generous	+ Abundant	0 Functional + Practical + Durable + High

Scram's primary mate, his soulmate, the love of his life.
They met when he was 11 turns old and she was a very
lonely 28. He was very mature for his age and functioned
at about 15 turns old. She has more Fae genetics than him,
so she was the equivalent of approximately 15 turns of age
in maturity at the time (she will outlive him by a couple of
hundred turns). They got together shortly after meeting,
got handfasted a few turns later, produced several
offspring, and have been happily handfasted for over 200
turns to date. At this point, they are Great-Great-Great-
Great Grandparents. That is why their home is so
large…lots of room for visitors (Munchkins, Rug-Rats,
Curtain-Climbers, etc.), who visit quite often. Reggie and
Maddy have over 1000 descendants, not all of which are
still alive, due to accidents, illnesses, wars, etc., but still,
the remainder is a lot of kinfolks. Even more when you add
in the descendants from his union with the other four
ladies. They have the entire 'family tree' algorithmic chart
covering a 2 story wall of the Ball Room in their mansion.
He is in the center, with Madeleine and Tilly to his right
and Nell, Kizzy, and Kichawi to his left. The trees extend
below the five ladies names.
She was raised by her Forest Elven kin. Her Mother,
Clarisse, and her Father, Pierre, a Half Elf who passed over
a few Turns ago

	Master Kata Instructor at the School Complex. Member of the Air Force and Ranger Company. Platoon Leader of a Ranger Platoon. Member of W.I.S. (Waterport Investigation Services). Member of L.A.F. (League of Adventuring Fellows).

Name	Deity		Alignment		Build
Teacher Tilly Fleetfingers of Thistledown DOB 4 Frostshine, 5000 (Born on the same day as Scram)	**Trickster**, Goddess of Luck, God of Crafts, God of the Harvest, God of Trade, Goddesses of Music, Celebration, and Dance (the three Sisters of Entertainment)		Good	Neutral	Meso-Ectomorph
	Gender	Race	Height		Weight
	Female	½ Elfkin Halfling, ¼ Human, ¼ Forest Elf	3'10"		46# / 3 stone, 4 lb
	Class				
	Fighter, Priest of Trickster				
	Specialty				
	Homemaker, Cook, Baker, Farmer, Gardener, Herbalist, Grover, Shearer, Groomer, Butcher, Crafter, Spinner, Dyer, Seamstress, Embroiderer, Drapemaker, Candlemaker, Soapmaker, Potter, Basketmaker, Woodcarver, Skinner, Tanner, Cordwainer, Plasterer, Painter, Merchant, Dancer, Musician – Kit, Singer				
	Hair		Beard		Skin
	Long, wavy, red-brown		none		Smooth olive
	Eyes		Ears		Teeth
	Large, almond, blue-green		Slightly pointed, dainty		Even, white
	Personality				

Category	Attribute	Trait	Trait
Rationality	Intellect	+ Active	+ Stable
Mannerism	Bravery	+ Courageous	+ Playful + Relaxed + Perceptive + Curious + Inquisitive
Self-esteem	Morals	- Amoral + Lusty	+ Modest
Philosophy	Piety	- Irreverent	0 Optimist + Extroverted + Altruist
	Motivation	- Motivated + Energetic	
Demeanor			- Happy

Relationships	
Manner	+ Sensitive + Trusting + Helpful + Kindly + Compassionate + Diplomatic
Mood / Disposition	+ Pleasant + Soft-Hearted + Forgiving + Cheerful
Honesty	
Length	+ Exceptionally Long

0 Capricious 0 Mischievous 0 Practical Joker 0 Prankster + Well-Spoken	+ Even-Tempered + Easygoing + Peaceful		+ Truthful	+ Very Stable

Interests			
Hobbies	Loves	Fears	Hates
Handicrafts History Horticulture Husbandry Legends Nature Altruism Community Service Dancing Fishing Foods & Preparation	Artwork Books & Scrolls Porcelain, China, & Crystal	Poison Torture Undead Dying Heights Loneliness Pain	Selfishness Stupidity Bad Food Braggarts Bullies Greed

Appearance		
General	Personal Habits	State of Clothing
0 Typical	0 Nonchalant + Organized	+ Clean

Possessions		
Thrift	Quantity	Quality
+ Thrifty + Generous	+ Above Average	0 Functional + Practical + Durable

Scram's 2nd Mate and 1st Cousin.

Her Mother and his Mother were identical twins. Their Fathers are also closely related genetically, though look no more similar than Cousins or vaguely Brothers.

The Deities have been manipulating folks in a breeding program for hundreds of years whose entire goal is the progeny of these two people. Their children will play a major role in the upcoming war between the forces of Good and Evil. Some of this was revealed to them by Trickster so that they would stop balking and start producing children.

Name	Deity	Alignment		Build
Lieutenant (Madam) 'Lucky' Nell McThyme of Slagdown DOB 4989	**Goddess of Luck**, God of Crafts, Goddess of Health, God of the Harvest, Goddesses of Music, Celebration, and Dance (the three Sisters of Entertainment)	Good	Chaotic	Meso-Endomorph
				Meso-Ectomorph

Gender	Race	Height	Weight
Female	Dwarfkin Halfling	1'9"	40# / 2 st, 12 lb
			27# / 1 st, 13 lb

Class
Priest of the Goddess of Luck, Archer Ranger

Specialty
Gardener, Herbalist, Poulter, Breadmaker, Cobbler, Musician- Mini-accordion

Hair	Beard	Skin
curly mop, reddish blonde	none	rosy cheeks, pale

Eyes	Ears	Teeth
leaf green	Small, fat, rounded	Bright white
	small, rounded	

Personality

240

Category	Traits	Category	Traits
Rationality	- Slightly Insane (Diety)	Intellect	+ Flighty
Mannerism	- Fanatical / + Perceptive / + Curious	Bravery	+ Fearless (Diety)
Self-esteem	+ Modest	Morals	+ Lusty / + Aesthetic / + Virtuous
Philosophy	0 Optimist / + Extroverted / + Altruist	Piety	- Martyr / - Zealot / + Pious
Demeanor	No Worries / Positive / Extrovert / Happy / Silly	Motivation	+ Energetic

Relationships	
Manner	+ Forceful / + Sensitive / + Trusting / + Helpful / + Kindly / + Compassionate
Mood / Disposition	+ Silly / + Easygoing / + Pleasant
Honesty	+ Truthful
Length	+ Stable / + Very Long

- Rash
0 Capricious
0 Mischievous
0 Practical Joker
0 Prankster
+ Soft-Hearted
+ Forgiving
+ Cheerful

Interests

Hobbies	Loves	Fears	Hates
Altruism	Armour	Undead	Bad Food
Community Service	Books & Scrolls		Bullies
Dancing	Coins & Tokens		Greed
Fishing	Minerals & Gems		
Foods & Preparation	Ornaments & Jewelry		
Gambling	Shields & Weapons		
Handicrafts			
History			
Horticulture			
Husbandry			
Legends			
Nature			
Politics			
Religion			
Wine & Spirits			

Appearance

General	Personal Habits	State of Clothing
0 Typical	- Scatterbrained 0 Nonchalant + Organized	+ Clean

Possessions

Thrift	Quantity	Quality

+ Thrifty + Charitable + Generous	+ Above Average	0 Functional + Practical + Durable

Scram's 3rd Mate and friend.

Member of the Training Squad of the City Guard Ranger Unit. Leader of the Air Force. Member of L.A.F. (League of Adventuring Fellows).

They got handfasted when she was 25. They had several children together. She passed away as a triple Great-Grandmother at 126 years of age in 5115. We all miss her.

Name	Deity	Alignment		Build
	Her Father, a Fire Djinn, Goddesses of Music, Celebration, and Dance (the three Sisters of Entertainment)	Good	Chaotic	Meso- Ectomorph

Gender	Race	Height	Weight
Female	½ Djinn ½ Human	5'8"	133 # / 9 st, 7 lb
		5'0"	114 # / 8 st, 2 lb
		4'4"	98 # / 7 st, 0 lb
		3'8"	83 # / 5 st, 13 lb
		3'0"	68 # / 4 st, 12 lb
		2'4"	53 # / 3 st, 11 lb
		1'8"	38 # / 2 st, 10 lb
		1'0"	22 # / 1 st, 8 lb

Class

Elementalist Wizard, Fighter

Specialty

Scribe, Poet, Dancer, Singer, Housekeeper

Hair	Beard	Skin
Short, soft, kinky, black	none	Café au lait coloured, minimal body hair, shimmers when the light hits it just right
Bald except for an exceptionally long ponytail of straight jet-black hair growing from the center top of her head	none	Dark red (maroon), no body hair, shimmers when light hits it. Can have a fiery nimbus at will.

Eyes	Ears	Teeth
hazel (green, brown, golden) slanted, almond,	Very tall and pointed	Very white and even

Name (sidebar): *Fae* Kichawi 'Firey' Nuru of Afuraka DOB 4910

slanted sleek eyebrows		
reds, oranges, and yellows that flicker like dancing flames, slanted, almond, slanted sleek eyebrows	Very tall and pointed	Bright white and even

Personality

Rationality	Mannerism	Self-esteem	Philosophy	Demeanor
0 Normal	+ Relaxed + Studious + Perceptive + Curious + Inquisitive	+ Obsequious + Humble	0 Optimist + Benevolent	
- Slightly Insane - Unstable	- Careless - Obsessive	- Haughty - Proud	- Hedonistic + Extroverted	

Intellect	Bravery	Morals	Piety	Motivation
+ Active	+ Courageous	+ Aesthetic	- Irreligious	+ Motivated + Energetic

Relationships			
Manner	**Mood / Disposition**	**Honesty**	**Length**
- Scheming + Flighty + Calculating	- Amoral + Lusty + Lustful	- Irreverent - Impious	- Driven
0 Mischievous + Well-Spoken + Sensitive + Helpful + Compassionate	+ Easygoing + Pleasant + Forgiving + Cheerful	+ Truthful	+ Stable + Long
- Vengeful - Rude - Opinionated 0 Capricious 0 Prankster + Forceful	- Scheming - Hot-Tempered - Secretive - Moody 0 Aloof	- Deceitful	- Fleeting - Casual
Interests			
Hobbies	**Loves**	**Fears**	**Hates**

Athletics Gambling Exotic animals Dancing Community Service Foods & Preparation Handicrafts History Legends Nature Politics Religion	Knives & Daggers Coins & Tokens Minerals & Gems Ornaments & Jewelry Artwork Books & Scrolls Porcelain, China, & Crystal	Dark Water Water Dying Dead Things Enclosed Spaces Loneliness Pain Sharks Sight of own blood Traps Undead	Laws Rival Clan Stupidity Bad Food Bullies

Appearance		
General	Personal Habits	State of Clothing
+ Dignified	+ Organized + Immaculate	+ Clean
+ Stately	0 Nonchalant	+ Immaculate

Possessions		
Thrift	Quantity	Quality
+ Generous	0 Average	0 Functional + Practical + Durable
- Greedy	+ Exceptional	+ Kingly

Officially, Scram's 5th Mate, though for a long time prior, she had been acting as a Mate surreptitiously by shape-changing to the form of one of his acknowledged mates. They were handfasted when she was 104 turns old, which is very young for her race.

Since she is a Fae, she can do Natural Magick at will. She is studying Humans, Human culture, and Human Magick. Changes size and appearance at will. Usually, she is in her default form or her generally Human appearing mode, but she can mimic practically any Humanoid female's size and appearance. Has 2 sides to her nature, fortunately, the nicer version usually wins out.

She has never tried to mimic a male Humanoid or an animal yet.

Name	Deity	Alignment		Build
Romni Kisaiya 'Kizzy' Ravelino of the Kale Romani DOB 4998	Kali Sara (a Mother Goddess), Goddess of Luck, God of Crafts, Goddess of Health, Goddesses of Music, Celebration, and Dance (the three Sisters of Entertainment)	Good	Neutral (both Chaotic and Lawful tendencies)	Meso- Ectomorph

Gender	Race	Height	Weight
Female	Rom Human, Dryad (tree Nymph)	4'6"	70# / 5 st, 0 lb

Class
Sneaky Fighter, Rogue (Pickpocket, Smuggler, Grifter, Forger) , Undercover Constabulary

Specialty
Dancer, Musician, Artist, Singer, Housekeeper, Rom Crafts, Accountant

Hair	Beard	Skin
Long, thick, black, wavy, natural	none	Smooth medium dark brown, minimal body hair

Eyes	Ears	Teeth
Black	Petite, rounded	Off-white, even

Personality				
Rationality	Mannerism	Self-esteem	Philosophy	Demeanor

Intellect	- Scheming (Gadjo), + Flighty, + Active, 0 Normal, + Stable, + Studious, + Perceptive, + Curious, + Inquisitive
Bravery	+ Calculating, + Courageous, - Suspicious (Gadjo), 0 Cautious (Gadjo), + Retiring (Gadjo), + Relaxed (Rom)
Morals	+ Lusty, + Aesthetic, + Virtuous, - Proud (Rom), 0 Proper, + Modest
Piety	+ Pious (Rom), 0 Optimist, + Extroverted, + Benevolent
Motivation	+ Motivated, + Energetic

Relationships	Traits
Manner	+ Forceful, + Sensitive, + Helpful (Rom), + Courteous (Rom)
Mood / Disposition	- Moody, + Reserved (Gadjo), + Pleasant (Rom)
Honesty	+ Truthful, + Honorable
Length	+ Long

- Vengeful (Gadjo)	- Scheming (Gadjo)
- Rude (Gadjo)	- Hot-Tempered
- Opinionated	- Unforgiving (Gadjo)
+ Well-Spoken	- Secretive (Gadjo)

Interests

Hobbies	Loves	Fears	Hates
Dancing (Rom)	Artwork (Vardo)	Cats	Bullies
Exotic animals	Books & Scrolls (Rom)	Caves	Stupidity
Fishing	Coins & Tokens	Dying	
Foods & Preparation (Rom)	Knives & Daggers	Illness	
Gambling	Minerals & Gems	Loneliness	
Handicrafts (Rom)	Ornaments & Jewelry (Rom)	Pain	
History (Rom)	Porcelain, China, & Crystal	Poison	
Legends (Rom)		Torture	
Politics (Rom)		Undead	
Religion (Rom)		Wizards	
Wine & Spirits			

Appearance

General	Personal Habits	State of Clothing
+ Dandyish	+ Organized	+ Clean
+ Foppish	+ Prim & Proper	
+ Stately	+ Immaculate	

Possessions

Thrift	Quantity	Quality
- Miserly + Thrifty	+ Above Average	- Garish 0 Functional + Practical + Durable

Scram's 4th Mate. Her Father adopted Scram and his Family into the Romani and, in the process, became a business partner of sorts and… traded her for a Rom Caravan sized Vardo. Scram was not aware of anything but the adoption part prior to the ceremony.

Very much a part of Rom culture. Only really comfortable around Familia. Distrustful of other Human cultures, Gadjo. Neutral towards others; Little People, Fae, etc.

Half Fae, but does not know it. Mother was a Dryad (tree connected Nymph) who seduced her Father to keep him from harvesting her tree, became pregnant, brought the baby to him to raise. She has always been more graceful, shorter, petite, and slender than her half-Brothers and half-Sisters from her Father's many Mates, but did not know why.

This was why he was willing to Handfast her to a non-Rom that was not a Gadjo. A part Fae man with part Fae or Little People Mates. He thought that this would be a perfect match considering his daughter's lineage.

Her first name comes from Romani 'kissi' meaning purse, (ultimately from Sanskrit koza "box; pocket; cask; treasure; bud", and this fits as she has natural talent as an Accountant. She took over keeping the books for our household, my companies (all of them), and eventually took Trent's place keeping the ones for the Smuggling Operation. She joined the Thieves Guild and applied her skills to keeping theirs also. She finished her training, up to Master in Smuggler, Pickpocket, and Grifter.

Member of W.I.S. (Waterport Investigation Services).
Member of L.A.F. (League of Adventuring Fellows).

Name	Deity		Alignment		Build
Trentish 'the Face' Oglesby (AKA Professor Finklepot) of ? DOB 4988	Goddess of Luck, Goddess of Beauty, God of Communication, God of Crafts, Trickster, Goddesses of Music, Celebration, and Dance (the three Sisters of Entertainment)		Good	Neutral	Ectomorph

Gender	Race		Height	Weight	
Both	¾ Human, ¼ Plains Elf		5'4"	120# / 8 st, 8 lb	

Class					
Thespian/Jongleur/ (Charlatan) Bard, Grifter/Smuggler Rogue					

Specialty					
Chef, Artist, Seamstress, Tailor, Wigcrafter, Singer					

Hair	Beard	Skin
flowing, wavy, thick, shoulder length golden locks	None, dimples	perfect, creamy complexion, no body hair

Eyes	Ears	Teeth
light hazel	Medium, rounded	perfect white

Personality

Rationality	- Neurotic 0 Normal
Mannerism	0 Cautious + Studious + Perceptive + Inquisitive
Self-esteem	- Haughty
Philosophy	0 Optimist + Extroverted + Benevolent
Demeanor	Worrier Extrovert Positive Serious/Silly Sad/Happy
Intellect	+ Flighty + Brilliant
Bravery	+ Calculating + Courageous
Morals	+ Lusty + Aesthetic
Piety	- Irreverent - Iconoclastic - Irreligious
Motivation	+ Energetic
Relationships	
Manner	0 Mischievous + Well-Spoken + Sensitive + Trusting + Helpful + Kindly + Compassionate + Courteous + Diplomatic
Mood / Disposition	+ Silly + Easygoing + Pleasant + Soft-Hearted + Forgiving + Cheerful
Honesty	- Deceitful + Truthful
Length	+ Medium

Interests			
Hobbies	Loves	Fears	Hates
Legends	Ornaments & Jewelry	Pain	Stupidity
Nature	Porcelain, China, & Crystal	Sight of own blood	Bad Food
Politics	Swords	Snakes	Bullies
Religion	Artwork	Spiders	
Wine & Spirits	Books & Scrolls	Torture	
Dancing	Coins & Tokens	Undead	
Foods & Preparation	Minerals & Gems	Dark	
Gambling		Dying	
Handicrafts		Dead Things	
History		Illness	
		Insects	
		Loneliness	

Appearance		
General	Personal Habits	State of Clothing
+ Dandyish + Foppish	+ Organized + Perfectionist + Immaculate	+ Clean + Pristine + Immaculate

Possessions		
Thrift	Quantity	Quality
+ Generous - Spendthrift	+ Exceptional	- Garish 0 Functional + High

Scram's adoptive Mother. One of Scram's Teachers in the Thieves Guild. Professor at the Engineers College and the Scribes College. Handfasted to Cranndair and Clarisse.

	Member of W.I.S. (Waterport Investigation Services). Member of L.A.F. (League of Adventuring Fellows).

Name	Deity		Alignment		Build
Colonel Cranndair *the Warden* of Ville Des Neuf & Waterport DOB 4910	**Goddess of Nature,** God of Strategy		Neutral	Lawful	Ecto- Mesomorph

Gender	Race	Height	Weight
Male	¼ Human, ¾ Mountain Elf	5'8"	125# / 8 st, 13 lb

Class
Investigator Rogue, Warden Ranger, Summoner Mage, Priest of the Goddess of Nature, (Elven Minstrel, stringed instruments)

Specialty
Constabulary

Hair	Beard	Skin
Red, but dyes it black, short, perfectly coifed, wavy	Meticulously elaborately trimmed, dyed	Flawless ivory

Eyes	Ears	
Yellow-gold, slanted, almond, fine eyebrows	Medium, very pointed	Perfect, white

Personality					
Rationality	Mannerism	Self-esteem	Philosophy		Demeanor

Intellect	+ Brilliant	+ Stable	- Exacting / - Suspicious / - Precise / 0 Cautious · + Somber / + Studious / + Perceptive / + Inquisitive
Bravery	+ Calculating / + Courageous		
Morals	+ Aesthetic / + Virtuous	0 Proper / + Modest	
Piety	0 Average	0 Optimist / + Extroverted / + Benevolent	
Motivation	+ Motivated	Calm / Extrovert / Positive / Serious	

Relationships

Manner	+ Well-Spoken / + Sensitive / + Helpful	+ Kindly / + Courteous / + Diplomatic
Mood / Disposition	+ Reserved / + Even-Tempered / + Peaceful / + Pleasant / + Forgiving	
Honesty	+ Truthful / + Scrupulous	
Length	+Exceptionally long	

Interests

Hobbies	Loves	Fears	Hates
Legends Nature Politics Religion Athletics Dancing History Wine & Spirits Community Service Foods & Preparation Handicrafts Horticulture Husbandry	Ornaments & Jewelry Porcelain, China, & Crystal Shields & Weapons Swords Artwork Books & Scrolls Knives & Daggers Minerals & Gems	Heights	Bad Food Braggarts Bullies Stupidity

Appearance		
General	Personal Habits	State of Clothing
+ Dandyish + Dignified + Stately	+ Organized + Prim & Proper + Perfectionist + Immaculate	+ Clean + Pristine + Immaculate

Possessions		
Thrift	Quantity	Quality
+ Charitable + Generous	+ Exceptional	0 Functional + Practical + Durable + Kingly

Scram's adoptive Father due to handfasting his adoptive Mother, Trent. Also, his boss in the Rangers.

Warden for the lands surrounding Waterport.

Member of W.I.S. (Waterport Investigation Services).
Member of L.A.F. (League of Adventuring Fellows).

Name	Deity		Alignment		Build
	Goddess of Nature		Good	Neutral	Meso- Ectomorph
	Gender	Race	Height		Weight
	Female	Forest Elf	5'6"		110# / 7 st, 12 lb
	Class				
	Blade Bard, Elven Minstrel, stringed instruments				
	Specialty				
	Scribe, Poet, Dancer, Singer, Artist				
	Hair		Beard		Skin
	Reddish brown undertones with golden highlights, long cascading waves		none		lightly tanned, flawless, no body hair
	Eyes		Ears		Teeth
	Mesmerizing, multi-hued, primarily gold, slanted, almond, slanted sleek eyebrows		Small, delicate, pointed		Perfect, white
(Queen) Lady Clarisse Feuille Plume of Village De L'arbre DOB 3834	Personality				
	Rationality	Mannerism	Self-esteem	Philosophy	Demeanor
	0 Normal	+ Perceptive + Curious + Inquisitive - Precise + Somber + Relaxed + Studious	- Haughty 0 Proper - Proud + Modest	- Hedonistic 0 Optimist + Extroverted + Benevolent	

A Runt's Tale, In the Beginning…

Intellect	+ Flighty, + Active, + Brilliant
Bravery	+ Calculating, + Courageous
Morals	- Amoral, + Lusty, + Aesthetic
Piety	+ Reverent
Motivation	+ Motivated, + Energetic

Relationships

Manner	+ Sensitive, + Compassionate, + Courteous, + Diplomatic / - Vengeful, 0 Capricious, 0 Mischievous, + Well-Spoken, + Forceful
Mood / Disposition	+ Easygoing, + Pleasant, + Soft-Hearted, + Forgiving / - Hot-Tempered, - Moody, 0 Aloof, + Reserved
Honesty	+ Truthful, + Honorable
Length	+ Extremely Long

Interests

Hobbies	
Loves	
Fears	
Hates	

Legends, Nature, Politics, Religion, Wine & Spirits

History, Horticulture, Hunting, Husbandry

Athletics, Dancing, Exotic animals, Foods & Preparation, Handicrafts

Ornaments & Jewelry, Porcelain, China, & Crystal, Shields & Weapons, Swords, Trophies & Skins

Armour, Artwork, Books & Scrolls, Coins & Tokens, Knives & Daggers, Minerals & Gems

Torture, Traps, Undead, Wizards

Illness, Pain, Sight of own blood

Being Bound, Caves, Dying, Enclosed Spaces

Rival Clan, Stupidity

Braggarts, Bullies

Bad Food

Appearance		
General	**Personal Habits**	**State of Clothing**
+ Dignified + Imposing + Stately	+ Organized + Immaculate	+ Pristine + Immaculate

		Possessions
Thrift	**Quantity**	**Quality**
+ Charitable	+ Exceptional	0 Functional + Practical + Durable + Kingly

Madeleine's Mother. Scram's Adoptive Mother. Handfasted to Cranndair and Trent. Queen of the Forest Elves of Village De L'Arbre.

Nobody knows why she is hanging out with a bunch of mixed-breeds, but she sure livens things up. It's funny to watch the effects of the 'Elven Stun' on the poor Humans due to her unoerthly beauty. I wonder who's running the show back in her realm with her gone?

Member of L.A.F. (League of Adventuring Fellows).

Name	Deity		Alignment		Build	
Sergeant Brud 'the Strong' Tarkin of Waterport *DOB 4986*	**Trickster**, God of Crafts		Good	Neutral	Mesomorph	
	Gender	Race		Height	Weight	
	Male	¾ Human, ¼ Orc		6'8"	350# / 24 st, 2 lb	
	Class					
	Mugger/ Thug/ Smuggler Rogue, Brawler Fighter					
	Specialty					
	Dockworker, Warehouseman, Carpenter, Constabulary					
	Hair		Beard		Skin	
	thick, short, raggedly cut dishwater colored		Scraggly dark brown, short		thick, coarse, and ruddy, wiry body hair	
	Eyes		Ears		Teeth	
	pigglsh, close-set, mud brown, beetled brows		Slightly pointed, large, sticks out from the head		large, gapped, and crooked	
	Personality					
	Rationality	Mannerism	Self-esteem	Philosophy	Demeanor	
	+ Stable	0 Cautious + Relaxed + Perceptive + Curious	+ Humble	0 Optimist + Extroverted + Benevolent	No Worries Extrovert Positive Happy	
	Intellect	Bravery	Morals	Piety	Motivation	

265

Relationships		
Manner	+ Ponderous, + Active, + Courageous	0 Mischievous, + Trusting, + Helpful, + Kindly, + Compassionate
Mood / Disposition	0 Normal	+ Pleasant, + Soft-Hearted, + Forgiving, + Cheerful, + Reserved, + Even-Tempered, + Easygoing, + Peaceful
Honesty	0 Average	+ Truthful
Length	0 Normal	+ Long, + Very Stable

Interests	
Hobbies	Altruism, Athletics, Community Service, Fishing
Loves	Coins & Tokens
Fears	Illness, Loneliness, Poison, Sharks, Torture, Undead
Hates	Bullies

Appearance

General	Personal Habits	State of Clothing
- Slob - Spartan 0 Typical	- Sloppy - Disheveled 0 Nonchalant	- Unkempt 0 Rough + Clean
Possessions		
Thrift	Quantity	Quality
+ Thrifty 0 Average + Generous	- Few	0 Functional + Practical + Durable

Scram's adoptive Father. One of Scram's Teachers in the Thieves Guild.

A Waterport local. His Father was a Blacksmith, his Mother a Sail Mender, and he had been a Dockworker prior to being hired by the Thieves Guild to transport heavy objects.

He is the boss of the security detail for Scram's businesses.

He is a 'Holy Knight' of Trickster. He is not aware of this.

He is one of a very few 'Truly Good' people in the world. He looks like a big, scary, evil type Humanoid, but has the kindest heart of anyone around. He cries when he has to hurt anything or anyone in the pursuit of his duties.

Evil things better beware. He has been known to literally dismember them with his bare hands. Very gory, but fun to watch.

He is only avaerage IQ, but his EQ is off the scale.

Member of the City Guard and Constabulary, Member of W.I.S. (Waterport Investigation Services). Member of L.A.F. (League of Adventuring Fellows).

Name	Deity		Alignment		Build
Head Chef / Master Chef Annie Really Of Waterport **DOB 4984**	Goddess of Health, God of Crafts		Good	Neutral	Meso- Ectomorph

Gender	Race	Height	Weight
Female	Human	5'10"	180# / 12 st, 12 lb

Class
Fighter (oak rolling pin & iron skillit)

Specialty
Chef, Homemaker

Hair	Beard	Skin
Dishwater blonde, straight, coarse	Light mustache and a few chin hairs	Very ruddy, pale, reddened and rough from working in the kitchen, heavy peach fuzz

Eyes	Ears	Teeth
Dark hazel	Thick, rounded	Large, yellowed, somewhat even

Personality				
Rationality	Mannerism	Self-esteem	Philosophy	Demeanor
0 Normal + Stable	- Exacting - Precise + Relaxed + Perceptive	- Proud 0 Proper + Modest	0 Optimist + Extroverted + Altruist	
Intellect	Bravery	Morals	Piety	Motivation

268

Relationships		
Manner	+ Trusting, + Helpful, + Kindly	- Opinionated, + Forceful, + Sensitive
	0 Average, + Active	0 Normal, + Courageous
Mood / Disposition	+ Pleasant, + Soft-Hearted, + Forgiving, + Cheerful	+ Reserved, + Even-Tempered, + Easygoing, + Peaceful
	0 Normal, + Lusty, + Aesthetic, + Virtuous	
Honesty		0 Average, + Truthful
	+ Reverent	
Length		+ Long, + Very Stable
	+ Motivated, + Energetic	

Interests			
Hobbies	Loves	Fears	Hates

	Horticulture / Husbandry / Legends / Wine & Spirits	Porcelain, China, & Crystal	Torture / Undead / Wizards	Greed / Selfishness / Wizards
	Altruism / Community Service / Fishing / Foods & Preparation / Handicrafts		Illness / Poison / Sharks	Bad Food / Braggarts / Bullies

Appearance		
General	Personal Habits	State of Clothing
- Spartan + Imposing	+ Organized + Prim & Proper	0 Rough + Clean + Pristine

Possessions		
Thrift	Quantity	Quality
+ Thrifty + Charitable + Generous	0 Average	0 Functional + Practical + Durable

Brud's Mate, so, Scram's adoptive Mom.

A truly sweet and caring person. She 'Mama's everybody. Protects people. Loves to give hugs.

She was the first woman to be able to see through Brud's scary exterior and to conquer his shyness.

Member of L.A.F. (League of Adventuring Fellows).

Name	Deity	Alignment		Build	
Sergeant Bersvend 'Bear' Dagvaldsson-Thorsson of Stavsund DOB 4992	Odin, **Thor**, Tyr	Good	Neutral	Mesomorph	
	Gender	**Race**	**Height**	**Weight**	
	Male	Norseman Human	7'2'	460 # / 32 st, 12 lb	
	Class				
	Archer Ranger, Berserker Fighter, Priest of Thor				
	Specialty				
	Musician - war drums, weaponsmith				
	Hair	**Beard**		**Skin**	
	Platinum blonde, long, braids, wavy	Short, slightly darker blonde		Very fair (bright red when angry)	
	Eyes	**Ears**		**Teeth**	
	Bright blue	Rounded		White, even	
	Personality				
	Rationality	**Mannerism**	**Self-esteem**	**Philosophy**	**Demeanor**
	- Slightly Insane + Stable	+ Relaxed + Perceptive	- Proud	0 Optimist + Extroverted + Benevolent	
	Intellect	**Bravery**	**Morals**	**Piety**	**Motivation**

Relationships

Manner	Mood / Disposition	Honesty	Length
+ Forceful, + Sensitive, + Helpful, + Kindly, + Courteous	+ Pleasant, + Soft-Hearted, + Forgiving		
- War-Like, - Barbaric, 0 Mischievous, + Well-Spoken	- Hot-Tempered, + Easygoing, + Peaceful	+ Truthful	+ Long
+ Active, + Courageous, + Fearless	0 Normal	+ Reverent	+ Motivated, + Energetic

Interests

Hobbies	Loves	Fears	Hates
Hunting, Legends, Religion, Wine & Spirits	Axes, Trophies & Skins	Spiders, Undead, Wizards	Greed, Thieves

Athletics Fishing Gambling Handicrafts	Armour Shields & Weapons	Illness Loneliness Poison Snakes	Braggarts Bullies

Appearance		
General	Personal Habits	State of Clothing
+ Imposing	0 Nonchalant + Organized	+ Clean

Possessions		
Thrift	Quantity	Quality
+ Generous	0 Average	0 Functional + Practical + Durable + High

Scam's cousin on his paternal grandmother's side of the family, strange how two such drastically sized and coloured people could be related. Beth's Mate.

Member of the City Guard Ranger Unit. Member of L.A.F. (League of Adventuring Fellows).

Name	Deity		Alignment		Build	
Bethilda 'Beth'Beckett of Fisherton DOB 4994	God of Crafts, Goddess of Luck, Goddesses of Music, Celebration, and Dance (the three Sisters of Entertainment)		Good	Neutral	Endo- Mesomorph	
	Gender	Race	Height		Weight	
	Female	Human	5'6"		165# / 11 st, 11 lb	
	Class					
	Fighter					
	Specialty					
	Waitress, Homemaker, Seamstress, Fisherperson					
	Hair		Beard		Skin	
	Light brown wavy long hair, usually in a net bag at the back of her neck or braided		none		Light tan	
	Eyes		Ears		Teeth	
	Dark blue		Small, rounded		Off-white, generally even	
	Personality					
	Rationality	Mannerism	Self-esteem		Philosophy	Demeanor
	+ Stable	+ Relaxed + Perceptive + Curious	0 Proper + Modest		0 Optimist + Extroverted	+ Benevolent

Intellect	Bravery	Morals	Piety	Motivation
0 Average + Flighty + Active	+ Courageous	+ Lusty	0 Average	+ Motivated + Energetic

Relationships

Manner		Mood / Disposition		Honesty	Length
+ Helpful + Kindly + Compassionate + Diplomatic	0 Mischievous + Well-Spoken + Sensitive + Trusting	+ Pleasant + Soft-Hearted + Forgiving + Cheerful	+ Silly + Even-Tempered + Easygoing + Peaceful	+ Truthful	+ Long +Stable

Interests

Hobbies	Loves	Fears	Hates

Community Service / Horticulture
Dancing / Husbandry
Fishing / Legends
Foods & Preparation / Politics
Handicrafts / Wine & Spirits

Artwork / Ornaments & Jewelry
Minerals & Gems / Porcelain, China, & Crystal

Being Bound / Sight of own blood
Dying / Snakes
Illness / Spiders
Insects / Torture
Pain / Undead
Sharks

Bullies / Selfishness
Greed / Thieves

Appearance		
General	Personal Habits	State of Clothing
0 Typical	0 Nonchalant + Organized + Prim & Proper	0 Rough + Clean

Possessions		
Thrift	Quantity	Quality
+ Thrifty + Charitable	0 Average	0 Functional + Practical + Durable

Bear's Mate.

Very voluptuous. Wide hips. Perfect blend of soft and smooth (no corded muscles or veins showing) and firmly muscular. Agile and graceful. Pretty and pleasant features. This is why she was such a popular waitress and why she attracts attention wherever she goes.

Member of L.A.F. (League of Adventuring Fellows).

Name	Deity		Alignment		Build	
Sergeant (Herr) Jagger Pfannkuchen of the Northern Forest Tribes DOB 4984	God of Crafts, Goddess of Luck, God of Strategy		Neutral	Lawful	Mesomorph	

Gender	Race		Height	Weight	
Male	Humkin Halfling		4'0"	55# / 3 st, 13 lb	

Class
Archer Ranger, Sneaky Fighter

Specialty
Weaponsmith, Chef, Cakemaker, Musician- Bodhran

Hair	Beard	Skin
straight blonde, flat-top style	None (shaven)	light

Eyes	Ears	Teeth
steel grey	Medium, rounded	Even, white

Personality					
Rationality	Mannerism		Self-esteem	Philosophy	Demeanor
	+ Somber + Studious + Perceptive				
+ Rock-like	- Fanatical - Exacting - Suspicious - Precise		- Proud 0 Proper	- Introverted 0 Optimist	Calm Neutral Serious
Intellect	Bravery		Morals	Piety	Motivation

Relationships

Manner	Mood / Disposition	Honesty	Length
+ Active	0 Normal	- Irreligious	- Driven
+ Calculating			
+ Courageous			
+ Well-Spoken	- Insensitive		
+ Forceful	0 Aloof		
+ Helpful	+ Reserved		
+ Courteous	+ Even-Tempered		
- War-Like	- Hard-Hearted		
- Violent	- Harsh		
- Vengeful	- Unforgiving		
- Opinionated	- Taciturn		
- Overbearing	- Unfeeling		

Interests

Hobbies	Loves	Fears	Hates
		+ Scrupulous	+ Long
			+ Stable

	History Hunting Smoking & Pipes Wine & Spirits	Shields & Weapons Swords Trophies & Skins	Traps Undead Wizards	Wizards
	Athletics Community Service Exotic animals Fishing Foods & Preparation	Armour Books & Scrolls Knives & Daggers	Torture	Rival Clan

Appearance		
General	Personal Habits	State of Clothing
- Spartan + Dignified + Imposing	+ Organized + Prim & Proper + Perfectionist + Immaculate	+ Clean + Pristine + Immaculate

Possessions		
Thrift	Quantity	Quality
- Ascetic + Thrifty	- Few	0 Functional + Practical + Durable + High

Entse's Mate. The most militaristic Halfling that Scram ever met.

Member of the Training Squad of the City Guard Ranger Unit.

Member of L.A.F. (League of Adventuring Fellows).

Name	Deity	Alignment		Build	
	Odin, Thor, Tyr, Goddesses of Music, Celebration, and Dance (the three Sisters of Entertainment)	Good	Neutral	Endo-Mesomorph	
	Gender	Race	Height	Weight	
	Female	Norse Human	5'6"	165# / 11 st, 11 lb	
	Class				
	Archer Ranger				
	Specialty				
	Farmer				
	Hair		Beard		Skin
	Dark blonde, long, wavy, braided		None		Fair
	Eyes		Ears		Teeth
	Blue		Rounded		Even, off-white
	Personality				
Corporal Emerentse 'Entse' Brynhildes-dotter of Ekridge DOB 4998	Rationality	Mannerism	Self-esteem	Philosophy	Demeanor
	0 Normal	+ Relaxed + Curious	+ Modest	0 Optimist + Extroverted	
	Intellect	Bravery	Morals	Piety	Motivation

Relationships

Manner	- Violent - Barbaric + Well-Spoken + Sensitive	+ Trusting + Helpful + Compassionate	0 Average + Flighty
Mood / Disposition	- Hot-Tempered + Easygoing + Pleasant	+ Soft-Hearted + Forgiving + Cheerful	+ Courageous
Honesty	+ Truthful		+ Lusty
Length	+ Long + Stable		0 Average
			+ Motivated + Energetic

Interests

Hobbies	Handicrafts Horticulture Husbandry Legends
Loves	Porcelain, China & Crystal Shields & Weapons Swords
Fears	Caves Enclosed Spaces Torture Undead
Hates	Greed Selfishness

Athletics Community Service Dancing Fishing Foods & Preparation	Armour Knives & Daggers Minerals & Gems Ornaments & Jewelry		Braggarts Bullies
Appearance			
General	Personal Habits	State of Clothing	
0 Typical	+ Organized + Prim & Proper	+ Clean	
Possessions			
Thrift	Quantity	Quality	
+ Thrifty + Generous	0 Average	0 Functional + Practical + Durable + High	

Jagger's Mate. Scam's cousin by adoption, Bear's adopted little sister.

Very voluptuous. Wide hips. Perfect blend of soft and smooth (no corded muscles or veins showing) and firmly muscular. Agile and graceful. Pretty and pleasant features. This is why she attracts attention wherever she goes.

Member of the Training Squad of the City Guard Ranger Unit. Member of L.A.F. (League of Adventuring Fellows).

Name	Deity	Alignment		Build
Lieutenant (Mr.) Mendel Padfoot of Thistledown DOB 4988	God of Crafts, Goddess of Luck, God of the Harvest, Goddesses of Music, Celebration, and Dance (the three Sisters of Entertainment)	Good	Chaotic	Endo- Mesomorph

Gender	Race	Height	Weight
Male	Humkin Halfling	2'6"	35# / 2 st, 7 lb

Class
Archer Ranger, Highwayman Rogue

Specialty
Farmer, Cook, Piemaker, Musician- Lute

Hair	Beard	Skin
curly mop, brown	Curly, light brown, short	Ruddy, moderately hairy

Eyes	Ears	Teeth
light brown, thick eyebrows	Medium, rounded	Somewhat even, off-white

Personality				
Rationality	Mannerism	Self-esteem	Philosophy	Demeanor
0 Normal	0 Cautious + Relaxed + Perceptive + Curious	+ Obsequious + Humble	-Introverted 0 Optimist +Benevolent	Calm Extrovert Positive Happy

Intellect	0 Average / + Active
Bravery	+ Courageous
Morals	0 Normal / + Aesthetic
Piety	0 Average
Motivation	0 Normal

Relationships

Manner	0 Mischievous / + Trusting / + Helpful / + Kindly / + Courteous
Mood / Disposition	+ Reserved / + Even-Tempered / + Easygoing / + Peaceful / + Pleasant / + Soft-Hearted / + Forgiving / + Cheerful
Honesty	+ Truthful
Length	+ Long / + Stable

Interests

Hobbies	
Loves	
Fears	
Hates	

Faeghan WhiteWolf

Hunting, Husbandry, Legends, Nature, Smoking & Pipes, Wine & Spirits	Minerals & Gems, Shields & Weapons, Swords, Trophies & Skins	Illness, Loneliness, Torture, Undead	Bullies
Community Service, Dancing, Fishing, Foods & Preparation, Gambling, Handicrafts, Horticulture	Armour, Artwork, Coins & Tokens, Knives & Daggers	Being Bound, Dying, Heights, Horses	Bad Food

Appearance		
General	Personal Habits	State of Clothing
0 Typical	0 Nonchalant + Organized	+ Clean

Possessions		
Thrift	Quantity	Quality
+ Thrifty 0 Average	0 Average	0 Functional + Practical + Durable + High

Member of the Training Squad of the City Guard Ranger Unit. Later, the leader of it.

Member of L.A.F. (League of Adventuring Fellows).

285

Name	Deity		Alignment		Build	
Master Farrlaighn MacDarach of Righ-na-coille Carraig (OakRock) DOB 4978	God of Crafts, God of War		Good	Neutral	Endo- Mesomorph	
	Gender	**Race**		**Height**	**Weight**	
	Male	¼ Mountain Dwarf, ½ Hill Dwarf, ¼ Human		5'1"	210# / 15 st, 0 lb	
	Class					
	Troubleshooter/Trapfinder/ Safecracker Rogue, Tank Fighter					
	Specialty					
	Locksmith, Goldsmith, Miner, Stonemason, Woodcarver					
	Hair		**Beard**		**Skin**	
	Black, long		Black, long, braided, full		Light tan, hairy	
	Eyes		**Ears**		**Teeth**	
	Bright blue, bushy eyebrows		Short, fat, rounded		Large, even, off-white	
	Personality					
	Rationality	**Mannerism**	**Self-esteem**	**Philosophy**		**Demeanor**
	+ Stable	+ Studious + Perceptive + Curious - Exacting - Precise + Relaxed	- Proud + Humble	0 Optimist + Extroverted + Benevolent		Worrier Extrovert Positive Serious

Intellect	Bravery	Morals	Piety	Motivation
+ Active	+ Calculating + Courageous	+ Virtuous	+ Reverent	+ Motivated

Relationships

Manner	Mood / Disposition	Honesty	Length
+ Forceful + Trusting + Helpful + Kindly	+ Pleasant + Soft-Hearted + Cheerful		
- Contrary - Barbaric 0 Mischievous + Well-Spoken	+ Reserved + Even-Tempered + Easygoing + Peaceful	0 Average	+ Long + Stable

Interests

Hobbies	Loves	Fears	Hates

Exotic animals	Legends	
Fishing	Politics	
Foods & Preparation	Religion	
Gambling	Smoking & Pipes	
Handicrafts	Wine & Spirits	
History		
Armour	Minerals & Gems	
Artwork	Ornaments & Jewelry	
Books & Scrolls	Shields & Weapons	
Coins & Tokens	Swords	
Knives & Daggers		
Cats	Sharks	
Dark Water	Undead	
Heights	Water	
Horses		
Bad Food	Rival Clan	
Bullies		

Appearance		
General	Personal Habits	State of Clothing
0 Typical	0 Nonchalant + Organized	0 Rough + Clean

Possessions		
Thrift	Quantity	Quality
+ Thrifty + Generous	+ Exceptional	0 Functional + Practical + Durable + High

Scram's Locksmith friend. Member of the Thieves Guild.
Lockpicking Trainer at the School Complex.

Member of W.I.S. (Waterport Investigation Services).
Member of L.A.F. (League of Adventuring Fellows).

Name	Deity	Alignment		Build
Sir Willem De Vie of Fewersham DOB 4985	**God of War**, God of Strategy, Goddess of Beauty	Good	Lawful	Ecto- Mesomorph

	Gender	Race	Height		Weight
	Male	Human (some Elf way back)	6'2"		175# / 12 st, 7 lb

Class
Noble Fighter, Holy Knight of the God of War

Specialty
Scribe, Poet, Aristocracy, Musician

Hair	Beard	Skin
Pitch Black, short to medium, wavy to curly, perfectly coifed with the signature forehead curl	None (shaven), chin dimple, chiseled jawline	Light, flawless

Eyes	Ears	Teeth
blue	Medium, rounded	Bright white

Personality					
Rationality	Mannerism	Self-esteem	Philosophy	Demeanor
0 Normal	+ Relaxed + Studious + Perceptive + Curious	- Proud 0 Proper + Modest	0 Optimist + Extroverted + Altruist	

Attribute	Value(s)
Intellect	0 Average / + Active
Bravery	+ Calculating / + Fearless
Morals	+ Aesthetic / + Virtuous
Piety	+ Pious
Motivation	+ Energetic

Relationships

Attribute	Value(s)
Manner	+ Helpful, + Kindly, + Compassionate, + Courteous, + Diplomatic / - War-Like, + Well-Spoken, + Forceful, + Sensitive, + Trusting
Mood / Disposition	+ Even-Tempered, + Pleasant, + Soft-Hearted, + Forgiving / + Reserved
Honesty	+ Scrupulous, + Honorable / 0 Average, + Truthful
Length	+ Moderately Long / + Moderately Stable

Interests

Attribute	Value(s)
Hobbies	
Loves	
Fears	
Hates	

Community Service, Foods & Preparation, Husbandry, Religion, Smoking & Pipes, Wine & Spirits	Minerals & Gems, Ornaments & Jewelry, Porcelain, China, & Crystal, Shields & Weapons, Trophies & Skins
		Heretics, Selfishness, Stupidity
Altruism, Athletics, Dancing, History, Hunting, Politics	Swords, Armour, Artwork, Books & Scrolls, Coins & Tokens, Knives & Daggers	None	Bad Food, Braggarts, Bullies, Greed

Appearance		
General	**Personal Habits**	**State of Clothing**
+ Dandyish + Foppish + Dignified + Imposing + Stately	+ Organized + Prim & Proper + Perfectionist + Immaculate	+ Clean + Pristine + Immaculate

Possessions		
Thrift	**Quantity**	**Quality**
+ Charitable + Generous	+ Abundant	0 Functional + Practical + Durable + Kingly

Scram's noble friend. 4th son of a noble...no inheritance.
Elven Family name, but so Human that he has no ability with
Natural Magick. A smidge of the Elven beauty is still there.

Member of L.A.F. (League of Adventuring Fellows).

Name	Deity	Alignment		Build
Captain Josh Silverflame of Waterport DOB 4989	Goddess of the Sea, Goddess of Luck, God of Crafts, God of Strategy, Trickster, Goddess of Beauty, Goddesses of Music, Celebration, and Dance (the three Sisters of Entertainment)	Good	Chaotic	Ecto- Mesomorph

Gender	Race	Height	Weight	
Male	Human	5'6"	120# / 8 st, 8 lb	

Class
Swashbuckler and Smuggler Rogue, Blade Bard, Acrobatic Fighter

Specialty
Fisherman, Pirate, Netmender

Hair	Beard	Skin
Dark brown, wavy, long, ponytail	Mustache & goatee (the rest shaven)	Tan, somewhat weathered, tattooed

Eyes	Ears	Teeth
brown	Rounded, lots of ear-rings	Even, off-white

Personality				
Rationality	Mannerism	Self-esteem	Philosophy	Demeanor

Intellect	+ Flighty, + Active	- Slightly Insane
Bravery	- Foolhardy, + Brave	- Careless, + Relaxed, + Perceptive, + Inquisitive
Morals	+ Lusty, + Aesthetic	- Haughty
Piety	- Irreverent, - Impious, - Iconoclastic	- Hedonistic, 0 Optimist, + Extroverted
Motivation	- Lackadaisical, + Motivated	No Worries, Positive, Extrovert, Happy

Relationships

Manner	- Vengeful, - Rude, - Opinionated, - Rash, 0 Capricious	0 Mischievous, 0 Practical Joker, 0 Prankster, + Well-Spoken, + Forceful, + Helpful
Mood / Disposition	- Hot-Tempered	- Moody, - Insensitive, + Easygoing, + Pleasant, + Cheerful
Honesty		0 Average
Length		- Short, - Unstable

Interests

293

Hobbies	Loves	Fears	Hates
Foods & Preparation Gambling Wine & Spirits	Ornaments & Jewelry Porcelain, China, & Crystal Swords	Sharks Torture	Rival Clan Wizards
Athletics Dancing Fishing	Artwork Coins & Tokens Knives & Daggers Minerals & Gems	Dark Water Dying Horses	Authority Guards Laws

Appearance		
General	Personal Habits	State of Clothing
+ Dandyish + Foppish	+ Organized + Immaculate	+ Clean + Immaculate

Possessions		
Thrift	Quantity	Quality
- Spendthrift - Wastrel	+ Abundant	- Garish + Durable + High

Scram's crazy friend. Sea Captain. Privateer in the Waterport Navy (basically a relatively nice version of a Pirate that works for a government).

Member of L.A.F. (League of Adventuring Fellows).

Name	Deity		Alignment		Build	
Sensei Nishimura (Nishimura-Sensei Yoshito) of Kepan [Master Ninja] DOB 4965	God of Death, the Elements, God of Time, God of Strategy, **Trickster**		Neutral	Neutral	Ecto- Mesomorph	
	Gender	Race	Height		Weight	
	Male	¾ Human, ¼ Water Elf	4'8"		75# / 5 st, 5 lb	
	Class					
	Ninja, Priest of Trickster / Elementalist Mage					
	Specialty					
	Scribe, Poet, Chef, Gardener					
	Hair		Beard		Skin	
	Black, short, bristly		Sparse mustache & goatee (no need to shave the rest)		Yellow-brown	
	Eyes		Ears		Teeth	
	Dark hazel		Small, rounded		Off-white, fairly even	
	Personality					
	Rationality	Mannerism	Self-esteem	Philosophy	Demeanor	
	+ Stable + Rock-like	+ Relaxed + Perceptive + Inquisitive - Suspicious - Precise 0 Cautious	+ Modest	- Introverted 0 Optimist + Benevolent	Extrovert Quiet Calm Neutral Positive	

Attribute	Values
Intellect	+ Active
Bravery	+ Calculating + Courageous
Morals	0 Normal + Lusty
Piety	- Irreverent - Iconoclastic - Irreligious
Motivation	0 Normal + Motivated

Relationships

Attribute	Values
Manner	0 Mischievous + Forceful + Kindly + Diplomatic
Mood / Disposition	- Unforgiving - Secretive + Reserved + Even-Tempered + Easygoing + Peaceful + Pleasant + Cheerful
Honesty	+ Truthful
Length	+ Fairly Long

Interests

Attribute	Values
Hobbies	
Loves	
Fears	
Hates	

History Horticulture Husbandry Legends Nature	Porcelain, China, & Crystal Swords		Greed Rival Clan
Athletics Exotic animals Fishing Foods & Preparation Gambling Handicrafts	Artwork Books & Scrolls Minerals & Gems	Jesters	Bad Food Braggarts Bullies

Appearance		
General	Personal Habits	State of Clothing
- Spartan	+ Organized + Perfectionist	+ Clean

Possessions		
Thrift	Quantity	Quality
- Ascetic + Thrifty	+ Exceptional	0 Functional + Practical + Durable + High

Scram's odd friend and Ninja Teacher. Very old, but unnaturaly young, for a Human. A bundle of secrets. Probably the deadliest person that Scram knows.

Member of L.A.F. (League of Adventuring Fellows).

Name	Deity		Alignment		Build	
Enigma (Emil Rathbone) DOB 4995	God of Strategy		Good	Neutral	Ectomorph	
	Gender	Race	Height	Weight		
	Male	Human	5'8"	120# / 8 st, 8 lb		
	Class					
	Riddlemaster Bard					
	Specialty					
	None					
	Hair		Beard		Skin	
	Light brown		Fastidiously trimmed, short		light	
	Eyes		Ears		Teeth	
	hazel		Medium, rounded		Fairly even, off-white	
	Personality					
	Rationality	Mannerism	Self-esteem	Philosophy	Demeanor	
	- Unstable	- Fanatical 0 Cautious + Inquisitive	- Arrogant	- Hedonistic + Extroverted	Neutral	
	Intellect	Bravery	Morals	Piety	Motivation	
	- Scheming + Brilliant	+ Calculating	- Amoral	- Irreligious	- Driven	
	Relationships					

Manner	Mood / Disposition	Honesty	Length
- Abrasive - Opinionated 0 Mischievous + Well-Spoken + Helpful	- Scheming - Secretive - Insensitive 0 Aloof + Even-Tempered	+ Truthful	-Short

Interests			
Hobbies	Loves	Fears	Hates
Nature Politics Religion Wine & Spirits Foods & Preparation Gambling History Legends	Minerals & Gems Ornaments & Jewelry Porcelain, China, & Crystal Artwork Books & Scrolls Coins & Tokens	Loneliness Pain Poison Sight of own blood Torture Undead Being Bound Body Fluids Dark Dead Things Illness Insects	Bullies Stupidity Bad Food Braggarts

Appearance		
General	Personal Habits	State of Clothing
+ Dandyish + Foppish + Dignified	+ Perfectionist + Immaculate	+ Pristine + Immaculate

Possessions		
Thrift	Quantity	Quality
- Miserly + Thrifty	+ Above Average	- Garish 0 Functional + High

Scram's crazy riddler friend.

Member of W.I.S. (Waterport Investigation Services).

Name	Deity	Alignment		Build
Drywd Pwyll Davyd O'Glen of Oakdell DOB 4975	**God of Nature**, the Elements, God of Crafts, Goddess of Health	Neutral	Neutral	Ectomorph

Gender	Race		Height	Weight
Male	½ Human, ½ Hill Elf		5'2"	65# / 4 st, 9 lb

Class
Peasant Druid, Elementalist Mage

Specialty
Grover, Barber, Weaver

Hair	Beard	Skin
Auburn, long, braided	Red, short	Freckled, pale

Eyes	Ears	Teeth
turquoise	Rounded, small	Off-white, fairly even

Personality					
Rationality	Mannerism	Self-esteem	Philosophy		Demeanor
	+ Relaxed + Perceptive + Curious				
+ Stable	- Suspicious 0 Cautious + Retiring + Somber	+ Humble	- Introverted 0 Optimist + Benevolent		Calm Introvert Quiet Serious Sad
Intellect	Bravery	Morals	Piety		Motivation

0 Average	+ Calculating / + Courageous	0 Normal	+ Reverent	0 Normal

Relationships			
Manner	Mood / Disposition	Honesty	Length
+ Sensitive + Helpful + Kindly + Diplomatic	+ Solitary + Reserved + Even-Tempered + Easygoing + Peaceful + Pleasant + Soft-Hearted + Cheerful	+ Truthful	+ Moderately Long

Interests			
Hobbies	Loves	Fears	Hates
Community Service Handicrafts History Horticulture Husbandry Nature Religion	Books & Scrolls	Crowds	Bullies Greed Big Cities

Appearance		
General	Personal Habits	State of Clothing
- Spartan	- Disheveled 0 Nonchalant + Organized	- Unkempt 0 Rough + Clean

Possessions		
Thrift	Quantity	Quality
- Ascetic	- Scant	-Low

+ Thrifty + Generous		0 Functional + Practical + Durable
Smash's adopted Father. Scram's Magick teacher. Member of L.A.F. (League of Adventuring Fellows).		

Name	Deity	Alignment	Build
Sir Smash of Oakdell DOB 4994	**Goddess of Nature**, God of War, God of Crafts	Good / Lawful	Mesomorph

Gender	Race	Height	Weight
Male	Ogre	8'6"	520# / 37 st, 4 lb

Class
Divinate Paladin. Holy Knight

Specialty
Herdsman, Wagoneer, Wainwright, Wheelwright

Hair	Beard	Skin
brown	None (shaven)	pale

Eyes	Ears	Teeth
Pale blue	Rounded, large, floppy	Large, with spaces, crooked

Personality					
Rationality	Mannerism	Self-esteem	Philosophy		Demeanor
+ Rock-like	- Fanatical + Relaxed + Curious	0 Proper + Modest	0 Optimist + Extroverted + Altruist		Calm Introvert Positive Quiet Serious
Intellect	Bravery	Morals	Piety	Motivation	
- Dull	+ Fearless	+ Aesthetic + Virtuous	- Zealot + Saintly	+ Motivated	

Relationships

Manner	Mood / Disposition	Honesty	Length
+ Kindly + Compassionate + Courteous	+ Pleasant + Soft-Hearted + Forgiving + Cheerful	+ Honorable	+ Stable
- Violent + Forceful + Trusting + Helpful	- Unforgiving + Reserved + Even-Tempered + Easygoing + Peaceful	+ Truthful + Scrupulous	+ Long

Interests

Hobbies	Loves	Fears	Hates
Horticulture Husbandry Nature Religion Altruism Athletics Community Service Handicrafts	Armour Shields & Weapons Swords	Crowds Jesters Loneliness	Bullies Greed Heretics

Appearance

General	Personal Habits	State of Clothing
0 Typical + Imposing	- Disheveled 0 Nonchalant	- Unkempt 0 Rough + Clean
Possessions		
Thrift	Quantity	Quality
+ Charitable + Generous	- Few	0 Functional + Practical + Durable + High

Scram's BIG friend. Born with Gigantism and Acromegaly which causes abnormal growth of long bones and all features and extremities. Pwyll's adopted son. Super nice, but really slow brained.

Member of L.A.F. (League of Adventuring Fellows)

Name	Deity	Alignment		Build
	God of Thieves, God of Strategy	Neutral	Neutral	Ecto- Mesomorph
	Gender	Race	Height	Weight
	Male	Human	6'4"	180# / 12 st, 12 lb
	Class			
	Burglar/Smuggler/ Safecracker Rogue			
	Specialty			
	Sculptor, Street Musician- Drums			
	Hair	Beard		Skin
	Kinky, black	None (sparse beard shaven)		Dark brown, nearly black, almost no body hair
	Eyes	Ears		Teeth
	bright, metallic gold	Rounded		Yellowish white
	Personality			

Name	Rationality	Mannerism	Self-esteem	Philosophy	Demeanor
Makebe of Zaire DOB 4982	+ Stable	- Exacting - Precise 0 Cautious + Relaxed + Perceptive	- Proud	+Extroverted	Calm Introvert Neutral Quiet Serious
	Intellect	Bravery	Morals	Piety	Motivation

Interests

Category	Entries	Rating
Hobbies	Handicrafts, Hunting, Legends	- Barbaric / + Helpful / + Courteous
Loves	Minerals & Gems, Ornaments & Jewelry, Swords, Trophies & Skins	- Hard-Hearted / - Scheming / - Callous / - Taciturn / - Unfeeling / 0 Aloof / + Reserved / + Even-Tempered / + Easygoing
Fears	Snakes, Undead, Wizards	0 Average
Hates	Laws, Rival Clan	+ Moderately Long

Relationships

Category	Rating
Manner	- Scheming / + Active
Mood / Disposition	+Calculating
	- Amoral / + Aesthetic
Honesty	- Irreligious
Length	0 Normal

Exotic animals Fishing Foods & Preparation Gambling	Artwork Coins & Tokens Knives & Daggers	Dark Water Poison Sharks	Authority Bad Food Guards

Appearance		
General	Personal Habits	State of Clothing
+ Dignified + Imposing + Stately	+ Organized + Perfectionist + Immaculate	+ Clean + Immaculate

Possessions		
Thrift	Quantity	Quality
+ Thrifty	0 Average	0 Functional + Practical + Durable + High

One of Scram's Teachers in the Thieves Guild. Part-time Teacher at the Rogue School in Burglary.

Primary Person at the Smuggling Operation, with help from Scram (operations interconnections), Brud (transport), Trent (the books), and Sarek (Dealing with the Bosses).

Name	Deity		Alignment		Build
Private (Mr.) Rudd Tinkerton of Tinkerton DOB 4990	God of Crafts, Goddess of Luck, God of the Harvest		Good	Chaotic	Ecto- Mesomorph

Gender	Race	Height	Weight
Male	Humkin Halfling	3'0"	25# / 1 st, 11 lb

Class
Archer Ranger, Trapfinder Rogue

Specialty
Gardener, Cook, Tinker, Musician- Fiddle

Hair	Beard	Skin
Wavy, nearly black, medium length	None (shaves the sparse mustache and goatee)	yellowish tinge

Eyes	Ears	Teeth
Almond, dark brown	Medium. rounded	Yellowish, somewhat uneven

Personality				
Rationality	Mannerism	Self-esteem	Philosophy	Demeanor
- Neurotic	- Suspicious 0 Cautious + Retiring + Somber	- Servile + Obsequious + Humble	- Pessimist - Introverted	Worrier Negative/Positive Sad
Intellect	Bravery	Morals	Piety	Motivation

Relationships

Category		Value
Manner	+ Sensitive, + Courteous	0 Average
Mood / Disposition	- Secretive, - Moody, - Taciturn, + Solitary, + Reserved	0 Normal
Honesty	0 Average	0 Normal
		- Martyr, - Irreligious
Length	+ Moderately Long	- Lackadaisical

Interests

Hobbies	Loves	Fears	Hates
Politics	Knives & Daggers	Dead Things	Spiders
	Ornaments & Jewelry	Heights	Torture
	Being Bound	Horses	Traps
	Body Fluids	Illness	Undead
	Cats	Insects	Wizards
	Dark Water	Jesters	
	Dying	Pain	
		Poison	
		Sight of own blood	
		Snakes	

Appearance

General	Personal Habits	State of Clothing

- Slob - Spartan	- Sloppy - Disheveled	- Unkempt

Possessions		
Thrift	Quantity	Quality
- Covetous + Thrifty	- Few	0 Functional + Practical + Durable + High

Member of the Training Squad of the City Guard Ranger Unit. Teacher at the Rogue School.

Scram transferred him to the City Guard because he was giving the Rangers and the Training Squad a bad name.

Name	Deity	Alignment		Build
Sarek *the Sly of Al-Andalus* DOB 4992	God of Death, God of Crafts, God of Strategy, God of Pain, Trickster	Evil	Lawful	Meso- Ectomorph

Gender	Race	Height	Weight	
Male	Human	4'10"	140# / 10 st, 0 lb	

Class
Cutpurse/ Pickpocket/ Smuggler Rogue, Assassin, Sneaky Fighter

Specialty
Cordwainer Rugcrafter, Dyer, Basketmaker

Hair	Beard	Skin
black ringlets, shoulder length	black shadow (no matter how often he shaves)	Swarthy, very hairy

Eyes	Ears	Teeth
long lashes, black	Large, rounded	White, fairly even

Personality					
Rationality	Mannerism	Self-esteem	Philosophy	Demeanor	
+ Stable	- Exacting - Suspicious - Precise 0 Cautious + Perceptive	- Egoist	- Malevolent - Hedonistic	Calm Neutral Negative Quiet Serious	
Intellect	Bravery	Morals	Piety	Motivation	

Relationships

Category	Traits	Summary
Manner	- Violent - Vengeful + Courteous	- Scheming + Active
Mood / Disposition	- Cruel - Hard-Hearted - Harsh - Scheming - Callous - Unforgiving - Secretive - Insensitive + Reserved + Even-Tempered	+ Calculating - Sadistic - Depraved - Amoral
Honesty	- Liar - Deceitful	- Profane - Irreverent - Irreligious
Length	+ Fairly Long	0 Normal

Interests

Hobbies	Hunting Legends Politics Wine & Spirits	Athletics Exotic animals Gambling Handicrafts
Loves	Minerals & Gems Ornaments & Jewelry Trophies & Skins	Armour Books & Scrolls Coins & Tokens Knives & Daggers
Fears	Fae Magick	Spiders Magickal Traps Wizards
Hates	Rival Clan Upper Class	Authority Guards Laws

Appearance

General	Personal Habits	State of Clothing
- Spartan + Imposing	+ Organized + Immaculate	+ Clean + Pristine

Possessions		
Thrift	Quantity	Quality
- Greedy - Miserly - Covetous + Thrifty	+ Above Average	0 Functional + Practical + Durable + High

One of Scram's Teachers in the Thieves Guild.

A frenemy that became an enemy when he made the mistake of assassinating a Mother and child which were friends of Scram. Scram ended him with prejudice.

Sensei used that as Scram's Mastery graduation excercize since he could not get Scram to to kill anybody without a very good reason. Assassinating a Master assassin was noteworthy.

Appendix C

Peoples and Creatures of the World

Name	Size Range		General Appearance	Age Range up to:	
	Males	Females		Males	Females
The Realm of Physical Laws					
The Humanoid Realm					
Humans	5'0" - 7'0"	4'6"-6'6"	Just Humans. The most diverse and populace creature on the planet.	110	120
Halflings	H. 2'3"-3'0" D. 2'0"-2'9"	2'0"-2'9" 1'9"-2'3"	Highly variable, 3 sub-races; Humkin, Dwarfkin, and Elfkin. Think short Humans for Humkin, short Humans with some Dwarf traits for Dwarfkin, and short Humans with some Elf traits for Elfkin. The latter 2 are crossbreeds. Elfkin live 200-300 Turns longer due to their Fae lineage. Can crossbreed with Humans. Tend to be farmers, craftsmen, or mischievous rogues.	110 +	120 +

	E. 2'6"-3'3"	2'3"-3'0"			
Dwarves	3'6"-4'6"	3'0"-4'0"	Highly variable, 8 sub-races; Mountain, Hill, Plain, Desert, Forest, jungle, Water, Ice. Coloration matches their climate. Think short, stocky, muscular Humans. Can crossbreed with Humans. All are craftsmen of some sort or merchants, even the warriors.	110	120
Orcs	3'0"-5'0"	2'6"-4'6"	Think Orang Pendek. A small jungle proto-human. Can crossbreed with Humans. Extremely strong and tough. Usually quiet and shy. The half-orcs are the most dangerous as they have all of the bad traits of Humans and are aggressive.	50	60
Trolls	6'0"-7'0"	5'6"-6'6"	Highly variable, 2 sub-races; Northern (light colored) and Southern (dark colored). Think tall Neanderthal Humans. Usually avoidant of a fight. Very tough and strong. Can crossbreed with Humans.	50	60
Ogres	8'0"-9'0"	7'0"-8'0"	Humans with Gigantism and Acromegaly which exaggerates height and features.	100	110

Giants	10'0"-12'0"	9'0"-11'0"	3 types; 1. Forest Giants, think Sasquatch, Skunk Ape, or Yeti– Gorilla-like vegetarian bipedal proto-humans in dark brown hair, probably evolved Gigantopithecus Blacki. 2. Scrub Giants, think Wendigo - Giant sized omnivorous bipedal Baboon-like proto-Humans. 3. Red Giants (like Humans, but harrier with red to brown hair). Tend to act like Humans and occasionally co-habit with them. The size and strength of all 3 make them incredibly dangerous if you somehow manage to corner one or make it angry.	80	90
			The Sea People Realm		
Merpeople	6'0"-8'0"	5'6"-7'6"	Think Humans that evolved back to the sea, the same way the whales did. Like a cross between a dolphin and a Human.	130	150
			The Avian Realm		

Birdpeople	5'0"-8'0"	4'6"-7'6"	Several varieties of highly evolved, sentient, tool using Raptors (think Bambiraptor, Velociraptor, etc.) with flatter faces, 3D vision, complex speech, more upright posture, dexterous hands, somewhat omnivorous appetites, bipedal people, though still basically a warm-blooded, mostly carnivorous, egg-laying, feathered dinosaur. In this area of the world, they evolved from the Maniraptorans Alvareszauridae Bradycneme, a version of Raptor that lived in Romania when it was an island. They never evolved vaned flight or display feathers, so are covered in a soft, furry, down-like coat of feathers which is usually brown with white spots with black edging in the females and a more red-brown colour in the males with the same markings. They have bright yellow eyes. They are about 6 – 7 feet long and weigh about 40 pounds. Their mindset, culture, mores, goals, etc. are completely alien to Humanoids. It is clear that they think of us as barely evolved, moronic apes. Their civilization has been around for at least 50 million Turns, far longer than even the Elves.	80	90

The Fae Realm

All Fae have Majickal abilities. Be very careful when dealing with them. They are fickle, unpredictable, mercurial, and perverse at best.

All Fae are randy, to say the least, and can crossbreed with anything. Be very careful around them.

They are extreme eco-warriors and infinitely viscious and inventive when roused. You do not want to experience their wrath.

It is extremely hard to quantify and qualify the members of the Fae Realm as they are all extremely Magickal and can alter reality at will.

Elves (Fae + Human)	4'0"-7'0"	3'6"-6'6"	Highly variable, 9 sub-races; Mountain, Hill, Plains, Desert, Forest, jungle, Water, Ice. Coloration matches their climate. The rarest are the High Elves. Think slender, graceful, beautiful hominids with large, slanted bright colored eyes, pointed ears, and no body hair.	700	800
Gen (Genie + Human)	Variable	Variable	Default appearance that shows their Elemental connection [Efreet (Fire), Djinn (Air), Marid (Water), Dao (Oerth), Jann (Mixed)], but can change appearance at will.	~900	~1000
Gnomes	5.5"-6.0"	5.0"-5.5"	Highly variable, 6 sub-races; Woodland, Dune, Garden, House, Farm, and Ice. All are generally nice, quiet, shy, and helpful except the Ice variety. Avoid them at all costs! All are craftsmen and farmers.	300	400
Leprechauns	1'0"-2'0"	9"-1'9"	Small, red haired, green eyed, hominids. Wears 3 cornered hats and fancy woodland colored clothing with lots of buckles. Very mischievous, hoards gold, Tends to be Cobblers.	200	300

Brownies	2'0"-2'6"	1'6"-2'0"	Appears as a miniature Human with brown skin and profuse hair. Wears brown clothing. Will 'adopt' a house, mill, farm, or other Human establishment and care for it at night. Expects a payment of cream and a cake smeared with honey each day. May change into its alter-ego, the troublesome Boggart when riled.	300	400
Faeries	3"-3'0"	3"-2'9"	Nature connected Fae usually only vaguely hominid in appearance with many cross-species appearing members, like, as one example, tiny Elven looking folks with dragonfly wings. Wildly variable in size, coloration, and form. Very prankish.	300	400
Pixies	3"-1'0"	3"-9"	Tiny, green, vaguely hominid in appearance with many cross-species appearing members, like, as one example, Urchins (a cross between a hedgehog and a Pixie). Occasionally helpful, but usually Tricksterish or Prankish in actions.	300	400
Sprites	6"-8'0"	6"-8'0"	Elementally connected Fae only vaguely hominid in appearance with many cross-species appearing members, such as Mermaids. Wildly variable in size, coloration, and form.	700	800
Nymphs	5'0"-7'0"	4'6"-6'6"	Several sub-races; Water (like Naiads), Land, and Plant (like Dryads). Elementally connected hominids that care for natural settings or objects. Usually appear as beautiful, young men and women. They do not appear to age and live as long as the thing or area that they are connected to lasts.	~900	~1000

Treemen	9'0"-12'0"	8'6"-11'6"	Tall, lanky, forest dwelling hominids which resemble the trees that they care for in their clothing and natural coloration. Tends to look like the trees in their vicinity.	700	800
Goblins	9"-1'0"	6"-9"	Small, swarthy, malicious hominids with too many sharp teeth. Tend to be thieves and mean tricksters.	70	80
Hobgoblins	3'0"-4'0"	2'6"-3'6"	A larger and more annoying version of Goblins.	90	100

The Animal Realm

All of the animals with which you are familiar on your world plus a few that have become extinct and are only remembered as legends or myths, like; Dragons [Eastern and Western, dinosaurs (that survived the near E.L.E. meteor strike) in the oceans, then evolved back to land dwelling forms with 6 appendages instead of 4], Unicorns (a large form of white mountain goat where the horns twisted around each other over millions of years until they appeared as one), most of the small land Dinosaurs and all of the water versions, the large (megafauna) mammals of the Ice Ages, etc.

Just as an odd aside, if you think that these beasts are fantasy, read your bible; Psalm 22:21 "Save me from the Lion's mouth: for thou hast heard me from the horns of the Unicorns" and Psalm 74:13 "Thou didst divide the sea by thy strength: thou brakest the heads of the Dragons in the waters".

The mammalian megafauna tend to love the very cold regions and generally stay up there, but they do occasionally wander down into our area, especially in winter. They include;

1. Woolly mammoth (Mammuthus primigenius)
2. Steppe Mammoth
3. Woolly rhinoceros (Coelodonta antiquitatis)
4. Irish Elk (Megaloceros giganteus)
5. Aurochs
6. Scimitar cat (Homotherium sp.)
7. Giant polar bear (Ursus maritimus tyrannus)
8. Cave lion (Panthera leo spelaea)
9. Cave bear (Ursus spelaeus)
10. Cave hyena (Crocuta crocuta spelaea)
11. Steppe Wisent (Bison priscus)
12. Elephants (Palaeoloxodon)
13. Straight-tusked Elephant
14. Elasmotherium (Elasmotherium sibiricum)
15. Merck's Rhinoceros (Stephanorhinus kirchbergensis)
16. Narrow-nosed Rhinoceros
17. Etruscan bear (Ursus etruscus), ancestor to both the cave bear and brown bear.

In this area of the world, the dwarf versions of many Dinosaurs, that evolved in Romania and other high spots when they were islands, survived;

1. A 'long neck'd quadrupedal Sauropod Dinosaur, the Romanian Magyarosaurus (20 feet long and 1 ¼ tons), known locally as the Knobby Longneck. Its dorsal surface is almost completely covered in 'dermal armour' plates. Other islands produced Europasaurus (20 feet long and over ½ ton), known locally as the Crested Longneck. Only the smallest of the Titanosaurs survived and have become fully furry feathered against the cold. These usually eat deciduous trees.
2. The dwarf 'duck billed' Hadrosaurid Telmatosaurus (about 10 to 15 feet long and 3 to 5 tons), also survived and continued to evolve into a fully furry feathered version. They are known locally as Cowbirds. These mostly dine on

coniferous trees. These alternate between quadrupedal and bipedal locomotion.

3. Another one was the Rhabdodontid Iguanodont Zalmoxes (¼ and 10 feet for Robustus to ½ ton and 15 feet long for Shqiperorum), a dwarf version of Tenontosaurus, 2 ton and 26 feet long. It is known locally as the Small and Large Deerbird. They eat all low growing trees, ferns, and bushes. They also have a full coat of furry feathers and sharp beaks to clip the branches. These alternate between quadrupedal and bipedal locomotion.

4. Another was the odd bipedal, omnivorous (insects and plants), beaked (with flattened, peg-like teeth) Theropod, Therizinosaurus Cheloniformis (23 feet long, 10 feet tall at the hips, about 3 tons). Its hands and feet were the oddest part. It walked on stout 4 toed feet with no large gripping claws. Its arms were really long and well developed (about 8 feet long without the claws) with 3 scary, 3 foot long, scythe-like claws on its hands. They are more brightly colored, probably as a warning to foolish predators and have well developed display feathers...crest, wings, and tail. It is known locally as the Slasher.

5. One dwarf version of a large bipedal Carnosaur has survived, the Euornithopod Nanuqsaurus, like a wooly feathered miniature T-Rex at 18 to 20 feet long, 6 to 7 feet at the back, and ¼ to ½ tons. This thing is really scary! It makes a Tiger look like a house cat. It is known locally as the Toothy.

6. The small quadrupedal Nodosaurid Struthiosaurus, 8 feet long is known locally as the Knobby. Its dorsal surface is almost completely covered in 'dermal armour' plates. It grazed on low growing plant life and evolved furry feathers.

7. The Pterosaur Hatzegopteryx (33 to 36 foot wingspan) is known locally as the Roc or Big Sky Dragon. When walking on all four limbs, it is about as big as a full grown Giraffe, but with an 8 foot long head and beak. Swallows its food whole and can quite easily accommodate a full grown Human. Swoops down and grabs its prey or walks amongst them casually plucking them up, flipping them in the air until they are headfirst, and then gulping them. Has evolved to be fully feathered.

8. The Pterosaur Azhdarchid Eurazhdarcho (9 foot wingspan) is known locally as the Sky Dragon. A junior version of the one above.
9. An ancient turtle, Kallokibotion.
10. The bipedal Maniraptorans Alvareszauridae Elopteryx, a small, fully feathered Raptor is known locally as the Packbird.
11. The bipedal Dromaeosaurid Balaur Bondoc (about 6 feet long and about 100 pounds) is known locally as the Bigbird. An extremely stout and slow, specialized Raptor with 2 grabbing claws instead of 1 and missing 1 finger. Fully feathered. Omnivorous, which was rare in non-avian Theropods. Semi-arboreal. More bird-like than the usual Raptor.

There are some cross-species types that defy logic and are the product of Fae Magick.

There are a few animals that seem to be only from this area. All are hardy and tend to be somewhat smaller than the usual sizes of their type, probably due to the often harsh weather with westerly gales blowing in from the sea. Some of these include;

1. Dwarf Mammoths,
2. Dwarf Elephant (4 types),
3. Dwarf Hippo (4 types),
4. Black Cattle (short and heavy, good milk and beef),
5. Herd Dog (short haired or long haired versions with short legs, large ears, barrel shaped bodies, good for herding and hunting.),
6. Stout Sheep (white and black versions),
7. Striped Sheep (dark brown with a white blaze and legs),
8. Mountain Goats,
9. Mountain Ponies (3 sizes, all small, the Dainty, Riding, and Work),
10. Giant Dormouse (2 types),
11. Giant Pika,
12. Puffins (a comically small sea bird).

13. Giant Swan,

There are also average sized common animals;

1. Salmon,
2. Trout (ocean, brackish, fresh),
3. Lamprey,
4. Houting,
5. Whales (various, including Grey Whale),
6. Dolphin,
7. Seal (6 varieties, Grey Seal most common),
8. Walrus,
9. Beaver,
10. Harvest mice,
11. Wood Mice,
12. Narrow-headed vole,
13. Root Vole,
14. Pika,
15. Arctic Lemming,
16. Steppe Lemming,
17. Red Squirrel,
18. Mountain Hare,
19. Rabbit,
20. Hedgehog,
21. Stoat,
22. Pine Marten,
23. Lesser Weasel,
24. Polecat,
25. Badger,
26. Wolverine,
27. Otter,
28. Wildcat,
29. Eurasian Lynx,
30. Eurasian Brown Bear,
31. Red Fox,
32. Grey Wolf,
33. Bats,
34. Wild Boar,
35. Fallow Deer

36. Roe Deer,
37. Saiga Antelope,
38. Elk,
39. Tarpan (Wild Horse),
40. Wisent (Bison),
41. Great White Pelican,
42. Sparrow Hawk,
43. Barn Owl,
44. Great Auk,
45. Adder,
46. Grass Snake,
47. European Pond Terrapin,
48. Agile Frog,
49. Moor Frog,

The Realm of Metaphysical Laws

The Spirit World

Generally divided into Light (Positive), Grey (Neutral), and Dark (Negative) entities. An infinite area that coexists in the same space as the Physical Realm, though at a different vibrational level. Metaphysical (AKA Majickal) Laws apply here. All Majick and Majickal abilities that exist in the Physical Realm originates from here.

Ghosts	These are simply the Spirits (AKA Souls) of various things that have died and become stuck, attached to a person, place, or object, for various reasons instead of going on to the Spirit World. They obviously come in a wide variety of appearances and personalities.
Spirits	Entities of the Spirit Realm. They usually have a default appearance, usually the appearance from their first life housed in a physical body, but can change their appearance at will to anything that they can imagine.
Nature Spirits	Usually smallish sized Elemental Spirits of Fire, Earth, Air, and Water. Usually nice, but varies per individual and can be Tricksterish. Trickster Spirits are Neutral. Usually live in natural settings, but many have adapted to live with Humans and other races.

Genies	Larger, more powerful and sentient Elemental Spirits with variable appearances, goals, and motivations. Usually stay in remote areas close to their element.
Tar Babies	Generally malicious Trickster Spirits that delight in 'inhabiting' sentient creatures and causing them to act in an abnormally mean, strange, or bizarre manner. Outside of a body, they appear to be child sized, charcoal grey, blob-like humanoids. Almost always stay near sentient beings.
The Mal	Larger, more powerful and sentient Negative Entities. Very dangerous.

The Deities

Many and varied. Clumped into pantheons for each group of people. Often, the same Spirits wear many hats by showing up to different peoples as a differently appearing Deity in their particular pantheon (for instance, on Earth, the same Deity is Ashira to the Hebrew Tribes, Isis to the Egyptians, Athena to the Greeks, and Brighid to the Celts. The same situation holds true for the mythical world described in this book.) They're portfolios include; Life, Death, Luck, Thieves, War, Peace, Justice, Strategy, Trade, Beauty, Nature, Storms, Healing, Harvest, Crafts, Communication, Music, Art, Time, Travel, the Sea, Destruction, Pestilence, Pain, the Elements (Earth, Air, Fire, Water, Wood, Metal) and the blended Elements (Dust, Mud, Magma, Smoke, Steam, Electricity, Light, Mist, Rust). The most powerful of all is the Trickster, the God of change, learning, and growth.

Author's Note

In the world in which we reside, Earth, it is sad, but true that most of the creatures listed above have become extinct. The percentage of the population that comprises Little People is very small, and they are blended into the overall population without communities of their own. Some of the Neanderthal race were genocidally killed off and the rest has been absorbed into the European human (Cro-Magnon) gene pool (They recently proved that genetically, which is why Europeans look so different than the other peoples of Earth, with lighter skin, light eyes, and lots of body hair. The middle-easterners and the people that migrated to become the (Southern) Indians and Australian Aborigines did the same for the darker Southern variety of Neanderthals.). The few remaining proto-humans around the planet stay in hiding, but their safe areas are getting smaller every day as we humans breed rapidly to fill every square inch of the planet. The Sea People may or may not still survive. Only the tiniest and most camouflaged Fae still survive. Only a few dinosaurs still survive, and those only in the large bodies of water. If the extinctions keep up this way, the common animals with which we co-exist will slip into the mists of Myth and Legend. A thousand years from now, our descendants will debate whether the most improbable of creatures, the mythical Elephant, ever existed or not. At least the Spirit World continues to function well. We have not yet figured out how to muck that up.

Appendix D

General Note

While this book is written with a particular period of Earth history in mind, the Medieval period or late Middle Ages (Rising Ages) to early Renaissance (Age of Renewal), but since there never was a Dark Ages on Oerth, the level of technology there more closely resembles a span of the 1400's to 1700's on Earth. Waterport is similar in some ways to a particular city, London, it is an alternate universe, so a lot of the things that occurred in Earth history did not occur in Oerth history.

Monotheistic religions never existed here. Akhenaten (Amenhotep IV) never became Pharaoh (when he 'removed' the current Egyptian religion and built his own, with himself as the only deity...the first monotheistic middle eastern religion), Yaweh never presented himself to the Hebrew Tribes, so they remain polytheistic with approximately 15 Deities and Subdeities, and extrapolating from that, the 2 offshoots of monotheistic Judaism, Islam and Christianity, did not occur. The Hebrew Tribes remain wandering desert nomadic herdsmen. Therefore, there was no Christianization of Rome (and subsequently, the rest of the world), Dark Ages, crusades, inquisition, Black Plague, genocide of Native Americans and Jews, or any other historical event that stems from these monotheistic religions.

Incidentally, the Roman Empire, Alexander the Great, Mongol invasions, and a few other world changing events was not as successful. The Fae still exist in large numbers, so 'Magick' (metaphysical laws) are still powerful. The world's tectonic plates did not move exactly the same way as it did for the Earth. The meteor did not strike the Oerth ~65 million Turns (years) ago in the last massive ELE (Extinction Level Event). Other events wiped out the larger dinosaurs ushering in the era of mammals, such as an era of increased volcanic activity worldwide that spewed millions of metric tons of ash into the atmosphere and ushered in a period of fluctuating ice ages and mini-hothouse cycles. (see below) The warm-blooded feathered land dinosaurs and all of the sea creatures survived and continued to evolve. Due to the intervention of the Fae, Humanoids have not caused the extinction of any creature group, so all of the fauna that existed from the early Cenozoic Era are still alive somewhere on Oerth. The collision that created our original moon occurred a slight bit differently resulting in a smaller degree of tilt in the

Oerth's axis and a more circular, less elliptical orbit around the Sun. This causes the Polar Regions to be colder and the rest of Oerth to have a more moderate climate. As a result, there are less extreme 'seasons' and climate more depends on your location on the globe in relation to the equator and poles, though weather patterns and ocean currents do tend to mix things up a bit. More fresh water is bound as polar ice and sea levels are much lower. The Mediterranean never flooded and the Black Sea is much smaller and land-bound. Most of this area is called Osiria and contains the most advanced civilization in the world with over 200 large and thriving cities. Those cities exist in that location on Earth, but they are underwater. What is the Nile River on Earth is known as the River Styx on Oerth and flows through the middle of the Osirian Valley and out to the ocean.

An excerpt from book 3 on geography might give you a clue as to how different Oerth is from Earth,

---

The Rom in our area of the world, called the Kale, had migrated here from the Iberian highlands and still had that flavour to their music and dance. One of their most showy forms of dance was called Flamenco.

Before that, their branch had been South of the river Styx in southern Osiria and the uplands of Northern Afuraka, and before that in Persia to the East. They were somewhat different from the Romanichal Rom that were in most of the rest of the large island of Albion, one of the islands of Britonia (the Land of the Britons).

Those had come from Gaul, where they were called Manush, and before that, from countries further East by way of the Northern Forest Tribal area (Franken, Friesia, Goten, Thoringer, Vandalia, Teutonia, and others) where they were called Sinti or Lalleri.

The other large island, part of Britonia, to the west of us was called Ierne (Land of the Eire) and had not yet been inhabited by the Rom.

The Anglelund and Saxony parts of Southern Albion were separated from Gaul, Franken, Friesia, and Jutelund by a shallow salt marsh, so Albion was only technically an island. There were several raised stone roadways, called Causeways, connecting Albion to the mainland. They had bridge sections to allow the flow of water and buoys on long chains attached on both sides of them to warn ships so sound the depth as they passed over during high tide. There were even higher way stations to rest at if you got caught by the rising tide.

A Runt's Tale, In the Beginning...

The areas of Albion North of the Angles and Saxons, the lands of the Picts and Scots, had an actual shallow sea between them and the homelands of the Danes and Norse.

On our side of Albion, we were barely disconnected from Ierne by a very shallow sea. At low tide, you could practically walk across it in a wide section to the North of our area. There were several raised stone causeways similar to the ones on the Eastern side which connected the Islands there.

Iberia and Gaul separated our 'island chain' from the amazingly advanced lands of Osiria, the center of civilization and learning. East and West Osiria were surrounded by many upland nations that were less advanced versions of themselves. Clockwise from Iberia to the West was Gaul, Illyria, and Byzantium to the North, Anatolia to the NorthEast, Phoenicia to the East, and Aegypt, Libya, Numidia, and Mauretania to the South. The River Styx flowed North through Aegypt out of the Afurakan highlands to turn West and split the valley nation of Osiria in half. I had been told that it was so big, that traveling on it by ship was like being on the ocean. Well, enough of geography.

The largest 'civilizations' consist of a groups similar to; generic European, Greek, Osirian, Chinese, Japanese, Aroi Sun Kingdom (the Pacific), Raman (India), Tiahuanacan (South America), Aztec, Mayan, Incan, Mound Builder, Persian, Sumerian, Babylonian, Phoenician, Uigerian (what is now the Gobi Desert), Nubian, and an Egyptian areas.

This world had its own large events, but generally is more stable and balanced politically than Earth, so their scale was much reduced. People are generally less war-like and more business-like. This was generally caused by the extremely powerful, though fickle, Fae guiding the more hot-headed, reactive, emotional, destructive, and warlike sentient groups towards 'cooperative equilibrium', instead of archism. This was done by various means of coercion from the most subtle and covert to the most blunt and overt. The fact that they have the 'biggest stick' tends to make their viewpoint the most 'right'.

The Fae have also accelerated the evolution of many other types towards sentience and civilization. These include; all Humanoids, apes, cetaceans, elephants, wolves, ravens, parrots, deinonychosaurian raptors, octopi, squid, etc. On Earth, there are at least 20 species that are 'self-aware' or on the brink of becoming so. On Oerth, there are at least 50 species that fit the criteria of having; brains, sociability, 'language' of some type, manipulative appendages, and an environment that allows the use of tools and possibly fire or Magick.

The largest difference to Earth dwellers remains that on Oerth, absolute equality is the rule. There is no bias, prejudice, discrimination, persecution, oppression, segregation, or even mean teasing based on the usual targets that are present on Earth, like race, religion, color, age, gender preference, gender or blend of genders, caste, disability, nationality, political beliefs, ethnicity, employment, culture, language, tribe, etc. This is so ingrained in all sentient beings since the Supertemporal Compact between the Sentient Races during the Great Conclave that if a person were to commit an act of this type in public, they would be mobbed and dragged to the nearest person of authority for punishment. Humanoids definitely prefer Humanoid punishment to Birdpeople, Fae, or Deific punishment.

Due to the lack of Christian, and more specifically puritanical and other narrowly strict belief structures, the world remains Tribal in nature and beliefs, what the Christians call 'Pagan'. The Golden Rule on Oerth is "An ye harm none, do as thou wilt."

There is no matrilineal or patrilineal viewpoint with the exception of names. Most Tribal groups still go with the traditional way of giving the child a single name and their last name being 'son of' their father's name for the boys and 'daughter of' their mother's name for the girls. Descriptive names of jobs have the neutral suffix of 'person'. Polygamy and polyamory in all their forms and possible combinations is the norm. Monogamy is very rare and generally thought to be somewhat strange. These differences will drive the bigots and descendants of the Puritans in America nuts, but since they need to evolve, that is a good thing.

People wear clothing, or a lack of it, to fit the current weather conditions, not because a religion says that they must remain covered. Sexual activities are considered natural and normal, not to be hidden or be ashamed of or flaunted. Therefore, there is no pornography, since nudity is not titillating. Prostitution does exist, but is considered a normal service industry; after all, not everyone is good at finding a willing partner. Gender preferences are also considered to be normal and people are not as polarized, being generally considered 'bisexual' in nature. Men, Women, and Transgender Males and Females are considered absolutely equal and part of the balance of Nature. Since monogamy is a rarity, all forms of temporary and permanent bonding occurs between any numbers of people. Every child knows who their

Mother is, but may not know which male in their Mothers life was their Father and in the case of fraternal multiple births, several different men might be the Fathers.

Since a lot of the religions and lifestyles of Oerth are 'Earth-based', 'nature oriented', or 'Buddhist-like', and all are pantheistic or polytheistic, people tend to be more peaceful and tend to think of war as a waste of resources, money, personpower, and time. That is not to say that it does not exist, for there will always be evil, powerful figures that seek destruction for a variety of reasons, usually the 'bad' ones, and lead others of like mind to do the same. Some groups are innately evil in nature and will always be a problem. So, in general, people are more like turtles...peaceful in nature until bothered and armored against the possibility.

As the peoples of Oerth have become more cosmopolitan and connected, Religions specific to particular groups have generally dropped out of fashion to be replaced by generic, worldwide versions that worship generic Deific versions of their progenitors, like the big 4; Creator, Trickster, Nature, and the Elements, and the junior Deities; Goddess of Nature, Goddess of Luck, God of Thieves, God of Crafts, God of Strategy, God of Trade, Goddess of Beauty, God of Communication, God of Death, God of Pain, God of War, God of the Harvest, Goddess of Health, Goddess of the Sea, God of Time, God of Magick, Goddesses of Music, Celebration, and Dance (the three Sisters of Entertainment), etc.

Waterport is generally fairly cool all year round due to its distance from the equator, an offshore warm ocean current (that keeps it from being constantly winter), and certain terrain features, so people tend to usually remain clothed. The temperature and rainfall range throughout the year is listed below. Winters are generally snowy, Springs and Falls are rainy, and Summers are sunny and cool. An ocean breeze from the Southwest exists year round. People go swimming in the Summer, but the sea temperatures range from 6 c / 43 f in the Winter to 20 c / 68 f in the Summer.

Waterport Weather Averages							
Moonth	Leaf	Cold	Snow	Frost	Slush	Thaw	Grow
Average Maximum Temp C (F)	9.3 (48.7)	7.4 (45.3)	6.5 (43.7)	6.6 (43.9)	8.6 (47.5)	11.0 (51.8)	14.5 (58.1)
Average Minimum Temp C (F)	3.7 (38.7)	2.2 (36.0)	1.3 (34.3)	1.1 (34.0)	2.4 (36.3)	3.4 (38.1)	6.0 (42.8)
Sunshine Houres	54.9	35.4	42.8	63.4	94.2	148.0	186.8
Rainfall mm (in)	156.6 (6.2)	173.1 (6.8)	158.4 (6.2)	113.8 (4.5)	118.5 (4.7)	85.7 (3.4)	80.6 (3.2)
Rainfall ≥ 1 mm Days	16.7	17.1	17.4	13.4	15.1	11.7	11.5
Waterport Weather Averages							
Moonth	Flow	Perf	Green	Gold	Fruit	Harv	Turn
Average Maximum Temp C (F)	16.8 (62.2)	19.1 (66.4)	18.8 (65.8)	16.2 (61.2)	12.8 (55.0)	11.0 (51.8)	12.3 (54.1
Average Minimum Temp C (F)	8.6 (47.5)	10.9 (51.6)	10.7 (51.3)	8.8 (47.8)	6.5 (43.7)	4.4 (39.1)	5.5 (41.9)
Sunshine Houres	167.0	181.8	168.7	125.8	90.4	72.6	1431.9
Rainfall mm (in)	86.0 (3.4)	78.3 (3.1)	105.8 (4.2)	123.8 (4.9)	152.9 (6.0)	154.7 (6.0)	1588.2 (62.4)
Rainfall ≥ 1 mm Days	11.4	10.3	12.2	13.0	15.8	16.0	181.5

Another major change is that, due to the Oerth equivalent of European Pagan, Asian, and Native American influence, people in the European-like areas bathe more frequently than on Earth and because of that change, people do not require perfumes as much to mask the rank body odor. Bath houses are popular and plentiful. One of the results of this change is that they live longer and are healthier than their Earth counterparts of the era. A healthier diet adds to this.

People in Waterport generally wash in cold water unless they are wealthy, then hot water would be provided for bathing purposes. Bathing is usually conducted in wooden barrels but simply designed bathrooms are part of Castle interiors for the wealthy nobles and lords. Before people enter the Great Hall for meals they wash their hands. As cleanliness and hygiene improved during the Rising Ages, lavers were introduced which were stone basins used for washing and provided at the entrances of castle dining halls.

During the Rising Ages people pay attention to dental hygiene. There is only one remedy for a bad tooth - it is pulled out without the use of any anesthetic or pain killer - the pain is excruciating. There are no false teeth, or dentures and women especially are very concerned about losing their teeth. Teeth are cleaned by rubbing them with a cloth or small brush. Mixtures of herbs, like mint, or abrasives, like baking soda, are also used including the ashes of burnt rosemary.

The practice of covering floors with rushes was a real threat to hygiene and health during the Rising Ages. A limited number of carpets and mats have been introduced to replace the floor rushes but floors strewn with straw or rushes are still favoured in the poorer areas. Sweet smelling herbs such as lavender, chamomile, rose petals, daisies and fennel are added to disguise the bad smells which were prevalent due to the inadequate plumbing systems and the rushes.

The great Scholar, Humanist and Reformer Erasmus (5226-5296) wrote to friend describing the state of the floors during the Rising Ages:

"The floors are, in general, laid with white clay, and are covered with rushes, occasionally renewed, but so imperfectly that the bottom layer is left undisturbed, sometimes for twenty years, harbouring expectoration, vomiting, the leakage of dogs and men, ale droppings, scraps of fish, and other abominations not fit to be mentioned. Whenever the weather changes a vapour is exhaled, which I consider very detrimental to health. I may add that the country is not only everywhere surrounded by sea, but is, in many places, swampy and marshy, intersected by salt rivers, to say nothing of salt provisions, in which the common people take so much delight I am confident the area would be much more salubrious if the use of rushes were abandoned, and if the rooms were built in such a way as to be exposed to the sky on two or three sides, and all the windows so built as to be opened or closed at once, and so completely closed as not to admit the foul air through chinks; for as it is beneficial to health to admit the air, so it is equally beneficial at times to exclude it".

In 5148 the governing body of the realm issued the following statute in an effort to clean up the country and improve Rising Ages Hygiene:

"Item, that so much dung and filth of the garbage and entrails be cast and put into ditches, rivers, and other waters... so that the air there is grown greatly corrupt and infected, and many maladies and other intolerable diseases do daily happen... it is accorded and assented, that the proclamation be made as well in the city of Waterport, as in other cities, boroughs, and towns through the realm, where it shall be needful that all they who do cast and lay all such annoyances, dung, garbages, entrails, and other ordure, in ditches, rivers, waters, and other places aforesaid, shall cause them utterly to be removed, avoided, and carried away, every one upon pain to lose and forfeit to our Lord the Mayor the sum of 20 pounds..."

The Small Spells

'Reparer' (Mend)/'Briser' (Break), 'Chauffer' (Heat)/'Refroidir' (Chill), 'Essuyer' (Dry)/'Tremper' (Wet), 'Durcir' (Harden)/'Ramollir' (Soften), 'Melanger' (Mix)/'Diviser' (Separate), 'Liquefier' (Liquefy)/'Solidifier' (Solidify), 'Cabosser' (Dent)/'Lisser' (Smooth), 'Nettoyer' (Clean)/'Souiller' (Dirty), 'Parfumer' (Freshen)/'Puer' (Stinky), 'S'Ouvrir' (Open)/'Fermer' (Close), 'Bloquer' (Lock)/'Degager' (Unlock), 'Supporter' (Stand)/'Tomber' (Fall), 'Charmant' (Glamour)/'Brut' (Decrepit), 'S'Etendre' (Expand)/'Comprimer' (Compress), 'Ranger' (Sort)/'Troubler' (Chaos), 'Absorber' (Absorb)/'Repousser' (Repel), 'Reduire' (Thin)/'Epaisser' (Thicken), 'Assimiler' (Sop)/'Deverser' (Spill), 'Pulveriser' Powder)/'Regrouper' (Cube), 'Saler' (Salt)/'Poivrer' (Pepper), 'Geler' (Freeze)/'Bouillir' (Boil), 'Organiser' (Order)/'Deranger' (Disorder), 'Envoyer' (Send)/'Recuperer' (Retrieve), 'Feuilleter' (Flip)/'S'Effondrer' (Flop), 'Sceller' (Seal)/'Desceller' (Unseal), and 'Vibrer' (Vibrate)/'Calmer' (Still).

Calendar

Planet Oerth, Rising Age 4826 - 5245
60 minutes in a houre, 28 Houres per Day, 7 Days per Sevenday, 4 Sevendays per Moonth, 28 Days per Moonth, 13 Moonths per Turn, plus 1 Turnover Day (365 days per Turn,)
The Moonths include: Leafall, Coldstart, Snowshell, Frostshine, Slushrime, Thawburst, Growapproach, Flowercascade, Perfumedelight, Greenswell, Goldengrain, Fruitaplenty, and Harvestgold

The Solstices and Equinoxes are at the same points in the Turn as in our year.

New Turns Eve and Turnover Day are roughly the equivalent to Earth's October 31st, the same as a lot of different Earth peoples Fall change of year. Oerth has 13 moon cycles, same as Earth.

Oerth Calendar								
Earth Gregorian Calendar								
Leafall								
1	2	3	4	5	6	7	8	9
November								
2	3	4	5	6	7	8	9	10
Leafall								
10	11	12	13	14	15	16	17	18
November								
11	12	13	14	15	16	17	18	19
19	20	21	22	23	24	25	26	27
20	21	22	23	24	25	26	27	28
	Coldstart							
28	1	2	3	4	5	6	7	8
	December							
29	30	1	2	3	4	5	6	7
Coldstart								
9	10	11	12	13	14	15	16	17
December								
8	9	10	11	12	13	14	15	16
Coldstart								
18	19	20	21	22	23	24	25	26
December								
17	18	19	20	21	22	23	24	25
Coldstart	Snowshell							
27	28	1	2	3	4	5	6	7
December						January		
26	27	28	29	30	31	1	2	3

Faeghan WhiteWolf

Snowshell								
8	9	10	11	12	13	14	15	16
January								
4	5	6	7	8	9	10	11	12
Snowshell								
17	18	19	20	21	22	23	24	25
January								
13	14	15	16	17	18	19	20	21
Snowshell			Frostshine					
26	27	28	1	2	3	4	5	6
January								
22	23	24	25	26	27	28	29	30
Frostshine								
7	8	9	10	11	12	13	14	15
February								
31	1	2	3	4	5	6	7	8
Frostshine								
16	17	18	19	20	21	22	23	24
February								
9	10	11	12	13	14	15	16	17
Frostshine				Slushrime				
25	26	27	28	1	2	3	4	5
February								
18	19	20	21	22	23	24	25	26
Slushrime								
6	7	8	9	10	11	12	13	14
February		March						
27	28	1	2	3	4	5	6	7
Slushrime								
15	16	17	18	19	20	21	22	23
March								
8	9	10	11	12	13	14	15	16
Slushrime					Thawburst			
24	25	26	27	28	1	2	3	4
March								
17	18	19	20	21	22	23	24	25

				Thawburst				
5	6	7	8	9	10	11	12	13

		March					April	
26	27	28	29	30	31	1	2	3

				Thawburst				
14	15	16	17	18	19	20	21	22

				April				
4	5	6	7	8	9	10	11	12

		Thawburst				Growapproach		
23	24	25	26	27	28	1	2	3

				April				
13	14	15	16	17	18	19	20	21

				Growapproach				
4	5	6	7	8	9	10	11	12

				April				
22	23	24	25	26	27	28	29	30

				Growapproach				
13	14	15	16	17	18	19	20	21

				May				
1	2	3	4	5	6	7	8	9

		Growapproach						
22	23	24	25	26	27	28	1	2

				May				
10	11	12	13	14	15	16	17	18

				Flowercascade				
3	4	5	6	7	8	9	10	11

				May				
19	20	21	22	23	24	25	26	27

				Flowercascade				
12	13	14	15	16	17	18	19	20

		May				June		
28	29	30	31	1	2	3	4	5

				Flowercascade				
21	22	23	24	25	26	27	28	1

				June				
6	7	8	9	10	11	12	13	14

Perfumedelight								
2	3	4	5	6	7	8	9	10
June								
15	16	17	18	19	20	21	22	23
Perfumedelight								
11	12	13	14	15	16	17	18	19
June							July	
24	25	26	27	28	29	30	1	2
Perfumedelight								
20	21	22	23	24	25	26	27	28
July								
3	4	5	6	7	8	9	10	11
Greenswell								
1	2	3	4	5	6	7	8	9
July								
12	13	14	15	16	17	18	19	20
Greenswell								
10	11	12	13	14	15	16	17	18
July								
21	22	23	24	25	26	27	28	29
Greenswell								
19	20	21	22	23	24	25	26	27
July		August						
30	31	1	2	3	4	5	6	7
	Goldengrain							
28	1	2	3	4	5	6	7	8
August								
8	9	10	11	12	13	14	15	16
Goldengrain								
9	10	11	12	13	14	15	16	17
August								
17	18	19	20	21	22	23	24	25
Goldengrain								
18	19	20	21	22	23	24	25	26
August						September		
26	27	28	29	30	31	1	2	3

		Fruitaplenty						
27	28	1	2	3	4	5	6	7
September								
4	5	6	7	8	9	10	11	12
Fruitaplenty								
8	9	10	11	12	13	14	15	16
September								
13	14	15	16	17	18	19	20	21
Fruitaplenty								
17	18	19	20	21	22	23	24	25
September								
22	23	24	25	26	27	28	29	30
Fruitaplenty			Harvestgold					
26	27	28	1	2	3	4	5	6
October								
1	2	3	4	5	6	7	8	9
Harvestgold								
7	8	9	10	11	12	13	14	15
October								
10	11	12	13	14	15	16	17	18
Harvestgold								
16	17	18	19	20	21	22	23	24
October								
19	20	21	22	23	24	25	26	27
Harvestgold				Turnover Day				
25	26	27	28					
				1	November			
28	29	30	31					

The meteor that caused the E.L.E. 65 million years ago on Earth missed. The Fae were the only sentient beings alive on the planet when this near cataclysm occurred. They probably thought that it was the end of the world as this spacial body slowly approached, looming larger each night. They might even have used their combined magicks to alter the potential disaster. A cloud of smaller pieces from the asteroid belt had been traveling along with the giant. They kept on going, pulled into the larger body's gravity well and pelted the Oerth with a less lethal barrage of projectiles, one of which made the crater that is now Waterport. The explosions from these impacts threw millions of metric tons of dust into the atmosphere and ushered in an era of increased volcanic activity worldwide that spewed more millions of metric tons of ash and hot house gasses into the atmosphere that altered the Oerth's then very stable and balmy hot-house event temperatures enough to immediately trigger a general cooling of the Oerth's average temperatures overall, that then progressed to the first of a series of ice ages alternating with mini hot-house events in a cycle of rapid, by geologic standards, changes in temperatures and weather patterns. The entirely warm-blooded, feathered dinosaurs survived along with the mammals, smaller reptiles, amphibians, insects, etc., but the larger land dwellers did not. Fur and feathers became an overnight positive survival trait. The water creatures were not as badly affected by the sudden change and survived quite well. These wild swings have slowly lessened over the intervening 65 million years, and now, generally tend to stay close to the midpoint with only slight differences over millennia.

Ancient Earth and Oerth both spun at 1000 mph and had a 25 hour day. Present day Oerth spins at 893 mph and has a 28 hour day, Present day Earth spins at 1042 mph and has a 24 hour day.

The Oerth's rate of spin was adversely affected by a near collision with another space body. The slower rotational speed caused a slight, but noticeable increase in gravity and a decrease in centrifugal force. This event happened at some point in the dim past, about 30 million years ago, and was caused by a near miss from a very large asteroid (of the size that could be labeled a planetoid), which had been knocked loose from the asteroid belt, thus slowing the planets speed of rotation as its velocity ground to a halt going the opposite direction from the direction of Oerth's spin until it came to a halt and reversed course to move in sync with the original moon. It was not going very fast when it got close to Oerth, so after getting trapped by the combined gravitational pull of the planet and its original moon, it ended up parked close to the original, thus becoming a second moon. It is smaller than the original, but closer, so they appear about the same size. Again, the Fae probably intervened to cause this, rather than face extinction. They probably helped park the thing in a stable orbit. Two moons make the tidal changes in sea level much more noticeable than on Earth.

In Earth's history, this planetoid missed us, during the opposite leg of its elliptical orbit that crosses the orbits of the planets, and sped up the rotation from 25 hours in a day to 24. The precursors of humans had already evolved at that time and were quite used to a 25 hour clock. Earth Human's internal clocks have been off ever since.

Tides on Oerth are therefore much higher than on Earth, reaching 70 feet in some areas. Waterport usually experiences minimum tides of at least 25 feet, so the seawall is very tall and the docks are hinged and float on double boat hulls (catamaran style). On Earth, the highest tides are experienced at the Bay of Fundy in Canada with the highest recorded at 53 feet. The tides on both versions of the planet are moved slightly ahead of the moons (1 or both) rotation. While the rotation of both versions of the planet speed up the rotation of the moon, thus causing them to slowly move away from Oerth/Earth, their gravitational effect also slows the planets rotational speed by about 4 hours per billion years. The distance from the Earth to its single moon is increasing by 1.5 inches per year. The effect of 2 moons on Oerth's rotational speed has slowed it faster than its twin.

Weights and Measures
Length, Width, & Height
- Line- a quarter of the length of a barleycorn
- Inch- 12 lines, the length of 3 barleycorn
- Span- width of the palm plus the length of the thumb, 6 inches
- Foot- the length of a large foot, 12 inches
- Cubit- length from finger tip to elbow, 18 inches
- Yard- 36 inches/2 cubits/3 feet/6 spans
- Fathom- widest length between fingertips of outstretched arms of a large man, 6 feet
- Rod- the combined lengths of the feet of 20 men, 16.5 feet
- Chain- 66 feet or 4 rods
- Furlong- length of a normal furrow in an ordinary field, 660 feet
- Mile- 8 furlongs/5280 feet
- League- distance a person walks in an hour, 3 miles

Weight
- Grain- 1 barleycorn
- Pound- 16 ounces, except for gold, silver, and precious stones which are 12 ounces
- Stone- 14 pounds

Volume
- Gallon- 27714 cubic inches, 4 quarts, 8 pints/cups, 32 gills
- Quart- fourth gallon, 2 pints

- Cup/Pint- 34.66 cubic inches, half quart/eighth gallon
- Gill- fourth pint/cup

Money
- 1 Noble or Sovereign [gold, smaller than a silver coin of the same weight due to the density difference] equals
  - 1 Pound [1 pound sterling silver (5400 grains/12.34 ounces)] equals
    - 4 Crowns [1 quarter pound sterling silver each (1350 grains/3.08 ounces)]
    - 8 Hacrowns [1 half crown/1 eighth pound sterling silver each (675 grains/1.54 ounces)]
    - 10 Florins [1 tenth pound sterling silver each (540 grains/1.23 ounces)]
    - 20 Shillings [sterling silver twelve pennies (270 grains/0.61 ounce)]
    - 40 Sixpence [sterling silver six pennies (135 grains/0.30 ounce)]
    - 80 Thrupence [sterling silver three pennies (67.5 grains/0.15 ounce)]
    - 120 Tupence [sterling silver two pennies (45 grains/0.10 ounce)]
    - 240 Pence [sterling silver, together weighed 1 pound sterling]
    - 480 Hapennies [sterling silver half pennies (11.25 grains/0.02 ounce)]
    - 960 Farthings [sterling silver quarter pennies (5.62 grains/0.01 ounce)]
    - 720 Copence [silver/copper]
  - 1 Shilling = 12 Pence
  - 1 Penny [1 pennyweight (22.5 grains/0.05 ounce) of sterling silver (92.5% silver, 7.5% copper), the standard upon which everything else is based] = 3 Copence [22.5 grains/0.05 ounce (33.3% silver, 66.6%copper), larger than a penny due to the density difference between silver and copper]

Appendix E

The History of Language on Oerth

It all originates with the first sentient beings on the planet, the Fae. They have been around for approximately four hundred and fifty million Turns. They came to this planet from somewhere else. They have been instrumental in the evolution of all species on the planet. When they first assisted in the evolution of humanoids from various ape stock, they were not aware of the future trouble that this would cause them. They only wanted to have some servants to assist them.

They speak a variety of languages specific to their particular type and a common tongue of their own. No known humanoid, other than Elves, has ever, to my knowledge, been able to learn any of their languages. They, on the other hand can speak ours, if they choose to do so.

When they created the first humanoids, the Forest and Ice Giants from a gigantic black ape and the Orcs from a human sized red haired ape, they did not even bother to enable them with functional speech mechanisms. They bred for a high Telepathy and Telempathy quotient and left it at that. When the Trolls, from a human sized black haired ape, and Red Giants, from a large red haired ape, evolved, either on their own or with assistance, they developed the ability to speak coherently and the first hominid languages were born. These were somewhat brutish and simple, but functioned. When Humans evolved from the same ape as the Trolls, but in a separate genetic line, speech had reached its current level.

The Fae are forever randy and tend to produce offspring with just about any creature. This is where all of the cross-species mixes came from. A lot of these are sterile mules, but if it happens often enough, fertile versions occur and when enough of them exist, a new species is created. When they mixed with Human's, they produced the Elves. The Elves are nearly as Majickal as the Fae and can actually understand their kin's languages. The Elves were the first Hominid civilization on Oerth and as the oldest, are a bit snobbish about it. The Humans were next to rise to that level. The other pre-curser species have yet to attain that vaunted position. Two offshoots from the Humans evolved, the Dwarves and the Halflings. These started as occasional growth mutations in Human children, but over time, as more of these anomalies occurred, they started their own colonies and began to breed true with all offspring being of their type. An occasional full-sized Human child is produced, but instead of thinking of themselves as Humans, they tend to think of themselves as giants among their kind.

Many languages developed in pocket communities around the world, but as the population increased, these began to have to deal with each other and so, a trade language developed. Over time, this language became known as the Common Tongue and at present, is spoken, at least to some extent, by almost every sentient being on the planet. It is a complete amalgam of all of its ancestor languages with no logical rules or structure and does not use phonetic spelling, which makes it awful to try to spell the words correctly. It has mutated over time into a separate language, but continues to absorb new words from every language that it encounters. Just trying to keep the dictionaries up to date is a full time job for some scribes. They generally apply 'the five Turn rule'...if a new word survives in the language for five Turns and becomes 'common' in usage, they add it officially to the lexicon.

Lord Reginald happens to speak True Common, courtesy of Trent's tutelage, along with various Common Tongues of the Waterport area, Highlander Dwarven, Woodland Elvish, and a far eastern language from the islands, called Daremo (the common speech of that area). He has also, in his long life, learned a smattering of many other languages with which he has come in contact, but remains fluent in only a few, as he converses with his friends, Sir Willem De Vie, Sir Smash of Oakdell, Farrlaighn MacDarach, Cranndair the Warden, Sensei Nishimura, and others in those languages. He also knows three Sign Languages; Thieve's, Merchant's, and Scout's, and can carry on two distinct conversations simultaneously in a spoken and sign language.

Languages of Oerth

All Human derivations communicate with extremely complex words, very complex gestures, and complex body language. All civilized beings speak the Common Tongue (think various forms of British English from around our world with Mid-western American, like the newscasters use, being the purist, unaccented form, called True Common).

Humans speak the language of their area of origin plus accented Common. Oerth Common is more similar to British English (as spoken and spelled in England, Scotland, Wales, Ireland, Canada, New Zealand, Australia, South Africa, etc.) than it is to American English.

Halflings speak whatever languages are spoken in their area plus True Common, though they have an ancient language of their own (that is similar to Irish Gaelic on Earth).

Dwarves speak one of two languages plus Common. The first appears to have derived from Highlander Tongue (think Gaelic, mostly Scottish version) and the second from the Northern Forest Tribal Tongues (think Germanic roots). These two groups tend to dislike one another and thus avoid each other, considering themselves to be two distinct Races. Other peoples tend to lump them together, which infuriates them and leads to incidents in which irate Dwarves loudly and publicly dress down the offending insensitive person (or beat them senseless). You can tell by their names and accents which group they belong to.

Orcs communicate with various sounds, some gestures, and body language. Half Orcs speak a rough form of Common.

Trolls speak their own language that consists of moderately complex words, complex gestures, and body language.

Red Giants speak their own language (think an ancient form of one of the 700+ Native American languages and dialects. I use Lakhota for any words written in their language.) and Common. Their voices are so deep that it is sometimes hard to hear them correctly (they laugh at Humans squeaky high voices).

Forest and Scrub Giants communicate with a fairly coarse language, complex gestures, and body language and can howl very loudly. Some of them can understand Common.

Mermen speak a language that is more akin to that of the toothed cetaceans than its Human roots. Some can speak Common.

Elves are the closest Fae to the Humanoid peoples. They speak their own language that appears to have been the precursor to the higher or more beautiful versions of Human languages (think the Romantic languages- French, Italian, Spanish, and Portuguese) and Common.

The other Fae have less direct contact with humanoids. They each speak their own language and a few can speak Common. Why would you be stupid enough to try to speak to a Fae anyway? They are just as likely to grant a wish as to curse you, change you into some other form, or just plain kill you. They might even eat you, afterwards.

Saying someone on Oerth has a Scottish (many types), British (hundreds of types), French (many types), German (many types),

Spanish (many types), or any other accent from some area on Earth is misleading at best and ludicrous at worst.

If I were to say truthfully that Madeleine/Chasseresse has a Forest Elven regional accent would not help the reader at all. They have no idea what that sounds like. To say that she has an odd combination of French and Spanish as an accent is true, but since those countries do not exist on Oerth... I can't even say that she has a Gaulish accent (the rough equivalent of the area occupied by France on Earth) because the Gaulic Tribes are Celts and speak a form of Gaelic. So, the accents are unavoidable. I use them only when necessary and generally stick to 'reporting' style, which is easier to read as it is written in unaccented True Common (American mid-western English with predominately British spellings).

Appendix F

Guilds

Each Guild, whose formal name is Livery Companies, has its own hall and their own Coat of Arms and Ceremonial Livery, but there is also The Guildhall where representatives of all the various city guilds meet together. [The word "guild" derives from the Saxon "gilden" meaning "to pay" and refers to the subscription paid to the Guilds by their members. Other words associated with the term guild include association, society, brotherhood, company, fellowship, fraternity and livery.]

Guilds in the City of Waterport (Medieval era equivalent) - Protection of Workers / Guild Members

The Guilds in Waterport protect the workers, or the guild members, as follows:

- Members of Guilds receive protection from excessive taxes imposed by the lords and land owners
- Competition between members is regulated by fixed pricing policies - advertising and price cutting is banned
- Illicit trading by non Merchant Guild members is banned
- All members of guilds are obligated to retain all trade secrets
- The number of Guild masters and members of guilds are restricted to ensure there is sufficient business for each of the guilds
- Sickness Protection
- Protection for their members, goods and horses when travelling
- Help with funeral expenses. Orphans of members of guilds are also cared for
- Guilds fund the first non-religious schools of the current era
- Working conditions and hours of work are regulated

Guilds in the city - Protection for Consumers

The Guilds of the city also protect the consumers. The spin-offs from the regulations of the guilds led to:

- Fair pricing policies - all prices are regulated by the guilds

- Quality of goods or workmanship. Goods and services are inspected and members of guilds are expected to undertake long apprenticeships

Guilds are also involved in civic duties. Guild members are expected to help to protect the city. These civic duties include providing a militia for the town, policing the streets and constructing public buildings and walls to defend the town or city. They are also expected to maintain high moral values in the guilds - usury and fraud is eliminated. Religion is an extremely important aspect of life during these times and guilds are expected to fund and to help in the construction of shrines, churches, and temples.

The Merchant Guilds of the Current Era

A Merchant Guild is an association of traders. The Merchant Guild is able to negotiate with the lord and, as a result, the trade levy stays regulated. The Merchant Guilds control the way in which trade is conducted in the city and applies equal and fair rules to all transactions. The members of the Merchant Guilds are very important members of the local community. The introduction of the Merchant guilds in a town or city leads to its own hierarchy and involvement in civic duties. Merchant guilds tend to be wealthier and of higher social status than craft guilds.

These rules were included in the charters of the Merchant Guilds:
- A ban on, or fines imposed, on any illicit trading by non Merchant Guild members
- Fines are imposed on any Merchant Guild members who violates the Merchant Guilds charter
- Members of the Merchant Guilds are protected and any Merchant Guild member who falls sick is cared for by the guild. Burials of guild members are arranged and the Merchant Guilds undertake to care for any orphans
- The members of Merchant Guilds also provide protection of their horses, wagons, and goods when moving about the land as travelling during the Middle Ages is dangerous

The Craft Guilds of the Current Era

The Merchant Guilds impose regulations on the individual traders or craftsmen to regulate prices and supply. The individual crafts and trades establish their own guilds.

These rules were included in the charters of the Craft Guilds:

- A ban on, or fines imposed, on any illicit trading by non Craft Guild members
- Fines are imposed on any Craft Guild members who violates the charter of their particular Craft Guild
- Members of the Craft Guilds are protected and any member who falls sick is cared for by the guild. Burials of guild members are arranged and the Craft Guilds undertake to care for any orphans
- The members of Craft Guilds also provide protection of their horses, wagons, and goods when moving about the land as travelling during the Middle Ages is dangerous

Commerce Guilds_____

- Mercers Guild (general merchants) [Head of the guild is the city Mayor and Chief Magistrate, leaders of the guild are the city Aldermen, other members of the guild are the city Burghers]
  - Grocers Association (food)
  - Street Merchants Association (anything in a cart or stand)
    - Fishmongers Society
  - Clothiers Association (Clothing)
    - Haberdasheries Association (Hats and Wigs)
  - Hardware Association (tools, fasteners, locks, wire, etc.)
  - Traders Association
- Bankers Guild (the head of this guild is the city Purser)
  - Accountants Guild
  - Transportation Association (money transport)
- Thieves Guild (grifters, forgers, counterfeiters, pickpockets, cutpurses, burglars, safecrackers, trapfinders, smugglers, thugs, muggers, highwaypersons, assassins, etc.)

Crafts Guilds_____

- ➢ Apprentice - A Craft Guild Apprentice was sent to work for a 'Master' during his early teens. The Craft Guild Apprenticeship lasted between 5 and 9 Turns depending on the trade. During this time the apprentice received no wages - just his board, lodging and training. An Apprentice was not allowed to marry until he reached the status of a Journeyman
- ➢ Journeyperson - A Craft Guild Journeyman was paid for his labour. During this time the Journeyperson would create his 'Masterpiece', in his own time, which he would present to the Craft Guild as evidence of his craftsmanship in the hope of being accepted as a Craft Guild 'Master'. It was difficult to reach the status of 'Master' and much depended on the Journeyperson's standing and acceptance by the top members of the Craft Guild
- ➢ Master - A Craft Guild Master could set up his own workshop and then train his own apprentices

- Leathercraftspersons Guild (anything made from leather)
  - o Cordwainers Association (fine leather products)
    - Parchmentiers Association
    - Papermakers Collective
  - o Tanners Association (Turns rawhide into leather)
    - Curriers Society (dressers of fine tanned leather)
  - o Skinners Association (skins the hides from the critters)
  - o Cobblers Association (makes shoes)
    - Pattenmakers Society (wooden clog-style footwear)
  - o Loriners Association (stirrups and other harness for horses)
  - o Saddlers Association
- Weavers Guild (all woven materials and fabrics)
  - o Spinners Association (thread and yarn)
  - o Woolpersons Society (winders and packers of wool)
- Seamstress and Tailors Guild (sews items)
  - o Hatmakers Guild

- - Wigcrafters Association
  - Dressmakers Association
  - Broderers Society (embroiderers)
  - Girdlers Society (girdles and belts)
  - Upholders Society (upholsterers)
  - Drapemakers Association (drapes and curtains)
  - Sail Crafters Association
- Rugcrafters Guild
- Dyers Association
- Basketmakers Society
- Glassblowers Guild (anything made from glass)
- Chandlers Guild (candlemakers)
  - Tallow Chandlers Association
    - Soapmakers Guild
  - Wax Chandlers association
- Jewelers College (jewelry makers)
  - Gemcutters association
- Potters Guild (pottery and ceramics, mostly cookware…china, etc.)
  - Plumbers Guild (ceramic water pipes and fittings)
- Smiths Guild
  - Blacksmiths Guild
    - Farriers Association (shoers of horses)
  - Armourers Association (steel armor)
  - Weaponsmiths Association (steel weapons)
    - Bowyers Society (longbows)
    - Fletchers Society (arrow makers)
  - Needlemakers Association
  - Brasiers Association (Brass items, musical instruments, etc.)
  - Tinsmiths Association (plates, cups, pots and pans)
    - Tinkers Guild (repair the above)
  - Silversmiths Association (silverware, jewelry, etc.)
  - Goldsmiths Association (jewelry, religious artifacts, etc.)
  - Locksmiths Association
  - Clocksmiths association
  - Lampsmiths Association (oil lamps)
  - Toolsmiths Association (all tools)
  - Cutlers Association (fine cutlery)

- o Fasteners Association (hinges, latches, nails, screws, brads, etc.)
  - o Type and Plate Makers Association
  - o Die and Casting Association (cast metal objects)
    - ▪ Mould Crafters Guild
- Masons Guild (stone and brick)
  - o Plaisterers Guild (plasterers)
  - o Whitewashers Association (painters)
- Carpenters Guild
  - o Cabinetmakers Collective
  - o Lumberwrights Association (lumber from trees)
  - o Shipwrights Association
  - o Barrelwrights Association
  - o Wainwrights Association (wagon makers)
    - ▪ Wheelwrights Association
- Roofers Guild (general roofing…lead sheets, etc.)
  - o Thatchers Association
  - o Shinglewrights Association

- Engineers College
  - o Mechanical Engineers Association
    - ▪ Siege Engineers Association
    - ▪ Vehicle Engineers Association
  - o Civil Engineers Association
    - ▪ Architectural Engineers association
    - ▪ Structural Engineers Association
    - ▪ Mining Engineers Association
  - o Alchemical Engineers Association
    - ▪ Materials Engineers association
  - o Systems Engineers Association
    - ▪ Agricultural Engineers Association
    - ▪ Applied Engineers association

<<<<<<<<<<<<<<<<<<<<<<<<<The Arts>>>>>>>>>>>>>>>>>>>>>>>>

The Majickal Arts_____

- Magicians Guild

News & Entertainment Guilds_____

Bards Guild (music and information)
- o Town Criers Association (news)
- o Thespians Society (actors)
- o Jongleurs Society (jugglers, acrobats, gymnasts)
    - ▪ Jesters & Fools Society
- Traveling Players Association
    - o Street Musicians Association (any street act)
- Gamblers society

Sustenance Guilds & Culinary Arts_____

- Butchers (beef, lamb, goat, deer, etc.)
- Poulters (birds)
- Bakers
    - o Breadmakers Association
    - o Pastry Chefs College
        - ▪ Cakemakers association
        - ▪ Piemakers Association
- Chefs College
- Brewers Society (ales, beers, mead, cider)
- Vintners Society (wines)
- Salters Society

Visual Arts Guilds_____

- Painters Guild
- Sculptors Guild
- Woodcarvers Guild
- Modelers Guild
- Printers Guild
    - o Typesetters Association
- Scribes Society (written works in general)
    - o Scriveners Society (writers of court letters and legal documents)
    - o Calligraphy Masters (fancy writing)

- - Illumination Masters (pictures added to written works)
  - Bookbinders Society
  - Limners Association
    - Cartographers Society

Health Colleges_____

- Healers College
  - Barbers College
  - Surgeons College
  - Dentists College
  - Apothecaries College

Workers Unions_____

- Labor Guilds
  - Dockworkers Union
  - Farmworkers Union
  - Street Sweepers Union
  - Chimney Sweepers Union
  - Warehousepersons Union
  - Wagoneers Union
    - Movers Union
    - Teamsters Union
    - Freighters Union
  - Building Maintenance Union
  - Cooks Union
  - Miners Union
  - Sailors Union
    - Navigators Union
- Produce Guilds
  - Farmers Association (all crops)
  - Herdsmen Association (cattle, sheep, goats, horses, mules, oxen, etc.)
    - Shearers Association (sheep, goats, llamas, etc.)
    - Groomers society (horses, dogs, etc.)
    - Animal Handlers Association (pack animals, beasts of burden, load hauling animals)

A Runt's Tale, In the Beginning...

- Animal Trainers association (dogs, horses, falcons, pigeons, elephants, ferrets, parrots, etc.)
- Poultry Association (fowl...chickens, ducks, geese, turkeys, dove, quail, guinea fowl, etc.)
- Grovers Association (orchards)
  - Foresters Association
- Fisherpersons Association (fish, shellfish, crustaceans, cephalopods, etc.)
- Hunters Society
  - Trappers Association
  - Furriers Society
- Gardeners Association (small plot farming)
  - Herbal association (seasonings and herbs)

Appendix G

Con Games Explained

Unlike most kinds of petty crime, a confidence game, or con, takes an enormous amount of skill and forethought to pull off. When done right, in many cases the grifters who perpetrate them have not actually done anything overtly illegal–they've simply used lies and manipulation to get their victim, or "mark," to willingly hand over their own money. Whether blackmail, fraud, or illegal gambling, the following are ten of the most famous ways that these swindlers try to take advantage of the confidence of their unsuspecting victims. Obviously, there are a number of takes on any kind of con, but these are the most popular variations of the most well known tricks.

❖Get Rich Quick Schemes

Salting

Salting or "salting the mine" are terms for a scam in which gemstones or gold ore are planted in a mine or on the landscape, duping the greedy mark into purchasing shares in a worthless or non-existent mining company. During gold rushes, scammers would load shotguns with gold dust and shoot into the sides of the mine to give the appearance of a rich ore, thus "salting the mine".

Advance-fee Fraud

Takes advantage of the victim's greed. The basic premise involves enlisting the mark to aid in retrieving some stolen money from its hiding place. The victim sometimes believes he can cheat the con artists out of their money, but anyone trying this has already fallen for the essential con by believing that the money is there to steal. Usually also contains an element of the romance scam.

Many con men employ extra tricks to keep the victim from going to the police. Many swindles involve a minor element of crime or some other misdeed. The mark is made to think that he will gain money by helping fraudsters get huge sums out of a country; hence a mark cannot go to the police without revealing that he planned to commit a crime himself.

The scam dates all the way back to the early 1900s, when it was often used against wealthy businessmen.

The Pyramid Scheme

There is no more potentially profitable con game than the Pyramid scheme. The trick dates back hundreds of years. The Pyramid scheme is a form of investment fraud in which a fake or corrupt stockbroker uses the money of his new investors to pay the imaginary reTurns of his old ones. Initial investments with the fake broker might yield enormous reTurns for the people being conned, but in reality their money has not been invested in anything—the con man has simply been putting it all into a bank account. Any time someone wants to withdraw money, or if he has to pay the reTurns of his old investors, the con man simply uses the money he's gotten from new investors to do it. Nothing is actually being invested, won, or lost in the market. The con man is simply giving that impression so that people keep handing over more and more cash. Because it can only grow so far, any Pyramid scheme is destined to eventually collapse under its own weight, so the con man usually pulls a disappearing act after collecting enough money, leaving the investors with nothing but the fake reTurns they received to keep them involved in the swindle.

❖Persuasion Tricks

Romance scam

The con actively cultivates a romantic relationship which often involves promises of marriage. However, after some time it becomes evident that this "sweetheart" is stuck in his or her home country or a third country, lacking the money to leave and thus unable to be united with the mark. The scam then becomes an advance-fee fraud. A wide variety of reasons can be offered for the trickster's lack of cash, he borrows the money from the victim through a local 'agent' (a second grafter). Of course, the con-person never makes the trip: the hapless victim ends up with a large debt and an aching heart.

Fortune-telling fraud

One traditional swindle involves fortune telling. In this scam, a fortune teller uses his or her cold reading skill to detect that a client is genuinely troubled rather than merely seeking entertainment; or is a gambler complaining of bad luck. The fortune teller informs the mark that he is the victim of a curse, and that for a fee a spell can be cast to remove the curse. In Romany, this trick is called bujo ("bag") after one traditional format: the mark is told that the curse is in his money; he brings money in a bag to have the spell cast over it, and leaves with a bag of worthless paper. Fear of this scam has been one justification for legislation that makes fortune telling a crime.

The Sick Person Hoax

A sick baby hoax is a confidence trick where a person claims that they have an ill child and are struggling to pay for its medical expenses. They ask people to make monetary donations directly.

Professional beggars have been exploiting sick children since ancient times. The success of such scams relies on a particular compassion in people towards children. When a child is sick, this particularly touches people's hearts.

A variation of this scam is the "sick parent" hoax, where an individual will enter a church, charity or other organization and claim they do not have the money for a bus ticket to see their sick or dying parent or to care for them. An often-flimsy story is usually accompanied by emotional language. They will then ask for cash, saying that such institutions have an obligation to help those in need.

❖Gold brick scams

Gold brick scams involve selling a tangible item for more than it is worth; named after selling the victim an allegedly golden ingot which Turns out to be gold-coated lead.

Pig-in-a-poke (Cat-in-a-bag)

One of the oldest cons in the book is the so-called "pig in a poke," which dates back to the Middle Ages. At the time, quality meat was scarce, and pigs and cows were often worth large sums of money. In this particular con, the trickster would offer to sell another person a baby (suckling) pig in a "poke" (bag). The bag ostensibly contains a live healthy little pig. After receiving the money they would hand over a "poke," or burlap sack, that clearly had a squirming live animal in it. If the victim neglected to check inside, they would be surprised when they arrived home to find that the sack contained a cat (not particularly prized as a source of meat) instead of a pig. The term "buying a pig in a poke" has since become a common expression meaning to make a risky purchase, and some say that the phrase "let the cat out of the bag" also dates back to this well known con. The person has bought something of less value than was assumed, and has learned first-hand the lesson caveat emptor. In Slovenia, Croatia, Serbia, Bosnia and Herzegovina, Montenegro, Poland, Denmark, France, Belgium, Lithuania, Latvia, the Netherlands, Norway, Israel, Germany, Russia and Ukraine, the "pig" in the phrase is replaced by "cat", referring to the bag's actual content, but the saying is otherwise identical.

Wagon/Van/Truck Sale

In this scam, low-quality items are sold as expensive units that have been greatly discounted. The salesmen explain the ultra-low price in a number of ways; for instance, that their employer is unaware of having ordered too many items, so they are sneakily selling the excess behind the boss's back. The "salesmen" are ready to be haggled down to a seemingly minuscule price, because the items they are selling, while usually functional, actually cost only a tiny fraction of their "list price" to manufacture.

People shopping for forbidden or controlled goods may be legally hindered from reporting swindles to the police. The buyer has no legal recourse without admitting to the attempted purchase of stolen goods. This con is also known as "The Murphy Game".

❖Extortion or false-injury tricks
The Badger Game

The badger game extortion is often perpetrated on married men. The mark is deliberately coerced into a compromising position, a supposed affair for example, and then threatened with public exposure of his acts unless blackmail money is paid.

The badger game dates back to the 19th century, and is arguably one of the most reproduced cons of all time. Other variations included false allegations of rape or sexual harassment. One famous version of it from the early 1930s involved a woman accusing her male doctor of improper conduct during a medical exam and then blackmailing him in order to keep her from pressing charges. Often the woman would be working in tandem with a second grifter who would show up in the middle of things and pretends to be her angry husband, which would help to scare the mark into going along with the blackmail. Like the embarrassing check scheme, the idea was always that the victim would be too ashamed of his own actions not to pay off the con men.

Clip joint

A clip joint or fleshpot is an establishment, usually a strip club or entertainment bar, typically one claiming to offer adult entertainment or bottle service, in which customers are tricked into paying money and receive poor, or no, goods or services in reTurn. Typically, clip joints suggest the possibility of sex, charge excessively high prices for watered-down drinks, and then eject customers when they become unwilling or unable to spend more money. The product or service may be illicit, offering the victim no recourse through official or legal channels.

Coin-matching game

Also called a coin smack or smack game, two operators trick a victim during a game where coins are matched. One operator begins the game with the victim, and then the second joins in. When the second operator leaves briefly, the first colludes with the victim to cheat the second operator. After rejoining the game, the second operator, angry at "losing," threatens to call the police. The first operator convinces the victim to pitch in hush money, which the two operators later split.

❖Gambling tricks
The Fiddle game

The fiddle game uses the pigeon drop technique. Many of the best cons work because of the inherent greed of the person being tricked, and the fiddle game is one of the best examples. It requires two con men to work, and is designed to take place in an expensive restaurant. One of the con men poses as an old man eating dinner. When he gets his bill, the man approaches the owner and explains that he forgot his wallet back at his inn. He promises to go get it, and as collateral leaves behind an old fiddle or violin, explaining that he is a traveling musician and that it is his sole source of income. After the old man leaves, a second con man who has been sitting nearby approaches the owner and asks to see the fiddle, saying that he is a dealer in rare instruments. After inspecting the fiddle, the man pronounces it a highly rare and valuable piece of work, worth thousands of dollars. He then pretends to be in a hurry and leaves, but not before giving the mark his card and telling him to call if the man is interested in selling. The old man will reTurn shortly thereafter with the money for his meal. If the con men have sold the trick well enough, the victim, believing that he will be able to sell it to the fake instrument dealer for a huge profit, will attempt to buy the fiddle off of the old man for a few hundred dollars. Of course, the number on the card will prove to be a fake, and the victim will inevitably be left with a worthless violin. The result is the two con men are richer (less the cost of the violin), and the mark is left with a cheap instrument

Glim-dropper

The glim-dropper scam requires several accomplices, one of whom must be a one-eyed man. One grifter goes into a store and pretends he has lost his glass eye. Everyone looks around, but the eye cannot be found. He declares that he will pay a thousand-dollar reward for the reTurn of his eye, leaving contact information. The next day, an accomplice enters the store and pretends to find the eye. The storekeeper (the intended griftee), thinking of the reward, offers to take it and reTurn it to its owner. The finder insists he will reTurn it himself, and demands the owner's address. Thinking he will lose all chance of the reward, the storekeeper offers a hundred dollars for the eye. The finder bargains him up to $250, and departs. The one-eyed man, of course, cannot be found and does not reTurn.

Three-card Monte

One of the classic short cons, three-card monte, "find the queen", the "three-card trick", or "follow the lady", is essentially the same as the centuries-older shell game, a similar scheme that was popular during the Middle Ages, or thimblerig (except for the props). Three cards are placed faced down on a flat surface, usually two black jacks and a red queen. The dealer shows the players the red queen, and then proceeds to thoroughly shuffle the cards to make it difficult to tell where it is. Players then bet on whether they can pick the queen out of the three cards. It sounds easy enough, but the game is more or less impossible to beat, because a good dealer can use sleight of hand to switch the cards at will, and can easily decide who wins or loses. At first the audience is skeptical, so the shill places a bet, and the scammer allows him to win. In one variation of the game, the shill will (apparently surreptitiously) peek at the lady, ensuring that the mark also sees the card. This is sometimes enough to entice the audience to place bets, but the trickster uses sleight of hand to ensure that he always loses, unless the con man decides to let him win, hoping to lure him into betting much more. The mark loses whenever the dealer chooses to make him lose. In Turkish the term "Üç Kağıtçı" meaning 'a three carder' i.e. the dealer of a three card monte scam; is used as a general term for any fraudster.

A variation on this scam exists, but with the addition of a pickpocket. The dealer and shill behave in an overtly obvious manner, attracting a larger audience. When the pickpocket succeeds in stealing from a member of the audience, he signals the dealer. The dealer then shouts "Watch Out!"—and the three split up. The audience is left believing that the police are coming, and that the performance was a failed scam.

Another variant of this scam exists. The shill says loudly to the dealer that his cards are fake and that he wants to see them. He takes the card and folds a corner and says in a hushed voice to the audience that he has marked the card. He places a bet and wins. Then he asks the others to place bets as well. When one of the audience bets a large sum of money, the cards are switched.

❖Spurious qualifications or endorsements
Diploma Mill / Writ of Nobility

These unaccredited educational institutions offer qualifications or academic titles in reTurn for a fee with few or no academic criteria. Purchasers may or may not know that the institution is unaccredited or the qualification is not legitimate.

❖Other confidence tricks and scams
Hooker's upstairs

A con waits outside of a closed strip club and approaches marks that are looking for the strip club. Usually he'll claim that he can take you up into the strip club, even though it is closed, and there are several girls to choose from. He will want cash up front before he lets you in the door. After the mark get's the money the con man may ask for an additional amount that will cover the fee for the room. Once he's gotten as much cash from the mark as possible the con man will say that it's better to go around the building to the back entrance. If the mark follows the con man to the back entrance a number of unfortunate things can happen. This is a low budget con because the con man needs little prep and no supplies to pull this one off. The con man needs only to wait out front of a closed gentleman's club.

Pigeon drop

The pigeon drop involves the mark or pigeon assisting an elderly, weak or infirm stranger to keep a large sum of money safe for him. In the process, the stranger (actually a confidence trickster) puts his money with the mark's money in an envelope or briefcase, with which the mark is then entrusted. The container is then switched for an identical one which contains no money, and a situation is engineered where the mark has the opportunity to escape with the money. If the mark takes this chance, he is merely fleeing from his own money, which the con artist will have kept or handed off to an accomplice.

The False Hero

There might not be any simpler or more ancient con than the so-called "false Hero". It usually involves a team of two con men working in tandem, and the victim is usually a lone person walking a city street at night. The first con man approaches the person and mugs them, stealing their wallet or purse and taking off down the street. The second con man, posing as a passerby, will give chase to the mugger, tackle them, and get back the wallet. The mugger, of course, always manages to escape during the fray. The false Good Samaritan will then reTurn the wallet or purse to the mark, who will have been witness to the entire performance. The hope is that the grateful victim will repay the con man for his help with some kind of cash reward, which they can then split with the mugger later on. When sold correctly and performed on the right kind of person, this con is capable of earning the grifters even more money than they would have ever gotten from just keeping the stolen wallet.

Appendix H

Musical Instruments of the Area and Era

'Blown into a Hole' Wind

Penny / Tin Whistle, Low Whistle, Fipple Flute, Ocarina, Recorder, Cornamuse (Alto and Bass), Crumhorn, Dulcian, Harmonica, Shepherd's Shawm, Kortholt, Rackett (Tenor and Bass), Rauschpfeife (screaming flute), Schalmei, Shawm, Chalumeau (Chalumeaux in plural) (Soprano, Alto, Tenor, Bass), Hornpipe (2 separate single reeds)

'Blown Across a Hole' Wind (end-blown)

Shakuhachi (Bamboo Flute), Panpipes

'Blown Across a Hole' Wind (side-blown)

Transverse Flute, Piccolo, Fife, Gemshorn

'Brass Type' Wind

Trumpet (Bugle…no holes), Shofar (no holes), Cornett Family [all with a cornet mouthpiece and holes like a Recorder - Zink (Soprano and Alto), Nicolo, Mute Cornett, Lizard, Serpent], Sacbut (Trombone – Tenor, Alto, Bass, Great Bass sizes)

'Bagged' Wind

Bagpipe, Bladder Pipe

'Plucked & Strummed' Stringed

Clarsach (small Highlander Dwarven harp), Harp, Lyre (a harp), Autoharp, Psaltery (plucked Dulcimer), Gittern (Guitar), Lute, Mandolin (small Lute), Sitar

'Bowed' Stringed

Faeghan WhiteWolf

Violin, Kit (small Violin, Halfling Fiddle), Viol, Viol Da Gamba, Rebec

Stick Percussion

Drum (single stick), Kettledrum (Timpani – metal or wooden bowl with a head), Bass Drum (double-headed, wood), Tambora (double headed drum played with a stick and a hand)

Hand Drum Percussion

Frame Drum (single headed), Mirwas (double headed Frame Drum), Congas, Bongos (2 small attached drums, 1 bigger than the other), Djembe, Doumbek, Ashiko (straight sided), Bougarabou (short Djembe)

Finger Percussion

Castanets (worn on finger and thumb, struck together, hardwood), Finger Cymbals

Percussion 'with Vibrating Response'

Side Drum (wood or metal with snares on the bottom), Tambourine

Percussion 'Tonal'

Xylophone (wood), Metallophone (metal xylophone), Tsuzumi (double headed hand drum, played with one hand on the tone adjustment strings and the other striking one end), Rommelpost Drum, Claves (2 hardwood sticks), Cymbals (Brass), Gong (metal), Triangle, Log Drum (hollow tapered log, open on both ends, mallet-like sticks or hands for softer notes), Bodhran (Frame Drum played with a short double ended stick. The holding hand is used to vary pitch and timbre by touching or rubbing the inside of the head.)

Percussion Miscellaneous

Maracas

Percussion 'Stringed'

Clavichord (small, oblong box, strung like a guitar, played with 2 metal hammers), Hammer Dulcimer

Keyboard

Harpsichord, Pipe Organ, Mini-accordion, Accordion, Organetto

Two Instrument Combinations

Pipe (3 finger whistle in left hand) and Tabor (single stick drum attached to left front waist, played with right hand)

Appendix I

WARNING:

If you are of the faint of heart or weak of stomach, do not read this information!

This information is historically accurate to Earth's Middle Ages and has been translated slightly for use in Oerth's Rising Ages.

In the book, there is no specificity or overtly communicated text regarding 'torture', just the mild fact that a prisoner was tortured. Considering that most middle school kids might consider 'torture' to be having their smartphone taken away for a day, it might be nice for them to understand the difference between the real torture techniques of the time period and that mild, and very temporary, inconvenience.

Yes, people were actually this vicious to each other at one time.

Again, if you have a weak stomach or are prone to nightmares, please do not read this information

Torture Techniques of the Era

The Rising Ages, 4826 – 5245, are a violent and bloodthirsty era as regards those that are considered to be incorrigible. As the population of Oerth becomes more civilized and worldly, these methods are becoming rare (unlike Earth, where Torture techniques are utilized daily all over the world to this day), to be replaced by much kinder means to the same ends, with rehabilitation being the new main goal. Within Reggie's lifetime and with his support and applied pressure, Gaols, Donjons, and Torture facilities were replaced entirely with Treatment Centers run by Priests of Trickster with the purpose of rehabilitating perpetrators of all types.

In barbarous times the cruel and pitiless feeling which induced legislators to increase the horrors of tortures, also contribute to the aggravation of the fate of prisoners. Torture chambers are included in many castles. Law or custom does not prescribe any fixed rules for the treatment of hapless prisoners who face torture. Different types of torture are used depending on the victim's crime and social status. Torture is seen as a totally legitimate means for justice to extract confessions, or obtain the names of accomplices or other information about the crime. Torture is a legitimate way to obtain testimonies and confessions from suspects for use in legal inquiries and trials during the Rising Ages.

The definition of torture is the deliberate, systematic, cruel and wanton infliction of physical or mental suffering by one or more torturers in an attempt to force another person to yield information or to make a confession or for any other reason. Devices or tools are used to inflict unbearable agony on a victim.

There are many methods of torture which have been practiced during the Rising Ages of Oerth:

- Ripping out teeth / nails
- Beating
- Blinding
- Boiling
- Bone breaking
- Branding and Burning
- Castration
- Choking
- Cutting

- Disfigurement
- Dislocation
- Drowning
- Flagellation, whipping and beating
- Flaying
- Roasting
- Genital mutilation
- Limb/finger removal
- Starvation
- Tongue removal

There is even a torture which uses tickling as a method to inflict suffering. Other tortures include the compression of the limbs by special instruments, or by ropes, injection of water, vinegar, or oil, into the body of the accused, application of hot pitch, and starvation, and other processes used in tortures.

A skilled torturer will use methods, devices and instruments to prolong life as long as possible whilst inflicting agonizing pain. However, the customs of the period dictate that many prisoners are tortured before they are executed in order to obtain additional information about their crime or their accomplices. There are many forms of torture with execution following. The execution method itself is part of the torture endured by prisoners.

These final methods of torture with execution include the following methods:
- Torture and execution by Fire
- The Sword or the Axe
- Mechanical force
- Quartering
- The Wheel
- The Fork
- The Gibbet
- Spiking
- Dismembering

Some of the more specific methods are listed below.

❖ The Rack

The rack is a machine consisting of a rectangular, wooden, bed-like frame. The wooden frame has a roller at each end. The victim's feet are manacled to one roller, and the wrists are manacled to the other. A handle and ratchet are attached to the rollers at either end of the board and are Turned very gradually stepwise to increase the tension on the chains, pulling the body in opposite directions. The victim's body is initially stretched. Limbs will be dislocated and prolonged use will end with limbs being torn from their sockets inducing excruciating pain.

❖ The Scavenger's Daughter

The device consists of one single iron bar that connects iron shackles closing round the victim's hands, feet and neck. This rack positions the head to the knees of the victim in a sitting position. It compresses the body as to force the blood from the nose and ears.

❖ The Brank (aka The Scolds Bridle)

The Brank, also known as the Scold's Bridle, is specifically used as a torture for women to inflict humiliation and discomfort as opposed to pain. A scold is a term given to a gossip, shrew or bad tempered woman during the Rising Ages. A scold is defined as: "A troublesome and angry woman who by brawling and wrangling amongst her neighbours breaks the public peace, increases discord and becomes a public nuisance to the neighbourhood." The device is a locking iron muzzle, metal mask or cage which encases the head. There is an iron curb projecting into the mouth which rests on the top of the tongue. This device prevents the shrew from speaking. In some instances the iron curb is studded with spikes which inflict pain if the victim speaks. Some Branks have a bell built in which draws attention to the scold as she walks through the streets. The woman will be humiliated by the jeering and comments from other people.

❖ The Ducking Stool (Dunking Stool)

The Ducking stool is a punishment designed to check for dark magick use. The device is a chair which is hung from the end of a free-moving arm. The person is strapped into the chair which is situated by the side of a river. The device is then swung over the river by the use of the free-moving arm. The person will then be ducked into the freezing cold water. The length of immersion into the water is decided by the operator and the crime of which the person is accused. It could last for just a few seconds but in some circumstances this punishment process could be continuously repeated over the course of a day. The crimes which deemed such a punishment were primarily dark magick and occasionally Scolds were also punished by this method. Ducking is seen as a foolproof way to establish whether a suspect is a dark magick user. The ducking stools are generally used for this purpose but ducking is also inflicted without the chair. In this instance the victim's right thumb was bound to left big toe. A rope is attached to their waist and the 'dark user' is thrown into a river or deep pond. If the 'dark user' floats, it is deemed that they are in league with an evil deity. If the 'dark user' drowned they are deemed innocent and revived.

❖ Torture by Dislocation

In the ordinary torture, the accused is stripped half naked, and his hands are tightly tied behind his back, with a ring fixed between them. Then by means of a rope fastened to this ring, they raise the poor man, who has a weight of one hundred and eighty pounds attached to his feet, a certain height from the ground. For the extraordinary torture, which then took the name of 'Estrapade' they raise the victim, with two hundred and fifty pounds attached to his feet, to the ceiling by means of a capstan; he is then allowed to fall several times successively by jerks to the level of the ground, by which means his arms and legs are completely dislocated.

❖ Iron Balls Torture

The ordinary torture consists in hanging the accused by the wrists, with a heavy iron ball at each foot; for the extraordinary torture, under the name of Veglia, the body was stretched horizontally by means of ropes passing through rings riveted into the wall, and attached to the four limbs, the only support given to the culprit being the point of a stake cut in a diamond shape, which just touches the end of the back-bone. A doctor and a surgeon are often present, feeling the pulse at the temples of the patient, so as to be able to judge of the moment when he can no longer bear the pain. At that moment he is untied, hot fomentations are used to revive him, restoratives are administered, and, as soon as he has recovered a little strength, he is again put to the torture, which goes on thus for six consecutive hours.

❖ Water Torture

The water torture is the most easily borne, and the least dangerous. A person undergoing it is tied to a board which is supported horizontally on two trestles. By means of a horn, acting as a funnel, and whilst his nose is being pinched, so as to force him to swallow, they slowly poured four coquemars (about nine pints) of water into his mouth; this is for the ordinary torture. For the extraordinary, double that quantity is poured in. When the torture is ended, the victim is untied, "and taken to be warmed in the kitchen," says the old text.

❖ Death by a Thousand Cuts

In this torture, the torturer administers '1000' slight cuts to the entire skin surface of the restrained victim, so slight as to barely break the skin. Concentrated salt water is then applied by dunking the person or pouring over the person. The person is then allowed to dry. The salt causes the skin to stretch taut, causing the cuts to split open, and allowing the salt to enter the wounds. The salt water application may be repeated. The person eventually bleeds to death or dies of dehydration. This is a very long and painful process.

❖ Drip Torture

The person is positioned in a frame or other method that allows no movement of the upper body and head. A large water container is positioned above their head so that only a steady drip of water hits the person at the precise same location on the top of their head. The dripping water allows no sleep or rest, though they stay hydrated if some of it gets to their mouth. They eventually go mad from this treatment, maybe before the water bores a hole through their skull and into their brain, thus killing them.

❖ The Boot Torture

The advantage of this type of torture is that the victim rarely dies. The boot torture is done with high boots made of spongy leather that have been placed on the culprit's feet. He is tied onto a table near a large fire, and a quantity of boiling water is poured on the boots, which penetrated the leather, ate away the flesh, and even dissolved the bones of the victim.

❖ The Foot Press

The advantage of this type of torture is that the victim rarely dies. There are several types of the foot press. The foot press consists of a pair of horizontal iron plates which are tightened around the foot by means of a crank mechanism in order to lacerate the flesh and crush the bones of the foot. Variations have been added including the addition of hundreds of sharp spikes to the plates and horrifically a crank mechanism is connected to a drill, so that when the instrument was tightened around the foot a hole was drilled in the center of the instep.

❖ Foot Roasting

The advantage of this type of torture is that the victim rarely dies. Foot roasting is also a method commonly used. The soles of the feet are smeared with lard and slowly roasted over red-hot coals. A bellows is used to control the intensity of the heat and a screen can be interposed between the feet and the coals as the victim is questioned. If the questions are not answered satisfactorily, the screen is withdrawn and the naked soles are again exposed to the flames. In one instance, a knights feet were burnt until they were charred to the bone resulting in his foot bones (metatarsals) falling to the floor.

❖ Brodequins

Tortures specifically for the legs are called Brodequins. The victim is placed in a sitting posture on a massive bench, with strong narrow boards fixed inside and outside of each leg, which are tightly bound together with strong rope; wedges are then driven in between the centre boards with a mallet; four wedges in the ordinary and eight in the extraordinary torture. Not infrequently during the latter operation the bones of the legs are literally burst.

The Brodequins which are often used for ordinary torture are stockings of parchment, into which it was easy enough to get the feet into when it was wet, but which, on being held near the fire, shrunk so considerably that it caused insufferable agony to the wearer.

❖ Thumbscrews

The use of the thumbscrew is a common method of inflicting intense pain on prisoners. The thumbscrew is a simple device designed to crush whatever is inserted. Typically thumbs, but even fingers or toes, are placed in the vice and slowly crushed. The crushing process is achieved by varying degrees of the screws which are applied and its toothed iron bars. The force of thumbscrews is such that the bone could be crushed and broken. The thumbscrews are useful to interrogators as they are a portable means of torture and not restricted to the confines of the torture chamber.

❖ Pillory

When it is only required to stamp a culprit with infamy he is put into the pillory, which is generally a kind of scaffold furnished with chains and iron collars, and bearing on its front the arms of the feudal lord. In Waterport, this name is specifically given to a round isolated tower built in the centre of one of the markets. The tower is sixty feet high, and has large openings in its thick walls, and a horizontal wheel is provided, which is capable of Turning on a pivot. This wheel is pierced with several holes, made so as to hold the hands and head of the culprit, who, on passing and re-passing before the eyes of the crowd, comes in full view, and is subjected to their hooting and jeers. The pillories are always situated in the most frequented places, such as markets and crossways.

❖ Burned at the Stake

The punishment by fire is always inflicted in cases of heresy, or blasphemy, but can be applied to other unusually heinous crimes against the community.

Many executions are public. In Waterport, it is the custom for the condemned to take part in a Death procession. The victim in his shirt, barefooted, the rope round his neck, followed by the executioner, and holding in his hand a wax taper, with a weight, which was definitely specified in the sentence which had been passed upon him, but which was generally of two or four pounds, prostrated himself at the door of a church or Temple, where in a loud voice he had to confess his crime, and to beg the pardon of the appropriate Deity and the citizenry of the city.

When a victim has been condemned to be burnt, a stake is erected on the spot specially designed for the execution, and round it a pile was prepared, composed of alternate layers of straw and wood, and rising to about the height of a man. Care is taken to leave a free space round the stake for the victim, and also a passage by which to lead him to it. Having been stripped of his clothes, and dressed in a shirt smeared with sulphur, he has to walk to the centre of the pile through a narrow opening, and is then tightly bound to the stake with ropes and chains. After this, faggots and straw are thrown into the empty space through which he had passed to the stake, until he is entirely covered by them; the pile is then fired on all sides at once. In some cases, the person is placed on a platform above the fire.

Sometimes the executioner, in order to shorten the sufferings of the condemned, whilst he prepares the pile, places a large and pointed iron bar amongst the faggots and opposite the stake breast high, so that, directly the fire is lighted, the bar is quickly pushed against the victim, giving a mortal blow to the unfortunate wretch, who would otherwise have been slowly devoured by the flames. Other merciful method designed to reduce the suffering is to place explosive powder or Greek Fire in the wood to ensure a quick death. If a condemned person is really fortunate he will be strangled to death before being chained to the stake.

❖ Branding and Burning

In 5107, the Statute of Vagabonds ruled that vagabonds, gypsies, thieves, adulterers, and brawlers were ordered to be branded, the first two with a large V on the breast, the last three with a T, A, and F (for fighter) respectively on the forehead. This Law has since been repealed in 5196 and replaced with one that only targets criminals. Slaves, too who run away are branded with 'S' on their forehead. Here is a list of the current common infractions and their minimum consequences (various torture techniques are also utilized);

- ✓ Arson- the dominant arm and hand are burned to uselessness
- ✓ Adultery- the person has both feet removed and an 'A' branded on their forehead. The Mate or Mates have to wish the person punished.
- ✓ Assault- the person is put in the stocks to be ridiculed and treated rudely for an amount of time
- ✓ Battery- the person is beaten an equal amount to the damage they inflicted and a 'B' is branded on the forehead
- ✓ Bribery- the person is fined double the amount
- ✓ Burglary- the person has both hands removed and a 'T' branded on their forehead
- ✓ Disorderly Conduct- the person spends a variable length of time in Gaol (the Dungeon)
- ✓ Disturbing the Peace- the person is fit with an iron muzzle for a length of time
- ✓ Embezzlement- the person is fined double the amount, has their holdings forfeited to the city, and has a 'T' branded on their forehead
- ✓ Extortion- the person has their dominant hand removed, a 'T' branded on their forehead, and spends time in Gaol
- ✓ Forgery- the person has their dominant hand removed, a 'T' branded on their forehead, and spends time in Gaol
- ✓ Fraud- the person is fined and spends time in Gaol and an 'L' branded on their forehead
- ✓ Kidnapping- the person spends a long time in Gaol
- ✓ Money Laundering- the person is fined double the amount
- ✓ Murder- the person is tortured and executed
- ✓ Perjury- the person has their tongue removed and an 'L' branded on their forehead
- ✓ Piracy- the person is usually executed in some hideous fashion as this crime includes a number of the others listed here

- ✓ Rape- the person has their genitals removed and an 'R' branded on their forehead
- ✓ Robbery- the person is beaten and has a 'T' branded on their forehead
- ✓ Tax Evasion- the person is fined double the amount and has a 'T' branded on their forehead
- ✓ Theft- the person has a 'T' branded on their forehead

There are various methods and devices used to torture or punish a victim using branding or burning techniques. The red-hot brazier, which is passed backwards and forwards before the eyes of the culprit, until they are destroyed by the scorching heat. Red hot pokers are applied to various parts of the body. Various marks branded on to the flesh using red hot branding irons. A branding-iron had a long bolt with a wooden handle at one end and a brand with a letter at the other. Two iron loops were used for firmly securing the hands during the excruciating process.

Execution by Quartering / The Wheel

Quartering may in truth be considered the most horrible penalty ever invented. This punishment dates from the remotest ages. In almost all cases, the victim had previously to undergo various accessory tortures: sometimes his right hand was cut off, and the mutilated stump was burnt in a cauldron of sulphur; sometimes his arms, thighs, or breasts were lacerated with red-hot pincers, and hot oil, pitch, or molten lead was poured into the wounds. After these horrible preliminaries, a rope is attached to each of the limbs of the criminal, one being bound round each leg from the foot to the knee, and round each arm from the wrist to the elbow. These ropes are then fastened to four bars, to each of which a strong horse is harnessed, as if for towing a barge. These horses are first made to give short jerks; and when the agony has elicited heart-rending cries from the unfortunate man, who feels his limbs being dislocated without being broken, the four horses are all suddenly urged on with the whip in different directions, and thus all the limbs are strained at one moment. If the tendons and ligaments still resist the combined efforts of the four horses, the executioner assists, and makes several cuts with a hatchet on each joint. When at last, for this horrible torture often lasts several hours - each horse has drawn out a limb, they are collected and placed near the hideous trunk, which often still shows signs of life, and the whole are burned together. Sometimes the sentence is, that the body should be hung to the gibbet, and that the limbs should be displayed on the gates of the town, or sent to four principal towns in the extremities of the kingdom. When this is done, "an inscription shall be placed on each of the limbs, which states the reason of its being thus exposed."

Execution by Hanging
In every town, and almost every village, there is a permanent gibbet, which, owing to the custom of leaving the bodies to hang till they crumbled into dust, is very rarely without having some corpses or skeletons attached to it. According to prescribed rule, the gallows are placed in an important part of town in the political as well as the criminal history of that city.

The criminal condemned to be hanged is generally taken to the place of execution sitting or standing in a wagon, with his back to the horses. When the criminal arrives at the place of execution the noose is placed around his neck from which he is suspended and thereby strangled to death. When the words "shall be hung until death doth ensue" are to be found in a sentence, it must not be supposed that they were used merely as a form, for in certain cases the judge orders that the sentence should be only carried out as far as would prove to the culprit the awful sensation of hanging. In such cases, the victim is simply suspended by ropes passing under the arm-pits, a kind of exhibition which is not free from danger when it is too prolonged, for the weight of the body so tightened the rope round the chest that the circulation or breath might be stopped. Many culprits, after hanging thus an hour, when brought down, are dead, or only survive this painful process a short time.

Hung, Drawn, and Quartered
This evil and sadistic form of execution was invented in 5001, specifically to punish a man called Willis Maurice who had been convicted of piracy. This form of execution is no respecter of rank. It is used to execute traitors to the Crown, including those of royal birth. In 5043, Dafydd ap Gruffydd, the last Prince of Westdale (c. 4995 – 3 Harvestgold 5043) , was tried for treason against King Howard I and was sentenced "to be drawn to the gallows as a traitor to the King who made him a Knight, to be hanged as the murderer of the gentleman taken in the Castle of Hawarden, to have his limbs burnt because he had

profaned by assassination the solemnity of Peace's passion and to have his quarters dispersed through the country because he had in different places compassed the death of his lord the king". Conan MacFirth (circa. 5030 – 5065), a Dwarven rabble rouser (whose army very nearly beat our own), was hung, drawn and quartered at Smithsfield on 23 Goldengrain 5065 in front of the remnants of his men. His limbs were displayed, separately, in Newkeep, Burntwick, Starling, and Firth. In the 5000's, a total of 105 Baalite martyrs were hanged, drawn and quartered at North Market in Waterport.

The most terrible punishment of the Rising Ages is being Hung, Drawn and Quartered. This barbaric form of execution is reserved for the most hated prisoners who have usually been convicted of treason or worse.

The form of execution referred to as being Hung, Drawn and Quartered is described by a chronicler called Wilfred Harson (circa. 5020):

"The greatest and most grievous punishment used in the Realm for such as offend against the State is drawing from the prison to the place of execution upon an hurdle or sled, where they are hanged till they be half dead, and then taken down, and quartered alive; after that, their members and bowels are cut from their bodies, and thrown into a fire, provided near hand and within their own sight, even for the same purpose."

The Quarters of the body are then hung in prescribed locations in the City of Waterport as a deterrent to all its citizens.

Appendix J			Cities, Towns, & Villages of the Waterport Area
Name	Size	Population	Known For
Mixed			
Merchantville (Bay of the Sea People)	Large	Mixed	Merchant's subdivision of Waterport
New Harbour (Bay of the Sea People)	Large	Mixed	Shipping & ship building
School Complex & Airfield (Bay of the Sea People)	Large	Mixed	Education & Air Force
Trasnustrath	Small	Mixed	Inn, General Store, Stable
Village De Passerelle (Bay of the Sea People)	Medium	Mixed	Inn, General Store, Stable, transport, shipping
Human			
Baybridge (Bay of the Sea People)	Small	Humans	Fish, Fishing products, Produce, Animal products (sheep, goats, wool, mohair), etc.
Bell's Crossing (Bay of the Sea People)	Small	Humans	Fish, Fishing products, Produce, Nets, Woven goods, etc.

	Small	Norse Humans & Humans	Inn, General Store, Stable
Beskyttesvale	Small	Norse Humans & Humans	Inn, General Store, Stable
Brikinton	Small	Humans	A large Brick Inn with support services, General Store, Stable, Produce
Brin's Hold (Sword Bay)	Small	Humans	Harbour, Fish, Fishing products, Boats, Nets, Produce, Animal products (sheep, goats, wool, mohair), Crafts, transport, shipping, etc.
Cackleton (Bay Hay)	Small	Humans	Grains, Produce, Animal products (sheep, goats, wool, mohair), Poultry products, etc.
Cliffside (Bay of the Sea People)	Small	Humans	Produce, Animal products (sheep, goats, wool, mohair), etc.
Cooperville (Bay of the Sea People)	Small	Humans	Poultry products
Creag Inlet (Bay of the Sea People)	Small	Humans	Fish, Fishing products, Produce, Nets, etc.
Ekridge	Small	Humans	Produce, crafts, etc.

Ella's Cove (Bay of the Sea People)	Small	Humans	Fish, Fishing products, Produce, Nets, etc.
Farmington (Sword Bay)	Small	Humans	Grains, Produce, Animal products (sheep, goats, wool, mohair), Poultry products, etc.
Fewersham (Sword Bay)	Medium	Humans	Fish, Fishing products, Produce, Animal products (sheep, cattle, wool, milk, cheese), etc.
Fisherton (Bay of the Sea People)	Small	Humans	Fish, Fishing products, Produce, Boats, Nets, etc.
Gale Safe (Leeward Bay)	Small	Humans	Harbour, Fish, Fishing products, Boats, Nets, Produce, Animal products (sheep, goats, wool, mohair), Crafts, transport, shipping, etc.
Gooseberg (Goose Bay)	Small	Humans	Harbour, Fish, Fishing products, Boats, Nets, Produce, Crafts, transport, shipping, Poultry products, etc.
Gooseborough (Goose Bay)	Small	Humans	Fish, Fishing products, Nets, Produce, Animal products (sheep, goats, wool, mohair), Crafts, transport, shipping, Poultry products, etc.
Goosederry (Goose Bay)	Small	Humans	Wood products, Produce, Animal products (sheep, goats, wool, mohair), Crafts, Poultry products, etc.

Goosehamlet (Goose Bay)	Small	Humans	Harbour, Fish, Fishing products, Boats, Nets, Produce, Animal products (sheep, goats, wool, mohair), Crafts, transport, shipping, Poultry products, etc.
Goosestead (Goose Bay)	Small	Humans	Harbour, Fish, Fishing products, Boats, Nets, Produce, Animal products (sheep, goats, wool, mohair), Crafts, transport, shipping, Poultry products, etc.
Gooseton (Goose Bay)	Small	Humans	Harbour, Fish, Fishing products, Boats, Nets, Produce, Crafts, transport, shipping, Poultry products, etc.
Goosetown (Goose Bay)	Small	Humans	Harbour, Fish, Fishing products, Boats, Nets, Produce, Animal products (sheep, goats, wool, mohair), Crafts, transport, shipping, Poultry products, etc.
Gooseville (Goose Bay)	Small	Humans	Harbour, Fish, Fishing products, Boats, Nets, Produce, Animal products (sheep, goats, wool, mohair), Crafts, transport, shipping, Poultry products, etc.
Hayton (Bay Hay)	Medium	Humans	Grains, Produce, Animal products (sheep, goats, wool, mohair), Poultry products, etc.

Highbridges	Small	Humans	Grains, Produce, Animal products (sheep, goats, wool, mohair), Poultry products, etc.
Klippe Cove (Bay of the Sea People)	Small	Humans	Fish, Fishing products, Produce, Nets, etc.
Lath's Mill	Small	Humans	Grain products
Longbridge	Small	Humans	
Lowbridge	Small	Humans	
Meadsville (Bay Hay)	Small	Humans	Produce, Animal products (sheep, goats, wool, mohair), etc.
Olafsport (Bay of the Sea People)	Small	Norse Humans & Humans	Harbour, Fish, Fishing products, Boats, Nets, Produce, Animal products (sheep, goats, wool, mohair), Crafts, transport, shipping, etc.
Port Royal (Leeward Bay)	Small	Humans	Harbour, Fish, Fishing products, Boats, Nets, Produce, Animal products (sheep, goats, wool, mohair), Crafts, transport, shipping, etc.

Sky's Harbor (Leeward Bay)	Small	Humans	Harbour, Fish, Fishing products, Boats, Nets, Produce, Animal products (sheep, goats, wool, mohair), Crafts, transport, shipping, etc.
Stavsund (Bay of the Sea People)	Small	Norse Humans	Harbour, Fish, Fishing products, Produce, Boats, Nets, etc.
Stjorheim (Bay of the Sea People)	Medium	Norse Humans	Harbour, Fish, Fishing products, Produce, Boats, Nets, etc.
Tripartite Crossing (West, East, South) (Bay of the Sea People)	Medium	Norse Humans & Humans	Harbour, Fish, Fishing products, Boats, Nets, Produce, Animal products (sheep, goats, wool, mohair), Crafts, transport, shipping, etc.
Wickerberg	Medium	Humans	Wicker products
Halfling			
Foothilldown (Or Cnoc)	Small	Dwarfkin Halflings	
Greendown (Fewersham) (Sword Bay)	Small	Humkin Halflings	Woven goods, Produce, Animal products (sheep, cattle, wool, milk, cheese), etc.

Irondown	Small	Dwarfkin Halflings	Limestone carving, coal transport (goat carts), Animal products (goats, mohair, milk, cheese), Produce
Joliedown (Trois Epees)	Medium	Elfkin Halflings	Produce, Woven goods, Woodcraft goods, Ranged weapons, Animal products, etc.
Pooldown (Righ-Na-Coille Carraig)	Medium	Dwarfkin Halflings	
Rootdown (Village De L'arbre)	Small	Elfkin Halflings	Food products, Forest Produce (roots, tubers, fruits), Woodcarvings
Slagdown (Or Torr)	Small	Dwarfkin Halflings	Animal products (goats, mohair, milk, cheese)
Thistledown (Waterport) (Bay of the Sea People)	Medium	Humkin Halflings	Produce, Garden supplies, Herbs
Wickerdown (Wickerberg)	Medium	Humkin Halflings	Wicker products
Elf			
Ville Des Neuf	Large	Plains Elves	Fine steel weapons & armour, Fine cloth

Village De L'arbre	Medium	Forest Elves	Fine Leather goods, Woodcarving
Half Elf			
Trois Epees (Un, Deux, & Trois) (Sword Bay)	Medium	Half Elves – all types	Ships, Nets, Fishing products, Produce, Woven goods, Woodcraft goods, Ranged weapons, Animal products, etc.
Dwarf			
Righ-Na-Coille Carraig	Large	Highlander Dwarves	Golden objects and coins. Iron ore, coal, and limestone. Iron and fine steel weapons, tools, and implements. Limestone building materials.
Or Torr	Large	Highlander Dwarves	Golden objects and coins. Iron ore, coal, and limestone. Iron and fine steel weapons, tools, and implements. Limestone building materials.
Or Cnoc By Village de L'arbre	Large	Highlander Dwarves	Golden objects and coins.
Gual Sloc	Large	Highlander Dwarves	Iron ore, coal, and limestone. Iron and steel weapons, tools, and implements. Limestone building materials.
Clach Sloc	Large	Highlander Dwarves	Iron ore, coal, and limestone. Iron and steel weapons, tools, and implements. Limestone building materials.

Iarann Creag	Medium	Highlander Dwarves	Iron ore, coal, and limestone. Iron and steel weapons, tools, and implements. Limestone building materials.
Red Giant			
Paha Wicoti	Small	Red Giant	Forest products, hides, Leather goods
Fae			
Fae Isle (Sword Bay)	Small	Human-Water Sprite mixes	Item enchanting, Illusions, Fishing products
Druidic			
Dairedell	Small	Mixed	Druid Circle / Grove
Fairdell	Small	Mixed	Druid Circle / Grove
Oakdell	Small	Mixed	Druid Circle / Grove
Passdell	Small	Mixed	Druid Circle / Grove

Fortresses and Castles			
Castle Goosefeather (Goose Bay)	Small	Humans	Barony (1 of 3 brothers, Artemus Goose, triplets)
Castle Goosequill (Goose Bay)	Small	Humans	Barony (1 of 3 brothers, Artoine Goose, triplets)
Castle Gooseplume (Goose Bay)	Small	Humans	Barony (1 of 3 brothers, Artur Goose, triplets)
Castle Hayton (Bay Hay)	Small	Humans	Barony (Herbert Hayworthy)
Castle Ramshorn	Medium	Humans	Barony (Lyonel Ekridge)
Festning Halvoy (Bay of the Sea People)	Small	Norse Humans	Town Fort
Fort Pishnook (Bay of the Sea People)	Large	Mixed	Military, Constabulary, Guards
Fortress Rashard	Small	Humans	Barony (Drake Rashard)

Waterport (Castle & Walled City) (Bay of the Sea People)	Large	Mixed	Import/Export, Trade, Manufacture, Government, the Arts (free city, Mayor instead of a Baron)

66021676R00217

Made in the USA
Charleston, SC
07 January 2017